THE VANISHED
A TREVOR JOSEPH NOVEL

KATHERINE JOHN

Published by Accent Press Ltd 2016

Paperback ISBN: 9781783759514
Ebook ISBN: 9781783758753

DEDICATION

In 1989 I published my first Trevor Joseph novel, *Without Trace*. One of the first letters of congratulation I received was from the brilliant playwright and actor Professor Norman Robbins, who invited me to see him perform professionally on stage as the Dame in an *Aladdin* he'd written and directed.

(My editor at the time scribbled a footnote on the letter – it was brief and to the point – this man could be a lunatic, or possibly but unlikely on the level.)

Norman's letter marked the beginning of a long, wonderful, warm and close friendship with him and his wife Ailsa.

I have so much to thank both of them for, especially the humour and laughter they brought into my own and my family's lives. I find it difficult to believe I'll never be able to telephone Norman again to discuss plot glitches, recipes or the exact dose of poison needed to kill someone.

Norman, thank you for all the friendship, laughter and the wonderful plays and pantomimes. Already you're sorely missed by so many.

THE FLASHING BLADES

The Flashing Blades exist. I had the pleasure of working with Rick Manning and Stuart McNeill and the rest of the 'warriors' on the set of *By Any Name*, the film I scripted for Tanabi from my book of the same name. Utterly professional and dedicated, their skill was amazing. Thank you so much for allowing me to use your name in *The Vanished*. I really hope to see you back in action on set again soon.

AUTHOR'S NOTES

LITTLE MISS NOBODY

Karen Price, christened 'Little Miss Nobody' by the media, was a fifteen-year-old from my home town of Pontypridd. She disappeared in 1981.

Two construction workers renovating a house in Cardiff in 1989 discovered a rolled carpet while working in the garden. When the carpet was unrolled, the skeletal remains of a young female were revealed. Tests determined that the girl had been dead for approximately ten years.

As there was nothing on the remains to assist with identification, British facial reconstruction artist Richard Neave used the skull to create a model of the girl's physical appearance. The reconstruction and the matching of DNA in the body to that of Karen's parents allowed her to be identified. The case was cited as one of the first instances in which DNA technology was used in this way.

Prior to the discovery of her body, it had been assumed that Karen had run away from the children's home where she had been a resident and turned to prostitution. In 1991 Idris Ali and Alan Charlton, who were alleged to have managed her solicitation as a prostitute, were charged with her murder. Ali's charge was eventually reduced to manslaughter, and he was released in 1994. Charlton is still serving a life sentence. On March 8th 2016 the appeal of both men against their convictions was dismissed.

No one had reported Karen Price missing.

JUNE 8th 2014

Almost 5,000 children including babies have disappeared from council care – figures obtained under freedom of information request by the *Daily Mail*

JANUARY 15th 2015

A 36% rise in children missing in care. 13,305 logged in the UK in a year as watchdog points to high risk of child abuse and exploitation – Ofsted report findings

PROLOGUE

Justin Hart was a child again, back in the orphanage. It was night, the room as dark as the dormitory in Hill House was allowed to be after lights out. The taste of fear, harsh, metallic, filled his mouth. He stared at the thin lines of pale yellow light that marked the outline of the door that opened on to the landing. He could hear footsteps in the distance. Hard-soled shoes walking over polished wooden floors.

The smell filled his nostrils, acrid, choking. A mixture of boys' sweat and underclothes that had been worn too long, seasoned by dust and the rubbery stench of canvas shoes.

He was lying on his iron-framed bed. The foam mattress was thin. He could feel the coiled springs as they bit into his back. The footsteps drew closer – ever closer, accompanied by murmured conversations too distant for him to make out what was being said.

He took his pillow, turned over and clamped it over his head. If he lay very still and very silent *they* might not realise he was there. *They* might walk past to the next in line, or *they* might not even reach his bed. His spot was fourth in a line of six. Half a dozen beds down one side of the dormitory, half a dozen the other.

He continued to lie stiff, immobile and listened hard.

He could hear the other boys' breathing, soft, quiet. Were they really asleep or – like him – pretending?

The footsteps resounded, closer – closer – He tried not to react when the doorknob grated as it turned. Hinges creaked. The door swung back. He peeped out from beneath his pillow. The lines of light were now a lozenge of pale amber.

He screwed his eyes tightly closed. The footsteps came closer … closer … He tensed every muscle in his body. He sensed a presence swoop down on him from on high. The pillow was torn from above his head. He opened his eyes and saw a shadow.

It was huge, black, terrifying in the pale light of the moon that filtered through the glass. He opened his mouth to scream. A hand clamped over his lips, bruising them against his teeth. Fingers hooked into the back of his pyjama jacket. He was hauled unceremoniously from the cocoon of sheet and blanket.

He was aware of other shadows gliding between the beds. He tried to scream a warning to his twin, Stephen. Fingers prised his teeth apart, foul-tasting, choking, they wormed their way to the back of his throat. He tried to bite – to kick – to fight – but he was weak, the shadow too strong.

He knew what was about to happen because it had happened before. And each time had been more degrading, humiliating and painful than the last. Stairs and landing swirled in a kaleidoscope of subdued lighting and fractured images as he was thrown over a shoulder and carried upwards.

Muffled cries and eerie laughter wafted down from the attic rooms. He watched a black-garbed monster set a boy dressed in a short white nightshirt on the landing. The boy looked tiny, frail, as he stood wide-eyed, dwarfed by taller children and the enormous silhouettes of the adults. The boy ignored all of them and stared intently towards him.

Justin recognised the boy as his mirror image and twin Stephen. There was anguish and reproach in Stephen's eyes. They continued to look accusingly at him …

Justin was suddenly and gratefully aware that he was dreaming, and at the point where he usually woke.

Only this time he didn't. Dumbstruck, he watched in horror as an enormous black cloud gathered in intensity. Slowly, infinitely slowly, it assumed a human shape that reminded him of the illustrations of the ogre in the copy of *Jack in the Beanstalk* that had given him nightmares as a child. The shadow ogre wrapped his arms around Stephen's shoulders, enveloping and eventually absorbing him. There was no more Stephen to be seen, only the ogre who seeped through an open door into a room. The door slammed. Stephen disappeared and he was left, abandoned among the weeping children and adults herding them.

He knew those rooms. Every one he'd been in contained a bed, a chair and a vicious, cruel adult. He was carried fighting and kicking into the room next door to the one Stephen had vanished into. Knowing what lay ahead, he closed his eyes again and did what he always did. Sent his mind outside of his body, so he wouldn't have to deal with the pain and degradation.

He concentrated and returned to the last time he'd been happy. Him, Stephen and their mum sitting together on the sofa cuddling, his mum reading them a story from their book of fairy tales.

They had heard the story before – many times. Jack and the beanstalk and the ogre. *Fi, fie, foe, fum … I smell the blood of an Englishman …*

He tried to hug his mum, hold her arm, kiss her hand.

Even as he did so he knew he shouldn't … every time he tried to touch her or Stephen, he woke.

It wasn't real.

Just a nightmare.

Only a nightmare.

He constantly repeated that to himself even when awake.

But the cries, the screams, the pain, the humiliation, the stench of adult sweat and sexual excitement – the horrifying intimate feel of raw flesh against his naked childhood body – lingered.

Poisoning and tainting his unconscious and conscious mind. Haunting not only his dreams but his every waking moment.

CHAPTER ONE

The defence barrister was calm, logical and relentless in her cross-examination of Witness C.

'You persist in maintaining your allegation that while you were at Hill House you were abused by staff and visitors?'

'I do.' Witness C held himself ramrod-straight and drew sufficient confidence from his appearance to look the defence barrister in the eye. His suit was new, expensive, bespoke from Savile Row tailors entitled to display the Royal Crest above their door. He knew how to act the Eton-educated intelligence officer. He'd won awards for playing the role.

'Remind the court, when exactly do you believe this alleged abuse occurred?'

'It began when my twin brother and I were taken to Hill House as six-year-olds. It continued for six years.'

'You were singled out for abuse?'

'No.'

'You witnessed other inmates being abused?'

'Not as such, but we were taken from the dormitories and common rooms in groups before being separated. Afterwards I heard their screams –'

The barrister interrupted. 'Didn't it occur to you that the screams could have been of pleasure?'

'There is a distinct difference between cries of joy and pain. The cries I heard were the result of pain.'

'Or punishment?'

'If it was punishment, it was punishment bordering on torture.'

'Again, a punishment – or *torture* – you personally witnessed?'

'No, but when I next saw some of the children who had been taken from the dormitories by the staff or visitors they were bruised and physically injured. A few were never seen again in Hill House.'

'Are you suggesting that children disappeared from Hill House under suspicious circumstances?'

Justin Hart, designated Witness C by the court, gritted his teeth. 'My own twin brother ...'

'Your twin brother disappeared from Hill House, Witness C?'

The barrister's scepticism was more than Justin could bear. 'Along with others, yes.'

'What do you think happened to him – and them?'

'All I can tell you is that after they were removed from the rest of us, they were never seen or heard of again by me, or any of the other inmates.'

'Did you ask the staff where these "vanished inmates" had been taken?'

'I did. I was told that my twin brother and the other children who had disappeared had either been fostered or adopted by new parents.'

'You chose not to believe this explanation?'

'Not after we requested to write to them.'

'Your requests were refused?'

'No, but none of us ever received a reply from the children who'd disappeared.'

'Isn't it likely that their adoptive parents wanted them

to break all ties to their old lives, so they would settle with their new families?'

'A simple letter wouldn't have interfered with their new lives,' Justin protested. 'He wasn't only my brother, he was my twin –'

'And you couldn't accept that he meant more to you than you did to him?' the defence barrister suggested.

Justin finally snapped. 'There were rumours that the children who'd vanished had been murdered by the people who were abusing us.'

He heard a sharp intake of breath in the court. He shuddered, realising he'd broken the solemn promise he'd made to the prosecution and the officer who'd investigated the allegations of abuse in Hill House. He'd sworn that he would stick to the facts, and only the facts when giving evidence.

'I can only reiterate that when I looked for the inmates who'd disappeared from Hill House I never found any trace of them.'

'Including your brother.'

'Including my brother,' Justin repeated.

'I have here,' the barrister reached for a file on her desk and opened it, 'a report made by a social worker when you and your twin brother, who we'll refer to for the purposes of this court as Child S, were admitted to Hill House. In it, she gives detailed accounts of the violent behaviour you both exhibited.'

'We were six years old. Our mother had just died and our father had abandoned us to the care system.'

'Do you deny that you were a violent child?'

Justin steeled himself. 'Given the report, how can I? Although I would question the competence of the social worker who compiled it.'

'Did you look for your brother after you left Hill

House?'

'I've never stopped looking for him nor the other children who vanished while they were in care alongside me in Hill House.'

'I will return to your ongoing search for them later.' The barrister closed the file and dropped it back on her desk. 'We've heard your testimony regarding the abuse you allege you endured, yet you could not give a description as to where it occurred. Don't you find it somewhat incongruous that you claim to be able to recall every revolting aspect of the assaults you allege you were subjected to, in graphic detail, yet you cannot describe even one of the buildings or rooms in which they happened, other than the attic rooms in Hill House?'

'I was a child. I was terrified.'

'You lived in Hill House Orphanage and Asylum until the age of twelve and during that time you had the run of the house, including the attic rooms?'

'I would argue with "had the run of the house". We weren't allowed upstairs, not even to our dormitories, during the day. The only times we went to the attic rooms was when we were carried up to them by our abusers.'

'The adults you allege abused you,' the defence barrister corrected.

Justin didn't trust himself to speak, so nodded assent.

'You allege that on various occasions over a period of approximately six years, you were abused in the attic rooms and staff accommodation at Hill House, as well as in various buildings outside of the premises.'

'More often outside of Hill House than inside.' Justin hoped that those of the jury who recognised him would see beyond the actor and realise he wasn't giving a performance.

'Did you leave Hill House often?'

4

'Too often.' Well-written scripts had taught Justin the value of brevity.

'Once a week, twice a week?'

'If there was a timetable or a pattern to the occasions that I, along with other inmates, was taken from Hill House, I was not aware of it. All I can say with certainty is that I was taken from there several times during those six years. Generally for the same purpose – to be abused, physically, sexually and mentally.'

Justin glanced at Shane and Mac, now designated Witness A and Witness B. Both were wearing new and expensive suits he'd paid for. Mac had taken his advice on a shirt and tie. Shane had point blank refused. The black shirt and white tie he'd failed to talk Shane out of wearing looked like a costume from *The Godfather*.

His friends sat together, tense and pale-faced on the public benches. He knew they'd already given their evidence and both looked shaken, which was unsurprising if they'd received the same grilling he was being subjected to.

The defence barrister continued. 'Generally – but not always – for the same purpose, Witness C?'

Justin made eye contact with the barrister. 'That is correct.'

'How exactly?'

Justin frowned. 'I don't understand the question.'

The barrister adopted a pained expression and moved closer to the witness box. 'I repeat, how exactly did you leave the orphanage? Did you walk? Or were you driven from the premises in a car or a bus? Or,' she turned to the jury, 'did you ride a horse?'

Justin realised the barrister was trying to goad him and reined in his irritation. 'Hill House was twelve miles from the nearest town and seven miles from the closest village.

So we didn't walk, and I never saw a horse the entire time I was incarcerated there.'

'Those are very precise distances for a child to remember.'

'We were all aware of the distances because the staff constantly reminded us just how isolated Hill House was.'

'You use the word "incarcerated". Isn't that more applicable to a prison?'

'Hill House was a prison for the children forced to live behind its walls.' Justin struggled to remain impassive.

'You were kept behind bars?'

'As I just said, Hill House was isolated. Only one road passed the gate. It led from the village and ended in an old quarry a few minutes' walk from the orphanage. We knew that if we tried to run away we'd soon be picked up.'

'But you had the freedom to leave the buildings, to play in the grounds and the immediate countryside.' The barrister flicked through the papers in her hands. 'Some seven acres of grounds bordered by woods and farmland, according to this leaflet.'

'The leaflet is probably correct.'

'Probably, Witness C?'

'I was a child when I left Hill House. I had no means of measuring the grounds.'

'So – even "probably" – you can hardly call Hill House a prison. And you admit you were taken on outings?'

'As I've just said.'

'At the risk of repeating myself, how were you taken from the orphanage?'

'Sometimes in a car, sometimes by minibus.'

'Hill House had its own minibus?'

'Yes.'

'And also a larger bus.'

'Yes. I recall a sign above the driver stating it seated forty-four people.'

'When do you recall seeing that?'

'When I travelled in the bus.'

'To where?'

'Charity-funded outings to cub and scout camps, outward bound centres, theme parks, the beach, sometimes to church.' Justin tried not to sound impatient.

'And you weren't abused at these places?'

Justin steeled himself. 'Sometimes but not always.'

'You travelled to school by bus?'

'No.'

'You walked to school?'

'We weren't sent to school.'

'Are you telling this court that while you were in care in Hill House no effort was made to educate you?'

'Teachers visited Hill House in term time.'

'Did any of the children at the orphanage attend school?'

'Not to my knowledge, but we received lessons at Hill House.' Justin continued to meet the barrister's eye. Uncertain of Shane and Mac's testimonies, he hoped he hadn't directly contradicted anything they'd said.

Mac's memory was at best uncertain. Both he and Shane had difficulty in separating their personal experiences from the accounts other inmates had related to them, dovetailing the traumatic suffering they'd heard second- and sometimes third-hand into their own stories. The one thing he could be certain of was that every survivor of the abuse meted out in Hill House had spent more time than was healthy dwelling on the misery of their existence within its walls.

He'd asked permission to sit in the courtroom while both Mac and Shane had been cross-examined, but the court officials had been adamant. No witness was allowed to attend court proceedings prior to giving their own evidence.

'So how do you explain this, Witness C?' The barrister walked across to her desk, picked up a ledger and handed it to Justin.

Justin glanced at the cover before opening it. 'I can't.'

'Please tell the court what that is.'

'It appears to be a class register of year five children in a school.'

'The name of the school?' the barrister demanded.

'Hen Parc.'

'Is that the name of the closest village to Hill House? The one you stated was seven miles away.'

'It is.'

The barrister again faced the jury. 'For those of you not conversant with the terminology of the education system, year five children are between the ages of ten and eleven.' She turned back to Justin. 'Look at the dates, Witness C. That register covers the period you would have been in year five?'

'Correct.'

'The children are listed in alphabetical order. Would you please read the list of surnames?'

'My name is listed here ...'

The barrister interrupted Justin. 'Just read the list as I've instructed, please, and tell me if the particulars next to the name that matches yours, also match your own, details?'

'They do,' Justin conceded.

'The same date of birth as yours?'

'It is.'

'And those for your twin brother? Do they match his details?'

8

'They do.'

'The same date of birth as yours, and the address that is given for both of you is Hill House Orphanage and Asylum?'

'It is, but we – I – never went to that school –'

The barrister broke in again. 'I see you have opened the page at the month of March. Would you tell the court the attendance record against your name for that month, please.'

'One hundred per cent, but I – we – never went to that school.'

'Was there another boy with the same name and birth date as you in Hill House Orphanage and Asylum when you were resident?'

'Not that I was aware of. But I am certain I never attended that school,' Justin repeated.

'Then how do you explain this register?'

'I can't, other than to say that it has been falsified.'

'In what way? The school didn't exist? The teacher named as Alice Price on the register didn't exist?' the barrister persisted.

'A Miss Price taught us in Hill House.'

'So you admit to knowing Miss Price?'

'A Miss Price taught us in Hill House, yes, but not in Hen Parc School. If such a school existed, I never set foot inside it.' Justin moved uneasily in the witness box.

'Could your memory be at fault?'

Justin loosened his tie. 'Not in my opinion. It's never failed in any other respect.'

'Are you absolutely certain that you did not attend Hen Parc Primary School, Witness C?'

'Absolutely.' Justin could feel his confidence ebbing. It wasn't the first time he'd been accused of lying when he'd voiced memories of his time at Hill House.

'Do you really expect this court to believe that the authorities would forge a register containing the names of children from Hill House? A register that stated they attended Hen Parc Primary School when they were actually educated at the orphanage?'

Justin gripped the side of the witness box to steady himself. 'All I can tell you is that I have never entered Hen Parc Primary School, as a pupil or at any other time. As for this register, this is the first time I've seen it.'

He forced himself to look the defence barrister in the eye. She stared back at him, but he knew he wasn't the only one who was relieved when the judge adjourned the court proceedings for lunch.

CHAPTER TWO

'Food? We can send for a takeaway if you don't want to go out?' Lucky suggested to Justin when he left the witness box.

'I'm not hungry. I need fresh air and a walk.'

'If you want to be left alone to enjoy it, follow me.' Lucky led Justin into a side room, took two police jackets and caps from a cardboard box and handed over a set. 'No one looks twice at police officers leaving a crown court. This wouldn't be a good time to be mobbed by your admirers, since the powers that be have gone to all the trouble of creating the anonymous Witness C.'

'The papers know damn well who I am.'

'But with a DA notice slapped on the proceedings they don't dare publish your name.'

'It'll soon be all over Twitter.'

'Only as a witness.'

Justin put on the hat and jacket. He was grateful to his fans for following his career and very aware that he owed them his success, but the last thing he felt like doing midway through his stint in the witness box was making small talk or signing autographs.

The court was only a few minutes' walk from the river. Nauseous, dreading what the afternoon would bring, Justin pulled the cap low over his forehead and walked quickly. He knew without checking that Lucky was at his side. Best friend, bodyguard and business partner in one, there had been occasions when he believed that Lucky knew him better than he knew himself.

They passed a café. Justin saw Shane and Mac sitting at a table in the window with Inspector Wells who'd investigated their case. They didn't recognise him and he didn't acknowledge them.

He walked to a bridge, leaned on it, looked down at the flowing water and breathed in deeply. After what seemed like a minute or two, although he knew it must have been closer to three-quarters of an hour, Lucky spoke.

'Time to go back.'

Justin retraced his steps. They entered the courtroom a few minutes before the judge reconvened the proceedings. The defence barrister wasted no time in picking up where she'd left off.

'To recap on your previous evidence, Witness C, you stated that you recall being taken on "outings" away from Hill House to premises where you allege you were abused.'

'I recall the occasions. They happened,' Justin replied.

'Did you complain about this alleged "abuse"?'

'Always. I was not a willing participant. I was molested and raped.' Justin turned to face the row of accused in the dock. All a score or more years older than him, they too were wearing expensive bespoke suits. They were also corpulent with the no-expense-spared, arrogantly confident look of the elite, wealthy and powerful.

'Can you name the people you complained to?'

'The adults who abused me and the duty staff when I was returned to Hill House.'

'What was the reaction of the staff when you alleged that you had been abused.'

'They told me I was worthless scum, and I shouldn't make up stories about important people.'

'In short, they didn't believe you?'

Justin took a deep breath to steady his nerves. 'That is one interpretation.'

'How often did you complain?'

'Every time it happened. When nothing was done, a few of us made a group complaint.'

'How many of you?'

'Twelve.'

'Was that the total number of inmates who made allegations of abuse?'

'No.'

'Why didn't everyone protest, if they alleged they'd been abused?'

Justin took care in phrasing his answer. 'In my opinion, because some children were afraid of what the staff might do to them if they complained.'

'Are you suggesting that a proportion of your fellow inmates were afraid of the staff?'

'Yes, particularly the male senior staff.'

'What happened when the twelve of you complained?'

'We were interviewed by a policeman. He made notes and told us that he would make a formal report to his superiors. But he never returned. We never saw him again.'

The barrister smiled as she faced the jury. 'So, a vanishing police officer as well as vanishing children, Witness C?'

Justin ignored both her riposte and the sniggers that rippled through the court.

'Were you interviewed again about this alleged abuse?'

'Not by a police officer.'

'Did you continue to complain?'

'Yes, but the staff accused me, and the others who complained of being abused, of lying. They punished us.'

'How?'

'They beat us.'

'Do you have the scars of these beatings?'

'No, because they took care not to leave any permanent marks.'

'How convenient.'

Justin fought his rising temper. 'A convenience that didn't lessen the pain we suffered.'

'Did you receive medical attention after these "punishments"?'

'We were taken one at a time to a room in Hill House to see a man they called "doctor". I have no idea whether he was a qualified physician or not.'

'He treated you?'

'He put ointment on my cuts and bruises, and tried to convince me that the beatings and abuse had taken place in my imagination and were caused by my self-harming. He also assaulted me on several occasions. He frequently injected me with what I assume with hindsight must have been a sedative as I invariably fell asleep while seeing him. Whenever I woke after a visit to the man, it was to find myself in solitary confinement.'

The barrister addressed the jury. 'It is well known that sedation and isolation after a violent episode is a tried and tested treatment for aggressive outbursts and mental instability. But,' she again faced Justin, 'I find solitary confinement in an orphanage that records show was constantly overcrowded hard to believe.'

'There were several rooms in the attics that were used as punishment cells. I was acquainted with many of them.'

14

'Can you explain why there is no record of complaints being made by yourself or indeed any other inmate of Hill House?'

'I can only assume they were either destroyed or never documented in the first place.'

'Do you really expect this court to believe that the people who worked in or visited Hill House in a professional capacity would destroy records?'

'Like the false school register, I can offer no other explanation.'

'So to clarify, you are accusing the staff of falsifying and destroying records as well as lying when testifying to this court, Witness C?'

Justin felt he had no option other than to reply, 'Yes.'

'To return to these outings where you allege you were abused. Were you driven by car, bus or minibus? To a town or rural location?'

'I can't remember.'

'Come now, you can recall one bus having a sign that stated it seated forty-four. The cars and buses you travelled from Hill House in must have had windows. Did they or didn't they?' The barrister pressed when Justin didn't answer immediately.

'They had windows.'

'Do you seriously expect this court to believe that a small boy being taken out of an institution he spent most of his time in, to the point of boredom, didn't look out of the windows as he was being driven away?'

'I was nervous ... afraid ...' Justin swallowed hard.

'You were afraid of what exactly?'

Justin lifted his head and looked the barrister in the eye again. 'Being hurt and abused.'

'Even the first time you were taken from Hill House, when you had no prior experience or knowledge of what you allege happened, you were afraid of being hurt and abused?'

'Yes,' Justin reiterated.

'Why?'

'Because the others ...'

'What others?' the barrister broke in swiftly.

'The other children ...'

'Boys or girls?'

'Both.'

'Continue.'

'They told me that we were hurt when we were taken away from Hill House to attend parties.'

'Parties?'

'That's where the staff told us that we were being taken – parties.'

'Did it occur to you that the other children might have been trying to frighten you as a joke?'

'No, because I knew they were serious.'

'You knew they were serious even at six years of age?'

'I sensed they were frightened.'

'Yet you still went with them?'

'Hill House wasn't a place where any child dared disobey an adult. As I've already said, we were afraid of several members of staff.'

'Something the staff who have given evidence to this court all deny. They spoke of warm, loving relationships between themselves and the children in their care.'

Justin knew better than to directly contradict the barrister again. 'If such relationships existed, I saw no evidence of them, and since then several members of the staff of Hill House have been found guilty of the physical and sexual abuse of the children in their care –'

'And they were all punished with lengthy prison sentences. That historic case is quite separate from this one. You are accusing well-respected members of society of abusing you, not those members of staff.'

'I am accusing both staff and visitors of abusing me and my fellow inmates –'

'We are not here to retry cases that have already been tried, Witness C. To move on. You testified that despite your misgivings and the warnings of your fellow inmates in Hill House, you went to this party.'

'Parties, there were several. Yes.'

'Did you recognise any of the people at these parties?'

'Not at the time, but I did later.'

'Not at the time,' the barrister repeated slowly, turning from Justin to the jury and finally to the accused in the dock. 'So when exactly did you identify the people you accuse of abusing you?'

'After I left Hill House and saw their photographs in newspapers and on television.'

'There was no television or newspapers at Hill House?'

'We were only allowed to watch children's television. There were no newspapers.'

'How old were you when you left the home?'

'Twelve.'

'And you left the home for where?'

Justin swallowed hard. 'A Young Offender Institution.'

'Why were you transferred?'

Justin braced himself. 'For attacking staff.'

'You were violent towards them?'

'I was frustrated, angry –'

'You were violent,' the barrister cut in ruthlessly.

Again Justin felt he had no option but to agree. 'Yes.'

'Were you informed that you had been diagnosed with mental health problems?'

Justin faced the jury. 'It was hardly surprising –'

'Please answer the question, Witness C.'

Justin clenched his fists in an effort to control the anger that invariably burned when he was forced to recall his childhood. 'Yes.'

'How long did you reside in the Young Offender Institution?'

'A few months.'

'Was it in fact less than two months?'

'Possibly.'

'Did you lose track of time after you were transferred from Hill House?'

'I may have lost track of time but I had no doubt as to what had been done, and was being done, to me.' Justin replied.

'Where were you taken after you left the Young Offender Institution?'

'I wasn't "taken" anywhere because I ran away.'

'Ran away?' the barrister questioned sceptically. 'Didn't you and four other inmates in fact attack and overcome a member of staff, injuring him before absconding?'

'I would prefer to say we fought our way out.'

'I have no doubt that is the interpretation you would like to put on the incident. Although as the officer concerned was hospitalised for four days, he would in all probability disagree with you.'

'I have since apologised to the officer.'

'He accepted your apology?'

'He did. He also accepted that I acted out of sheer desperation.'

'If I may say so, Witness C, you were fortunate to find such a forgiving officer. And then where did you live?'

'London.'

'Your address.'

'I didn't have one.'

'Am I correct in saying that you lived on the streets?'

'Wherever I could find shelter,' Justin conceded.

'In squats?'

'On occasion.'

'You must have needed money for food. How did you survive?'

'By any means open to me.'

'Theft?'

'When I had no other recourse,' Justin confessed.

'How did that make you feel?'

'Ashamed.'

'As ashamed as when you sold yourself as a homosexual prostitute and mugged innocent defenceless people?'

'I'm not proud of the way I was forced to live. Whatever I did, I did in order to survive.'

'Forced to live, Witness C? I quote,' the barrister opened a file and read from a document. '"As a result of Witness C's violent outbursts he has been transferred from Hill House orphanage to a Young Offender Institution." I think recourse to violence can be taken as an indication of criminal behaviour.'

'It was a response to being beaten and abused –'

'Allegations you made and continue to make without a shred of evidence to substantiate them. However given your "violent outbursts" I sympathise with the authorities, who, concerned for the safety of their staff and your fellow residents of Hill House, reacted appropriately –'

'By beating and abusing me –'

'By transferring you to a safe and secure Young Offender Institution where you were comfortably housed while professionals attempted to curb and moderate your behaviour?'

'I wouldn't agree with comfortably. The conditions were harsh and the abuse continued.'

'The alleged abuse,' the barrister corrected.

'The Young Offender Institution was no different from Hill House. If anything it was worse.'

The barrister turned her back on Justin and faced the jury. 'So, to summarise – on your own admission, Witness C, you absconded from the Young Offender Institution you were sent to after attacking members of staff in Hill House Orphanage. You subsequently lived rough on the streets of London and indulged in criminal activities. Police and magistrates' court records show that you were charged multiple times with ...' the barrister flicked through a wad of papers in the file she was holding. 'Soliciting, theft, GBH, unlawful entry of a property, burglary ...'

'In my defence, my actions were a direct result of the abuse I had suffered,' Justin remonstrated.

'To return to an earlier question I put to you regarding your twin brother. Did you continue to look for him?'

'And the others who disappeared. Constantly.'

'Where did you look?'

'I searched for their names on electoral rolls and physically searched on the streets but I've never found a trace of my twin brother or any of the other children who disappeared from Hill House. I compiled a list of names that I, and the other survivors of Hill House, could recall, and gave it to the police, but they refused to act on it.'

'When did you first give this list to the police?'

'About ten years ago, when I left the streets and began training and working as an actor.'

'"Training and working"? Mr Hart?'

Once again Justin managed to ignore the sniggers.

The barrister resumed her cross-examination. 'Your continued allegations over the decade that has elapsed since you first gave the police the list of names of children you claimed vanished while in the care of Hill House, and your continued badgering of the authorities since, has resulted in a recent investigation that has culminated in this trial, has it not?'

'The trials and incarcerations of high-profile paedophiles has helped publicise this case, as has the trial and incarceration of the last manager of Hill House for child abuse.'

'As I stated earlier, Witness C, we are not here to regurgitate history that is irrelevant to this case. I asked about the list of children's names that you compiled.'

'The officers I gave the list to drew a blank as I did. None of the children who vanished from Hill House, including my twin brother, have been traced.'

'Why look for a sinister explanation for their disappearance, Witness C? Isn't it more likely that, as the staff told you, they were fostered or adopted? Or simply absconded to live on the streets, as you did, because they saw it as a glamorous alternative to the orderly, disciplined life of care.'

'It is possible,' Justin allowed, 'but I doubt they could have remained incognito for so many years, especially given the publicity that this case has received. Also, if they had run away and were living on the streets I'm certain that someone I'm acquainted with would have received news of them. When you are brought up in care, your fellow inmates become your family. You seek them out.'

'Even on the streets?'

'Especially on the streets. Homeless people have their

own communication network.'

'I'll paint a different scenario for you, Witness C. Wouldn't a simpler and more logical explanation for their disappearance be that after descending into a life of criminality as you and your fellow "rent boys" had done, they changed their names in order to seek a fresh start? I'll even give you a motive for their desire to remain "lost." Did you, Witness C, band together with other homosexual prostitutes in order to fabricate scandalous allegations against well-known figures in the fields of politics, entertainment and the church, with a view to blackmailing them for considerable sums of money. Isn't this "abuse" you allege you suffered nothing more than a figment of your imagination, formulated by you and others of your ilk with the aim of extorting money?'

The court began to spin around Justin.

'Did you or did you not add your name to a letter demanding money from one of the accused in the dock, after alleging that he abused you. A letter that resulted in charges of extortion being made against you?'

'That letter was written years ago when I was sixteen. I was young, destitute –'

'Yes or no, Witness C?'

Justin whispered, 'Yes.'

'Louder, Witness C, so the jurors can hear you.'

'Yes. But I have no need of money. I'm rich –'

'Now, you most certainly are,' the barrister interrupted. 'Thanks to your acting ability, which I believe the masters of your profession refer to as "the art of lying convincingly".'

'The abuse I suffered was real …'

'To you, maybe,' the barrister grudgingly allowed. 'You have undergone "recovered memory therapy"?'

'Yes.'

'A high proportion of the instances of abuse you documented for the prosecution are the result of that therapy.'

'Yes.'

The barrister again looked to the jury. 'I refer you to Dr Harris's earlier expert witness testimony regarding "Repressed Memory Syndrome". A psychotherapy technique that has been discredited by many eminent psychiatrists and at best can be termed controversial.'

'The abuse happened,' Justin stated forcefully. 'I am a survivor. Able to relate my experiences unlike those who disappeared ...'

'Evidence, Witness C,' the barrister cut in ruthlessly. 'Courts deal with evidence, not allegations.' She addressed the jury again. 'It is documented that Witness C was violent towards the staff of the orphanage who cared for him. Diagnosed with psychiatric problems, he was sent to a facility more suited to treating his mental illness. From there he absconded after attacking a member of staff – and by his own admission subsequently lived on the streets of London and indulged in criminal activities which resulted in him being hauled before the courts on several occasions. He has a criminal record, not just for one crime, but several. The only question I would put to you regarding Witness C, and the other witnesses that you have heard for the prosecution, ladies and gentlemen of the jury, is this: can you believe a single word any one of them has said in this courtroom?'

CHAPTER THREE

The jury were out for half an hour. No one was surprised when the verdict was read. Least of all Justin.

'This isn't the end.' Inspector Anna Wells steered Justin, Mac and Shane behind the accused who were shaking hands and congratulating one another and their barrister on their acquittal. She led them through a side door at the back of the court. 'More witnesses might surface as a result of the publicity of this case.'

'Even if they do, you can be certain that they won't be listened to. The rich and powerful of this country have always looked after themselves. This trial was nothing more than a sham from the outset.' Justin didn't attempt to conceal his bitterness.

Anna opened the door to a small room and ushered them inside. A few moments later, the door opened and a court officer escorted in Lucky, who was carrying a large cardboard box.

'This man says he knows you, Inspector Wells.'

'He does.' Anna nodded to Lucky. Neither of them smiled, not after having listened to the verdict.

The officer looked unconvinced. Lucky was tall, well-built and held himself with the unmistakeable stance and puffed chest of the professionally trained soldier.

'Lucky's my business partner.' It was Justin's usual description of his closest friend.

'Sorry, sir, can't be too careful.' The officer closed the door behind him.

Lucky dropped the box on to a table.

'I'm sorry about the verdict, Inspector Wells. You put a lot of time and effort into investigating this case.'

'Not enough to convince the jury unfortunately, Lucky. Thank you for coming to court every day. I know how busy you are. It was good of you to spare the time to support us.' Anna shook the callused hand he offered her.

Anna knew, because Justin had told her, that Lucky managed a stunt combat team, *The Flashing Blades,* that specialised in recreating warfare and battle scenes for film companies. He'd even given her a wad of Lucky's business cards to distribute, although she couldn't imagine why Justin thought a police inspector would have contacts within film companies.

Soldiers for hire. Any period – any war – Pre-History – Viking – Roman – Napoleonic – Twentieth Century, Modern or Fantasy call **THE FLASHING BLADES***. We'll not only fight it for you but supply authentic uniforms and weaponry. Make-up artists, prosthetic experts, vehicles, animals and technical advisors available on request.*

'It was no hardship to clear my schedule for this court case.'

'I warned you it was a waste of time, Lucky,' Justin muttered.

'The time I spend with you, Justin, even in court, is never a waste of time given the number of girls who throw themselves at you. I'm not too proud to take your leftovers.'

'Have you worked with Justin long, Lucky?' Anna

26

asked, suddenly curious. She knew from various things that Justin had said to her that the two men were close, but Justin had never explained the origin of their friendship.

'Since he received the salary cheque for his first film and could afford to bankroll *The Flashing Blades*, but I've known him since we were both on the streets.'

Anna was surprised. 'You were homeless as well?'

'Not for long. I left to join the army at sixteen.'

'Social Services ...?'

'Didn't give a toss. They were glad to get me off their books although they never did anything for me when I was on them.' He opened the cardboard box and handed Justin a heavily padded and pocketed police vest. 'This is yours.'

Anna looked in the box. 'The Flashing Blades has police kit as well as military?'

'Have you seen the crowds outside the court? I don't know which is the most likely to cause trouble, the journalists or fans. Word's got out somehow. But it always does whenever Justin makes a public appearance. I swear he'd get mobbed in a monastery.' Lucky took three more vests from the box, handed two to Mac and Shane and proceeded to put one on. 'Keep your shirts on, boys, they won't be seen under the jackets.'

'What about the side door?' Anna asked. 'I was hoping to smuggle Justin, Mac and Shane out of the car park entrance.'

'You've no chance of smuggling Justin anywhere beyond this building while he's recognisable.' Lucky helped Mac, who was still shaking, to zip up his police vest. 'That's why I brought these.' He handed out police jackets and riot helmets. 'There's no need to study the insignia, Inspector Wells. They're meaningless.'

'Where did you get them?'

'The Flashing Blades wardrobe department. I had these made for Justin's *Mac McLochrie Time Traveller* series. We do British, American, European and International police forces as well as soldiers.'

'I'm sorry, somehow I seem to have missed those films,' Anna apologised.

'You haven't missed much. My character's a rogue time-travelling drug squad officer.' Justin picked up a helmet, put it on and pulled down the visor.

'Your own mother wouldn't recognise you,' Anna said, thoughtlessly.

'If I had one. Anna,' Justin hesitated. 'Thank you.'

'I was doing my job, Justin. I just wish the jury had brought in the right verdict.'

'The van's outside the back door. Sully's keeping the engine running.' Lucky made an adjustment to Mac's helmet.

'Are you going home?' Anna asked Justin.

'No, the press will be camped on my doorstep. I asked Lucky to make other arrangements.'

'If you give me the address I'll arrange a police guard in case the press or fans track you down.'

'No need, Anna. I'm a movie star, remember? I can afford my own security.' Justin held out his hand.

Anna took it and registered the extra pressure he placed on her fingers. She would have smiled at him if she could see his eyes. 'Our armed officers are trained ...'

'So is mine.' Justin glanced at Lucky. 'By Special Forces.' He finished dressing in the riot gear and pulled on a pair of gloves.

Lucky went to the door, opened it, walked down the corridor to the back door of the building and peered through the spy hole. 'I'll go first and open the back doors on the van. When you hear me shout, run out and straight into the van. Keep your face visors down and carry your riot shields in front of you.'

'Dare I ask about the van?' Anna questioned.

'Plain black, no markings, tinted windscreen and windows, Inspector Wells. Like these,' Lucky indicated the uniforms, 'it's a film prop.' He turned to Justin, Mac and Shane. 'Ready?'

All three nodded.

'On my shout.'

Lucky thrust open the door of the building, cold air blasted in as he ran to the van. He unlocked the back doors swung them open and shouted.

'Stand back! Police!'

The crowd obediently ebbed from the entrance. Lucky held the door until Mac, Shane and Justin had run out of the court building and jumped into the back of the van. Lucky joined them, closed and locked the van doors behind him. When Sully stopped at traffic lights, Lucky climbed into the front passenger seat. He checked the mirrors as Sully drove off.

'No one's following us,' Sully reassured.

'No chain? One taking over from another?'

'I'd notice, Lucky.'

'Take the back road to the north end of High Avenue. You've parked your car in the supermarket car park?'

'Before you ask, out of range of CCTV.'

'Good. Double back through the side streets.'

Although no car or cars appeared to be following the van, Sully drove the circuitous route to the car park and parked next to a nondescript saloon car.

'See you tomorrow.' Lucky slid behind the wheel of the van after Sully alighted.

'Make-up told me to remind you they want Justin in at five. They need the extra time to create his wounds.'

'I'll get him there.'

Sully closed the door and climbed into his own car. After Sully drove away, Lucky studied the wing and rear mirrors of the van for five minutes. When he was certain no one was watching them, he turned the ignition and drove back out on to the road.

The house Justin had bought through his company and had yet to move into was less than twenty minutes away. Lucky stopped outside the high, solid metal gates, opened them with a remote control, drove into the yard, closed the gates and turned off the ignition.

'Home sweet home, gentlemen. Strip off that riot gear in case the neighbours are watching from their bedroom windows, or they'll think a drug lord has moved in.'

'Given the price I paid for this place, a drug lord is about the only other person who could afford it.' Justin removed his helmet and jacket but not his vest.

Mac dumped his "uniform", opened the back doors and climbed down from the van. 'Hope you've got beers in, Lucky. I could do with a few after giving evidence. It was worse than an interrogation.'

'I stocked up on beer, whisky and frozen pizza. The telephone number of the nearest Chinese takeout is next to the phone and the housekeeper made up the beds and filled the bathrooms with essentials before she left for the day.' Lucky opened the van window and handed Mac the door key.

'Thanks, Lucky, you're a gem.' Shane shrugged off his vest and ran after Mac.

Justin picked up their discarded kit and helped Lucky pile it into a box in the back of the van. 'Mac's right, Lucky. I may not say it as often as I should but I appreciate you watching over me.'

'Thank you for recommending me for a job as a stunt

man when I left the army, and for stepping up to bankroll the company when it was only a germ of an idea in my mind.'

'Even though you've ended up working 24/7?' Justin asked.

'Not quite 24/7, and what other job would offer so many bonuses ...'

Justin ducked instinctively as the world exploded. Lucky was quicker, he slammed the van door shut behind them and flung himself to the floor of the vehicle beside Justin.

Outside, debris whirled and rattled through the air, bouncing off the windscreen, van and yard.

The silence when the last of the detritus had fallen was hollow and deafening, broken only by the crackle of fire. Justin lifted his hands from his head and tentatively opened his eyes. Lucky was staring up through the windscreen towards the house.

There was an enormous jagged hole where the steps leading to the front door had been. What remained of the door was hanging off its hinges at a precarious angle. The windows either side of the front door had blown out and flames were licking through the gaps in the brickwork.

The sound of sirens filled the air, drawing closer and closer.

'Too soon.' Lucky's voice sounded odd, robotic, after the noise of the explosion.

'What?' Justin mumbled in shock.

'Response time. They're here before they could have been notified.' Lucky locked the doors at the back of the van and, confident that he couldn't be seen through the tinted windows, slipped into the driver's seat, checked the keys were in the ignition and all the windows closed, before activating the central locking.

Justin continued to stare mesmerised through the windscreen. In a single devastating instant he realised not all the splashes of crimson were down to fire. A torso lay where the steps had been, headless and limbless, it rested in a nest of bloodied, shredded flesh. Justin wished he could turn aside, but he was mesmerised. Then he realised something was moving close by.

Mac, one side of his face scorched, blackened and burned, the rest of his body broken and soaked in blood was crawling inch by inch towards what was left of Shane.

'Mac!'

Lucky clamped his hand over Justin's mouth as the gates shuddered but held under heavy impact. The top of a ladder appeared above the wall. A figure in protective clothing and helmet climbed up, straddled the wall and heaved up coils of rope. He tugged on them to check they'd been secured, unfurled them and threw the ends into the yard. He checked the area in front of the house before climbing down. Three more figures followed and joined him. All were wearing high visibility luminous vests with GAS printed on the back in large letters.

They ran as fast as their protective gear would allow to Mac, who'd stopped moving. Justin watched them shake their heads. One of the men went to the gates and studied them. He blocked Justin's view of the lock. A few minutes later they were heaved open and more figures flooded into the yard.

Justin caught a glimpse of fire engines and police vehicles parking in the street outside. Sirens resounded and more emergency vehicles pulled up in front of the entrance to the yard. Justin was shaking so much the van was beginning to vibrate. Lucky held him firmly in a vice-like grip.

'Not a sound,' Lucky whispered in Justin's ear. He half dragged, half carried Justin to the back corner of the van. 'Move carefully,' he murmured, 'don't rock the van or give any indication we're inside.'

'Mac … Shane …'

'Are dead and gone.' Lucky spoke with the finality and authority of the experienced non-commissioned officer accustomed to doling out bad news. 'We'll wait our chance then get away.' He handed Justin a riot helmet and jacket. 'Put these on. You're still wearing your bulletproof vest?'

Justin turned and Lucky checked. The padding crinkled at Lucky's touch. He'd packed Justin's vest with banknotes in case they'd needed to go to ground after the court case. Credit card receipts could be monitored and traced – cash couldn't.

Lucky lifted a panel from the floor of the van. 'We need a diversion. When it happens …'

'If it doesn't?' Justin was still shaking.

'It will. And when I'm certain no one's looking in this direction we'll make our move.' Lucky took his phone from his pocket, dialled 999 and whispered down the line.

Justin looked inquisitively at him when he ended the call.

'I gave them the code for a bomb alert. When bomb disposal get here, we'll climb out and mingle with them.'

They didn't have long to wait. Bomb Disposal Officers arrived and cleared the yard. While they were searching in front of the house Lucky pushed Justin through the hole in the floor of the van.

Once they started moving, the fear that had threatened to paralyze Justin dissipated. He followed Lucky's lead, dusted himself down and headed straight for the barricade.

Lucky opened the door of a police car blocking the gate. The keys were in the ignition. Justin thought he heard someone shout behind them, but Lucky jumped into the driver's seat and started the car. He was driving out before Justin had time to close the passenger door behind him.

'What now?' Justin asked as Lucky pressed his foot on the accelerator and sped away.

Lucky tossed him his phone. 'Phone Sully. Tell him to meet us in the supermarket car park with a limo.'

'Why a limo?'

'They're hardly ever stopped by the police.'

'And then?'

'We get away.'

'To where?'

'I know someone I can trust.'

CHAPTER FOUR

Anna Wells walked into her apartment, kicked off her shoes, went into the living room and opened the fridge. There were two bottles of wine in the door. She took one, opened it and filled a large glass. Before she finished pouring, her phone rang.

'Wells.' She listened for a minute, before interrupting the caller. 'I've had a drink, send a car.' She replaced the receiver and emptied the glass. Then refilled it.

Lucky finished his call to his assistant Jules and turned to Justin. 'Keep your helmet on and your head down until I return.' Realising Justin was in shock, Lucky repeated the order twice before he was satisfied Justin had understood him. He left the police car, checked Justin was slouched below window level and walked over to the black limo that had parked four ranks away. He opened the passenger door, climbed in and sat beside Sully.

Sully was pale. He kept his gaze and both hands fixed on the steering wheel. 'I was looking for the van ...'

'I left it behind.'

'I heard the news ... there was an explosion ... you are all right?' Sully whispered hoarsely.

'As you see.'

'Mac ...' Sully choked, unable to say more.

'Justin, Shane and Mac are dead. Blown into scraps too small for dog food.' Lucky had no qualms in lying about Justin's fate. Not after seeing the damage the explosion had inflicted on Mac and Shane.

The silence between the two men closed in, dark, oppressive. Finally Lucky broke it. 'Why did you do it, Sully?'

'Do what, Lucky?'

'Whoever arranged that explosion knew where the four of us were headed early enough to rig everything. They knew the address and the time we'd arrive. The only people who were aware which one of Justin's houses we were going to, were me, Justin and you, Sully. The only person outside of that van I was driving who knew what time we'd arrive at the house was you. I didn't phone anyone. So tell me, Sully. Who did you phone? And why did you tip them off?'

Lucky had spoken softly, calmly and conversationally. He hadn't raised his voice, not once. Sully had never been so terrified in his life.

'I don't know ...'

'What do you know, Sully?'

'They offered me money, Lucky –'

'For your friends' lives?' Lucky cut in. 'Justin gave both of us a job and a place to live when we didn't have a roof over our heads. He fed us and looked after us when everyone else we knew slammed their doors in our faces.'

'I know, it's just that ...'

'What, Sully? Tell me? What is the going rate for selling out a true friend to a killer?'

'They promised me no one would get hurt.'

'Who promised you?'

'I don't know, Lucky,' Sully pleaded. 'I swear to you I don't know. They contacted me by phone and text. They said they only wanted to send a warning – a warning, that was all, so Justin, Mac and Shane would never accuse anyone ever again. It was only to be a warning – that was all it was going to be, I swear it …'

'How much?' Lucky repeated.

'Two hundred grand, Lucky. I texted them my bank details and half the money was in my account an hour later. The rest to be sent after … after … That money, it's enough to set me up for life …'

'It had better be, Sully, because you'll never get another penny from the Flashing Blades.'

Sully's voice was very small, and very fearful. 'What are you going to do to me, Lucky?'

'Do to you, Sully? Nothing now. I'll let you live out the rest of your miserable existence with your conscience.'

'Lucky …'

'Get out of the car, Sully.'

'The car you came in …'

'Stays where it is. Get out of the car, Sully.'

'You want me to come in early tomorrow …'

'Don't ever come into work again, Sully.'

'You're firing me?'

'You're fired.'

'The flat …'

'Is no longer yours.' Lucky checked his watch. 'Jules will have changed the locks by now. If you're quick, you might be able to pick your stuff up from the street before the scavengers take it.'

'Lucky …'

'Stay well away from me, Sully. Because the next time I see you, I'll kill you. And I promise you, I keep my word.'

'After everything we've been to one another …'

'Closer than brothers?' Lucky looked Sully in the eye.

'Exactly, Lucky –' Sully began eagerly.

'Just like Mac, Shane and Justin. The next time I clap eyes on you, Sully, you're a dead man,' Lucky reiterated.

Sully left. Lucky watched him run across the car park. He took his phone from his pocket and hit the speed dial. 'He's just left, Jules. Pick up the limo from the motorway service station in four hours. Should you or any of the boys see Sully, make sure he stays away from the Flashing Blades – and me.' He rang off, opened the door of the limo and went to fetch Justin.

Anna stood next to the senior fire and police officers. All three watched the remains of the fire smoulder in the front yard of Justin's house.

'You sure there was no incendiary device or bomb?' Anna checked.

'Quite certain,' the fire officer reiterated.

'What caused the blast?'

'It's too early to say.'

'Come on, do you really expect me to believe that?' Anna snapped.

'A neighbour phoned the gas alert line. He said he'd smelled gas when he'd walked his dog past the property. The call was received twenty minutes before the blast. The emergency team responded and arrived seconds after the explosion occurred.'

Anna frowned. 'You've interviewed the neighbour?'

'He lives three doors away. Been there over forty years. A retired engineer.'

Anna tried and failed to ignore the forensic teams crouching over the pools of blood and shards of flesh in front of the house. They were scraping up samples and bagging them. Then she caught a glimpse of a scrap of black cloth overlaid with white blowing in the wind. Justin's voice echoed in her mind. Had it really only been that morning?

'Shane, you look like you're auditioning for a bit part in the Revenge of Al Capone, *not about to give evidence for the prosecution in a British court of law. Do you want the defence barrister and judge to think you're threatening them? A black shirt and white tie ... for crying out loud.'* He'd appealed to her. *'Anna, talk sense into him.'*

But instead of talking sense as Justin had hoped, she'd complimented Shane on his appearance. She'd meant it. Shane obviously loved the clothes and felt good in them and it showed. He was beaming like a child who'd cornered a trove of chocolate.

She realised the officers were staring at her. 'You found two bodies?' Too grief-stricken to do more than repeat what she'd been told, she concentrated on assimilating the scene in front of her.

'Two males, ma'am,' the police officer confirmed. 'One was killed instantly by the blast. The other died within seconds of the emergency gas team's arrival. He was carrying a driving licence in the name of Robin –'

'MacDonald,' she murmured.

'You recognise him, ma'am?' The officer looked over to the area where a pathologist was examining the remains of Mac's scorched and battered body.

'His head is remarkably untouched.' She gazed at Mac's face. His green eyes stared vacantly up at the cold November sky, his red hair ruffled by the wind. 'In answer to your question, Sergeant, yes, I recognise him. He gave evidence in court this morning.'

'The Hill House case ...'

Anna couldn't wait a moment longer to ask the question burning uppermost in her mind. 'Have you identified the other victim?'

'Not as yet, ma'am,' the sergeant answered.

She indicated the scraps of cloth. 'Shane Jones left the court with Robin MacDonald, Justin Hart and Justin Hart's bodyguard Lucky after the verdict was announced around five o'clock. Shane was wearing a black shirt and white tie beneath a police jacket. They drove off in that van.' She pointed to the vehicle. 'Have you found evidence that suggests there could be other victims besides the two you found?'

The fire officer replied. 'No, ma'am, but we've only had time for a cursory examination of the scene. I didn't realise that van belonged to the victims. I assumed it was an emergency vehicle.'

Anna checked that the paper over-boots she'd pulled on over her shoes were secure, before walking to the van. Using the tips of her gloved fingers she tried to open the driver's door. It was locked.

'Can you open this?' she asked the sergeant.

'See to it now, ma'am.' He left them and approached a group of constables who were sifting through debris.

Anna waited impatiently. A constable joined them and succeeded in opening the van in minutes. Anna climbed into the driver's side. The glove compartment held a logbook, owner's manual and MOT certificate. The van was registered to Flashing Blades Ltd, Lucky and Justin's stunt team company. She leaned over the seat. The back was empty apart from two large cardboard boxes. She reached into one of them and rifled through the selection of clothes and helmets it contained. When she pushed it aside she saw that a panel had been removed from the floor.

'Open the back doors, please,' she called to the sergeant, 'and search underneath the van.'

'We're here.'

Justin opened his eyes and looked around. Lucky had parked the limo on the fringe of a motorway service station car park. He felt faintly nauseous, then remembered Shane and Mac. The trauma and tragedy of the past few hours hit full force – yet again.

'Want to eat or drink?' Lucky asked.

'No thanks.'

'I need to leave the keys of the limo inside.'

'You've made arrangements?'

'No need, fifty quid to whoever's manning the fast food counter will do it. Jules will know where to get them.'

'And then?'

Lucky scanned the car park. Headlights flashed. 'Our onward ride is already here.'

Anna remained in the yard long after night had fallen. Lights were brought in at dusk and the forensic work continued hours after the remains of Shane Jones and Robin MacDonald had been removed to the mortuary under the supervision of the Home Office Pathologist. The relief she felt when the forensic teams declared they'd found no more human remains was tempered by concern for Justin and Lucky.

Where were they? Dead – murdered? Or alive and in hiding?

She continued to watch the fingerprint and forensic teams swarm around the site, not really knowing why she stayed. There was nothing she could do to help. It wasn't her case, not any more. Her jurisdiction and responsibility had ended with the not guilty verdict that had been delivered in court that afternoon.

She stared at the pools of blood marked out in the yard. Were they all down to Shane and Mac's fatal injuries, or had Justin or Lucky been wounded in the blast? Why had they run? Was the explosion the result of an accidental gas leak, a corroded pipe or break in the supply line, or something more sinister? Had Justin and Lucky been kidnapped ... threatened ... taken to be murdered elsewhere – or had they simply run to a place of safety where they could hide? Had the explosion been engineered by the members of an influential VIP paedophile ring to silence their victims?

'Inspector Wells?'

She snapped to attention and out of her reverie. 'Chief Superintendent Mulcahy.'

'I'm surprised to see you here?'

'I came as soon as I received the call, sir. I was concerned for Hart, Jones and MacDonald.'

'There's nothing you can do for the two who are dead, Inspector Wells. As for Mr Hart, we have every copper in the area out looking for him.'

'Yes, sir.'

'Go home, get some sleep, Wells.'

'Sir. You will tell them to inform me ...'

'You'll be the first to know if anything happens. My commiserations on the verdict. I know how hard you worked on the Hill House case.'

'Sir.'

'Constable,' Mulcahy hailed a rookie officer. 'Drive Inspector Wells home.'

'Sir.'

It wasn't until the constable parked outside her apartment block, that Anna realised the Chief

Superintendent must have noticed her car wasn't at the scene of the explosion. Either that or he'd enquired how she'd reached Justin Hart's house when he'd arrived at the site. It was the only explanation as to why he'd ordered an officer to drive her home.

The empty bottle of wine stood accusingly on the breakfast bar when Anna walked into her living room. She picked it up, dumped it in her waste bin, then opened the fridge and lifted out the second bottle.

Food – she couldn't remember the last time she'd eaten. She'd settled for coffee at lunch. The almost-empty fridge yawned back at her when she poked around in its depths. A carton containing half a takeaway pizza of uncertain age joined the empty bottle in the bin. A pack of wrinkling apples, a lump of plastic-wrapped cheese covered in a layer of blue mould and a family-sized yoghurt that had been out of date for a month followed. She was left with a fridge devoid even of wine.

She fared better in the cupboard, finding a tin of corned beef and one of baked beans. She opened the tins, tipped the beans into a bowl, added a few chunks of corned beef, covered it and put in into the microwave. While it was heating she checked her phone for the tenth time since she'd unlocked her front door.

'If you don't want to phone, at least text me to tell me you're alive, damn you!'

As if on cue the phone rang.

'Wells.'

'Chief Superintendent Mulcahy.'

'Sir.'

'I'm sending a car. Pack a bag, you could be gone for a few days. See you in the office.'

'Sir, has there been a development –'

Mulcahy ended the call before she could finish the sentence. She replaced the wine in the fridge and went into her bedroom to find a suitcase.

CHAPTER FIVE

A shrill alarm resounded in Trevor Joseph's ear, shattering dreams. He fought with the bedclothes, reached out and pressed the button on the clock. The noise persisted and he realised it was his phone. His wife, Lyn, stirred beside him, turned over, rested her face against his back and her arm around his waist.

He squinted at the time as he picked up his phone. Three thirty! He pressed the green button.

'Joseph?'

Trevor recognised the Chief Superintendent's voice. 'Sir.' He instinctively sat up in bed in a parody of 'attention' and banged his head on the headboard.

'Meeting. Superintendent Evans's office. Fifteen minutes.' The line went dead. Mulcahy never used two words where one would suffice. Polite niceties weren't in his vocabulary.

'Don't go.' Lyn snuggled even closer, allowing her hand to wander downwards.

'Wish I didn't have to and you're not helping, sweetheart.' Trevor reluctantly swung his legs out of bed. He turned and looked at Lyn, a shadow amongst a tangle of bed linen. 'Keep the bed warm?'

'Meanie.'

Already her voice was slurring in sleep. Naked, Trevor

padded into the walk-in wardrobe, switched on the light, grabbed a selection of clothes and headed for the bathroom. He was still pulling on his sweater a few minutes later when he opened the door of his son's bedroom and glanced in. The nightlight burned low sending cartoon octopi, fish and seahorses gently spinning around the room. Marty lay on his back, his tiny fists closed loosely, his lips slightly open.

Trevor smiled as he closed the door. After years of lonely bachelorhood he could never take Lyn, Marty or his good fortune at having a family of his own for granted.

He ran down the stairs, found his shoes in the hall cupboard and slipped them on, tied his laces, felt in his jacket pocket for his keys then stepped outside. His closest friend, neighbour and colleague Peter Collins was leaning against his car.

'You've been called in too?' Trevor wasn't surprised. He'd become accustomed to Peter's abrasive manner and generally – but not always – worked well with him simply because, unlike most of their colleagues, he saw past Peter's belligerence to the dedication and integrity the man went to great lengths to conceal. As a result they were usually assigned to the same case.

'Upstairs wouldn't dream of calling you in without me. They know you need someone to keep you in line.'

Trevor locked his front door and opened his car. 'Why am I driving and not you?'

'Because my darling daughter has been screaming with colic for the last eight hours. Daisy was sleeping on her feet, so being the noble husband and father that I am, I volunteered to nurse Miranda so Daisy could go to bed with a pair of earplugs. I'd only just got Miranda down when Mulcahy phoned. As Miranda didn't wake at the ring, hopefully she'll sleep through until dawn, which will make Daisy a better person to live with.'

'I still don't understand why I'm driving and not you.'

'Because I'm so exhausted I can see four of you. It's like being drunk without running to the expense of alcohol. Quadruple vision isn't good when you're behind the wheel of a car. Still want me to drive?'

'No.' Trevor climbed into the car.

Peter joined him and buckled on his seat belt. 'What's up?'

'No idea.' Trevor edged the car out of the quiet cul-de-sac on to the main road.

'Big chief boss couldn't sleep so he decided no one else should?' Peter suggested.

'Possibly.'

'Aren't you interested?'

'We'll find out soon enough.' Trevor watched Peter stifle a yawn. 'If you manage to stay awake long enough to hear the briefing.'

'So what can my favourite computer wizard tell me about the flap?' Peter asked Sarah Merchant as he stumbled into the station.

Sarah didn't raise her eyes from her screen. 'Superintendent Evans called in everyone who can work a computer. Given the number of times you shout for help whenever you're behind a keyboard, I'm amazed to see you here.'

'I have other skills too numerous to mention.'

'You bury them deep.'

Peter looked around. Officers were manning every computer in the outer office. 'I see keyboard chimps but no fire.'

Sarah knew better than to rise to Peter's bait. 'If

47

anything's burning it's in the super's office.'

'Come on, you always know what's happening,' he coaxed.

'Not when I've been made to sign the Official Secrets Act, I don't.'

'That a joke?'

'Do you see me laughing?' Sarah sat back in her chair. 'You look like death, Collins. So glad to see your daughter putting you in your place.'

'People in glass houses shouldn't crow so loud.'

'Mixing metaphors now?'

'Given that you look as though you should be in a maternity ward, you too will soon be as lively as me. I've never seen a woman burgeon so quickly. Is it twins – triplets – quads?'

'Not according to the scan.'

'Then he'll be an elephant.'

'*She* will be a dainty, petite ballet dancer.'

Mulcahy's voice boomed from the office. 'Collins, is Joseph with you?'

'Parking his car, sir.'

'Sharpen your pen,' Sarah muttered as Peter walked away.

'Why?' Peter waved to Trevor as he walked through the door.

'The Official Secrets Act.'

Peter frowned.

'What's the problem?' Trevor caught up with him.

'Evidently a hush-hush one.' Peter led the way to Mulcahy's office.

Chief Superintendent Bill Mulcahy and Superintendent Dan Evans were sitting watching a computer screen that had been turned on the desk to face the room.

'Halloween decorations?' Peter quipped as he and Trevor entered.

'Close the door. Pull up a chair,' Mulcahy ordered.

Trevor handed a chair to Peter before reaching for a second one.

'Those *are* the limbs and heads of dummies?' Peter stared at a photograph of a metal sign festooned with what appeared to be swollen white body parts and broken toys.

'We won't know whether they are or aren't until the pathologist is on site, but initial inspection by the locals suggests they could be some kind of wax,' Dan replied. 'Possibly prosthetic film props.'

'Patrick O'Kelly's on his way there?' Trevor set his chair down next to Dan.

'Along with the forensic expert Jenny Adams,' Dan confirmed. 'This photograph and a dozen others, all similar but taken from different angles, were posted up on the internet shortly before midnight. Within minutes they were on every government, police and local authority website in the country as well as the usual social media platforms. As fast as our IT people have taken them down, they've resurfaced.'

'Do we know who put them up, sir?' Trevor asked.

'The IP address has been traced back to the press room of the Welsh Assembly.'

'That's priceless,' Peter beamed.

'It's obviously been hacked. Our people are working on it now trying to trace the jokers.' Dan took a box of mints from his pocket and offered them around. No one took any.

'Clever little jokers,' Peter added.

'As you see, the first photograph has the name of the place in focus.'

'Hill House Orphanage and Asylum,' Trevor read.

'The trial yesterday …'

'Exactly,' Dan concurred.

'Do we know the location?'

'Wales,' said Dan.

'It had to be, didn't it,' Peter complained. 'Middle of bloody nowhere, I bet.'

Mulcahy looked to Trevor. 'Have you followed the case?'

'Along with half the country, given the amount of press historic VIP paedophile investigations have attracted the last few years.'

'I've sent for the officer who worked on the case, she's on her way,' said Mulcahy.

'If those photographs are of real body parts, they're bloody sick.'

'Tell us something we don't know, Collins,' Dan said.

'You investigating the carjacking murder, Joseph?' Mulcahy asked.

'Arrested the man's partner yesterday, sir.'

'Forensics proved there was no carjacking. The two of them were arguing about which route to take to a pub. He pulled into a lay-by, she was manicuring her nails and lashed out with the scissors, jabbing them into his neck. The blades match the wound. The moral of the story is check your missus' handbag for nail scissors before you take her out to lunch.' Peter left his chair, opened the door of Dan's office and took a tray of coffee from Sarah Merchant. 'Much appreciated, thank you.' He winked at her before closing the door again.

'So you're not working on anything, Joseph?' Mulcahy checked.

'I opened an investigation into the Michael Trenwith case this morning – sorry, yesterday morning,' Trevor corrected with a yawn.

'The MP who disappeared?'

'That's the one, sir,' Peter moved back to the computer screen.

'Made headway?'

'Not much in half a day,' Trevor admitted.

'It's as if he stepped off the planet,' Peter continued to stare at the screen.

'No leads?' Mulcahy pressed.

'Nothing obvious,' Trevor volunteered when he realised Peter had no intention of answering.

'Money worries?'

'None. As well as his salary, he receives rents on a portfolio of residential and commercial properties he inherited from a great-uncle. They alone equate to more than a good income. No debts, not even a mortgage. His wife is well-heeled, his two children attend private school and all three are provided for with trust funds set up by their maternal grandfather.'

'Another woman?' Dan suggested.

'If there is, he must have been seeing her in his dreams. His secretary handed over both his public and private diaries. The man barely had time to breathe between engagements.' Peter tore himself away from the screen as the door opened again.

'Inspector Wells, Anna, good to see you.' Dan left his chair and swept her into a bear hug. As he was over six foot tall and almost as wide, it seemed like he was absorbing her into his giant frame. He released her and introduced her to the others. 'Chief Superintendent Bill Mulcahy.'

'We've met. Hello again, sir.' Anna saluted.

Dan continued to effect the introductions. 'Chief Inspector Trevor Joseph, Sergeant Peter Collins – my goddaughter, Inspector Anna Wells.'

51

'What can you tell us about these, Wells?' Mulcahy indicated the photographs on the computer screen.

'Nothing beyond what's obvious, sir.'

'You've seen them?' Dan checked.

'I studied them on my phone in the car on the way here. Thank you for sending transport and a driver to pick me up, sir. It was much appreciated at this time of night.'

'You have no thoughts on the photographs, Inspector Wells?' Mulcahy steered the conversation back on course.

'They appear authentically scaled, but so do many of the prosthetics used in theatrical and film make-up, sir. I'm no expert when it comes to pathology or forensics.' Anna set her laptop case on the table and opened it. 'I put together a file of all the evidence we gathered relevant to the recent Hill House investigation.'

'Anything new?' Mulcahy asked.

'Nothing's been added since the onset of the court case that ended yesterday, sir. I'd know if it had because I've been checking the file on a regular basis.'

'Is it the same information that's stored on the police mainframe?'

'Essentially it is, Chief Superintendent Mulcahy,' Anna confirmed. 'But I've extracted it from the all-encompassing, UK-wide, historic paedophile files and separated it from the evidence that's been gathered at other locations. I've also made a second file that covers the evidence collected during the investigation into the paedophile activities of the staff of Hill House, including the manager nicknamed "the ogre", that resulted in their convictions in the late 1990s.'

'I scanned the general file on the journey here. You up to date?' Mulcahy asked Dan.

'I've only had time to read the headings and allegations of abuse that were made during the trial

52

against the staff of Hill House Orphanage and the VIPs who were alleged to have met and abused the children outside of the home.'

'The principal witness for the prosecution of your investigation, Witness C, was the actor Justin Hart?' Trevor turned to Anna for confirmation.

'You're well informed.'

'Word gets out.'

'So it would appear, even when DA-notices are posted.' Anna capitulated. 'Justin wasn't the only witness, or even the most important, but I doubt the case would have received as much media exposure if the defendants hadn't been so high-profile and the press hadn't been aware of Justin Hart's role as a witness, even though they couldn't comment or report on his involvement.'

'According to the report I saw on the news, Witness C admitted to a criminal background and mental illness on the stand,' Trevor observed.

'A psychiatrist hired by the prosecution certified Justin Hart as sane before the case went to court. We found a few historical records of the inmates of Hill House. They were far from comprehensive or complete but we did notice that every child who made a formal complaint of being abused whilst resident in the home, or as an adult after leaving care, was subsequently convicted of criminal behaviour or treated for psychiatric problems, or both.'

'Strange that records of mental illness survived when you consider how many other records were lost,' Trevor mused.

'What records?' Mulcahy asked Trevor.

'Details of trips made by inmates and staff and records of the children who disappeared from Hill House in the twenty years before it closed. I read somewhere that more than 24,000 children went missing from local authority care homes from January 2012 to December 2013. Of course, some of them were only missing for a couple of hours, or a few days, before turning up again, but those are just the recorded cases. I have no idea as to the more recent figures. The real extent isn't known as many local authorities not only refuse to publish data, but even to monitor the number of children who go missing while in their care.'

'You know a great deal for someone who didn't work on the investigation, Chief Inspector Joseph.' Anna switched on her laptop.

'I read the witness statements out of interest. Hill House is not the only institution that has generated claims of abuse from its inmates. When I joined the force as a green constable, I was a lowly and insignificant member of the team that investigated Red Oak House.'

'I've heard of the case, but I don't recall the outcome,' Anna said.

'There wasn't one. At least not one that reached the press.' Trevor noticed that Peter had returned to his intense study of Dan's computer screen. 'Allegations were made, the accused interviewed, evidence collected and collated, files prepared and delivered to the Crown Prosecution Service. Six months later the senior officers in charge of the investigation received notification that the CPS had decreed there was insufficient evidence to proceed.'

'You disagreed with the decision?' Anna asked.

'The first lesson I learned as a copper was making decisions is not the prerogative of those who do the legwork. But working on the Red Oaks investigation gave me an interest and insight into similar cases, which is why I know a little – a very little – and only what's in the files or has been reported in the media on Hill House. I saw a late report on the television news this evening that two people involved in this latest Hill House case had been killed in a gas explosion. I also saw the later retraction denying their involvement. Were they defendants or witnesses?'

'Witnesses A and B were killed within an hour of the verdict being delivered.' Anna failed to keep the emotion from her voice. 'Their names were Robin MacDonald and Shane Jones.'

'I'm sorry, you must have grown close to them while working on the case.' Trevor sympathised.

'I did.'

'If I were a cynic I'd say their deaths are extremely convenient for the defence, who might otherwise be preparing for a legal challenge to the verdict,' Peter said.

'Without new evidence the prosecution has no grounds for a challenge,' Anna pointed out.

'Was Justin Hart with them when the explosion occurred?' Trevor took a cup of coffee from the tray and offered it to Anna.

She shook her head and declined. 'No, thank you. I don't know any more than has been reported in the news and, as there's a DA-notice prohibiting the divulging of the defendants and witnesses' names in the Hill House case, I'm not expecting to hear anything.'

Trevor noticed Anna bit her lip and tensed her fists when Justin's name was mentioned. 'You have no idea where he is?'

'Frankly, after seeing his two friends blown to kingdom come, I think he ran for his life without waiting to check if the explosion was an accident.'

'You think the gas explosion was suspicious?' Dan asked, while frowning at Peter who was still crouched in front of the computer screen.

'A company owned by Justin Hart bought that house a few weeks ago. He had the place professionally surveyed. I know because he complained about the cost when we were making small talk during a court break. If there had been a problem with the gas supply I think whoever carried out the survey would have noticed.'

'Did you believe Justin Hart, Shane Jones and Robin MacDonald's stories of being abused while they were in Hill House?' Dan questioned.

Anna didn't hesitate. 'Yes, sir, I believed them. Just as I believed the sworn statements that were voluntarily given to the investigation by other victims deemed too fragile to give evidence in court by the prosecution's medical experts.'

'You think the jury delivered the wrong verdict?' said Trevor.

'I do, Chief Inspector Joseph.'

'What are you finding so fascinating in those photographs, Collins?' Dan questioned.

'Have you looked at the dolls' heads?' Collins paused, before adding, 'sir'. It was just one of the many habits Trevor suspected had cost Peter promotion. His friend was in danger of becoming one of the longest-serving sergeants in the station.

'I was too busy trying to work out if the body parts are real to consider the dolls, Collins,' Dan replied in his Welsh lilt. If he was irritated by Peter's answer, he showed no sign of it.

'Some of those heads, legs and arms are bisque.'

Even Trevor was astounded. 'Pardon?'

'Bisque,' Peter repeated, 'it's a type of porcelain that was used to make dolls' heads and body parts in late Victorian and Edwardian times, and right up until the 1930s. The best were manufactured in Germany. They were fired several times and painted in layers to represent skin tones. Some of the bisque dolls were entirely made of porcelain, some had cloth bodies – they're still being mass-produced in China. But the features on these dolls are quite distinctive and look authentically antique. As do these toy cars. When did you say Hill House was built?'

'I didn't.' Anna scrolled through the files she'd downloaded on to her laptop. 'The building was finished in 1875 and opened its doors the same year.'

'As a children's home?' Peter asked.

'Yes.'

'So the toys could have been there since it opened.'

'Been where?' Dan asked. 'The place was closed. It should have been emptied.'

'Unless whoever decorated this sign transported the body parts and toys to the site, they must have been hidden somewhere in the buildings or the grounds,' Peter declared.

'And if the bodies and toys had been concealed there, what else has been hidden on the site?' Trevor wondered.

'Who made you an expert on antique toys?' Mulcahy demanded of Peter.

'I have hidden depths.' Peter saw the look of annoyance on his superior's face. 'My grandparents, sir,' he explained. 'They were antique dealers. An occupation I found boring, especially when my parents left me in their care at the shop. The only stock I was interested in was the toys. Some of the lectures they gave me must have stuck.'

The telephone rang. Dan picked it up.

Peter collected the empty coffee cups and returned them to the tray.

'You're absolutely certain those body parts are real … Thank you for letting us know, Patrick. Hang on a minute.

I'm putting you on speaker.' Dan pressed a button and replaced the receiver.

'You're in Wales again, Patrick?' Peter glared at Dan, as though he were defying him to send him there.

'That you, Collins? Congratulations, as you're with the Superintendent I take it you're heading for the land of hills and song as well. But for all your grumbling, I know you love the place really.' Patrick's Irish brogue crackled over the speaker phone from the police radio that had been patched through to a landline. 'I'll get ready to extend that warm hillside welcome to you.'

CHAPTER SIX

'I'm not doubting your word, Patrick, but I've never seen anything as pale and wax-like as the body parts strung on that gate,' Dan commented.

'Adipocere,' Patrick stated. 'Google it. The segments are from corpses that have been kept in a dark, damp place. Wet ground or mud where oxygen couldn't reach them. If it had, they would have decomposed.'

'Corpses? More than one?'

'I've identified parts from three distinct individuals. Body fat is transformed into adipocere when corpses are stored in moist places away from light and air. The remains of children, women and the overweight are perfect candidates because they have a high ratio of fat. Two of these heads are from children, one an adult male. As a rough guide I'd estimate the age of one child somewhere between five and ten. The other was an adolescent in the range thirteen to eighteen. The male could be any age from twenty-five to fifty. That's based on a rough and quick examination of the teeth. I can't be more specific than that at the moment.'

'Any idea when they died?' Dan continued.

'I wouldn't even attempt to hazard a guess on the strength of a visual examination. Once adipocere has formed it's impossible to determine from a cursory look if the remains are weeks, months or centuries old.'

'Centuries?' Mulcahy repeated sceptically.

'Early medieval adipocere corpses have been found in Italian churches and monasteries. The Windover site in a Florida swamp held corpses that are thousands of years –'

'These?' Mulcahy snapped.

'As I've said, I've absolutely no idea. I'll need access to a fully equipped mortuary so I can carry out several tests before I can even think of making a report. You need to send in enough trained people to carry out a full and intensive search of this place. None of these bodies are complete so there may well be more parts waiting to be found. Requisition cadaver dogs and a couple of strong-armed officers who know what they're doing and how to dig and you might strike lucky.'

'We'll get everything you need to you, Patrick. This line is terrible.' Dan replaced the receiver.

'Officers who know what they're doing?' Collins lifted his eyebrows.

'And none more so than you, Collins,' Dan smiled. 'Can you think of a better team? Anna led the Hill House investigation. She has all the background knowledge on the place that the force is party to. Trevor started his career investigating abuse at a children's home, and you resemble a dog biting a flea once you start on a case. You won't rest until the flea is contained, categorised, beaten and punished under the full force of the law.'

'Which is never as stringent as I'd like these days, thanks to soft judges, lenient sentencing and holiday camp prisons.' Peter met Dan's steady gaze. 'I take it Patrick's right, I'm going to Wales – again.'

'As Patrick said, you know you love it there, really.' Dan reached for another peppermint. 'Besides, the sheep have missed you.'

Mulcahy turned to Trevor. 'I'll arrange for portable accommodation to be delivered to the site along with the facilities Patrick has asked for. I'll try to get everything you need set up today.'

'What happens if it isn't?' Peter asked.

'There's a town half hour's drive away.'

'With a hotel or pub that does B&B?'

'If there isn't, Collins, you'll have to drive until there is. The force isn't responsible for your personal comfort.' Mulcahy snarled. 'Thoughts on manpower, Joseph?'

'We'll need a computer and first-class operator,' Trevor answered.

'Merchant,' Dan suggested. 'I'll get the locals to install a landline. Given that they had to patch a radio through for Patrick, I'm guessing there's no broadband or Wi-Fi in that area, so a landline will be your best chance of access to the internet.'

'Merchant is pregnant,' Peter objected.

'Pregnancy's not a disease, Sergeant Collins,' Anna said in amusement.

'What if she goes into labour in the back end of beyond. I'm no midwife –'

'No one will expect or want you to deliver a baby, Collins,' Mulcahy cut him short. 'You can have Merchant, Joseph. Who else?'

'Chris Brookes has a strong back and he's Merchant's paramour,' Peter suggested.

'I've worked with Brookes. He's competent, reliable and prepared to put in extra effort when it's needed,' Trevor acknowledged, knowing Mulcahy wouldn't take Peter's recommendation at face value.

'Clive Barry's an excellent dog handler, but you'll need another copper prepared to do some digging. Any ideas?' Dan turned to Trevor and Peter.

'Tristram Hever is a fast-track graduate. He'd appreciate the experience,' Mulcahy suggested.

'Good idea.' Peter smiled maliciously.

'Any reason you look so pleased, apart from the fact that his name is Tristram and he went to public school?' Dan asked Peter before Mulcahy did.

'He's rich and bored enough to have an active gym membership and has exercise-honed muscles. They might come in handy.'

Mulcahy summed up. 'Right, that's a pathologist and forensic team on site, Joseph, two constables to search under your supervision and,' he paused too long for the hesitation to be unintentional, 'Sergeant Collins. You'll have a handler and cadaver dog, a computer expert and an officer who worked on the Hill House case to fill you in on information pertinent to past investigations. Will you need more personnel or facilities besides what the locals can supply? If so, now is the time to speak. I'm reporting to the Home Office in two hours.'

'The Home Office?' Peter reiterated.

'You think they'll do nothing while someone posts photographs of body parts on government web sites, Collins?' Mulcahy's temper was beginning to fray.

'We need someone to liaise with the media and keep the press at bay,' Trevor glanced at Anna.

'Good luck with that, sir,' Anna said. 'It wasn't easy to keep the red tops under control during the court case. My landline is ex-directory and I've only given my mobile number to a few friends and colleagues, but both my voicemails are packed with messages from journalists.'

'I'll talk to the local Welsh force and the press,' Dan volunteered. 'The army were first on site after the photographs were posted because their camp is closer than a police station. I'll ask if they can move in, set up a temporary camp and concentrate their training exercises around Hill House and the surrounding area for a while to keep the media and civilian ghouls at bay.'

'Wouldn't bringing the military in be overstepping the mark, sir?' Trevor asked.

'Not if their operation was totally separate to ours. I'd only ask them to secure the perimeter of the area. It will free up more of our officers for the search.'

'Have you visited Hill House orphanage recently?' Trevor asked Anna.

'Yes, sir, when I began investigating the VIP paedophile case. But I only looked through the gates and viewed the buildings from vantage points on the hillside outside the walls. I managed to get hold of some historic photographs of the interiors and uploaded them on to the evidence file, but when we applied for permission to visit the building with our witnesses, it was denied. Hill House has been scheduled for demolition for ten years and the local council has declared the entire site, including the grounds, unsafe.'

'Hope you kept the hard hat from that last Welsh case, Joseph.' Peter finished stacking the tray with coffee cups. 'You don't have to worry about wearing one, Inspector Wells. You can remain safely tucked up out of danger in the nice cosy "female only" portable accommodation with Sergeant Merchant.'

'Perhaps you'd like to take responsibility for night security for the site, Sergeant Collins? We'll set up a sentry box where it can be seen from our "female only" window to make sure you stay awake,' Anna countered.

'Warn the local authority, unsafe or not, we need full access to Hill House,' Mulcahy ordered Dan.

'I'll organise a warrant right away, sir.'

'Keep me posted on developments.' Mulcahy

walked to the door.

'Yes, sir.'

'Prepare the Michael Trenwith case file for handover, Joseph. As soon as you've done that, head to Hill House. I want you there this afternoon.'

'I'll get the file ready, sir.' Trevor followed the Chief Superintendent to the door.

Mulcahy lowered his voice. 'The Home Office is looking for a swift conclusion to this case, Joseph. I told them you'd deliver.'

'Yes, sir.'

'I'm relying on you.'

'Yes, sir.' Trevor wondered what else Mulcahy expected him to say, when all coppers knew the speed of investigations was driven by the availability of evidence not the officers' desire to close a case. He closed the door after Mulcahy left.

'Warn Merchant and contact Brookes and Hever, Joseph. I'll organise that warrant and get on to the dog handlers and ask if they can spare Clive Barry and two cadaver dogs. Just as well to have back-up if it's available.' Dan picked up the telephone. 'In the meantime, I'll check for marshland and boggy areas in the vicinity of Hill House in case those body parts were kept outside the walls of the old orphanage. If you're familiar with the immediate area, Inspector Wells, perhaps you can spare a moment to look at the map with me.'

'Be glad to, sir.'

'Report to me before you leave, Joseph.'

Peter carried the coffee tray out of Dan's office and dumped it on Sarah Merchant's desk. 'Do you want the good or bad news?'

'I'll take the good but only if you clear that tray from

my workspace.' Sarah pushed her chair back from the computer screen.

'I've been sent to Wales.'

'To investigate this?' She indicated the photographs on her screen.

'They're sending the best.'

'That will be Chief Inspector Joseph.' She looked across to Trevor's desk, where he was checking files. 'We'll miss him around here. I could say we'd miss you, sergeant, but I'd be telling an untruth.'

'In more ways than one. You won't be missing either of us because you'll be with us.'

'Are you serious?'

'You'll be sent there as soon as we have accommodation and a computer station set up.'

Trevor overheard Peter and joined them. 'Has Peter told you that Brookes will be coming with us, Merchant?'

'No, sir.' Sarah stuck her tongue out at Peter.

'Always thinking of you, even when you're being childish. We wouldn't want you to be lonely,' Peter winked.

'I've never had the time to be lonely on an investigation.' Sarah turned back to her keyboard.

Trevor held up the file to Peter. 'Soon as I've handed this over, I'll be leaving.'

'Five minutes to clear my desk?'

'You have until I've given this to Dan.'

'That's quarter of an hour gone.'

Dan was on the telephone when Trevor knocked the door. He beckoned him into his office, finished his conversation and replaced the receiver. 'That's the warrant for Hill House organised.'

'Inspector Wells left?' Trevor asked.

'She's gone to the canteen in search of breakfast. I told her if she finds something worth eating, to bring it back here. I could eat anything edible.'

'She'll be lucky to find anything that falls into that category. She obviously has no idea what the food's like here.'

'Close the door.'

Trevor did as Dan asked and pulled up a chair to Dan's desk.

'Mulcahy and upstairs have finalised everything. You'll be in sole charge of the investigation and responsible for collecting and collating O'Kelly's pathology and forensic reports as well as your own. I've printed a copy of the instructions that have come down from above. I'd like your views on them. Now,' Dan added when Trevor moved to pocket the papers.

Trevor scanned them and began to read.

Only one file to be made and stored on the sole mainframe computer and the two networked laptops the investigating team will have at their disposal on site. Only two back-up mirror image files to be made on storage connected to the sole mainframe computer. No member of the team to bring or use any personal computing equipment into the police accommodation on site including USBs, discs, portable storage or external hard drives of any kind. The computer network will be monitored remotely and checked regularly for evidence of downloads to portable storage and exterior systems.

Trevor looked up. 'What about phones?'

'They've stipulated that none are to be carried by the team. There's no Wi-Fi or mobile signal in the area so there's no point. They're running a landline in there now. Needless to say that will also be monitored.'

'Private calls?'

'You'll be allowed time on one of the phone extensions.'

'Privacy?'

Dan moved uneasily on his chair. 'It's obvious there won't be any.'

'Have these measures been put in place,' Trevor tapped the paper, 'so the powers above can assume total control of all our findings and interpret the result of our investigation as they see fit?'

'Is that why you think they've been put in place?' Dan turned the question back on him.

'Have you challenged these orders?'

'The reply was the standard "sensitive information has to be treated in a sensitive manner, and all allegations of child abuse and paedophilia against public figures are to remain classified until they are either dismissed or proven in court, to protect the reputation and security of both accused and accuser".'

'The web is rife with allegations against public figures. The only mystery is why the people named in them haven't brought private prosecutions against those who've posted them.'

'You think everyone accused in those unsubstantiated accounts is guilty?'

'I have no idea and I wouldn't without conducting a full and proper investigation,' Trevor replied.

'Glad to see you being diplomatic. It could be argued that diplomacy is the reason that the Home Office has slapped a DA-notice on Hill House and a full news blackout on anything that's found there.'

'We are talking off the record?' Trevor asked.

'That's why I asked you to close the door.'

'DA-notices do nothing to solve the most pressing problem. How can a full and comprehensive investigation be conducted into allegations of child abuse or sexual assault that occurred decades ago? At best it will come down to opposing witness statements, the accuser challenging the accused and vice versa. Forensic evidence will have long gone, unless the scene has been preserved ...'

'Exactly,' Dan interrupted.

Trevor stopped mid-sentence. 'Do you think it's possible that a crime scene has been preserved in Hill House?'

'As it appears that body parts and toys have been stored somewhere in the vicinity, the short answer to your question is yes. If there's more to be found, find it, Joseph. Given recent and ongoing advances in forensics, it's theoretically possible that some evidence may be recoverable and if it is, no matter how old or slight, such evidence might result in a successful prosecution. As Anna's investigation has proved, once the defendants reach a courtroom, all the defence has to insinuate is that the accusers are criminals who have suffered mental health problems for the jury to doubt their version of events.'

'It would take a strong person to survive child abuse without suffering any ill effects.'

'Near impossible,' Dan agreed. 'You'll report to me every day.'

'Yes, sir.'

'Never forget that people will be listening in on every telephone conversation, work-related and private.'

'If that's a hint to keep Collins away from the phone, I'll try, sir.'

Dan walked out from behind his desk and looked through the glass panel into the main office. He watched the officers manning the computers. 'I've heard some odd stories from coppers who've investigated historic child abuse cases involving VIPs.'

'So have I, sir.'

Dan turned to face Trevor. 'Such as?'

'Searches of investigating officers' work space and private residences. Intense and prolonged interrogation of officers and their families about private matters unconnected to the case. Confiscation of personal items of no interest to the case by people who claimed to be conducting the searches for reasons of national security, yet refused to show their identity cards. Rumours of involvement by one or more of the secret services, and the enforced early retirement of officers who persisted in asserting that they were removed from investigations because their conclusions were too close to the truth. Would you like me to continue?'

'I get the gist. You'll have Collins with you Joseph, and I dare say Mulcahy will keep a close eye.'

'I sense you're about to say "but", sir?' Trevor raised an eyebrow.

'Watch your back, Joseph. Watch it carefully. Trust no one.'

'Except Collins, sir?'

Dan smiled. 'He'd hate to hear me say it, but he'd go through hellfire for you, Joseph. However, given his propensity for plain speaking, it might be well you keep him in check. If you don't, both of you might end up in the Tower or wherever it is they stow recalcitrant police officers these days.'

'If the more extreme articles on the internet are to be believed, it's sedation in a psychiatric hospital. Don't concern yourself, sir. I'll contact you after we've reached Hill House.'

'You have my private number?'

'On my phone but I'll put it in my notebook.'

Dan watched Anna walk into the outer office. She carried a tray over to Sarah's desk and pulled up a chair so she could see the computer screen while she ate. Dan waited until Anna was seated and she and Sarah were deep in conversation before stepping in front of the door. He leaned against it to prevent anyone from entering.

'There's something you should know about Anna Wells, Joseph.'

CHAPTER SEVEN

Trevor waited expectantly. There was little point in trying to hurry Dan. His superior spoke only after he'd thought out precisely what he wanted to say. Coupled with his slow speech, the superintendent's habit frequently made for unnecessarily long conversations.

'Anna Wells was in Hill House.'

'As in an inmate?' Trevor was surprised.

'When she was six, her father's car was hit by a bus. The driver had fallen asleep at the wheel and veered on to the wrong side of the road. Her father was killed, her mother seriously injured. Anna was in the back and walked away without a scratch. Social Services moved in. They took Anna from the hospital where her mother was being treated in intensive care early the following morning.'

'Anna had no family or friends willing to care for her?'

'Plenty, but the Social Workers overrode her grandparents' objections and mine as Anna's godfather, and insisted she be sent immediately to the orphanage at Hill House. They'd decided that Anna's grandparents were too old to care for her, even on a temporary basis, which was ridiculous as they were in their early fifties at the time. My wife had just died so they discounted me. They applied for, and secured, an order from a closed family court placing Anna in the care of the local authority. The more Anna's grandparents and I argued, the more adamant and entrenched the Social Workers became.'

'Damn secretive family courts,' Trevor murmured.

'The senior Social Worker insisted he was acting in Anna's best interests, although he knew nothing about her except that her father had been killed and her mother hospitalised. He sent Anna to Hill House because in his opinion the staff there had experience of working with traumatised children. Using Anna's mother's condition as an excuse, he was considering adoption as Anna's best option and, with that in mind, said he needed a professional psychological assessment of Anna. I knew little about the place in those days other than it was miles from where Anna lived and the station where her father and I worked. But there were odd stories about the orphanage even back then. Her father had been a close friend, Anna was an exceptionally pretty little girl so I went to my super –'

'You were a constable?'

'Sergeant. My super was one step ahead of me. Knowing Social Services wouldn't release Anna from care, he'd ordered two female sergeants to work in shifts and stay with Anna in Hill House. He asked me to keep an eye on them. I spent as much time there with them as I could. The staff tried to turf us out. We refused to leave, using the excuse that as Anna was a witness to the crash we had to interview her. The female officers even took turns beside Anna's bed at night, telling the staff it was essential they sit next to her in case she relived the crash in a nightmare and talked in her sleep.'

'I'm surprised you got away with it.'

'No one argued with the super. When he spoke it

happened. But it took eight weeks of string-pulling by him and his contacts to get Anna removed from Hill House, and then only after the super and his wife had made an official application to become foster parents and had been thoroughly scrutinised by the relevant authorities. Anna's grandparents made another attempt to get custody, they even hired a barrister, but again Social Services blocked the attempt, stating they were too old to look after Anna, even on a temporary basis.'

'Were Social Services being thorough because Anna Wells was a copper's daughter?' Trevor ventured.

'Possibly, but there were so many children in Hill House it would have taken considerable time to investigate Social Services' approach to individual cases. Time we didn't have. As it was, watching Anna stretched our manpower to breaking point.'

'Was Anna harmed in any way?'

'Other than emotionally by the trauma of losing her father, seeing her mother severely injured and being abandoned in strange surroundings among strangers?'

'You know what I mean.'

'Unfortunately I do.' Dan faced Trevor. 'Everyone who'd worked with Anna's father, Joe Wells, made a point of visiting her as often as possible when she was in Hill House. In fact they – we – all of us made nuisances of ourselves to the point where the staff said we were disrupting the routine of the orphanage. I think that made the staff wary of mistreating Anna in any way. I recall seeing a lot of frightened children there, including a set of twins about Anna's age. Dark-haired, handsome boys. I glanced through the trial testimony earlier, given Witness C's testimony they could have been Justin Hart and his brother, but I never spoke to them. There was also a woman working there who lived in Hen Parc village. A newly qualified social worker, Mair Davies. She was a head-turningly beautiful young redhead. We exchanged pleasantries but I was always left with the feeling that she wanted to tell me more than she had after our conversations. She behaved as though she was terrified of some of the staff, especially the manager.'

'The ogre?'

'That's the nickname he acquired. Mair Davies slipped a note into my pocket during one visit, asking me to meet her in the pub in Hen Parc. I kept the appointment. She didn't. I tried telephoning her on the number she'd written in her message but received no reply. When I made enquiries, the staff at Hill House told me she'd resigned suddenly because of a family emergency. After Anna Wells left the home, I visited Hen Parc village and called into the pub. The landlord told me no one had seen Mair Davies for weeks. I alerted the local force. To cut a long story short, she'd disappeared. The local businessman – I believe he was a solicitor – who owned the cottage Mair Davies was renting said she'd left without taking all her things but she'd sent him a note apologising for not giving him notice and telling him to keep her deposit for any inconvenience. If she had family, no one reported her missing.'

'Hill House?' Trevor asked.

'When I persisted in asking about her they showed me a typed letter of resignation. Apparently Mair said her sister had fallen ill abroad and she had to leave the country suddenly.'

'Had she?'

'Passport control had no record of a Mair Davies leaving the country for two months after I last saw her in Hill House but that might not have been her real name. I found a record of a Mair Davies attending and graduating

Swansea University who was about the right age. It's entirely possible she's turned up somewhere by now. It's years since I looked for her. I'm only telling you this so you can bear it in mind. It might mean something. It might not.'

'Did you see any evidence that the staff of Hill House were involved in child abuse while you were there with Anna?'

'There was certainly an atmosphere of fear among the children and junior staff. The more we – by that I mean me and the two female officers – tried to talk to the children, the more they clammed up. But you know how difficult it is to question the witnesses and victims of abuse. Child abuse is intolerable but when it's inflicted by an adult the child loves and believes loves them, the victim can consider it normal. Unless the perpetrator is actually caught in the act, it can be the devil to prove, as Anna has discovered. Historical cases are a nightmare. I've often wondered what Mair Davies wanted to tell me that night. But for all I know she could have been a fantasist unhappy in her work who wanted to cause problems for her colleagues.'

'Do you believe she was?'

'Let's just say it's a question I've asked myself.' Dan moved away from the door and returned to his desk.

'And Anna Wells?'

'She lived with the super and his wife for six months. As soon as her mother was well enough to leave hospital she moved in with her parents – Anna's grandparents. Anna joined her there.'

'Did you keep in touch?'

'Birthdays, Christmas, university graduation. I'm her godfather,' Dan reminded him.

'And Hill House?'

'Neither she nor I ever mentioned the place again until today.'

'She didn't ask your advice when she was handed the historical abuse case?' Trevor questioned.

'No, and I didn't volunteer any. What could I tell her? That there were rumours about what went on there? Wait until you see it for yourself. The building reminded me of the original Hammer Horror haunted house and I saw it when it was occupied. Now you know as much as I do about Hill House. What you do with the information is up to you.'

There was a knock at the door. Dan called, 'Come in.'

Anna opened it. 'If I'm interrupting ...'

'Not at all, Anna,' Dan beckoned her in.

She entered the office, closing the door behind her.

'You found something worth eating in the canteen?' Trevor asked.

'Rice Krispies.'

'With fresh milk?'

'I had a glass of water. I didn't like the look of the milk.'

'Very wise.'

'I've filled Trevor in on the guidelines from above stipulating how the investigation should be – or rather will be – conducted. I thought it might be as well if you drive to Hill House with him and Collins so you can update them on your findings.'

Anna agreed. 'Good idea.'

'Any thoughts on who's behind this gruesome display?' Trevor asked Anna.

'I've no idea.'

'Could it be Justin?' Trevor fished.

'He didn't leave the court until five o'clock. The explosion at his house occurred at six thirty. He wouldn't have had time to travel to Wales, remove the body parts from wherever they'd been hidden and arrange that display. The journey alone would have taken over five hours and that's in good traffic conditions. Those photographs were posted up around midnight.' Anna reminded.

'He could have flown,' Trevor suggested.

'I'll check with the airports that cater for private planes. The nearest one to Hill House would probably be Swansea. There'll be a record if a plane flew into there from London.'

'The photographs could have been posted by someone who knew Justin and was peeved about the jury's verdict.' Dan turned his chair to face Anna.

'Justin gave as honest an account as he could recall of his experiences in Hill House. It wasn't easy for him. The pain he still feels as a result of what happened to him and his brother was palpable. He spent days with my team trying to remember all he could about specific events in the home and the children who'd disappeared from there. If he'd known anything about a secret burial chamber, I'm certain he would have mentioned it, because he knew how desperate we were for concrete evidence to prove the allegations that he and the others had made. Similarly, if anyone who had the slightest regard for Justin knew about those body parts, I'm certain they would have said something either to him or us before the court case.'

'What about the others who gave evidence? Do you think they knew anything about hidden bodies?'

'Shane Jones and Robin MacDonald?' Anna felt the need to supply their names. 'Like Justin they'd been damaged by their experiences in Hill House and they also had criminal records for drug taking, petty dealing and minor theft, which the defence used to discredit their testimony. If either of them had known anything about bodies being hidden or buried in Hill House, I'm sure they would have mentioned it in the hope of strengthening the prosecution case.'

'You really have no idea where Justin has gone?' Trevor pressed.

'I've thought about nothing else since I received the call about the explosion. Justin's business partner was with him …'

'You think he might have had something to do with it?' Dan broke in.

'The explosion – no. From what I saw of them together they're close. It's obvious Justin trusts him implicitly.'

'His name?' Dan reached for a notepad.

'Lucky – and before you ask, that's all the information I have. I've asked, but he's never given me his real name or said anything about his past other than that, like Justin, he'd lived "on the streets" and joined the army when he was sixteen. I had the impression that he met Justin when they were both homeless, but that might be just my take on what Lucky said. When I offered Justin police protection he said his guard had been trained by the army. Lucky certainly looked ex-military, possibly even Special Forces.'

'We're one of the few countries in the world that still recruits boy soldiers.' Trevor couldn't bear the thought of his own son wanting to join the army in his teens.

Anna glanced at her phone, which was vibrating. She checked who was calling before cancelling the call. 'More damned journalists. I recognise the number.'

'You said the local authority refused you entry to Hill House,' Trevor began.

'They did,' Anna confirmed.

'I suppose it's feasible that whoever arranged those

body parts on the Hill House sign stayed away from the orphanage during the court case because they suspected the place was being watched. Especially after the Local Authority refused you access. When the jury delivered their verdict, he, she or they were angry enough to go in and show the world what was hidden there.' Trevor left his chair. 'The "who" is somewhat academic now after someone has broken in and, thanks to the internet, broadcast their gruesome findings to the world. But I'd like to talk to whoever's responsible to find out what else they know.'

'You have to find whoever "they" are first,' Dan reminded.

Trevor glanced at his watch. 'Peter said I'd be in here a quarter of an hour, it's been double that. I'll go home and pack. Pick you up here in an hour, Inspector Wells?'

'Thank you.'

'Looking forward to working with you.'

'And I with you, Inspector Joseph. I've heard a great deal about you. You're almost a legend.'

'Legends attract stories, Inspector – in my experience, most untrue.'

'There is one thing that might be worth following up. The ogre. He worked in Hill House for the last twenty years that it operated as a children's home and was in charge of the place for fifteen.'

'Is he still in prison?' Trevor asked.

'Yes, he was prosecuted for physical and sexual child abuse the year after Hill House closed and sentenced to life, with a recommendation he serve a minimum of eighteen years. He applied for parole two years ago and received a hearing but the parole board took the statements of his victims into account and concluded he was still a danger to the public, especially children. He can apply to the parole board again, although one of the prison psychologists told me that the ogre's unlikely to be given parole any time soon as he's shown no remorse or signs of wanting to reform. He's in Point Green.'

'I've seen nothing about that in the press,' Dan commented.

'The parole board hearing attracted very little media attention. A paedophile care home manager doesn't generate the same headlines as a paedophile VIP,' Anna said.

'Have you visited him?' Trevor asked.

'During the investigation. I interviewed him. Not that I got anything out of him. He agreed to see me but clammed up and refused to talk about his time at Hill House as soon as I started asking questions about the place.'

'Point Green's only a couple of miles out of your way, might be worth stopping off there and showing him the photographs that were posted on the internet. Even if he refuses to talk, you can gauge his reaction to the sight of the body parts,' Dan suggested.

'If he thinks more of Hill House's secrets are about to be revealed, he might say something significant,' Trevor said.

'I doubt it,' Anna warned.

'From where we are right now anything has to be worth a try. See you later, Inspector Wells.'

'Anna.'

'Anna,' Trevor smiled. 'Good to be working with you. I'll be in touch, Dan.' Trevor went to the door. He stopped at Sarah's desk when he entered the main office. 'Do me a favour, go through the Hill House staff files. See if you can find any mention of a Mair Davies?'

'Anything else, sir?'

Trevor thought for a moment. 'Yes, track down as many of the staff who worked there during the last thirty years as you can, especially those who left suddenly, and when you've finished that start checking the inmates.'

'Inspector Wells warned the records of Hill House are incomplete.'

'I've no doubt they are. Just do the best you can please, Merchant, as you always do.'

CHAPTER EIGHT

'I'm about to conduct a search of a derelict orphanage in Wales, my love, not sit behind a desk in a clean office – not that my office is clean considering the state of some of the human traffic that flows through the station,' Trevor protested when Lyn dropped a stack of freshly laundered shirts on top of the underclothes and socks he'd packed into his suitcase.

'You still have to look like a Chief Inspector.'

'Only since you de-scruffed me.'

'Is there such a word?'

He saw the concern etched in her eyes.

'You will be careful, won't you?'

He pulled her towards him, wrapped his arms around her and kissed her. 'It's an historic cold case search in an abandoned isolated orphanage in Wales with Peter. The worst that can happen is that Peter will get drunk on the local brew and attacked by a sheep. Not necessarily in that order.'

'Sheep are too docile and wary of people to attack anyone.'

'Not the rams and they sense Peter hates them.' Trevor released her, went into the walk-in wardrobe and checked through the shelves. He lifted down a hard hat and pulled a belt from a rack. 'I may need the helmet and the belt I'm wearing is cracking. The result of too many of your home-made chicken pies, my love.'

A gurgling resounded from the nursery. 'That's Marty awake.' Lyn left the bedroom.

'I should only be away a few days, a week at most. You two will be all right without me, won't you?' Trevor called after her.

She reappeared carrying Marty. The child opened his eyes wide and held out his arms to Trevor. 'We'll be fine.'

'Not too fine, I hope. I'd like you to miss me, if only a little.' He took Marty from her, kissed, hugged and tickled him.

'Daisy will be over and we'll have a few girly days playing with the children, shopping and watching the weepy romantic films you and Peter call soppy.'

Trevor returned Marty to Lyn, opened his sock drawer and lifted out a large box of chocolates. 'I'll leave these on the dresser for you to take downstairs.'

'There was me thinking that you were holding on to them until you had a chance to eat them in secret.'

'You knew they were there?'

'I know all your hiding places.'

'So much for me being sneaky.' He picked up a photograph of Lyn and Marty from his bedside table, dropped it on top of the clothes and zipped up the case. The doorbell rang. 'That will be Peter.' He lifted his bag from the bed, ran down the stairs and opened the door. Peter, Daisy and Miranda were on the doorstep. 'It's our favourite neighbours, Lyn, with their adorable daughter.'

'You wouldn't have called her adorable at two o'clock this morning,' Peter grumbled.

'You look exhausted, Peter,' Lyn said in concern. 'You're not driving, I hope.'

'I'll start,' Trevor volunteered. 'It's only a couple of hundred miles give or take a few. Three and half – four hours should do it. If I get tired the Inspector we've arranged to pick up at the station can take over.'

'It would be four hours if it was motorway driving. It's not,' Peter grumbled. 'It'll be country lanes with detours that land us in farmyards, slow-moving tractors and horseboxes travelling in convoys that are impossible to overtake, crossroads without signposts, mountains you get lost on and more twists and turns than a sheep's innards. We'll be lucky to get there before dark.'

'Not that you'll know much about the journey because you'll be sleeping on the back seat for most of it.'

'That a promise, Joseph?'

'Better that than having to listen to you swear at every sheep we pass on the way.'

'Give me your car keys.' Peter held out his hand. 'I'll load up the cases.'

'I'll help you.' Trevor went into the hall and picked up his bag. He stepped outside. Peter's case was propped against the rear bumper of his car, so were four cases of beer, one of red wine and a wholesale-sized box of crisps.

'Supplies,' Peter explained succinctly. 'We'll be miles from anywhere.'

'Just as well if you intend drinking that lot.'

'It's for sharing.'

'Thank you. I'll remind you of that when you're down to your last half a dozen cans of beer.' Trevor opened the boot and lifted the beer and wine in first.

Peter glanced at the front door. Lyn, Daisy and the children had retreated to the living room. 'This search and investigation?'

'Yes.'

'You happy to take it on?'

'We've been given our orders. What do you want me to do?'

'Tell Dan and Mulcahy we don't like the smell of it.'

'When have you ever liked the smell of a case?'

Peter grimaced. 'This is different. Officers investigating historic child abuse have been harassed and threatened. Some have even been kicked off the force.'

'I know. Dan and I talked about that earlier.'

'And you still took the case on? You're crazy, Joseph.'

'Someone had to take it.'

'Someone – not us.'

Lyn appeared in the doorway. 'You two want to eat or have coffee before you go?'

'Thank you, but we haven't time before picking up the inspector.' Trevor returned to the house and scooped Marty from the floor of the living room where he and Miranda were picking up and examining plastic shapes.

'Bye, big fellow, look after your mum.'

Marty reached up and pulled Trevor's hair.

Lyn kissed Trevor. 'We'll look after one another.'

He heard the catch in her throat, handed Marty over and headed for the door before his emotions also got the better of him. 'I'll phone when I get there.'

'Mind you do.'

'Don't worry, Lyn,' Peter consoled after kissing Daisy and Miranda. 'I'll look after Trevor.'

Daisy smiled, 'Who's going to look after you, sunshine?'

'I'm big enough and ugly enough to look after myself.'

'I'll second that,' Trevor called through the open door. 'Sooner we go, sooner we'll be back.'

The moment Anna climbed into the car she began updating Trevor and Peter with an account of the investigation she and her team had made into the history of Hill House.

'Before we submitted our findings to the Crown Prosecution Service we re-examined all the witness statements we'd taken. We discounted those we couldn't corroborate.'

'You didn't regard the people who'd made them as trustworthy?' Taking advantage of Trevor's offer to drive, Peter was lolling on the back seat, but Trevor could tell from his tone that he was listening attentively to every word Anna said.

'Not at all. We discounted them because we had a surfeit of statements and didn't need those that might prove vulnerable to a challenge from the defence. We concentrated on the statements from those witnesses, Justin, Mac and Shane included, who gave accounts so similar they endorsed one another, even though they were rarely subjected to abuse in the same room at the same time.'

'I read in one of the court reports that Justin Hart couldn't identify any of the places outside of Hill House where he alleged he'd been abused. He couldn't even say if the buildings were in a town or the countryside,' Trevor glanced at Anna looking for confirmation.

'That's correct.'

'I can understand why the defence went after your principal witnesses when they all swore on oath that, although they couldn't remember the locations where they were abused, they could remember the perpetrators.' Peter checked his phone as it pinged. 'Damned spam messages. I'm looking forward to being out of range.'

'Did your witnesses pick out their abusers from photographs?' Trevor asked.

'Yes, but they were all interviewed in isolation. The

only people present were police officers. There was no question of collusion.'

'That isn't significant when the defendants were all public figures whose photographs are published almost daily in the media,' Trevor reminded.

'Every man in the dock at the trial had been identified by at least a dozen victims,' Anna protested.

'But when it came to describing the houses they'd been taken to and the rooms where they'd been assaulted the victims could only give the vaguest of descriptions.' Peter folded his coat into a cushion and settled it behind his head.

'Could the victims have been drugged?' Trevor accelerated and overtook a delivery van.

'It's possible,' Anna agreed. 'It's also probable that the victims were drunk. All the witnesses mentioned being plied with alcohol and sweets. The psychiatrists and psychologists we consulted warned us that children have a tendency to block painful or distasteful images from their conscious minds.'

'In my experience children don't always succeed in blocking them, which is one of the reasons why we run into so many messed-up kids on the streets,' Peter observed.

'Time to talk about what we should be looking for in Hill House.' Trevor dropped speed and pulled in behind a convoy of military vehicles.

'After listening to Patrick's comments about the formation of adipocere, I vote we start with the cellars, paying particular attention to any that are damp, dark and closed off from light and air.' Peter slipped his phone into his shirt pocket.

'I know you'll both have copies of the file I put together on the laptops we've been issued with, but I've also printed half a dozen large scale drawings of the original 1875 architect's plans of Hill House, and photocopied the notes and plans I found on the alterations that have been made to the building over the years. I've put them into document folders for you.'

'Major alterations?' Peter asked Anna.

'According to the notes I read on the history of the place, there've been ongoing improvements since the place was opened but only two major refurbishments, one in 1964 and another in 1982.'

'Ah, the sixties, when all public buildings were subjected to "modernisation" that required the ripping out and discarding of all original features – features that mysteriously reappeared in reclamation yards to the enrichment of shadowy council officials who were never charged with theft, only congratulated and rewarded for doing their job,' Peter sniped.

'Major as in knocking down walls and extending the building?' Trevor asked Anna.

'Both, as well as erecting temporary buildings in the grounds.'

'Sounds like we're going to have fun searching the place. If you two want to visit Point Green, the turning's a mile ahead.' Peter lay back, closed his eyes and made himself as comfortable as space would allow on the back seat.

'You coming in?' Trevor asked Peter after he'd parked the car in a visitors' parking bay.

'I'll stay and guard the car in case any escapees try to steal it.'

'Is your sergeant always so belligerent?' Anna asked Trevor as they left the car and headed for the main entrance.

'I'm so used to him I've long since ceased to notice

whether he is or isn't.'

'He seems to enjoy provoking people?'

'He does.'

'Does he care about anything?'

'A great deal, especially his family and the victims of crime.' Trevor stepped up to the door and pressed the button on the intercom. 'Are we expected?'

'I emailed the governor's office early this morning to request an interview.'

'Do you think this "ogre" will see us?'

'Unless he's feeling particularly cantankerous.'

'Did he co-operate with you on any aspect of your investigation?'

'No.'

'But he saw you and talked to you?'

'Oh he was prepared to talk all right. About anything and everything other than the case. As he's been attacked several times by other inmates he now spends most of his time in solitary confinement. To quote him, "I'll see anyone if it means a break in the monotony".'

An enormous uniformed guard appeared behind the glass door. Anna took her identification from her bag and held it up. He nodded and let them in.

'Good to see you again, Inspector Wells. We were sorry to hear about the outcome of the case.'

'Thank you. This is Chief Inspector Trevor Joseph.'

Trevor shook the guard's hand before he led them into a cool, clinical reception area, which was decorated in muted shades of blue and dark grey. The guard pointed to a bank of lockers.

'Thank you, I know the drill.' Anna kicked off her shoes and handed them to the man behind the reception desk so he could examine them.

Trevor took the key the guard gave him. He checked

the number, opened the corresponding door in the bank of lockers and removed the tray from inside the box. He stripped off his watch, emptied his jacket pocket of wallet, phone and pens and tipped the remainder of his loose possessions into the tray while Anna did the same. When her pockets were empty she set her handbag on top of the tray, replaced it in the locker and locked it. She retrieved her shoes, slipped them on and held out her arms so she could be scanned by a hand-held metal detector.

'You're clean.'

Trevor went through the same procedure before walking ahead of Anna into the first 'holding pen'. The door clanged shut behind them, the lock was activated and they waited for what seemed hours but was only minutes before the metal door ahead of them sprang open.'

'Inspector Wells, good to see you.'

'You're looking well, Colin,' she greeted the prison warder.

'Appearances can be deceptive, Inspector Wells. My back's giving me a lot of gip these days. It's so bad I can hardly move.'

Given the snail's pace of the grossly overweight man he and Anna followed down the corridor, Trevor could easily believe he had health problems. When they passed the open door of the warders' cubicle at the end of the bank of prisoners' cells he noticed that in addition to a table and two chairs there was an open bookcase. The top shelf held a few ledgers and a couple of official-issue notebooks, but most of the others were filled with cans of fizzy drinks, family-size packs of crisps and chocolate bars. The body of the guard sitting at the table positively rippled to the floor as he overflowed his chair.

Anna spoke to their escort as he ushered them into another holding pen. 'How's the ogre?'

'I couldn't tell you, ma'am. I don't have much to do with our Category A guests. But if there had been anything untoward I would have heard. Drama class,' he indicated as they heard chanting coming from the corridor that stretched ahead on the other side of the holding pen.

'Sounds like Greek tragedy,' Trevor quipped.

'It is, sir.'

Trevor thought the warder was joking until he looked at him.

'This is as far as I take you, ma'am, sir.' The warder closed the metal gate behind them. Trevor stood next to Anna and waited for the inevitable locking of the door they'd walked through and the opening of the door in front of them.

'Every time I enter a clean, sterile prison like this where a fair proportion of the inmates are incarcerated in their cells for twenty-three out of twenty-four hours a day, I think the staff are sentenced as much as the prisoners. It must be mind-numbingly boring.'

'You prefer nineteenth-century Victorian gaols without plumbing?' Trevor asked Anna in amusement.

'At least they have character.'

'Cold, damp, smelly character.'

'With interesting graffiti carved into the walls. There are some stunning examples in the old condemned cells.'

'You go looking for them?' Trevor was amused by the thought.

'It's a hobby. Two more air locks and we'll be in A wing.'

The senior warder was waiting for them. He showed them into a large room furnished with metal tables and benches. Every table had been welded into a single framework with two benches. The legs of both benches and tables were bolted to the floor.

'Has he agreed to see us?' Anna asked.

'He's agreed,' the warder replied, 'but whether you'll get anything out of him remains to be seen. He only returned to his cell from the hospital wing this morning after treatment.'

'Attacked again?'

'Yesterday,' the warder answered. 'In the showers.'

'Always the showers.'

'Some inmates complain if we watch them in the bathrooms. He should have been alone in there, but,' the warder shrugged, 'it's impossible to monitor all of the inmates all of the time.'

Anna changed the subject. 'Have you shown your prisoner the photographs I emailed through this morning?'

'Yes, the office printed them out and sent them down. I gave him hard copies an hour ago.'

'Did he look at them?'

'He took them out of the envelope and glanced at them, ma'am. He didn't exactly study them that I saw.'

'That would have been too much to hope for, but thank you anyway.'

Trevor sat on one of the benches. It was cold, hard, narrow and fixed too close to the table for his knees or comfort. Anna climbed in and sat beside him. The door opened and two warders escorted an inmate into the room.

CHAPTER NINE

The man who'd ruled tyrannically over Hill House Orphanage and Asylum for fifteen years, terrorising, abusing and raping the helpless inmates, was not a prepossessing figure. The same height as Trevor, he looked approximately treble the weight. Pasty-faced with watery brown eyes, he carried a heavy paunch, which contrasted with his spindly legs and arms. His greasy grey, thinning hair had been meticulously and painstakingly combed up and over the sides of his head to cover a bald patch – Trevor reflected he had nothing much else to do with his time. Handcuffed, dressed in a washed-out grey fleece tracksuit, he looked more pathetic than terrifying.

The first adjective that came to Trevor's mind was seedy, but then, he wasn't a frightened, insecure child who'd been dumped in unfamiliar surroundings.

The warder ushered his charge to the table and bench seat where Trevor and Anna were sitting side by side. He set the envelope he carried under his arm in front of them, stepped back and waited for the inmate to climb on the opposite bench.

The prisoner didn't advance. He stood and stared at Trevor and Anna.

'Please sit down.' Anna indicated the seat opposite them.

'I'll stay where I am.' His voice was soft, oily and oddly feminine.

'As you wish.' Anna reached across the table, opened the envelope and extracted the photographs it contained. 'Have you seen these?'

'Yes. I don't know why I was given them.'

'I emailed them to the governor's office this morning. I asked that they be shown to you in the hope that you could identify the individuals these body parts belonged to.'

'Identify – they're waxwork.'

'Unfortunately not,' Anna contradicted. 'The pathologist has confirmed they are all too real. As you see from the photographs, sometime last night they were arranged, along with the toys on the Hill House sign.'

'You can't pin that one on me.'

Anna remained deadpan. 'Before I leave here, I'll make sure to check your whereabouts last night with the warders.'

'Can your pathologist tell the difference between real and fake?' The ogre reached out and pushed the photographs across the table. 'They look like the sort of thing you'd find in a low-budget horror film.'

'Study the heads and features. They're bloated but recognisable if you'd seen the people when they were alive. Two are children, one an adult. Were the children inmates or the adult a member of staff at Hill House when you worked in the place?'

The ogre made a great pretence of picking up the photographs. He raised his eyes from them until he looked directly at Anna. 'You expect me to identify those battered heads?'

'I'm asking you to look at them. Do they remind you of anyone?'

'No. I know nothing about them. Just as I knew nothing about the abuse I was accused of inflicting on the boys who made false accusations against me.'

Trevor admired Anna's self-control as she returned the inmate's gaze without flinching.

'You were found guilty of child abuse by a jury in a court of law.'

'It was a miscarriage of justice,' he spat angrily.

'You were given legal representation and a fair trial. You appealed against the verdict and your appeal was dismissed. As was your application for parole.'

'You know a great deal about my trial and me.'

'I've studied the evidence against you,' Anna acknowledged.

'Then you must have realised that the charges against me were trumped-up.'

'On the contrary.'

'It doesn't bother you that an innocent man,' he pointed to his chest, 'was put away and that they wouldn't consider releasing me even after I finished serving my recommended minimum sentence. Although they've done as much for most of the murderers in here.'

'The parole board decided you needed to serve longer.' Anna wiped flecks of his saliva from her face with a tissue. 'Shout a little louder and spit a little further and I'll have a word with the prison governor about rescinding your privileges.'

'You wouldn't dare.'

Anna didn't answer, just looked at him.

The ogre pointed to a bandage wrapped around his neck. 'You don't care about my suffering. Out of sight is fine by you. I was attacked yesterday by an inmate with a sharpened spoon.'

'The bandage is an indication that you received

medical treatment. No doubt you made an official complaint with a view to receiving compensation.'

'I made a complaint, not that anyone in this place takes a blind bit of notice of anything I say.'

'You have to be alive to make a complaint. Please look at these photographs again?'

'No.'

'Are you refusing to look at them?'

'I've already looked at them.'

'Do you, or don't you, recognise anyone in them?'

'I recognise nothing.'

'Please look closer. The torso is wrapped in what appears to be the remains of a shirt. Is it part of the uniform the children in the orphanage were issued with when you were in charge?'

'There was no uniform when I managed the place. The children were allowed to wear their own clothes.'

'And if they were in Hill House long-term and had outgrown the clothes they brought in with them?'

'They were given catalogues and told to choose their own clothes.'

'The pattern on that shirt is distinctive. The colours are faded but you can see they were once red and green stripes.'

'You expect me to remember what clothes the children wore twenty-five years ago?'

Anna kept her voice soft, low. 'Twenty-five years is very specific. I never said that shirt was twenty-five years old.'

'It's obvious, isn't it?' the ogre blustered. 'Stripes were all the rage twenty-odd years ago. And as you just said, that's striped.'

'Then you do recall the children wearing striped shirts?'

'What if I do? I'll tell you something for nothing. Those who ended up in Hill House were scum. Absolute scum. Worthless! All they did was make trouble and play up, especially when they had an audience. The problem with gullible fools like you, and that goes for doctors, nurses, teachers, social workers and all the bleeding heart, liberal do-gooders, is that you believe every damned word the lying worthless tramps tell you. You never bother to look beyond the "poor me" hard luck stories they invent to tug at your heartstrings. You think, "poor kids". Poor kids *nothing*. Abuse! They didn't know the meaning of the word. Was it abuse to feed and clothe them, give them toys, take them on outings, let them run round and play all night when they refused to go to bed?'

Trevor spoke for the first time. 'You didn't have a timetable or a routine bedtime in Hill House?'

'What's it to you whether we did or didn't? You never spared those kids a single thought. And I'll tell you why. Because society took care to keep them well away from decent people. People who looked after them, like me and the rest of the staff in Hill House, should have been given medals for what we did.' Spittle dribbled down the ogre's chin as he began to lose control. 'You think those kids had feelings like you and me? They weren't even human! All they wanted to do was fight. They didn't care who they hurt and they didn't need a reason to lash out. There was no chance that they'd grow up into useful members of society. They behaved like vermin because they were vermin. No decent person gave a damn about them because they weren't worth caring about. Rats have more compassion in one claw than they had in their whole bodies. They cared for nothing and no one except themselves. They were prepared to lie, cheat and steal to get what they wanted, and they'd cut the throat of anyone who got in their way. Poor little children?' he sneered. 'Vicious, violent thugs more like. And the girls were worse than the boys.'

'Did you tell them what you thought of them?' Anna spoke calmly, conversationally.

'Of course I bloody well told them. Someone had to try and show them the error of their ways. There was good reason why they ended up in Hill House. Their parents didn't want them, even if they were alive and hadn't drunk or overdosed themselves to death. No decent person would want them. But I would have had more success trying to guide and advise a cockroach. The only people prepared to risk life and limb to look after those brats were me and the people I had working under me until that bloody soldier –'

'What "bloody soldier"?' Trevor interrupted.

'As if you didn't know.'

'I don't.'

Anna enlightened Trevor. 'A soldier on a night exercise found a naked, critically wounded boy crawling on the hillside. He contacted the ambulance service. The boy was airlifted to hospital. After examining him the doctor called the police. Before he died the boy told them he was from Hill House and that this man,' Anna pointed to the ogre, 'amongst others, had abused him. You'll find the rest of the story in the files.'

'The boy was a liar,' the ogre declared.

'And his injuries?' Anna queried.

'Self-inflicted.'

Anna picked up the photographs from the table, shuffled them together and returned them to the envelope.

'You're not going to leave them with me?' the ogre asked.

'There's no point if you're not going to study them.'

'I'll look at them later. I might see something then.'

'If you didn't see anything now, I doubt you'll see anything later.'

'But if I do think of something?' he called after Anna and Trevor as they climbed out of the fixed bench seat and walked towards the warder.

'Put in a request to see us. But we'll be busy, so it may take us a while to get back to you. If you should send for us and waste our time again when we get here, I'll make sure that you'll regret sending for us.'

'I might know something …'

Anna and Trevor both turned back from the door.

'Like what?' Anna demanded.

'Enough to keep me alive in here – but I'd rather be out.'

'Dream on,' Anna quipped.

'I know things.'

'What kind of things?' Trevor pressed.

'Insurance. Tell your bosses one more attack like the last one and my solicitor will hand the press the evidence I've hidden. Evidence that fingers the VIPs who raped the kids in Hill House. That's not an idle threat.'

'So, you know exactly who abused the children in Hill House – besides you and the rest of the convicted staff?' Trevor questioned.

'The only abusers were those bastard VIPs and I can prove it.'

'Then do so,' Trevor snapped, tired of the ogre's games.

'You give me something, and I'll give you something. Isn't that how it works?'

'Not when it comes to child abuse and murder it doesn't.' Anna nodded to the warder. He unlocked the door.

'Ask me something – anything!' the ogre shouted in desperation.

Anna watched him carefully. 'Where's your evidence?'

'You don't think I'd give up the only thing that's keeping me alive?'

'Do you know who arranged those body parts on the sign last night?' Anna demanded.

'If I do?'

'Tell us who it was.'

'Get me out of here.'

'No.'

'I'm not bluffing,' the ogre shouted.

'Neither are we. You have something to say to us that's worth listening to, send us a message through the governor.' Anna walked through the door, followed by Trevor.

Peter opened his eyes when Trevor opened the driver's door of the car.

'Enjoy your nap?' Trevor asked.

'No.' Peter rubbed his face with his hand. 'I was disturbed by all the activity in the car park. Noisy place and noisy exhaust on that new Merc. It needs seeing to. It belongs to your man's solicitor.'

'How do you know the driver was the ogre's solicitor?' Trevor asked.

'Files. Inspector Wells, my compliments, you made a decent job of compiling them. His photograph is on a press report of the ogre case.' Peter held up one of the laptops Anna had loaded with files and put in the car.

'Coming from you, Sergeant Collins, that sounds suspiciously akin to praise.' Anna climbed into the front passenger seat.

'Did you get anything out of the ogre?' Peter asked.

'Do sheep fly?' Anna retorted.

'He did recognise the shirt the torso was wrapped in,' Trevor reminded.

'He admitted it?' Peter rubbed his eyes and sat upright.

'No, but he recognised the pattern and said it was twenty-five years old.' Anna fastened her seat belt.

'Do you think the ogre killed those victims who ended up decorating the sign?'

'We can't even be sure they were murdered,' Trevor reminded Peter.

'You think they killed themselves and hung their own body parts on the gate?'

'I suggest we make a detailed and thorough investigation before voicing any theories that may influence our thinking.' Trevor turned the ignition and edged the car out of the parking bay.

'I'm surprised to hear you've already studied the files, Sergeant Collins,' Anna commented.

'Why? I learned to read a few years ago and like to practise every chance I get.'

'Picture books?' Anna mocked.

'I prefer the well-written police file. So much more creative imagination goes into its construction. Do either of you have an opinion as to why the ogre's solicitor turned up just after you arrived.'

'Presumably because the ogre sent for him,' Anna suggested.

'Before or after he saw the photographs you sent through to the prison, Inspector Wells?'

Anna turned to face Peter in the back of the car. 'The ogre was attacked yesterday in the shower by a prisoner wielding a sharpened spoon. He probably sent for his solicitor afterwards. Prisoners like to sue the Home Office every chance they get.'

Peter beamed. 'I love the image that conjures. A naked paedophile and a sharpened spoon. Thank you –'

'Do you really think the ogre sent for his solicitor because those photographs spooked him?' Anna interrupted, mulling over the thought.

'I think it's one hell of a coincidence that he asked to see his solicitor just after you sent them through.'

'He could have made the request yesterday after the court case ended,' Trevor suggested. 'He boasted that he has proof that could convict VIPs of abusing the children in Hill House. It's possible that he believes the evidence – if it exists – could be used as a bargaining tool to get him parole.'

'You really believe he's sitting on evidence that could convict influential people of child abuse?' Peter asked.

'There has to be a reason why he hasn't disappeared,' Anna said thoughtfully. 'On the other hand he could be bluffing.'

Trevor turned on to a slip road that led up and on to a stretch of dual carriageway. 'When those VIPs walked free yesterday, the ogre might have thought their acquittal would give him grounds for another appeal against his own conviction.'

'Or he saw the photographs and was worried that a trace of his DNA still remained on those body parts or clothes.' Peter reached into his pocket, pulled out three chocolate bars and offered two to Trevor and Anna.

'Not when I'm driving thank you,' Trevor refused.

Anna reached out her hand. 'Please, I can't resist crunchy chocolate.'

Peter passed her a bar, opened another and bit into it. 'I read an article about recent developments in forensics. It said that traces of DNA at a crime scene can last for years.'

'More reading,' Anna teased.

'So Jenny Adams confirmed the last time we worked together.' Trevor pulled out into the stream of traffic. 'I hope she and Patrick have their lab and mortuary set up by the time we reach Hill House.'

'Was the ogre convicted of acting alone?' Peter checked with Anna.

'He was tried alone, but six other members of the staff of Hill House were charged with child abuse at the same time. They opted to be tried separately and all were found guilty, but in every case the ogre was named and accepted as the ringleader of the paedophile group.'

'They're all in prison?'

'They were, Sergeant Collins –'

'Please, we're travelling in the same car, you're eating my chocolate, call me Peter.'

'The former members of staff were all found guilty and imprisoned for terms varying from two to nine years. I checked their whereabouts before we went to court. All are on the sex offenders register and all are now free under licence.'

'Did you track down their present locations?'

'They're all living in bail hostels in a coastal area of the south of England. But as every police officer knows, it's a rare convicted paedophile who returns to their family.'

'I hope they're being closely monitored.' As soon as he said it, Peter realised he was being optimistic.

'In this era of cutbacks?' Anna unzipped her bag and removed her laptop. 'I'll draw up a plan of action. Where do you want to start with this case, sir?'

'Call me Trevor when we're in an informal situation

like now. Forensics first. We'll talk to Patrick and Jenny as soon as we reach Hill House.'

'Have you met Patrick O'Kelly?' Peter crumpled his chocolate wrapper and pushed it into his pocket.

'And Jenny Adams,' Anna added. 'We've worked together a few times.'

'You like their sense of humour?'

'I prefer it to yours, Peter. And after we've been updated on forensics?' she turned back to Trevor.

'A detailed and thorough search of the site. My instinct tells me those body parts came from somewhere close by.'

'You think they were kept in the house?'

'Not necessarily. There are the grounds as well. You've studied the map. Are there any marshy or boggy areas or old buildings? An icehouse perhaps?'

'For the most part the grounds are barren Welsh hillside. There were outbuildings marked on the original plans of Hill House, principally workshops that were used to teach carpentry and metalwork. A few annexes were added later. Some after alterations had been made in the 1960s and 1980s. I didn't see any outbuildings when I viewed the place from the hillside a few months ago so I assume they've either fallen down as a result of decay or been demolished. I didn't think to look for an icehouse. But there might be one. The house is the right era.'

'Hills suggest valleys. Did you go to the floor?'

'No. I'm not even sure there's a road down to it from the orphanage.'

'The building was Victorian. Was there a bog or rock garden in the grounds?' Peter asked.

'It was built as an orphanage. I doubt the grounds would have been expensively landscaped or cultivated.'

'Might be worth checking, Victorian garden features lend themselves nicely to corpse disposal.'

'The voice of experience talking?' Anna joked.

'It wouldn't be the first time Joseph and I have found corpses in an ornamental garden.'

'After we've talked to Patrick and Jenny and conducted the search, we'll think again,' Trevor mused. 'Of course, if we strike lucky and find hard evidence that's worth following up ...'

'We'll crack the case and return to our cosy domestic lives within twenty-four hours?'

'That is too much to hope for,' Trevor glanced at Peter in his rear view mirror.

'I'm hoping we'll be away for at least a week.'

'You have an unhappy home life, Sergeant Collins?' Anna asked in amusement.

'On the contrary, but I do have a colicky baby daughter. Her paediatrician keeps telling us she'll grow out of it. I'll be more than happy to stay – even in Wales – until she does.'

'And your wife?'

Peter smiled as an image of Daisy, hair tousled, frowning from lack of sleep came to mind. She was beautiful even when exhausted. 'She's a saint as well as a qualified doctor. She'll cope. Unlike the ogre when he's faced with inmates with sharpened spoons. Doesn't it bother either of you that the people who've kept the lid on the happenings at Hill House for so many years have a very long reach?'

CHAPTER TEN

'So this is the nearest town to Hill House.' Peter looked out of the car window at the winding terrace of Georgian shops and houses built a metre or so above the road on a raised pavement.

'It was the county town.' Anna pointed across the street, where the road and pavement were the same level. An archway led into the yard of an old coaching inn. 'When I came here to view Hill House with Justin, Shane and Mac we had a good meal in there. It has a fantastic atmosphere. I doubt it's changed or been decorated since Jane Austen stepped out of a carriage.'

'Stop, Joseph, I'm hungry.'

'It may have escaped your notice, but I'm in the middle of traffic.'

'There's a public car park behind that supermarket,' Anna pointed to a turning a few yards ahead.

'Looks like I'm not the only one who's hungry.' Peter sat up and ran his fingers through his hair as Trevor entered the car park.

'You can always eat,' Trevor commented.

'We don't all live on fresh air like you. There's a parking space over there.'

Trevor pulled up. Peter climbed out, locked the laptop he'd been using into the boot of the car and headed for the ticket machine.

Trevor looked around. The car park was busy. A traffic warden was checking the times on the displayed parking vouchers and entering them into his notebook. He waved as they passed. 'This might be the middle of Wales but given the number of Audis, Mercs and BMWs, it appears to be fairly affluent.'

'Farming area, rife with inherited wealth and an abundance of celebrity second homes. Just look at the clothes.' Anna gazed enviously at a middle-aged woman wearing an artistically draped velvet scarf and coat so stunning even Trevor recognised it as unique. 'That has to be a Charles and Patricia Lester original. I saw their couture in a feature in *Vogue*. They're Welsh designers who make bespoke items to order as well as supplying film and theatre costumes. One day ...'

'You two coming or what?' Peter shouted from the ticket machine.

'Impatient isn't he?'

'Unbearable when he needs feeding.' Trevor slipped on his coat and replied to a couple's friendly greeting. 'I can't believe this town. Well-dressed, polite people. A traffic warden who smiles and waves. I feel as though I've stepped through a time warp into the 1950s.'

'It seems a nice place.'

'You didn't spend much time here?'

'Just long enough to eat a meal.'

Peter joined them. They negotiated the alleyway that led into the High Street.

A camper van painted with sunflowers and roses drove through the archway into the stable yard of the inn as they approached. A young woman in a long, flowered dress and knitted shawl climbed out of the driver's seat. A kitchen hand appeared from a side entrance as she opened the back doors of the van. It was stacked high with trays of farm produce. He lifted out two boxes and carried them into the inn.

The woman noticed Peter watching her. 'Can I help you?'

'Sorry,' he apologised, aware he'd been staring at her. 'I've never met a real live hippy before.'

'We've moved on in the last half a century and prefer to be called earth people or free thinkers now.'

'Forgive me. I'm a simple urban man, uneducated in the ways of the world. Are you selling these?' He pointed to a tray of beeswax candles.

'No I'm taking them on a trip around the countryside. It's boring for them being locked up in a storeroom all day.'

'Met your match in humour, Peter,' Anna smiled.

The woman relented. 'I'm delivering orders to the local pubs and shops but I can spare you a few things. What would you like?'

Peter eyed the trays. 'A dozen beeswax tea lights and two jars of honey?'

'Should be twenty-two pounds, let's call it twenty with discount.'

Peter reached for his wallet.

Trevor called. 'We'll see you inside.'

'Order for me.'

'Steak and chips?'

Peter nodded, turned back to the woman and handed over a twenty-pound note.

'Thank you.'

'Thank you, Ms …'

'Alice.' She tucked the note into a bag she wore hooked on a belt at her waist.

The kitchen hand returned. 'Chef's asking if he can have another three boxes of vegetables, please, one of salad, another of votive candles and four jars of honey as all the rooms are booked in the inn. The dining room is full tonight and four parties are vegetarian.'

'He can have the honey, salad and two vegetable boxes. Tell him I'll have to return with the other vegetable box and votive candles and it will take me at least an hour to get there and back and load up.'

'Will do, Alice.' He picked up two boxes and carried them back through the yard to the kitchen door.

'Your goods are in demand,' Peter made room for the honey he'd bought in the box of candles she handed him.

'People here appreciate organic produce and they know ours is top quality, as are our honey and candles.'

'"Our"? Your family has a farm?'

'Land I cultivate with friends.'

'Friends who live close by?'

'You ask a lot of questions, Mr …'

'Peter,' he flashed a smile. She didn't return the gesture.

The boy returned. Alice took the empty boxes from him and placed them in the back of the van. 'Perhaps you'll buy more from me the next time I'm in town, Peter.'

'If I see you, I will. Thank you for these.' Peter carried the box into the inn.

Trevor and Anna had found seats at a table in a window alcove.

Peter dropped the box on a spare chair and joined them. 'You ordered steak and chips for me?'

'Rare grilled rump of Welsh beef with hand-cut chunky fried potatoes.'

'As opposed to foot-cut,' Peter joked. 'No salad?'

'I asked that nothing green be placed on or wafted over your plate.'

112

'You've been making friends with the locals, Peter?' Anna leaned back so the waitress could set a jug of water and plates of olives, olive oil and bread on the table.

'I have. I'm sure you'll be pleased to know that if you've ordered vegetables or salad, the supplier assured me it will be organic.'

'You met Alice?' The waitress noticed Peter's candles and honey.

'I did.'

'Everything she sells is first class. The chef here will do without rather than go to another supplier.'

Peter picked up one of the jars of honey and read the label. '*Hen Parc Mel*. That conjures images of hens running around a park with a pretty girl called Mel.'

The girl laughed. 'Mel is Welsh for honey, and Hen Parc ...'

'Translates from Welsh as old wood,' Anna supplied. 'It's also the name of a village near here.'

'So much for my understanding of Welsh.' Peter took a slice of bread and dipped it into the garlic-flavoured olive oil.

'Is Alice's farm in Hen Parc?' As he hadn't yet had time to study the map of the area around Hill House, Trevor was interested in any houses or farms in the vicinity.

'The food Alice sells is produced in Tepee Village.'

'Tepee Village?' Peter repeated in amusement. 'You have Indians here?'

'They're known as Native Americans now,' Anna corrected.

'Forgive my Neolithic language.'

'A group of hippies came here in the 1960s –' the waitress began.

'Back in the olden days,' Peter quipped.

'My grandparents remember them arriving.'

Trevor smiled, it wasn't often Peter was lost for words.

'They built tepees and started living off the land.'

'They're still there?' Trevor asked.

'Not in tepees. They've advanced with the times. Now they scoop hobbit cave houses in the woods and hillside, although some of the older members of the commune still use tepees for storage and to house their animals.'

'Where exactly did you say this Tepee Village was?'

'I didn't, sir,' the waitress replied. 'I'll see if your order is ready.'

'Did you know there was a tepee commune near Hill House?' Peter asked Anna.

'This is the first I've heard of it.'

'Might be worth looking into, especially as it seems to have been founded before the ogre worked in Hill House.' Trevor took a slice of rye bread from the communal plate. 'People there might have heard something about the orphanage.'

'Doubtful, sir. After talking to staff and inmates of the orphanage, I came to the conclusion that the ogre ran the place as though it was an isolated colony, not a part of Wales – or even Britain come to that.'

'Now that is what I call a steak. Thank you,' Peter said as the waitress served him after setting Anna's mushroom, spinach and parmesan risotto in front of her. 'Fish and chips again, Joseph?'

'Fish and risotto,' Trevor corrected.

'Would you like any sauces or condiments, madam, sirs?' the waitress asked.

'No, thank you, but you could tell us exactly where the tepee village is and how to get there.'

'Are you police officers or government officials, sir?'

'Why do you ask?' Peter questioned.

'Because the authorities have been trying to evict that community for years, although they do no harm. They pay their way and get on with everyone around here.'

'I'm sure they do …'

'If there's nothing else, sir. I have other patrons to serve.'

'Good to see the locals closing ranks on outsiders while remaining loyal to one another.' Anna thrust a fork into her risotto.

'Depends on what they are closing ranks on.' Peter cut into his steak.

'Surely you don't think that the local people were aware of the abuse being carried out on the inmates of Hill House?' Shocked by the notion, Anna dropped her fork back on to her plate.

'The media reported that some of the victims of the alleged abuse complained to the staff about what was happening to them. Those members of staff would have either had to live in Hill House or close by. It's probable that they discussed the allegations with family or friends. Unless that is, they all wore blinkers, or were warned not to say a word on pain of losing their jobs.' Peter forked a piece of steak into his mouth. 'It would be interesting to look at the figures for staff turnover during the years the ogre was in charge,' he added when he finished chewing.

'It's one more aspect worth considering. I'll ask Merchant to check the staff records.' Trevor reached for his notebook and pen.

'I feel like a condemned man eating his last meal. Do you know what catering arrangements have been made for us?' Peter sprinkled more salt onto his potatoes.

'No.'

'Honestly, I can't leave anything important to you, Joseph.'

'We're only about twelve miles from Hill House. You can always come in and pick up a takeaway for us,' Anna suggested.

'At the end of a mind-crushing twenty-hour day?'

'It crushes your mind to think?'

Trevor gazed out of the window at the street. It was busy. Elderly couples were window shopping in the galleries and antique "emporiums". Young mothers pushed prams into the coffee shop across the road. A group of well-dressed middle-aged women were purposefully heading for the inn.

The scene looked so peaceful, so normal. He didn't want to consider these people in the context of the corpse parts and crimes associated with Hill House, but the images were already forming in his mind. He knew from bitter experience there was nothing he could do to eradicate them, other than investigate and trust he uncovered something close to the truth.

'You're too busy thinking to eat, Joseph?'

Trevor realised his meal was growing cold on his plate. 'I was imagining what it would be like to be orphaned and wrenched from everything and everyone I knew to be brought to this remote part of Wales.'

'This part – and by that I mean this town – might be bearable if you were with people who were kind to you and inspired trust. But to be taken to an enormous Gothic building on a barren hillside and placed in rooms full of other confused and frightened children … it doesn't bear thinking about,' Anna said feelingly.

Trevor sensed she was remembering more than imagining

'How many children were in Hill House at any one time?' Peter asked.

'It was built to house a hundred and fifty but it has

housed well over three hundred on occasion, especially during the depressions of the 1920s and 1930s and post-Second World War. That was when the British Government decided to take some of the pressure off the orphanages by sending out boatloads of children from care to Australia and Canada.'

'I've read about that scandal. You've done your homework, but then a case that involves the ill-treatment of children is all-consuming.'

'That sounds like the voice of experience talking, Peter.'

'Joseph and I have had our share. What amazes me is that people in authority keep appointing bastards like that ogre to positions of trust that allow them to ill-treat children.'

'The problem is they don't look like ogres.'

'Or, they are ogres appointed by ogres,' Peter suggested. 'What's that saying about like being attracted to like?'

'You think a paedophile network operated out of Hill House?' Anna questioned.

'From the evidence of the victims in the trial of the VIPs you investigated, I believe Hill House may well have been just one of many staging and procurement posts in a nationwide network. Haven't you read the headlines in some of our more salacious red tops? *They looked at us as if we were sweets on display in a sweet shop* is one that comes to mind and I'll give you one guess as to who was playing the part of the sweets and who was playing the greedy schoolboy.'

'Has it never occurred to you, Anna, that the abuse was highly organised and the staff put in place in Hill House to facilitate it?' Trevor asked.

'I thought …' Anna fell silent.

117

'You thought what?' Peter asked.

'I suppose if I considered the situation at all, I assumed that it was just a few perverted evil people who kept in touch with one another.'

'I don't entirely disagree with you. They certainly were perverted and evil, but I question their numbers and the extent of their influence.'

'You think they'll try to put a stop to our investigation?' Anna asked.

'Let's just say I think it's possible that they engineered the outcome and verdict in yours.' Trevor rose from his chair. 'Time we were on our way.'

CHAPTER ELEVEN

Peter stepped out of the car, breathed in and started coughing. 'This really is the end of the road,' he wheezed when he could talk. 'The back end of beyond. The last transit stop of the world. The air is raw.'

'It's fresh, Peter. You want pollution, go back to the city.' Anna climbed out of the passenger seat and studied the cars, vans, military vehicles and Portakabins that lined both sides of the country road which ended a hundred yards ahead in a quarry encircled by a mountain track.

'I find dirt reassuring and warming. This wind could slice through steel. It's playing havoc with my lungs, not to mention my aged, aching bones.'

Anna smiled. 'Old people do feel the cold more.'

'And young people's brains haven't developed enough for them to recognise an Arctic breeze when it blows in their face.'

Trevor slammed the car door and stretched his cramped muscles. 'I see Portakabins and vehicles but no Victorian orphanage.'

'The gate's behind you,' Anna pointed to the hillside below them.

Trevor turned. A tarmac drive led down to a pair of massive, close-worked wrought iron gates. It wasn't easy to see through the intricate pattern of rusting metal but he could just about make out grey flashes of roof slate.

'I assumed Hill House would be on top of a hill.'

'Weather they get up here, it probably made sense to build halfway down and into the slope to get what shelter they could from the lie of the land.'

An extremely fit army officer in his early thirties approached. He held out his hand. 'Major Simmonds, presumably you are the police as you couldn't have driven through the road blocks we've set up without showing your ID.'

Trevor shook the hand he offered. 'Chief Inspector Trevor Joseph,' he indicated Anna, 'Inspector Anna Wells. Sergeant Peter Collins.'

'Nice to see you have this site secured tighter than a civil service tea and biscuit ration. Some might say three road blocks are excessive, but not me.' Peter shook the major's hand.

'Good exercise for the men, setting up and manning security barriers. I ordered all the portable buildings now at your disposal to be erected along the end of this road. Initially I suggested placing the Portakabins in the grounds on the old hard standings that once housed long-demolished demountables, but your pathologist told me to keep the grounds clear until you've had time to conduct a thorough search.'

'We've no specific ideas on where to look, what we'll find, or where we'll find it.' Trevor studied the gates of Hill House. 'That chain and padlock look new. Can you give me a list of people who've entered the grounds since last night?'

'Before your pathologist, only Lieutenant Baker. He was out on the third night of survival exercise travelling after dark, when he spotted the body parts shining in the moonlight. At first he thought he was hallucinating. When he realised he wasn't, he made his way into the grounds.'

'Through the gates?'

'Over the wall.'

Peter narrowed his eyes. 'It's a high wall.'

'Baker's a fit man,' Major Simmonds replied without a trace of humour. 'He examined the heads and body parts and contacted HQ on his radio. When he touched them he thought they were fake. Some kind of Halloween props, although he did say the texture was odd.'

'Why did he contact army HQ and not the police?' Trevor asked.

'Convenience. He was carrying a radio tuned into military frequency. He suggested the duty officer call the local police so they could check out the body parts. The police requested he remain on site until they reached here. HQ gave him permission to abort the exercise so he could wait for their arrival. As you can see from the "DANGER DO NOT ENTER" signs, the local authority has declared this building and site unsafe. Lieutenant Baker was concerned that vandals may have broken into the house and might injure themselves.'

'Did he see or hear anyone while he waited?'

'I asked him that question. He replied in the negative but that doesn't mean there wasn't anyone hiding close by. Aware that Hill House is in a state of dereliction, I drove out here after HQ alerted me to his call. Local police officers arrived shortly after I did. It was they who contacted your pathologist.'

'The local police didn't examine the body parts?' Trevor checked.

'Only visually through the gates. The pathologist, Dr O'Kelly, and his assistant turned up a couple of hours later. He asked the local police to cut the chains on the gates, and ordered them and us to stay back while he examined the sections of corpse. As you're probably aware, by then news had broken that someone had posted up photographs of the body parts on the internet. We gave the pathologist a hand to move the sign and everything that had been hung on it into the temporary mortuary when it arrived this morning. The pathologist had the gates fastened with a new chain and lock after we moved the sign out. He said something about waiting for a dog handler.'

'The dog or dogs will be the next to go in,' Trevor acknowledged.

'This is the mortuary and forensic laboratory,' the major stopped outside the first Portakabin in the row. 'The next three cabins are earmarked for police and pathologist accommodation. Each has three bedrooms, with en suite shower rooms. The water pressure is lower than we would like but allowances have to be made when you're in the field.'

'Quite,' Peter agreed brightly.

Trevor frowned at him.

'The fourth cabin is a mobile canteen that the regiment has set up, stocked and staffed. It will be open 24/7 to everyone on site for the duration we're here. We'll lose the cost of running it in our budget. We have a creative financial officer.'

'Thank you, that's generous and thoughtful of you,' Trevor said.

'As a police officer used to subsisting on cans of soft drink, Mars bars and the odd sausage roll in the field, real food will be much appreciated.' Peter stepped up alongside Trevor.

'The end building is one of our largest. There are tables, stacking chairs and a couple of screens and white boards in there as well as a small separate office and toilet facilities. We use them for briefings so I thought it might do as your makeshift HQ. All the Portakabins have running water and electricity but only the end one has telephone and internet access. It wasn't easy to get communications installed at short notice here, but both telephone and internet are now operational. If you require anything else, let me know. Our base HQ is only a few miles down the road. We received an official request from the Home Office to keep the sightseers away and secure the perimeter. We'll continue to do so as long as we're needed. We also have plenty of spare muscle if you need any fetching and carrying.'

'Thank you for the offer, we may well take you up on it.' Trevor went to the door of the mortuary and laboratory and knocked.

'I'll leave you to settle in. Our site HQ is behind you on the opposite side of the road, on the hillside behind the perimeter wall of Hill House.'

'Thank you, Major. We'll see you later?'

'No doubt, Chief Inspector, if only in the canteen.'

Trevor knocked on the door of the Portakabin a second time.

A sharp voice replied in an Irish lilt. 'Enter if you must, but don't walk beyond the mat at the door.'

'There are three of us, Patrick.' Trevor opened the door and stepped to the edge of the mat to make room for Anna and Peter.

'Then stand side by side and be skinny.' Patrick looked up from the head he was dissecting. 'My oh my, if it isn't Trevor Joseph and Peter Collins with Inspector Anna Wells. Two beasts with one beauty. What are you doing with these reprobates, Anna?'

'Finding out if there's a case worth investigating.'

Trevor looked up and down the makeshift mortuary. It

was surprisingly spacious. There was a bank of freezer drawers too small to take a corpse, but roomy enough for the body parts that were ranged on slabs on a set of side shelves. A dissecting table complete with tap and running water projected out from the wall next to the freezer drawers. A work surface at standard height ran around three sides with fitted cupboards beneath and shelves above.

'Nice place you have here.'

'Isn't it just?' Patrick agreed. 'It doesn't come with all the advantages of a full-sized mortuary but as someone has taken the trouble to chop these corpses into bite-size pieces, they're proving easy to handle, so we don't mind foregoing some mod cons.'

A door opened at one end of the area and Jenny emerged with a tray stacked with a cafetière, two specimen beakers and a roll of chocolate biscuits.

'We have visitors, Jenny.'

'So I see.' Jenny dumped the tray on to a work surface.

'I hope those biscuits have been cooled. If there's one thing I hate it's melted chocolate on biscuits.' Patrick said.

'You saw me take them out of the drawer that's holding the leg you dissected.'

'When will you two give up trying to shock us, Jenny?' Peter grumbled.

'That's Dr Adams to you, Sergeant Collins. And in answer to your question, when you stop annoying us. Coffee, Trevor, Anna?'

'I could murder one,' Anna said. 'It's been a long drive and I've missed a night's sleep but I prefer mine in a china cup to a specimen beaker.'

'Canteen is the last but one Portakabin on the mountain side of this row but even they don't have china cups, only waxed paper cartons. Sure you wouldn't prefer a glass specimen beaker?' Jenny filled both beakers with coffee and added sugar from a suspicious-looking urn and milk from a strangely shaped bottle.

'Quite sure, but thank you for asking.' Anna moved as Peter pushed past her and opened the door that Jenny had walked through. He peered in.

'Nosy aren't you, Collins?' Patrick snapped off his rubber gloves and took one of the specimen beakers Jenny had stirred with a scalpel.

'Essential attribute for every police officer.'

'Dolls' house-sized kitchen and bathroom,' Jenny explained as she handed Patrick a biscuit and offered the roll to the others.

'So I see.' Peter took a biscuit but he was the only one aside from Patrick.

'So what can you tell us, while we stand and think ourselves skinny on your mat?' Trevor asked Patrick.

'We have body parts from six corpses.'

'But only three heads?' Peter demolished half his biscuit in one bite.

'Three heads, two from children, one adult. We also have three arms, all children's and all from different corpses. Annoyingly, none belong to the heads. One head, torso and one leg belong to one child, another head second torso and one arm a different child. The only part we have from the adult is the head.'

'So we're looking for ...' Peter considered for a moment.

'An adult's headless corpse, two arms and a leg belonging to one child, two legs and an arm from another and three children's corpses minus arms, two right and one left,' Jenny answered for him.

'Thank you, that's helpful,' Trevor said. 'Have you

found anything that might assist us to identify these individuals?'

'I'm a pathologist, not a bloody magician.' Patrick stepped back from the table. 'Over here.'

'You're allowing me to tread on to your hallowed floor?' Trevor asked in amusement.

'I'm offering to instruct and enlighten you as to what we're working with. Jenny, slap a hat and overall on him, and while you're at it paper over-boots. I suppose as they've interrupted us, you may as well get sets for Anna and our friend as well.'

'We've only disturbed you so we can investigate your findings and determine if a crime has been committed,' Peter protested.

'Given that these corpses haven't been buried, I think it's safe to assume they didn't cut themselves up.' Patrick rolled on a fresh pair of gloves.

'So who did?' Peter asked.

'That's for you to find out, Collins.'

Peter zipped up his overalls. 'I never knew you thought of me as a friend, Patrick. I'm touched.'

'Don't push your luck, Collins,' Patrick pulled up his mask and glared at Peter over the top.

Trevor slipped on the paper over-boots before moving alongside Patrick.

Patrick held up a slice he'd removed from the cheek of the head he was examining. 'Adipocere.'

'Looks like candle wax.'

'Precisely. It can be rock hard but this isn't quite there yet. However, rock hard or the consistency of cream cheese, it's a swine to separate from bone.'

'How –'

'No questions until I've finished talking.' Patrick turned his head and took a bite from a chocolate biscuit

Jenny held out to him. 'Adipocere is formed from the fat of a deceased corpse's soft tissue. It can make identifying a body and pinpointing time of death difficult. What is absolutely clear is that a corpse with adipocere is not fresh. As I said to you on the phone, they can be months, years or even centuries old. Once formed, adipocere acts and behaves like a preservative and doesn't decompose like normal flesh.'

'Run through the environmental conditions necessary to produce adipocere again?' Anna asked.

'Oxygen-free, but you need the presence of some types of bacteria and a fairly generous layer of body fat on the corpse. Warm temperature, mildly alkaline environment and moisture, either in the environment or from the body itself, can trigger formation but it will take time, months, years even, but it can also begin within a few days after death provided the conditions are right.'

'At the risk of incurring your wrath – what can you tell us about these body parts?' Trevor ventured.

'I can tell you what I told Dan earlier. The children's are all male, as is the single adult. We've gauged the ages of the two children at death. One was between four and seven years old, the other nine and twelve. I've taken X-rays of the teeth. All three heads bear evidence of dental work and if their dentists kept records we should be able to identify them from those. I've stripped back the adipocere to reveal the bones and extracted DNA, which is why I know we have parts from six separate corpses. Jen is running profiles through our DNA database now, although as we haven't internet access in this mortuary we're doing it from our files which aren't up to date.'

'Merchant is on her way.'

'Good. Although it's worth pointing out that even if our database was up to date it's unlikely the children's

DNA would be on it. However, if they are related to criminals who've had their DNA recorded we may pick up a familial match.'

'Any progress on cause of death?' Peter questioned.

Patrick laughed, a short sharp sound that reminded Trevor of a seal's bark. 'Did you hear the man, Jenny? Are we looking at the same body parts? How in hell do you think I can determine cause of death from these pieces?'

'Something must have killed them,' Trevor said evenly.

'Something or someone. I've checked the remains of the necks on the heads. The hyoid bone in all three has been fractured.'

'So they were strangled?' Anna suggested.

'Not necessarily. Given the absence of any other injury in an intact corpse it can pinpoint strangulation as a possible cause of death. But these heads, torsos and limbs were removed from the corpses, and, by the look of the jagged edges, none too gently. It's possible the hyoid bones were fractured post-mortem. To determine cause of death I'd need more body parts than we have here.'

'Did you find any distinguishing marks on the body parts that might help us?' Trevor persisted.

'I can tell you one child had black hair, one brown and the adult male had fair hair. Birthmarks and skin imperfections may be detectable when I take a closer look but they may just as likely not show. When I've finished this head I'll examine the torso, and more specifically the stomach and intestines. Jenny is removing bone collagen from the long bones. We'll try to carbon date it and a piece of that striped shirt, along with any stomach or intestine contents we find in the torsos. If we're successful we may be able to give you an approximate date of death but I'm talking about narrowing it down to years not weeks.'

'Have you determined race from the skulls?' Anna took a closer look at the fragment of shirt Jenny was handling.

'Initial examination suggests all were white Caucasian,' Jenny replied.

'That's all the information we can give you at the moment. You want to know more, you're going to have to leave us in peace,' Patrick warned.

'Have you moved into the accommodation here?' Trevor asked.

'Jenny and I have taken a room in the cabin next door to this one.'

'They each have three en suite bedrooms?' Trevor checked.

'They do,' Jenny confirmed, 'and very comfortable they are too. All the beds are large single, or small doubles, dependent on your size.' She eyed Peter. 'That's a small single in your case, Peter. You've burgeoned since Daisy managed to drag you up the aisle. I'll never understand why she bothered, or what she sees in you.'

'My charm,' Peter winked.

'You keep it well hidden.'

'Peter and I will take the centre Portakabin, you're welcome to share with us if you want to, Anna, that leaves the third one for Clive Barry.'

'And his dog or dogs?' Patrick resumed his study of the head.

'They'll probably sleep in the cage in his van. Hopefully we won't need him or them for more than a day or two. Tristram Hever can bunk in with him.'

'And Merchant and her paramour?' Peter asked.

'I would say nice sensible people like them can share

with us, but we'll hold off until you go into the house, Trevor.' Patrick continued to slice the adipocere on the head he was working on. 'Depending on what you find in there we may need a few extra pairs of hands.'

'So, if you don't mind, we'll keep the two spare bedrooms in our Portakabin in reserve for the time being,' Jenny said.

'Two spare bedrooms? You and Patrick? Still together – my oh my. Must be coming up to some kind of anniversary.' Peter whistled.

'Nice of you to ask. I won't say more than it's time for you to send us a case of champagne, Collins.' Jenny teased a fragment of cloth from the striped shirt.

Patrick glared over his mask. 'You're making it impossible for me to concentrate. All of you out of here. Now!'

'You'll let me know –'

'The minute I find anything remotely of use. Yes.' Patrick looked up at Trevor. 'Don't I always? Now let me work!'

130

CHAPTER TWELVE

Trevor emerged from the van to see Sarah Merchant and Chris Brookes parking their car in front of his. Clive Barry had already pulled in ahead of them. He'd opened the back of his van and was filling his dogs' bowls with water.

After directing Sarah and Chris to their Portakabin, which he warned they'd have to share, Trevor joined Clive Barry.

'Welcome to Wales, Barry. I'm glad to see you have two dogs? I know we asked but I wasn't sure we'd get them.'

'They like working in pairs, sir. Meet Clovis and Clothilde.' Barry held up the spaniels' leads.

'Fine-looking dogs,' Trevor complimented. He knew better than to stroke them because it invariably resulted in the reprimand, "They're working dogs, not pets," from the handler.

'The best cadaver dogs I've worked with, sir. It was cadaver, not blood dogs you wanted?'

'It was,' Trevor confirmed. 'Get yourself settled into your accommodation. The first Portakabin is the mortuary and lab, the next three are accommodation. The first two have been taken but the third has been earmarked for you, Hever, Brookes and Merchant. The fourth is a canteen. The fifth HQ.'

'I'll grab a coffee and a sandwich then make a start, sir. The dogs could do with a run after being cooped up on the journey.'

'Patrick O'Kelly has identified the corpse sections we have as adipocere. Will that create a problem for the dogs?'

'No, sir, even if the adipocere is rock hard. They're trained to pick up corpse scent and both of these dogs have done that on skeletons that have been in the ground for thirty years and more. Chemicals are produced by every corpse when it decays, even if the soft tissue is transformed into adipocere later, and it's the chemicals the dogs are trained to react to.'

'This is the mortuary. Patrick O'Kelly and Jenny Adams are working on site. I'm sure they'll oblige should you need any scent samples.' Trevor knocked on the door of the Portakabin and shouted, 'We're not coming in, just advising you that the dogs have arrived with Clive Barry, Patrick.'

Patrick shouted a reply through the door. 'Hello, Barry. Unfortunately this case is more complicated than the last we worked on together. If you need anything, feel free to come in here but …'

'Think yourself skinny and stay on the door mat.' Peter stepped down from the canteen and handed Trevor a coffee. 'Real, ground coffee.'

'In a real waxed paper cup.' Trevor took it from Peter.

'Moan, moan. But the coffee is guaranteed ground and authentic.'

Barry shut the dogs back into the van. 'I'll take my case to my room, get that coffee and sandwich, then I'll be with you, sir.'

'I'll go into the grounds with you and the dogs. I want to be on hand if you find anything. Twenty minutes long enough for you?' Trevor looked up at the sky. 'Just as well we get as much done as we can in daylight.'

'I'll be ready, sir.'

Trevor opened the hatchback of his car, placed his coffee on the roof and lifted out his case. He noticed Peter had already removed his case and the beer, wine and crisps. He retrieved his coffee and carried it and his case inside the Portakabin. Anna had taken possession of the cubicle to the left of the door and was already hanging clothes in a tiny narrow wardrobe.

'Hope you don't mind me taking this room, sir?'

'Not at all.' Trevor turned right.

'It's a narrow corridor so take Patrick's advice and be skinny.' Peter opened a door on his left. 'There's a slightly larger third room ahead, but the beds in both are the same size.'

'Which do you want?'

Peter shrugged. 'Makes no difference to me.'

'You take the larger.' Trevor tossed his case on the bed and opened the two doors in the room. One was a wardrobe barely deep enough to take four clothes hangers front on, the other a shower room.

'Gives new meaning to "compact" doesn't it?' Peter peered in from the doorway.

'Showering with elbows in and head bent to accommodate the low ceiling will refresh my contortionist skills. See you outside in a few minutes.' Trevor closed the door, opened his case, removed the photograph of Lyn and Marty and placed it on a shelf next to the bed. He stowed away his clothes, washed his hands and face in cold water and left.

Peter, Anna, Barry and the dogs were waiting at the gates to Hill House.

Peter held up a key. 'You owe me. I prised this from

Patrick at the cost of his standard lecture on how not to contaminate crime scenes. As if I needed a refresher given the number of times he's recited it to us.'

They donned fresh protective suits over their clothes. Peter unlocked the chain and unthreaded it from the wrought iron gates. He opened one gate and pushed it inwards. It groaned and shuddered. A shower of rust particles fell from the hinges.

Trevor studied the wall. Moss had been scuffed from the stones in four places close to the top. 'Perhaps the army officer on night exercise wasn't the only one to vault this wall recently. Is there another gate in the perimeter wall?' he asked Anna.

'Not one that's marked on any plan I've seen, sir, but if you look down the grounds you can see the stone wall is much lower in front of the house than it is on either side or up here. If anyone knows the place, they might walk around and try to get into the garden from there.'

'Large walled-in area. You could mark out a couple of football pitches and a tennis court down there, if you weren't put off by the slope.' Peter stepped through the open gate to get a better view.

'Not so large when you consider the number of children the home housed at its peak.'

'You said it was built to take a hundred and fifty,' Trevor checked with Anna.

'Fifty girls, a hundred boys and twenty staff, sir. But in 1900, twenty-five years after the doors were opened, it housed three hundred and forty children. I found a copy of a letter written by the master complaining to the Parish Guardians that he'd been forced to place the children two and even three to a bed, including the babies. As a result, childhood diseases had rocketed and the death toll had risen. Seventeen in one week alone from measles.'

Peter shook his head. 'You have to love the Victorians. They cried buckets over Dickens' fictional killing-off of foundling Smike while consigning unwanted children to orphanages and workhouses that would have made Dotheboys Hall look like Eton.'

'I'm impressed. You really do read, Peter,' Anna teased.

Barry kneeled in front of the gates, unclipped the dogs from their leads and gave a command. They bounded forward. Both stopped dead in their tracks a few feet inside the grounds and barked.

'The exact site where the sign stood.' Patrick observed from behind them. 'You can see the holes in the tarmac where the local police yanked it out.'

Trevor turned to face him.

'Jen's holding the fort. Thought I'd be on hand in case you find something.'

Barry knelt beside the dogs and rewarded them.

'Any chance they can backtrack to wherever those body parts came from?' Anna asked Barry.

'Ever seen a dog search before?' Trevor didn't take his eyes from the dogs as Barry instructed them to move forward.

'No.'

'And there they go.' Peter watched Barry send the dogs haring around the back of the building, built into the mountainside. Clovis and Clothilde raced up and down the length of the high retaining wall that separated the narrow back yard at the rear of the orphanage from the steep slope of the hillside. They stopped and sniffed around two doors that had been boarded up and investigated the drains and perimeter of the area. The ground was covered with chippings blackened by age and mildew. They looked as though no one had trodden on them for years.

Barry waited until the dogs had examined every inch of the dark, dank back.

'They've found nothing here, sir,' Barry shouted to Trevor. He recalled the dogs, instructed them again and sent them around the far side of the building.

Both dogs ran ahead and sniffed the ground, stopping to check Barry's whereabouts every few minutes. Peter, Trevor, Anna and Patrick trailed behind. They walked around the side of the orphanage. There were no doors and every window had been boarded with planks, carefully sawn to sit flush with the surrounding wall and cover the entire frame, making it difficult for anyone intent on intruding to gain purchase or access to the building.

The front façade of Hill House was still imposing even in dereliction. As large as a stately home, it was massive, intimidating and dominated by a crumbling pillared portico. Half a dozen steps led up to the front door. Four stone-built stories towered above the steps and the narrow windows of a cellar sunk partially underground ran alongside them. Both dogs made straight for the door and started barking.

Barry rewarded them and examined the double doors. Like the windows they had been boarded over with planking but it wasn't flush with the wall of the house. It was also the worse for wear with weathering. Rusty nails protruded from the rotting wood that had greyed and splintered with age.

Barry tugged at one of the planks. It came away easily in his hand. 'Looks like this was either removed recently, or rotten or both. You want me to tear down the rest of the planks, open the door and send the dogs in, sir?'

Trevor looked up at the sky and checked the time on

his watch. 'No. It's getting late. It will be dark in half an hour and we could miss something if we use torchlight. We need to access portable floodlights and set them up first thing tomorrow in the ground floor and the basement. I'll talk to the army about removing the boards from all the doors and windows to get some natural light into the building and I'll inform the local authority that we're going in. I doubt any services are still connected. By the look of the tiles hanging off the roof we'll also need safety gear and hard hats.'

Barry gave the dogs the order to stand down. They sat side by side on the step, panting, waiting for a further command.

'Do me a favour please, Barry, take the dogs around to the side of the house we haven't checked and if there are any other doors, get the dogs to pay attention to them.'

'Will do, sir.' Barry ordered his dogs to move on.

Trevor stepped back from the front door. Like the narrow back yard, the flat area in front of the steps was covered with coarse grey chippings. A layer of moss had settled over those closest to the house and the low wall that separated it from the slope of hillside, but there were a few scuffed spots that looked as though they'd been trodden on, and recently. He craned his head back and looked up at the building.

It was in a sorry state. The narrow basement windows at ground level were barred, and those on the first and second stories were boarded over with planks that had splintered at the sides, showing the same signs of rot as those that covered the front door. The window frames on the third and top – presumably attic – floor were in a dire state, also rotten but fronted by iron bars set in the stonework. The glass had fallen out in places, he assumed back inside the rooms. Above the row of attic windows, lengths of guttering along with several tiles hung precariously from the roof.

He studied the basement windows. The iron bars that fronted them were thicker and more substantial than those in the attic. The bricks around the windows were yellowish brown in contrast to the grey stonework. The overall effect was intimidating, even now when the orphanage was derelict and abandoned. How much more so would it have appeared to the children who'd arrived here after being separated from their families?

'The whole damned place is rotting,' Peter observed. 'Not just the woodwork and boards over the doors and windows but the walls themselves and the steps leading up to the front door. You can see the entire place crumbling inch by inch in front of your eyes.'

'It's evil.'

Trevor realised Anna was speaking more to herself than anyone else. He allowed Peter, Patrick and Barry to walk ahead with the dogs and fell into step beside her.

'You should know.'

'Dan said he'd told you that I was in here.'

'What was it like?'

'For me, bearable because Uncle Dan and two of my father's female colleagues, Aunties Sue and Marilyn, were with me the whole time.'

'They worked with Dan and your father?'

'They did.'

'You still in touch with them?'

'No. Sue was killed on duty shortly after I was returned to my mother and grandparents.'

'Do you know how she died?'

'Someone reported a man behaving suspiciously in a children's playground at two in the morning. When Sue arrived she was shot in the head and died instantly. They never caught her killer. It made headlines at the time. I researched the case when I joined the force. In fact, with hindsight, I think it was Sue and Marilyn who put the idea of joining the force into my head. Along with me wanting to honour my father of course.'

'I think I remember the case.'

'My mother cried when she was told Sue had been killed. Sue was a close family friend but more than that, her death rekindled all the horror of losing my father.'

'And Marilyn?'

'Was killed in a riding accident shortly after Sue was murdered. They found her body next to her horse on a country road. It was assumed that something had spooked her horse and it had thrown her.'

'Do you believe that?'

'I didn't know what to believe at the time and I don't know now. It seems an incredible coincidence that both of them should die in fatal accidents a short time after caring for me here. But then, Uncle Dan was with me too and he's still alive.'

'Very much so.' Trevor picked up on the strain and emotion in Anna's voice and filed away the information in his mind. One officer from a local force dying in a car crash was a tragedy – three in a short space of time raised his suspicions. 'What about your time here? Is there anything you recall that could be useful to this investigation?'

'I remember the awful unnatural silences, especially at bedtime amongst so many children. The atmosphere was dark, heavy, hushed as if everyone was too afraid to make a noise. It was even worse whenever the man we called the "master" walked into the room.'

'The ogre?'

'I never heard anyone called that when I was here.

139

Given the dates, I know "the ogre" was appointed manager of Hill House before I was an inmate, but I have no memory of him. I even looked up photographs of him from the time, but I didn't recognise him.'

'So you never heard the name "ogre".'

'Not that I remember, but I was very young and no doubt traumatised at the time.'

'Have you told him you were an inmate?'

'No.'

'Has he guessed?'

'I doubt it.' She gave a cynical smile. 'Although he has complimented me on my research into this place.'

Trevor heard the dogs bark and quickened his pace.

Barry had stopped at the side of the building. 'The dogs are alerting to this side door, sir. There's the foundations of a step and what looks like an old porch, although if it was a porch it's been flattened.'

Barry pushed the boards that had been nailed over the door. They gave way and the door scraped a few inches back over the threshold. He peered inside. 'Looks like it's been recently opened judging by the dust that's been disturbed on the floor, sir, but it's as black as a tomb in there.'

'Patrick will want to go in there first and we'll need lights. Peter, inform Patrick that we've more than likely found our corpse-arranging joker's entrance to the house.' Trevor turned back to Anna. 'You missed a night's sleep yesterday.'

'So did you.'

'Not an entire night. The major said the canteen will be serving food 24/7. Go and eat, then get some rest. If we get access to the house, we'll have a full day ahead of us tomorrow. For elimination purposes I'll make a start on checking the rest of the grounds with Barry and the dogs now, but I doubt we'll make much headway before dark.'

Anna looked down over the grounds within the wall. 'Do you think anything's buried here?'

'I make a point of not thinking or assuming anything until I'm faced with hard evidence.' He smiled at her. 'Goodnight, Anna.'

'Goodnight and thank you … Trevor.'

Trevor walked down the hill and gazed at the view after Anna walked away. The land within the walls of Hill House's grounds was covered in scrubby grass, longer in some places than others. He wondered if sheep ever clambered inside the walls. Below the lower wall the hill tumbled steeply down to the valley floor. A river cut through the base of the hills. To the right of the wall that surrounded the grounds a stream raced through copses of wind stunted trees and bushes, before circumventing a dry-stone wall sheep pen. In the distance to the left, a mile or possibly more away, he saw the grey slate roof of a farmhouse. Smoke curled upwards from a chimney. He shivered. The sun was sinking. The air growing colder by the minute.

He turned and walked back up to the side door. Peter had returned. He'd pushed back the side door and he and Barry stood talking in front of it.

'Patrick says he'll take a look when he has time, but he'll need portable floodlights. I told Merchant to track some down and have them erected.'

'Thank you.'

'I'd say we have about twenty minutes of reasonable daylight left, sir,' Barry observed. 'Would you like me to let the dogs loose in the grounds.'

'Please, Barry. I'll be with you in a moment.'

Barry gave the dogs a command and followed them down the hill.

Trevor turned to Peter. 'Anna looked as though she was sleeping on her feet so I sent her back to get some food and rest. I suggest you do the same.'

'I suppose you want us up at the crack of dawn tomorrow.'

'I intend to go into the house as soon as it's light.'

'See you.' Peter was already walking away. Trevor saw Barry heading for the right hand wall. A few straggly buddleia and hydrangea bushes sporting dry withered blooms blew in the wind, evidence that shrubs had once been planted in the grounds. He looked around for other signs of cultivation but if there had been more shrubberies or flowerbeds within the walls, they had long since died back allowing the ground to revert to barren mountainside.

'One hell of a lonely place, sir,' Barry observed when Trevor joined him and the dogs.

'It is, but the house would have been full when it was occupied. With staff as well as orphans.'

'Clothilde's picked up a scent again, sir. Look.'

Trevor saw the dog standing barking a signal beside the centre of the low wall that fronted the grounds. Clovis joined her, sniffed and added his barks to hers.

'Could be whoever handled the corpse parts climbed over the wall and left a scent, sir. Do you want to follow?'

'Not in this twilight. The hillside outside of the grounds can keep until tomorrow, Barry. Time to go back, eat and see if Merchant and Brookes have set up the incident room.'

'Yes, sir.' Barry walked down to retrieve the dogs.

Trevor went with him. 'Strange, isn't it? The dogs reacted at the front door of the house, the side door and this wall. Yet nowhere in between.'

'Not strange, sir. They're trained to pick up on areas

that have been in direct contact with corpse scent, which can be transferred. It's my guess that whoever arranged those body parts carried them from wherever they'd been hidden in the house and set them down inside the front of the main door. That explains the dogs' reaction there. Our joker or jokers then carried the body parts to the side door because it's closest to the sign and possibly left them there for a few minutes until he could open the door. Then he or they arranged the corpse pieces on the metal sign. The scent would have been transferred to the ground in front of the sign if the body parts had been piled there before they were hung up. It's possible that whoever set up the decoration left the grounds by climbing over this wall. When he or they did so, his clothes touched this wall.'

'That makes sense. Do you think the dogs will pick up the scent again lower down the hill if he walked that way?'

'If he sat on the grass and stayed in one place long enough for it to be transferred again from his clothes, possibly.'

'I hate waiting but we've no choice but to see what tomorrow brings.'

Barry called to the dogs, commanding them back, then stopped as he spotted something pale fluttering in the wind. 'Look, sir, in front of the wall. That could be how our joker transported the body parts and toys.' Barry pointed to a large bag tucked just inside the wall. It reminded Trevor of the garden waste bags issued by his local council.

'Take the dogs back, alert Patrick and tell him we've found a bag. He'll want to check the surroundings.'

'Yes, sir.'

'Tell him I'll stay here until he arrives. Once you've notified Patrick, settle the dogs and go and eat. There's nothing more you can do tonight. Thank you for your help.'

Barry had worked with Trevor Joseph many times. He knew when his superior wanted to be alone.

Trevor stood by the wall after Barry left. Darkness fell swiftly, thick, black and icy around him. Stars came out in the sky, the moon rose. He turned and looked back at the house, huge, brooding. He wondered at the scenes that had been played out within its walls.

Anna was right. If it was possible for a building to look evil, Hill House did. The sooner it was demolished the better. But not before he'd made it relinquish its secrets.

CHAPTER THIRTEEN

Trevor left the grounds shortly after Patrick and Jenny arrived and for once Patrick didn't argue when he suggested they send for extra forensic staff to assist him and Jen.

He left them collecting DNA samples and fingerprints on the side door by torchlight and walked up the hill towards the lights shining out from the high strip windows of the Portakabin HQ. He found Tristram Hever and Chris Brookes moving furniture under Sarah Merchant's directions. Both were perspiring and both looked exasperated.

'Not over there, you'll block the light if you put it in front of the window, you idiots. Set the incident screen midway between the window and the corner so it can be seen from almost every point in the room. Now it's too far to the left. Move it four inches to the right.' Sarah indicated the spot she'd picked out.

'Hello, sir.' Brookes set down his end of the screen when Trevor walked through the door.

The look of relief on his face amused Trevor. 'I see Merchant is getting the force's money's worth out of you two.'

'Only when they do as I ask, sir,' Sarah said. 'The phones are working and the main computer is connected to the internet and police network. Do you approve of where I've put the desks?'

'I do. No one can organise an incident room like you, Merchant.' He nodded to Hever and Brookes. 'Thank you for providing the muscle. I also suspect this is the last time I'll see this place without a coffee cup, food carton or chocolate wrapper in sight. Excellent,' he walked over to the ordnance survey map of the area and plan of Hill House pinned to the wall. 'Now I can put what I've just been looking at in perspective. It's easier looking at these than at plans unrolled on a desk.'

'Come on you two, get that screen into position. Sooner it's done –'

'Sooner you'll find something else for us to do,' Brookes interrupted Sarah.

Despite the grumbles, he and Hever pushed the screen into the spot Sarah had chosen.

'Barry told us that the dogs alerted at the front and side door of the house and the front wall of the grounds, sir,' Hever commented. 'Will you need us to start digging there in the morning?'

'You'd prefer to dig than help Merchant?' Trevor found it difficult to keep a straight face.

'If I have a choice ...' Hever eyed Sarah and fell silent.

'Our next move will depend on what we find in Hill House in the morning. The dogs reacted to the area around the doors and the low stone wall that encloses what must have been the garden. The ground around both the wall and the doors appears undisturbed so there are no immediate plans to dig anywhere.'

'Are you looking for anything I can help with, sir?' Sarah picked up a notepad and pen and carried them over to Trevor.

'I'd like information on every building within easy

walking distance of the orphanage – say six miles. That will take you to the outskirts of the village of Hen Parc. Start with this farm here,' Trevor located the farmhouse he'd spotted from the grounds on the map. 'There are two more farmhouses across the valley and one on the road back to Hen Parc. Find out who owns them, the names of the people living in them and how long they've been there.'

'Yes, sir.' Merchant peered at the names on the ordnance survey map and wrote them down.

'There's also a Tepee Village somewhere around Hen Parc. Apparently it was set up as a hippy commune in the 1960s. Some sort of market garden operates from there. Track down the location.'

'Yes, sir.'

'You said the phones are working?'

'Yes, sir. Aside from the three in here I told them to place one in the small office and another in the hallway,' Sarah pointed to a side door. 'I thought people might appreciate privacy for their private calls. There's also a mattress and sleeping bag in an alcove next to the bathroom. Given the nature of this investigation it might be as well to man the HQ 24/7 in case someone rings in or walks in with information in the early hours.'

'Good idea. You've set up a rota?'

'I've volunteered to sleep here, sir.'

Trevor was surprised. 'That's very good of you, Hever.'

'The mattress is comfortable enough, there's room for my clothes and personal items in a cupboard at the back of the alcove and there's a shower in the bathroom.'

'Thank you. If something should happen in the early hours, fetch me.' Trevor turned away from the map.

'Yes, sir.'

'Sarah, contact the local authority, military and local police on their out-of-hours numbers and tell them we'll be going into the house first thing tomorrow. Have you made arrangements to borrow portable lights?'

'Yes, sir. Major Simmonds assured me they'll be in place before dawn.'

'If anyone wants me in the next half hour, I'll be in the canteen.'

'I recommend the sausage and mash, sir,' Hever said.

'It was good,' Sarah confirmed.

'I'll give it a try and call in on my way back. By the look of it you've done as much as you can in here for the moment, Merchant. Get some sleep, all of you. We'll have a busy day tomorrow.'

The canteen was deserted apart from a handful of army personnel. Trevor saw Major Simmonds sitting alone at a table next to the counter. He doubted it was co-incidence that the table was set at the furthest possible point from where the ranks were eating.

'Do you mind if I join you?'

'Be glad of the company.' The major stuck his fork into his meal. 'The cottage pie is good.'

'I was told to opt for the sausage and mash.'

'That's long gone. This field canteen operates on a first come first served basis with no allowance made for rank or seniority. It saves on waste.'

Trevor settled for the cottage pie – not that he had a choice, as it was the only food on offer.

'I hear your dogs came up with a positive reaction,' Simmonds observed when Trevor sat opposite him.

'They did.' Trevor wondered how he could put a stop to the rumour mill that was operating.

'One of our dog men spoke to your dog man.'

'I see.' Trevor wondered if Simmonds had read his thoughts.

'Nothing's going to go beyond this site. None of my men are due leave for two months.'

'That's reassuring to know.'

'This is an historic case, isn't it? Like the Savile celebrity paedophile cases?'

'To be perfectly frank we have absolutely no idea what we're looking for or what we'll find in Hill House. We're here solely to investigate the appearance of the body parts.'

'You think they've been kept in the house since it closed?'

'Either that or they were brought here from somewhere else.'

'So you're keeping all your options open?'

'I always do until I'm faced with facts that can't be disputed.'

'Do you think the display is connected to the not guilty verdicts delivered yesterday in the Hill House paedophile case?'

'It's possible.'

Simmonds looked Trevor in the eye. 'Don't give much away do you?'

'I've learned never to assume anything and only draw conclusions based on actual evidence. All I know for certain is that someone hung those body parts and toys on the Hill House sign. I have no idea of their motives, and no idea where the artefacts came from. Until forensic can provide me with absolute proof of their original location, I have no intention of making a guess.'

'So you haven't entirely discounted the school of thought that believes evil spirits draped them on that sign.'

Trevor smiled. 'I try to keep an open mind but I confess, I've never believed in ghosts, ghouls and the supernatural. I'm surprised to hear you advocate the idea.'

'I heard a couple of squaddies discussing the possibility that devil worship has survived in this remote part of Wales. I thought you might want to keep a lookout for robed druids who make a habit of disinterring bodies.'

'Off-colour jokes aside, that's a good point. I'll ask my team to check out local graveyards. Do you happen to know the location of the nearest one?'

'There's a chapel and church in Hen Parc. Both have graveyards.' Simmonds finished his meal and pushed his plate aside. 'Are you expecting to find anything in the house?'

'Hoping more than expecting. Cases are always easier to solve when we have tangible evidence. More body parts that would help us identify the victims, or provide DNA, could be useful.'

'I'd be surprised if you find anything inside Hill House. Aren't local authorities responsible for the care of institutional buildings within their jurisdictions, including clearing them before they close and demolish them?' Simmonds asked.

'I believe so, but given the history of the orphanage and the imprisonment of the last manager – warden – or whatever he was called, for child abuse, and the subsequent surfacing of body parts possibly from inside the building, it looks as though the doors were closed, the place boarded up and the remainder of the staff simply walked away.'

'I can see that it would be easier – and cheaper – for them to leave the place boarded up than clear and demolish the house. Have you really no idea what you'll find inside?'

'None.' Trevor decided it was time to change the subject. 'Have you been stationed in this area long?'

'Six months, but that's just this current posting as training officer. It's not the first time I've been based here. Regimental HQ is eight miles south of here.'

'So you know the area well?'

'I'm acquainted with the more remote areas where we hold our exercises, which are generally well away from the roads.'

'What about Hen Parc village?'

'I've been there a few times. There's a good country pub, which has a restaurant. A couple of the local houses offer bed and breakfast. There's also a village shop and a garage that sells fuel, does repairs and doubles as a Post Office.'

'Have you heard of Tepee Village?'

'Yes, but there aren't many tepees there these days.'

'You know its location?' Trevor questioned.

'I do.'

'Now who's not giving much away?'

'The residents don't like authority, which is understandable given the number of times the local council have tried to evict them.'

'Unsuccessfully I take it, as they're still there.'

'The land is privately owned by a local who's sympathetic to the lifestyle of the inhabitants. The buildings they've erected are temporary and out of sight of their closest neighbours and the road. But most important of all, they have the support of the local community. In general they keep themselves to themselves.'

'And pay their way by selling produce.'

'They're not a drain on the taxpayers, if that's what you are suggesting.'

'I'd like to talk to them.'

'I doubt very much that they'll have anything to tell you that will help you to investigate this case.'

'I'd still like to try,' Trevor persisted.

'How's your hill walking?'

'Not good.'

'The community is about two miles from the nearest road. There's a track but you'd need an off-road vehicle to drive there. If you're determined to visit the village, I can give you a grid reference and loan you transportation.'

'I'd appreciate it.'

The major took a notebook from his pocket, scribbled half a dozen numbers and tore the page from the book.

'Thank you,' Trevor took the scrap of paper. 'I'm surprised you remember the grid reference.'

'They've taken in the odd waif and stray from the regiment who fell by the wayside while out on exercise.'

'What about when Hill House operated as an orphanage? Did they ever take in runaways from there?'

'Not that I've heard, but the place has been closed five years or more, hasn't it?'

'Try doubling that and adding a couple of years.'

'You surprise me. But isn't losing track of time common as you get older.'

'So they tell me. Do the people in the village ever talk about the time Hill House was open?'

'The impression I have, and it is only an impression, is that apart from the odd member of staff who lived off the premises, the orphanage was self-contained. Even the supplies were brought in from shops in the county town.'

'Some of the children must have had visitors –'

'I wish I could help you, Chief Inspector, but if I said any more, I'd be moving into conjecture, and army officers like police officers are trained to deal in facts, not supposition.'

'Thank you for this.' Trevor slipped the piece of paper with the grid reference into his pocket.

'I've ordered my men to set up your portable lights. Will you be going into the house early tomorrow?'

'Dawn if we can get everything organised by then. I've contacted the local authority. I trust they won't try to interfere.'

'When it comes to an issue that falls under the jurisdiction of Health and Safety I'd say you have no chance. Town Hall bureaucrats never miss an opportunity to meddle. If you find yourself needing brawn not brains, give me a shout. The ranks can always do with exercise.'

'Will do. Thank you.'

Simmonds and Trevor left the canteen together. Simmonds stood on tiptoe and breathed in deeply.

'A fine cold night. Time for me to check on the progress of the night exercise.'

Trevor watched Simmonds walk away before entering the incident room. Hever was sitting at a desk scrolling through the files Anna had compiled. He jumped to his feet.

'Trying to familiarise myself with the case, sir.'

'There's no need to get up or explain, Hever.' Trevor pulled up a chair and looked at the screen. 'Have you come to any conclusions?'

'Not really, sir, although in my opinion the jury brought in the wrong verdict.'

'Based on what?'

'Evidence. Some of the witnesses hadn't seen one another in years yet their statements correlated and supported the accounts of the others.'

Trevor played devil's advocate. 'And if they'd

colluded shortly after the alleged events had supposedly taken place and invented the scenarios?'

'Given that the alleged abuse took place over twenty years ago, they would have had to have had excellent memories. Don't you believe it happened, sir?'

'First lesson I learned in policing, Hever, is that my beliefs are immaterial and evidence is crucial. Without it court cases can disintegrate into interminable "he said" "she said" arguments that can never be resolved.'

'But now we have body parts, sir.'

'And hopefully the pathologist will be able to tell us more about them tomorrow. But until we know the identity of the people those parts belonged to and how they died, they are unlikely to further the case for a prosecution. As yet we can't even be certain any laws have been broken. But I'm grateful for you for studying the files. The more eyes on them the better the chance of spotting something that will result in this case being brought to a resolution.'

'Yes, sir.'

'Don't forget to get some rest.'

Trevor walked into the back cubicle, picked up the phone and dialled home. Lyn picked it up at the first ring.

'Sitting on the phone.'

'Sensed you were thinking of calling.'

Trevor took a deep breath. 'Love you. Both of you.'

'I know and we love you back. What is it like in the depths of Wales?'

'Bleak, lonely.'

'Peter behaving himself?'

'Sleeping.'

Lyn laughed. 'Then he is. What's the orphanage like?'

'The set of a horror film and we haven't been inside the house yet. I can't help imagining how the children

154

who were brought here after losing their parents felt. They must have thought they'd been sent to the end of the world. I keep thinking of Marty, how he'd feel ...'

'Marty will always be loved.'

'The parents of the inmates here would have assumed the same before they died or were forced to relinquish custody,' Trevor observed.

'Those parents didn't have the network of support that we have. My parents and brother would be fighting your brother for custody and guardianship if anything happened to us, and that's without Peter and Daisy demanding godparents' rights.'

'You're right as usual but I still think we should draw up a detailed will when I get back.'

'That's a good idea. Insurance in case the unthinkable occurs. You need to sleep. You didn't get much rest last night.'

'I don't need reminding, my love. I'm on my way to bed now.'

'You will be careful ...'

'With what I have to come home to. I'm never anything but. Love you.'

She gave him her usual reply. 'Love you more.'

Trevor hung up and left the cubicle. Hever was still immersed in the files. Trevor waved to him and left the Portakabin.

The moon had risen, high, silver and cold above the hill opposite. He looked down and on impulse opened the gate to Hill House and entered the grounds. The moon was the large round moon so beloved by children's book illustrators. He walked down to the front of the house, which was bathed in soft light. A flash in the basement caught his eye. Wondering if he was hallucinating from exhaustion, he headed for the windows at the side of the house where he thought he'd seen it.

The more he stared, the darker the glass behind the bars at ground level appeared. Wishing he'd brought a torch with him or had a working phone so he could wake Peter and ask him for a second opinion, he waited. An owl swooped low, hooting as it soared downwards in search of small mammals hiding in the grass. Sheep bleated on the hillside outside the walls. Stars shone above the horizon of the hill across the valley and still he waited.

He heard footsteps crunching over gravel and froze.

Peter's voice cut through the icy air. 'Is this a private party or can anyone join?'

'What are you doing here?' Trevor tried not to sound too grateful for Peter's presence lest Peter pick up on his relief and gloat.

'I went to HQ to fetch a plan of the orphanage when I saw you walk through the gate. Want a torch.' He handed Trevor one.

'I thought you would have been asleep hours ago.'

'So did I, but something's bugging me about the basement, either that or I'm missing Miranda's screaming. I wondered how far the rooms in the cellar go under the hill.'

'Front or back?'

'Both ways. If it's any distance they're bound to be damp.'

'You're thinking of adipocere.'

'Aren't you?'

'There,' Trevor grabbed Peter's arm, 'did you see it?'

'What?'

'Light flash, second basement window from the right,' Trevor whispered.

Peter stared for a full minute. 'My eyes are burning but I see nothing. What do you want to do?'

'Check all the entrances and exits.'

'If there is someone there we'll run the risk of frightening them off.'

'The idea is to flush them out.' Trevor walked slowly towards the building and tested the side door while Peter checked the windows. The wood Barry had jammed under the door to hold it in place looked as though it hadn't been moved.

They proceeded slowly, circling the building, Trevor slightly ahead.

For no reason Peter could explain he looked up. A small child was watching him from an attic window. He called out to Trevor. By the time Trevor turned, the child had gone.

'We're not used to the country. The night's dark and full of peculiar noises. All I saw was a trick of the moonlight. It's set us jumping at our own shadows,' Peter snapped irritably as they passed the sentries Simmonds had posted at the gates of Hill House.

'They say ghost sightings went down ninety-nine per cent after the introduction of electric lighting,' Trevor agreed.

'Might be noisier but at least you can see what's going on in an urban area.' Peter stopped outside their Portakabin and pulled out his key. 'I'm for bed.'

'Do you want anything from the canteen?'

'No thanks.' Peter unlocked the door and went inside.

Trevor went to the canteen and picked up two bottles of chilled water. As he left he saw movement in the shadows that shrouded the wall opposite his accommodation.

He stopped and stared for a moment. A soldier emerged from the darkness, his beret pulled low, concealing the side of his head.

'Goodnight, sir.'

'Goodnight.' Trevor went into the Portakabin and locked the door behind him. The man looked familiar. He just couldn't place him ...

Peter was right. They were jumping at their own shadows.

CHAPTER FOURTEEN

Trevor opened the door of Peter's bedroom and set a coffee carton on the shelf next to the bed before perching on the edge of the mattress. 'It's morning.'

Peter opened one eye. 'You look disgustingly awake for seven o'clock.'

'Possibly because I've been up since six.'

'Why?'

'Things to do. The good news is the council won't be here until nine to oversee us entering the house.'

'You intend to be in there by then?'

'In and working. Do you think you could stir yourself? I may need your muscles.'

Peter rearranged his pillows, sat up and reached for the coffee. 'I'll take the muscle part under consideration. But congratulations on your decisive attitude. You obviously know the mandate when dealing with jobsworths, "There's no turning ..."'

'"... back from what's done,"' Trevor finished for him. 'Patrick, Anna, Hever, Brookes, Barry, the dogs and I will head there straight after breakfast. I hope to be inside Hill House a full hour before anyone from the council arrives.'

'And when they do?'

'You can utilise your superior talents in dealing with bureaucrats.'

'Thank you for delegating that task to me. I knew there had to be a reason behind the coffee. It's not even light yet.'

'It will be soon, but given that the house is boarded up, our military friends have delivered portable floodlights. They've also promised to knock the boards from the windows and loan us hard hats should we need them.' Trevor opened the door.

'And the dogs?'

'House first, hillside later.'

'Give me ten minutes to shower and dress and I'll be with you. Order me a full English breakfast with extra sausage, bacon and black pudding if they have it.'

'It's an army canteen, they'll have it, but Daisy asked me to watch your diet. Blueberry porridge is her preferred breakfast choice for you.'

'Daisy's not here.'

'I need to be able to face her when we get back.'

Trevor shut the door when Peter picked up one of his pillows. He heard the soft thud as it hit the other side of the door behind him.

When the entire team were gloved, suited and booted, Trevor led the way to the front of Hill House. Peter whistled the dwarves' theme tune from Snow White as he brought up the rear.

'Cheerful this morning, Peter,' Patrick commented.

'I try. It seems appropriate given our matching suits. Dawn's breaking on a new day and who knows what we'll find inside the house.'

'I doubt it will be treasure. Put a red star on the calendar, Joseph, Collins is in a good mood.'

'Experience says it won't last.' Trevor mounted the steps that led up to the main entrance.

160

The sky was streaked with lighter shades of grey and darkness was rising from the ground. Hever and Brookes switched on the lights that had been trained on the front door. They set down the toolbox they'd hauled from the Incident Room, opened it and removed crowbars. In the event, they weren't needed. The boards that had been nailed across the wooden doorframe were rotten and came away easily in their hands.

Trevor stared at the massive double doors. The keyhole set in the left-hand door measured at least four inches from top to bottom.

'That lock must had been built for one hell of a key,' Peter commented. 'Not the sort you'd slip into your pocket unless you're a giant who lives up a beanstalk.'

'I don't suppose you have it?' Patrick asked.

'You don't suppose right.' Trevor answered. 'And I've no intention of waiting in the hope that someone from the Local Authority will be bringing it.'

'Want me to use the "enforcer", sir?' Brookes took a police battering ram from the tool box.

'Go ahead.' Trevor, Patrick, Anna and Peter stepped back. Barry led the dogs away from the door and down the steps. Brookes swung the enforcer and hit the door full force. It shuddered but held. After half a dozen strokes Hever took an axe from the box and looked enquiringly at Trevor.

'Save your strength, Brookes. Time to let Hever expend some energy.' Trevor ordered.

The doors splintered but didn't open at Hever's third blow. Peter snatched the axe from Hever's hand, swung it back and brought it down hard. The lock gave way and the doors shook. Brookes pushed on the left-hand one. It fell off its hinges and crashed inside the house, landing on the floor of the hall with a deafening bang that sent clouds of dust, dirt and cobwebs flying. Brookes coughed and retreated sharply.

A foul stench wafted out of the door into the chill dark morning.

'Bring up those lights please, Hever,' Trevor ordered.

Peter helped Hever lift the battery-powered lamps up to the top step.

'Holy Mary Mother of God!' Patrick's exclamation hung in the air along with the dust.

Trevor was lost for words. Patrick wasn't.

'Brookes, run up to Jen in the lab. Tell her I need her and sterile packing bags, evidence bags, swabs and sterile test tubes.'

Peter adjusted the light until it shone directly into the hall. The floor was tiled with black and white marble squares in a checkerboard pattern. They were grey with dust, debris and shards of plaster that had fallen from the upper walls and ceiling. The walls were covered to shoulder height with the brick-shaped beige tiles topped with green and brown bands so beloved by Victorian institutions. The staircase was dark wood, massive and solid. It rose majestically along the back wall to the right of and opposite the door. But no one was studying the décor.

The area below the stairs was open and Peter had aimed one of the beams of light directly into it, illuminating a haphazard pyramid of adipocere body parts topped by heads. A broth of glutinous yellowish liquid lapped around them, seeping into canals that had made inroads into the dirt that greyed the floor.

'Where do you want to start, sir?' Barry asked Trevor tentatively.

Patrick answered for him. 'Not in the house with the dogs. Not until Jen and I have examined and bagged those body parts, taken samples and had a chance to check out the place forensically.'

'You'll need help, Patrick. Hever, go to Merchant and ask for an update on the extra forensic personnel I asked for.'

Patrick stepped into the hall and looked around. Trevor followed and looked up at the ceiling.

'Don't you dare mention "Health and Safety" or "Risk Assessment",' Patrick glared at Trevor.

'I wasn't going to.'

'If the place falls down on top of me, it falls,' Patrick muttered. 'That staircase looks strong enough to take at least some of what's above us. Jen and I will work under it.'

'Now I understand why the council refused us permission to enter this place.' Anna moved inside and stood close to Trevor.

'You think someone working for the council knew what was inside here?' Trevor asked.

'I'd say it looks suspicious. Wouldn't you?'

'I'd say those body parts haven't been in this hall long.' Patrick trod carefully and crouched under the stairs. He dipped his gloved fingers into the liquid surrounding them and lifted them to his nose. 'Still wet. If they'd been here more than a couple of days, this would have dried.'

Trevor looked down the left-hand side of the corridor. It stretched into darkness for about ten feet before ending in a set of double doors. He turned, expecting a corridor on the right, but if there was one, it was closed off by a door.

'No!' Patrick exclaimed.

'No?' Trevor repeated in confusion.

'That spot is as far as you and Anna go in this house until I and, after me, the dogs have had a chance to check out the place.'

The sound of ripping and tearing echoed in from outside, as the military personnel Simmonds had loaned Trevor set about removing the boards that covered the ground floor windows.

'How long will it take you to forensically check out the house?'

'And there's me thinking you were a policeman, Trevor. Now tell me, how long would it take you to clean a stable with all the horses in residence?'

'There's nothing in residence here.'

'No?' Patrick indicted the body parts. 'Want to take a guess how many bacteria and DNA samples are living in this lot.'

A shadow blocked out the light for a moment and Jenny appeared in the doorway. She dropped the box of evidence bags she was carrying on what remained of the front door. 'I see you've found our missing heads, Trevor, and presumably most of our missing limbs. Just as well I finished testing the bag you found last night.'

'And?' Trevor asked.

'It was definitely used to transport the body parts that were found on the gate. There were no fingerprints, just smudges of latex, suggesting our joker was wearing gloves.'

'That's useful,' Peter said caustically.

'You think so?' Patrick lifted one of the heads up to the light.

'I was –'

'Being sarcastic? We know. Sarah is summoning the forensic reinforcements we agreed on, Trevor. Where do you want me to start, Patrick?' Jenny snapped on a pair of gloves.

'Here. We need to photograph, examine, bag and tag

these before transferring them to the lab. Everyone except Jen out of here. Barry, keep your hair-shedding dogs away.' Patrick turned the head he was holding upside down.

Trevor and Anna retreated. Brookes and Hever were outside the door with Peter.

'Barry told me to tell you he's gone ahead with the dogs, sir. He's starting at the point where you broke off the search last night.'

'Thanks, Brookes. Hever, get waterproof ground markers from the office and go with Barry and the dogs. After checking the boundary wall where they signalled yesterday, ask Barry to circuit the grounds once more. When he's done that he can take them on the hillside and give them their heads. I want you to mark every spot they alert to inside and outside the grounds.'

'Yes, sir.' Glad to leave the gruesome scene, Hever headed back to the gates.

'What now?' Peter asked Trevor.

'We wait for the council to turn up and Patrick to give us the all clear to search the downstairs rooms.'

'And in the meantime?' Anna pressed.

Trevor thought for a moment. 'It might be worth you two driving down to Hen Parc village and interviewing the locals. Ask around. Find out if any of them recall the orphanage when it was open. Pay particular attention to any VIPs who visited Hill House during that time and any staff who lived locally. See if anyone remembers a Mair Davies –'

'Who's Mair Davies?' Peter asked.

'Someone Dan remembers.'

'Dan was here? In Hill House?' Peter questioned. 'And neither he nor you thought to mention it until now?'

'Nothing to do with this case. Just someone Dan

165

remembered,' Trevor said evasively. 'She would have started working here twenty-five years ago.'

'Longer than that,' said Anna. 'Come on, Sergeant, I'll fill you in on the drive down to the village.'

'I don't have a car here,' Peter reminded.

'Take mine. But Anna drives.'

'Don't trust me, Joseph?'

'With my car, because it's insured, but not with Anna. She's unaccustomed to your driving. The keys are on the shelf in my room.'

'I'll get them, sir,' Anna said.

'You sure you don't want me to stay until the jobsworths arrive?' Peter checked with Trevor.

'Given what we've found and the fact that Dan organised a search warrant for this place, I can't see them giving us much trouble.'

'What do you want me to do, sir?' Brookes asked after Peter and Anna left.

'Stay there for a moment.' Trevor returned to the door. 'Patrick, do you have any objection to my going in through the side door.'

'Not if you're suited, tread carefully and leave anything suspicious to me.'

'When have I not?'

'There's always a first time.'

Trevor returned to Brookes. 'Get two torches, one of these lights and this toolbox to the side door.'

The side of the house was more sheltered from the weather than the front. Trevor pulled the wooden jamb from beneath the door and it flew open when Brookes shouldered it.

Trevor switched on his torch and shone it into a corridor that bore the same pattern of wall tiles as the main entrance. The floor was wood block and just as dusty as the entrance, except where it was marked with recent footprints. The air was stale with the stench of decay that permeates rooms that have been closed off for decades. Trevor opened the first door on the left, marked TOILETS in Gothic gold lettering, and revealed a washroom with a row of a dozen enormous, cracked and stained Belfast sinks. Beyond them was a row of toilet cubicles. None had doors and no toilet had a seat.

'Given the smell, I don't think anyone cleaned here before they closed the house,' Brookes observed.

Trevor eyed the dust on the floor. 'Someone's been in here recently that's for sure. Photograph and measure those footprints.'

'Yes, sir.'

Trevor left the washroom and opened the first door on his right. GENERAL OFFICE was stencilled on the door. The soldiers had already prised the boards from the windows and natural light filtered in through grimy windows. Trevor switched off his torch and looked around what had been a fairly spacious office. Like the washroom, dust lay thick and undisturbed on the floor. It was furnished with an odd assortment of grey metal filing cabinets and battered and scarred Victorian, dark oak furniture. He pulled on the top drawer of the nearest filing cabinet. It grated open and yawned back at him, empty.

'Check the cupboards and other filing cabinets,' he ordered Brookes, reserving the desk for himself.

The desk had two banks of drawers either side of a kneehole, and a single drawer across the top. All were locked. Trevor returned to the toolbox and filched out the strongest screwdriver he could find. He returned to the desk and prised open the centre drawer to reveal a mass of dried-up biros, pencils, rubber bands and rulers.

Brookes glanced over Trevor's shoulder as he crossed the room from one bank of filing cabinets to another. 'Messy desk, sir.'

'I read somewhere that this place closed suddenly when the ogre and several of his staff were arrested, but I'd have thought the council would spare the manpower to clear the place.'

'You'd think so, sir, if only to move out the more valuable items.'

'At first glance there doesn't appear to be anything worth carting away.'

Brookes eyed the dilapidated, damp-swollen and rusted furniture. 'You have a point, sir.'

'Anything in the filing cabinets?'

'Nothing so far, sir. But I'll need to borrow the screwdriver for the wooden cupboards, they're locked.'

Trevor jemmied open the remaining drawers in the desk and handed the screwdriver over to Brookes before sorting through the contents. The ones on the left hand side of the kneehole were empty. The top two on the right held piles of forms marked with the council logo and Hill House's name and address. Below them was a filing drawer. He flicked through the hanging files. Most were empty, two held more forms. He lifted them out, dumped them on top of the desk, then pulled up a chair, sat down and began to go through the papers methodically, tossing the blank forms to the floor as he went through them. After ten minutes of searching, the desk was empty and there was a pile of discarded forms on the floor.

'Have you found anything in the cupboards, Brookes?'

'All sorts, sir. Cricket bats and balls, tennis rackets and balls, deflated footballs and rugby balls.'

Trevor joined him in front of a cupboard that was taller

and wider than most Victorian wardrobes. 'Outdoor toys. I hope the children were allowed to play with them.'

'Not often by the look of them, sir. There's hardly any signs of wear and they're too clean to have had much use.'

Trevor took the screwdriver and opened a second cupboard to reveal a bank of drawers. Some held blank envelopes and writing paper, most were empty.

'Nothing in here, sir.' Brookes heaved a stuck drawer back into a massive chest on the opposite side of the room, behind the door.

Trevor eyed the strip of carving on top of the drawers. 'My brother has a chest like that in his farmhouse. Pull the carving on the top.'

Brookes grabbed the sides of the carving and heaved. 'It won't budge, sir.'

'Let me try.'

Trevor took the screwdriver and wormed it into the gap between the carving and the body of the chest. He tried prising it open without success. 'Either the wood's swollen or there is no secret drawer in this particular chest.'

'I'll get another screwdriver and insert it in the other side, sir.'

Brookes soon returned and pushed the blade of a second screwdriver into the crack between the carving and the body of the chest on the opposite side to Trevor.

'On three,' Trevor said. 'One ... two ... three ...'

The blade of Brookes' screwdriver snapped but the carving budged. Trevor attacked his end with his screwdriver and managed to prise it open an inch.

'Get the axe, Brookes, I'll knock off the carving.'

Brookes left and returned with the axe. Trevor took it and hit the protruding carving. It fell off to reveal the back of a drawer and a stack of files.

Trevor reached in and pulled out the topmost one. He opened it and was showered with photographs.

CHAPTER FIFTEEN

'You were an inmate in Hill House?' Peter glanced across at Anna as she drove along the winding mountain road that led to Hen Parc village.

'I was for a short while when I was six years old.'

'And the super cared for you?'

'Dan Evans was a sergeant then, not a superintendent. He hardly left my side when I was in there. He's always taken his godfather duties seriously, even more so after my father died. I doubt my mother could have managed without him. He organised my father's funeral when my mother was in intensive care and too ill to even attend. Whenever we needed something, advice, someone to sort out official forms, insurance, bank and financial problems related to my father's pension, he was there for us. But it was Superintendent Andy Mulcahy, the present Chief Superintendent's father, who gave Uncle Dan permission to stay with me. He also ordered two female police officers to take it in shifts to watch over me while I was in Hill House. But saying that, I believe Uncle Dan would have stayed with me even if he'd had to take leave to do so.'

'There must have been rumours about this place even then,' Peter said.

'If there were, I knew nothing about them. I was six years old. All I was aware of was my parents' sudden absence from my life and the trauma of being torn from home to live in strange institutionalised surroundings. But with hindsight, I think it's possible that Uncle Dan and Superintendent Mulcahy were aware of rumours.'

'And Mair Davies?'

'I remember the name because Uncle Dan asked me about her after I went to live with my mother at my grandparents' house. I have no memory of her. There were a lot of adults in Hill House and I was too frightened to look any of them in the eye. Principally because they all seemed terrifying.'

'So Mair Davies didn't care for you?'

'Not that I can recall. But I'm the first to admit I blocked out my time at Hill House as soon as I left. It may not even have been that terrible for me, but losing my father certainly was and I was devastated – grief-stricken. We were very close.'

'Who told you he was dead?'

'Uncle Dan, but I'd already heard the social workers talking among themselves. It was obvious from what I overheard that my father was dead and they thought my mother was dying. They told me that I would soon be going to live with a new family.'

'That's unforgiveable.' Peter hesitated for a moment. 'I'm sorry.'

'Thank you, but it happened a long time ago.'

'I'm surprised you were given the Hill House case.'

'The Chief Superintendent said that he thought the short time I spent there might help.'

'Did you meet Justin Hart while you were in Hill House.'

'Yes, and Shane Jones and Robin MacDonald, along with Justin's twin Stephen. We were all roughly the same age.'

'How did you get on with them?'

'Well, during the short time I spent with them. They allowed me, a mere girl, to sit at their table in the dining room because there was no room at any of the girls' tables. If there were second helpings they made sure I had a share – not that there were many second helpings.' Anna changed the subject. 'This is Hen Parc village. Where do you want to start?' She looked around for a parking space.

'The best place to start in any unknown territory is the pub, preferably before the locals rumble you as a police officer.'

'It won't be open for a couple of hours.' Anna pulled into a square in front of an old stone-built inn. Low, with a slate roof, it looked as though it had probably begun life as a medieval Welsh longhouse. Peter stepped out of the car. There was a small shop across the road, its front windows heavily plastered with special offer posters. Further down on the same side of the street he spotted a garage forecourt, with two petrol pumps and a Post Office sign.

'Garage, or shop?' Anna asked.

'I still say no one knows a village like the landlord of the local pub.' He smiled maliciously. 'Shall we disturb him?' He walked over to the main door and knocked loudly. A woman's voice, slow, faltering, echoed back, 'We're closed.'

'Police, madam, making routine enquiries.'

'So much for travelling incognito,' Anna muttered.

'We'll send Brookes and Merchant down here tonight. No one will suspect them of being anything other than a charming couple on the verge of multiplying.'

There was a scuffling behind the door followed by, 'I'll get the landlady.'

Peter and Anna waited. After what seemed like an

eternity but was probably only a minute or two, bolts were drawn back on the door and it opened. An attractive middle-aged blonde brushed her hair from her eyes with her fingers.

'You are the police?'

'Routine investigation, madam.' Anna held up her identification.

'Come in. I suppose you're here about the theft in the garage.'

'There was a theft in the garage?' Anna asked.

'The shop was broken into and the lock on one of the pumps tampered with. A couple of jerry cans were stolen along with fuel. Nothing ever happens in Hen Parc so the village has been talking about nothing else.'

'When did this happen?' Peter checked.

'Night before last, but I assume you'd know if you're investigating the theft.'

'We're not here about a theft. We investigating Hill House,' Anna informed her.

'The derelict orphanage?'

'That's the one.'

'You're looking into how those body parts ended up on the sign.' The landlady winced. 'I saw the photographs on the internet. It's a horrible business. The idea that someone – anyone – could chop up and mutilate bodies, especially children's, is monstrous.'

'Do you remember Hill House being open?' Peter asked.

'Of course I do. I grew up in this village. Although Hill House closed years ago. No one around here was sorry when it did.'

'Why was that?' Peter asked.

'There were rumours about the place. Allegations that the children were ill-treated. Poor mites. They might as

174

well have been locked in a prison. Never allowed out …'

'They didn't attend the village school?' Anna broke in.

'No. Not that I went to the local school, I went to a private school in the town and drove in every morning with my mother. She owned a dress shop there.'

'So the children weren't educated?' Anna persisted.

'Teachers went to the orphanage to teach them there. One or two of them lived in the village and used to drink here. But as I said, the place closed down a long time ago.'

'Can you spare us the time to answer a few more questions, please? I know it's an imposition but we have so little information about the place, anything you can tell us might prove useful.'

'If I can help you I will, not that I know much about Hill House. My father knew more but he died last year.' The landlady opened the door wider. 'It would be more comfortable to talk inside than on the doorstep. Would you like coffee?'

'That would be lovely, thank you.' Anna and Peter followed her into a whitewashed bar furnished with dark wood tables and chairs. The beams on the ceiling were oak and the walls festooned with vintage wedding photographs dating from the Victorian era to the 1960s.

'Nice pub,' Peter complimented.

'I suppose it is, not that I notice it any more. Nothing's been changed since my parents bought and decorated the place when I was a child. My husband wanted me to sell it when my father died last year, but no one wants to run a village pub any more. It's hard work for little profit particularly if you have to pay staff. I've become accustomed to managing the place, doing the books and the ordering and so forth. As my husband and I spend most evenings here I persuaded him to let me keep it. We

175

live practically next door.'

'Does your husband help you run the pub?'

'Bryn?' She laughed as she led them to a table. 'No, he's a solicitor and has an office in town, but as it's only five miles down the road it's an easy commute. I'm Rose Jones.'

'Anna Wells.' Anna shook Rose's hand.

Peter glanced at Anna. Making pleasant small talk and conversation was the oldest tool in a copper's box when it came to investigating. It was obvious Anna was a past master at using it.

'Peter Collins,' Peter shook Rose's hand.

Rose called out to the woman who'd talked to them through the door, 'Bring a pot of coffee and a plate of croissants please, Judy.'

'Judy seemed reluctant to open the door to us,' Peter commented.

'Judy is wary of authority. She was in Hill House.'

'As an orphan?' Anna asked.

'The staff told my father Judy was an orphan. She couldn't recall enough of her past life to contradict them. My father first met her when he was called in to cater for visiting groups of VIPs to the orphanage. He held the catering contract there for years and as soon as Judy was old enough to enjoy helping in the kitchen, she used to look out for him whenever he went there.'

'Did he cater there often?' Anna set her bag down, unzipped it and removed a notebook and pen.

'Whenever anyone important visited Hill House, which was about half a dozen times a year.'

'What kind of important people?' Peter questioned.

'TV personalities, children's entertainers, pop stars, politicians, church dignitaries and the like. My father also used to cater for Christmas, Easter and summer parties for the children that the local charities in town organised and funded.'

'You said he met Judy there?' Anna reminded.

'The first time he noticed her she was a small child, about seven or eight years old. He said he felt sorry for her because she was timid and the other children constantly bullied her and pushed her to back of any queue. A couple of years before Hill House closed, the matron at the orphanage told my father that Judy was about to be moved to a psychiatric institution that catered for geriatrics suffering from dementia and Alzheimer's. He knew the place. It had a horrendous reputation. It was closed down a few years later, not long after Hill House. My father couldn't bear the thought of Judy going there. She'd been classified as having special educational needs, which my father in his non-politically correct mode translated as "being a bit slow", but he knew that given careful handling Judy was a good and conscientious worker. So he offered her a live-in job here in the pub as a kitchen help.'

'So he took her from Hill House shortly afterwards?' Peter asked.

'No, that day. It shocked my father at the time. He was obviously well known in the area but the master gave him a form to fill out, which was basically his name and address and a guarantee that he'd employ Judy and pay her a small sum in addition to board and lodge. Then the master ordered Judy to pack a bag. My father brought her here that evening. At first Judy just cleaned the pub and kitchen in the morning, later when my mother became ill she began cleaning their accommodation upstairs. She helped look after both my mother and father during their last illnesses. Some people in the village accused us of exploiting her, but we pay her a decent wage in addition to her food and accommodation and she's happy and feels secure. Something that is important to her.' Rose smiled as Judy carried in a tray of coffee and a plate of croissants and set them on their table. 'Thank you, Judy. I was just telling the police how you came to work here.'

Judy set her mouth in a firm line. 'I won't leave. Not now I'm in Mr and Mrs Jones's flat.'

'Judy's moved into what was my parents' accommodation,' Rose explained.

'We're not here to take you away, Judy. We're here to find out what happened in Hill House when it was an orphanage,' Anna assured her. 'You know the place is closed?'

'Yes.' Judy crossed her arms over her chest.

'Were you there a long time?' Peter asked.

Judy pursed her lips and nodded.

Rose went into the kitchen and returned with another cup. 'Pull up a chair, Judy, and have a drink.'

'Can you remember where you lived before you went to Hill House?' Anna asked.

Judy shook her head. She picked up the coffee pot, poured out four cups of coffee and handed them around.

'Thank you, Judy.' Anna took the cup and poured milk into it. 'What was it like living in Hill House?'

Judy shook her head fiercely. 'Not nice.'

Rose gave Anna a warning glance.

Peter waded in. 'What wasn't nice about it, Judy?'

'Always hungry and they hurt and hit me.'

Peter proceeded carefully. 'The other children hurt you?'

'The masters. They hit and hurt everyone, especially at night.' Judy drank her coffee quickly. 'I'll wash the cups now, Mrs Rose.' Judy piled the cups back on to the tray and left the bar for the kitchen.

'I'm sorry, but that is about as much as Judy has ever said about her time in Hill House,' Rose apologised.

'You never asked her about it?' Anna probed.

'Not after we saw how much it upset her.'

'Have you been following the recent court case involving the VIPs accused of abusing children who lived in Hill House?'

'The star witness case?' Rose checked. 'Yes.'

'The case will be known as the star witness case – until the names hit Twitter,' Peter warned Anna.

'As I'm beginning to find out. Did your father ever voice any suspicions about child abuse at Hill House?'

'Yes.'

Anna set down her coffee cup. 'Are you saying your father knew that children were being abused at Hill House?'

'Yes. He made a report to the police and our MP in the 1990s. I can't remember the exact year. But from some of the things that the children had said to him when he'd worked there he had suspicions as to what was going on. The problem was he couldn't prove anything before he made the report.'

'He had proof in the 1990s?' Peter said.

'Yes, I remember the night he came home with it. He was quite relieved. He drove straight down to the police station in town. He talked to someone there.'

'Who?' Peter demanded.

'I don't know. If my father knew the name of the officer he spoke to he never told me. He said that he'd been assured that there was a full inquiry in progress but that it would take time as it didn't only involve Hill House. That there were care homes in North Wales and other parts of the country where children had also been abused. I thought …'

'What?' Peter asked.

'That the recent case was the result of that enquiry.'

'We only started investigating the allegations our witnesses made last year,' Anna revealed. 'What proof did your father have that children were being abused in Hill House?'

'He had photographs. Horrible photographs of crying, injured children. There was a boy with bruises around his neck and on his back and buttocks. And a small naked girl with bite marks all over her. There were others but my father wouldn't show them to me or my mother. He said it was bad enough that he'd have to suffer nightmares after seeing them.'

'Did your father take the photographs?' Peter's voice was cold, unemotional.

'Good heavens, no.'

'How did he get them?'

'A social worker at Hill House gave them to him. She told him they'd been taken by one of the staff and she'd found them when he'd asked her to get something from his desk. She assumed he had forgotten he'd put them there. She told my father that she wanted to leave Hill House but couldn't because she didn't want to abandon the children with the staff who were responsible for hurting them. She begged him to take the photographs to someone in authority who could put a stop to the abuse.'

'Can you remember the name of the social worker?'

'Yes, she rented a cottage in the village from Mr and Mrs Protheroe. Her name was Mair Davies. She disappeared shortly after she gave my father the photographs.'

CHAPTER SIXTEEN

'Don't move!'

'I'm not, sir,' Brookes whispered to Trevor.

Trevor started to laugh. 'That's an excellent impression of a statue, Brookes. Reminds me of the kids' game we used to play in school. Move and you're out.'

'I wouldn't like to stay in this position for long, sir.'

'Neither would I.' Trevor stared at the mess of photographs on the floor. 'So much for the local authority's assertion that most of the records of this place were lost or destroyed when it closed. Judging by the dress of the children and adults in some of those pictures there's more than a century's worth of photographs there.'

'I'd go along with that, sir. Why do you think they were hidden?'

'I'm not sure they were – deliberately that is. Anyone who'd come across one of those chests, and they're far from uncommon or expensive, would know about that so-called "secret drawer". It's obvious from the body parts and the rubbish that's been left here that this place wasn't searched or cleared properly when it was shut down. From what I've gleaned from the files it was closed very soon after the child-abusing ogre and staff were taken into custody. Presumably to minimise the time they had to cover their tracks.'

'What do you want to do?'

'Aside from kick myself for not giving a thought as to what might happen before prising the front from that drawer, and not stand here for ever, I'm not sure.'

'You weren't to know the drawer was full, sir.'

'I'm paid to anticipate events and think. I've done neither. There may well be fingerprints and DNA on those photographs and now thanks to my idiocy they've been exposed to the contamination of a filthy floor. How are you on fingerprinting?' Trevor asked.

'Brilliant, sir, but useless on gathering DNA.'

'If we're going to finish examining this place this side of Christmas we'll need at least two or three more people. Go up to Merchant and ask her to phone the Home Office again and stress the urgency of our situation. If she runs into a brick wall tell her to contact Superintendent Dan Evans and ask him to beg for help on our behalf. I'll secure things here and join you in the office shortly.'

'Sir.' Brookes picked his way carefully out of the room. Trevor stepped back to the door. He walked out backwards and closed the door behind him before switching on his torch and looking up the corridor.

There were four more unopened doors, two either side in front of the double doors he presumed led into the main hall where Patrick was working.

He walked down the corridor and opened the door next to the washroom. STAFF TOILETS was printed on the varnished wooden door in faded Gothic lettering. Two more doors faced him when he entered a small vestibule. One marked LADIES, one GENTS. Both held a row of sinks, with brass taps and banks of cubicles with doors. He pushed open the cubicle doors. The toilets had wooden seats with brass fittings. Even dirty and decayed, the facilities were cleaner and more serviceable than those for the children.

He returned to the main corridor and pushed open the last door on the left before the double doors. Lettering announced it was the MASTER'S OFFICE.

Trevor had never considered himself nervous or susceptible to 'atmosphere', but the second he stepped over the threshold of the room he felt the hairs rise on the back of his neck. It didn't help that the view from the only window was of the retaining wall behind the house. It loomed barely three feet away and high above the top of the window frame. It hadn't been warm in the corridor but he felt a sharp drop in temperature and a rush of cold air. It was as though he'd opened the door on a freezer.

The walls were tiled in the same brick-like beige, brown and green tiles as the corridor. The floor was parquet, and beneath the dirt he could make out the dull sheen of once polished wood. The furniture, like that in the larger office, was heavy mahogany Victorian and included a cracked and mildewed leather sofa and two chairs set around a revolving bookcase filled with leather-bound volumes. He glanced at the spines. Most were religious books or hymnals.

He went to the desk. He had no need of a screwdriver. The drawers had already been jemmied open. He pulled the topmost one and recoiled. A whip lay in an otherwise empty drawer. There were black, shrivelled shreds caught in the thong. Skin? He closed the drawer quickly with his gloved fingertips.

He stopped at the door and turned for a last look. He preferred not to think of the scenes that had been played out within the walls. The children who'd been sent to the office for punishment. But images flooded, unbidden, into his mind.

The reluctant slow walk of a terrified child down the

corridor. The dragging steps that reached the door too soon. The raised small hand. The timid knock. The boomed command to enter …

He left the room and closed the door behind him. Natural light filtered through the dusty glass panels in the two doors that faced him across the corridor. Both were marked LIBRARY. He opened the nearest door, stepped inside and realised that the doors opened into the same large room.

It was lined with dark wood shelving. Some still held books. There were small chairs and low tables. A weak, watery sun shone through the filthy glass for the first time since the windows had been boarded up, illuminating layers of dust on the shelves and books and dust balls on the floor.

The room was freezing cold, hardly surprising in a stone-built mansion in November in Wales, but it had a totally different atmosphere to the master's office. He could picture children sitting in the chairs reading the books they'd taken from the shelves.

He walked down the length of the room and picked up one of the books. It was sodden with damp and disintegrated in his hands. He looked at a row of similar volumes, obviously a series. *The Life of Jesus*, *The Little Town of Bethlehem*, *Joseph and his Coat of Many Colours*. He continued to walk around and found a few copies of the classics – *Treasure Island, Children of the New Forest, The Secret Garden* – but there were very few books for a hundred and fifty children. He wondered if some had been removed before the orphanage had closed.

He looked out of the window that was set at least a foot too high for a child to peep out of, even on tiptoe. The morning mist was clearing over a damp grey slice of roughly grassed hillside. He glimpsed movement from the corner of his eyes.

A small child was perched in one of the undersized chairs. A book rested on her knees. She'd drawn them up until they were practically under her chin. Her bare feet were flat on the seat and she was dressed in a drab grey workhouse smock.

She stared at him. The colour of her eyes, a deep cerulean blue, registered as did the light brown of her curly hair. He smiled, stepped closer and found himself staring at a beam of light that cut across the empty chair.

He shook himself.

'You need to get a grip and more sleep, Joseph. You're seeing things.' He only realised he'd spoken out loud when he heard Brookes shout, 'You still here, sir?'

'Yes, Brookes. In the library.' Ridiculously relieved by the knowledge that he wasn't alone in the wing of the house, he stepped out into the corridor. Brookes was standing at the open outside door.

'The people from the Local Authority have arrived. They're asking for the senior officer.'

'Don't suppose you feel like impersonating me?'

'No, sir.'

'Do me a favour, please? Close the outside door and replace the planks over it. Nail them on again if necessary. The first people to follow us in here must be a forensic team. I'll call into the hall and have a word with Dr O'Kelly about what we've found, then go to the incident room.'

'The Local Authority officials ...'

'What about them?' Trevor interrupted.

'They said they're on a tight timetable.'

'So are we, Brookes. To proceed with this investigation and solve this case. I'll talk to the officials after I've updated Patrick. In the meantime ask Sarah to

185

call the local force and beg for help to interview the local authority people. Tell them it's urgent. The local force might get more out them than we would.'

'Not one step further,' Patrick shouted when Trevor pushed his way through the temporary plastic curtain the forensic team had hung across the door. 'I hope you're here to tell me when we can expect reinforcements.'

'I've no idea. I've just come from the corridor that led off the side door. It's the other side of those double doors …'

'I've no time to listen to one of your bedtime stories,' Patrick snapped.

Accustomed to Patrick's ways, Trevor ignored the rebuke. 'I found a pile of photographs and files hidden in a secret drawer in an office. They look as though they've been there since the place was closed. Is it worth fingerprinting them and checking them for DNA?'

'You know damned well it is.' Patrick's eyes narrowed suspiciously. 'Unless that is you've contaminated them with your sausage fingers.'

'I was wearing gloves but the drawer broke when I opened it.'

'And?'

'The photographs fell on the floor.'

'I wish you joy checking them for evidence among the dirt they've picked up. I have enough to do here.'

'I sent a message to Merchant. She's contacting Dan with a view to enlisting the help of more forensic people.'

'Good, they can sort out the mess you made when they arrive. Don't touch the photographs again until we've examined them forensically, and that's an order. Did you find anything else in that wing of the house?'

'Library, two washrooms, master's room and general offices.'

'You and Brookes were gloved and suited when you entered them?'

'Of course.'

'They'll all need checking for DNA and fingerprints.' Patrick sat back on his heels and looked at Trevor. 'The photographs? They of children?'

'Most are. Looking at the clothes they go back to the turn of the century, possibly further.'

'Interesting but not interesting enough to leave this.' Patrick finished scraping beneath the fingernails of the hand he'd been studying and bagged the residue he'd collected.

'Dare I ask if you've enough parts to make six whole bodies?' Trevor ventured.

'Not quite yet.' Patrick looked across to where Jen was assembling body parts. 'But I do have some good news.'

'What?' Trevor asked, wary of Patrick's odd sense of humour.

'We have more heads.'

'Three more to go with the body parts?' Trevor suggested hopefully.

'Five more.'

'I've been delaying making an appearance in the incident room because it's full of local bureaucrats. You've just given me good reason to go there, before you impart any more good news.'

Trevor heard the sound of hammering as he walked around the side of the building. Brookes was replacing the boards over the side door. He waved to him and continued on up to the gate. Since he'd left the canteen that morning, two vans bearing the logo of the local authority and three

187

cars had parked in the narrow road with no thought or care given to either the vehicles they were blocking in, or any of the military four wheeled drive, rough terrain vehicles that might want to drive through and on to the mountainside.

He pulled off his paper over boots and hat at the door and entered the incident room. Sarah was behind her desk. Major Simmonds was standing next to her. The party from the Local Authority were sitting on two rows of folding chairs they'd arranged in front of Merchant's desk. Half a dozen men sat in the first row, behind them half a dozen women were poised, notepads and pens at the ready. The scene reminded Trevor of a 1950s pre-feminist film. He could almost hear the voiceover: '*And here we have the executives with their attendant secretaries* …'

A private entered with a tray of coffee. He snapped to attention in front of Simmonds. 'The coffee you ordered, sir.'

Simmonds nodded a dismissal. The private left.

'Good morning.' Trevor made a beeline for the tray as Simmonds and Merchant returned his greeting.

Sarah looked at the markings on the lid and handed him one. 'Black coffee with no sugar, sir.'

'Thank you, Merchant.' Trevor turned to the officials. Not one of them had answered his 'Good morning.' 'I'm Chief Inspector Trevor Joseph. One of my officers said you wished to see me?'

'That is correct. We were informed that you intend to search Hill House this morning …'

'I have a warrant,' Trevor cut the man short.

'We must protest. Hill House is in a derelict and dangerous condition and overdue for demolition. The building is unstable …'

Trevor eyed the short square man. 'And you are?'

'Mr Williams, Chief Executive Officer, Health and Safety. It is quite impossible, Chief Inspector. No one can possibly enter the building.'

'Mr Williams, we have our own Health and Safety Officers.' It wasn't strictly true – although all police officers received health and safety training, investigative officers often bent the rules when they were working. He had a sudden image of Peter snatching the axe from Hever's hand and slicing it through the lock on the front door of Hill House.

Williams drew himself up to his full height and puffed out his chest. 'You may enter the grounds provided you and your men wear hard hats and safety boots with steel toecaps ...'

'My orders are to investigate the sudden and unexpected appearance of body parts draped over the sign of Hill House.' Trevor pulled up a large swivel chair and rolled it to the right of Merchant's desk facing the double row of officials. He sat down. 'We entered the house this morning.'

'That's impossible,' Williams spluttered. 'I have the key.' He opened his briefcase and produced a six-inch long key, which was as gigantic as Trevor had imagined.

'We axed the door.'

'You've damaged the property ...'

'You just said Hill House is derelict and dangerous and overdue for demolition.' Trevor felt Peter would have been proud of him.

'I ...'

Trevor interrupted, 'I have some questions for you.'

Williams jumped to his feet. 'If any of your officers are in the house now, they must leave. At once ...'

'There is a forensic team in the house working under the supervision of Dr Patrick O'Kelly, the Home Office

Pathologist. They are examining more body parts that we found heaped under the staircase inside the hall of the house this morning. The questions I would like to put to you, all of you, are exactly what can you tell us about the body parts that were found outside and inside Hill House? How much information can you give us about the staff and inmates of Hill House prior to its closure? Full and comprehensive yearly registers would be good, monthly or weekly ones would be better. How many of you visited Hill House before it closed? The fourth question, but not the last, is, were any of you aware of the abuse that was inflicted on the inmates of Hill House and if so, did any of you witness it?' Trevor rose to his feet and went to the door that led to the small private office. 'Detective Sergeant Merchant, you have copies of the photographs of the body parts and heads that we've found?'

'Yes, sir.'

'Please show them to our guests. While they are looking at them, please telephone local police HQ and remind them that we've asked for assistance. Tell them I would be grateful if they could help us interview local authority personnel in relation to our Hill House investigation.'

'Yes, sir,'

'Mr Williams, if you come with me I'll interview you first – in private. You have no objection to my recording the interview?'

'I'm not sure ...'

'It's for your protection as well as mine.'

Trevor showed Williams into the small office and pushed one of the visitors' chairs toward him before closing the door. He sat behind the desk, took a Dictaphone from the top drawer of the desk and switched it on. 'Your full name, age and address, Mr Williams?

Your occupation and position within the Local Authority in relation to Hill House?'

Williams turned bright red. 'I protest …'

Trevor repeated. 'Your full name, age and address, Mr Williams? Your occupation and position within the Local Authority in relation to Hill House …'

'I refuse to answer any of your questions.' Williams sat back in his chair and crossed his arms over his chest.

'In which case you give me no choice but to proceed under caution. Mr Williams, you do not have to say anything. But, it may harm your defence if you do not mention when questioned something which you later rely on in court. Anything you do say may be given in evidence …'

CHAPTER SEVENTEEN

'We would have been happy to have walked over to Mrs Protheroe's house,' Peter protested.

'I feel dreadful making a ninety-year-old woman come to us,' Anna added. 'Particularly when she's the one doing us the favour.'

'Martha was insistent on joining us here when I telephoned her. Judy will make sure that she arrives in one piece.' Rose set another place at the table. 'She loves company and she also loves our chef's croissants.'

The door opened and Judy led a remarkably sprightly old woman into the bar. Peter didn't usually notice women's clothes, but Martha Protheroe looked as though she'd stepped from the pages of a glossy magazine promoting elderly chic. She was what his mother would have called 'a born lady'. It wasn't simply her elegant clothes. Her long, grey hair was twisted into a perfect bun without a single straggly end to mar it. Her make-up was light and immaculate; even the ebony stick she leaned on gleamed with polish.

She walked slowly, obviously fighting stiff joints and arthritic pain, and Peter was concerned that she might not make it to the table without stumbling. He rose to his feet, went to meet her and offered her his arm. She relinquished Judy's and took it.

'Thank you. As you see I'm only too happy to

exchange the assistance of my friends for that of a strong, good-looking man when he makes me an offer.'

'We could have visited you, Mrs Protheroe.'

'No trouble, I've only walked across the road and it's not often I have the opportunity to chat to Judy so early in the morning, or leave the house to breakfast out.' She glanced at the table. 'Rose's chef is second to none when it comes to French pastries.'

Peter escorted Martha to the table and pulled out a chair. She sank down gracefully and propped her stick against the wall. 'Judy told me you're police officers and you want to know about Hill House and Mair Davies.'

'That's right, Mrs Protheroe.'

'Please, call me Martha.'

'You'd prefer tea to coffee wouldn't you, Martha?' Judy asked.

Martha reached out and patted Judy's hand. 'You know I would, dear. Thank you.'

Rose picked up a croissant with tongs and set it on a plate. 'Would you like butter and jam or honey with that, Martha?'

'Nothing thank you, Rose. Just the delicious croissant. Your chef made them for the café?'

'He did.'

'I'll telephone them and ask them to bring me some.'

'There's a café in Hen Parc?' Anna asked in surprise.

'At the back of the shop, overlooking the valley.' Rose handed the croissant to Martha. 'Although it's more of a drop-in community centre with a small food counter. The mother and baby group meet there every weekday morning.'

'Which makes it very noisy after ten o'clock. So many young voices you can't make yourself heard. Now, young man and young lady, how can I help you?' Martha smiled at Peter and Anna. 'You make a lovely couple.'

Peter glanced at Anna and laughed. 'I think my wife might have something to say about that, Martha. We have a baby daughter, Miranda.' Peter didn't know why he'd told Martha that, other than she reminded him of his grandmother. She even smelled of the same violet-scented perfume.

'A daughter, how lovely, and you named her Miranda presumably from *The Tempest*? Such a beautiful name.'

If it was a hint, Peter took it. 'I'm Peter, Peter Collins, and this is Anna Wells.'

'Judy told me that you've been asking about Hill House and Mair Davies.'

'We have.' Anna sat back and waited to see if Peter would achieve more than she could by flirting with Martha. He'd made an excellent start.

'Rose tells me you knew Mair Davies, Martha?'

'Acquainted with rather than knew, Peter. My husband Samuel rented Mair one of our cottages when she started working in Hill House. It must be twenty-five years or more ago now. I think Samuel was related to Mair in some way. A second or third cousin perhaps, but then it's difficult to find someone you're not related to in these small Welsh villages. Not enough people to choose from when it comes to marriage. Even Samuel and I were distantly related. Our great-grandparents were first cousins.'

'Mair Davies rented from you?' Peter reminded her tactfully.

'Samuel was an estate agent and preferred to invest in property rather than stocks and shares. He used to say they'd pay us more than any pension plan in the long run and he was right. You can see bricks and mortar, you can rent it and if you're desperate, you can sell it. Even at a loss it will bring in enough to put food on the table.'

'A wise man. Do you remember Mair Davies?'

'Of course. Mair was an exceptionally pretty girl. Beautiful green eyes, long, curly, red hair, so full of life and keen and eager to start working in her first "proper job" after graduating college.'

'Did you meet her before she worked in Hill House?'

'Yes, Mair rented the cottage a month before she started in the orphanage. It was furnished but she made her own covers for the sofa and chairs and hangings for the walls and windows. She was a natural artist and arranged her pieces to advantage around the rooms. She turned that cottage into a real home.'

'She lived alone?' Anna checked.

'No, one of the teachers who worked in Hill House moved in with Mair a week after she took the place. Samuel put them in touch. The teacher was older than Mair. Widowed and in her late forties. She'd been sharing one of Samuel's houses with two nurses in town, but she complained to Samuel that her housemates were messy so he suggested she contact Mair to see if she'd consider taking in a lodger. They seemed to get on all right together despite the age difference. Mair was certainly happy to divide the rent and bills.'

'Can you remember the name of the teacher?' Anna held her pen over her notepad.

'Alice Price. She'd worked in Hill House for a few months before she moved in with Mair, possibly even as long as a year, but they never travelled to the orphanage together. Mair told me that as a social worker she had to work shifts, which meant working longer hours than Alice. There was a good deal of evening and night work too. But within days of starting in Hill House, Mair was a different girl. Samuel was not the most perceptive of men,

196

but even he commented on the difference in her. I knew something was wrong but Mair wouldn't talk about it. Not to me, nor to Samuel. We both tried. It was dreadful to see her so miserable. Samuel was surprised when she left Hen Parc without saying goodbye to us but I wasn't. The last time I saw her she was deeply unhappy.'

'She was crying?' Peter checked.

'No, a public display of grief wasn't Mair's way. But you only had to look at her to sense she was troubled.'

'Did she leave a forwarding address?' Anna asked.

'No. Not even at the Post Office. When her mail started building up, I checked.'

'Do you have any idea where she went after she left Hen Parc?' Peter smiled at Judy when she refilled his coffee cup.

'Not for a long while,' Martha cut her croissant into pieces. 'Then I received a postcard about ten years after she left, thanking Samuel and I for everything we'd done for her. Not that we'd done anything other than take the money she'd paid us in rent.'

'I don't suppose you noticed the postmark on the card?'

'It was Ealing in London.'

'Did you hear from her again?'

'Yes, I received a card from her when Samuel died. I was surprised because it arrived the day before the funeral notice was published in the *Western Mail*. She must have been in touch with someone local to have known.'

'Was that posted in Ealing?'

'No, it was delivered with the post but there was no postmark. There rarely is these days. We have a good local postwoman but the main sorting offices just don't seem to care about letters and packages the way they used to. Letters arrive without cancelled stamps and frequently the packaging on parcels is torn.'

'How long ago did your husband die, Martha?' Anna asked gently.

'Three years next month. He died the week after Christmas.'

'I'm so sorry.'

'Mair was very kind, she's sent me "thinking of you" cards every Christmas since.'

'You said she must have been in touch with someone in the village. Do you have any idea who that could be?'

'No one's ever mentioned her to me until you did this morning, Peter, apart from Rose and Judy that is. Rose remembers Mair living in the village and Judy remembers her from Hill House.'

'Mair was kind.' Judy brought a pot of tea in from the kitchen for Martha and set it on the table in front of her.

'Mair was still working in Hill House when my father brought Judy here,' Rose explained.

'Did Mair socialise much in the village?' Anna sipped her coffee.

'Not after she started in Hill House,' Rose answered. 'A few people who worked in the orphanage lived in Hen Parc when the place was open. But a position in the orphanage was more than just a job. They worked such long hours they rarely seemed to have time for anything outside.'

'Thinking about the condolence card you received from Mair, Martha, you said she was a distant cousin of your husband's. Could someone in your husband's family have been in touch with her?' Peter suggested.

'If it was someone in Samuel's family, it was someone I know nothing about. I have two nieces who live in Cardiff but Samuel was the last of his line. We never had children, but,' Martha gave an unconvincing smile, 'we never missed them. The village became our family. People here are wonderful. Always happy to help anyone in any way they can. I've never been lonely for a moment.'

'Is there anyone living in the village who worked in Hill House when it was open?' Peter took a croissant from the plate Rose offered him.

'No. You do know the last manager in charge of Hill House was found guilty of child abuse?' Martha checked.

'We do,' Anna confirmed.

'After his trial and imprisonment there were more court cases and another six staff were sent to jail.'

'Did any of them live here in the village with their families?'

'Four of the men did, but not the man who managed the place, he'd never married and he lived in Hill House. The wives and children of the other convicted social workers moved away after the sentencing. It was impossible for them to stay here. The press wouldn't leave them alone. They were hounded day and night by journalists who wanted to know what it was like being married to a child abuser. The press even published photographs of their houses along with the name of the village. For a while it made life unbearable for everyone here.'

'I'm sure it did,' Peter sympathised.

'As for Hill House, no one around here wanted anything to do with the place before or after the council closed it. It had always operated outside of the village although some of the local people held fundraisers and donated to the orphanage's Christmas, summer and Easter children's parties.'

'So there really isn't anyone else in the village you can think of who might be help us find Mair?' Peter persisted.

Martha sipped her tea. 'There are the people in Tepee Village. They keep themselves to themselves but they know everything that goes on in the county. There may be one or two there who knew and remember Mair. There were some young people her age living there when she was renting the house.'

'What about Alice Price?' Anna asked.

'She was killed in a car accident driving home from Hill House. It was raining heavily and she went off the road where it narrows on the sharp bend about two miles from the orphanage. There were skid marks and the police thought she'd lost control swerving to avoid something. Probably an animal, the sheep get everywhere.'

'And have no road sense,' Peter commented. 'When did this happen.'

'Oddly enough, the same time Mair disappeared,' Martha said. 'It was heartbreaking, my husband was left with the unenviable task of clearing the cottage of both Mair and Alice's belongings.'

'Alice had no relatives?' Anna set her pen aside.

'None that could be traced,' Martha said. 'Bryn found her will. She left everything she owned to the Red Cross. The staff at Hill House had a collection and paid for her funeral. Such a sad ending for anyone.'

'Don't get your hopes up of finding out anything in Tepee Village, Peter,' Rose warned. 'The population there has ebbed and flowed over the years. People, particularly the young finding their feet, frequently stay only for a short time before moving on.'

Martha laughed. 'Especially in the sixties when marijuana growers were being hounded by the police. Now of course,' she eyed Peter over the rim of her cup. 'police officers have better things to do than chase every New Age hippy who brews herbal remedies.'

200

'Could you give us directions to the village?' Peter asked Rose. 'We'll stop off there on the way back.'

'There's no road there, only a mountain track. As you leave the village take the first fork in the road to your left. There's a rough lane for about a mile. If you leave your car there and keep walking west you'll eventually see it below you.'

'Time for a hike?' Anna suggested.

'Time to see if our superior officer needs us. Just one last thing before we go. One of the army officers mentioned that the Tepee Village has a reputation for taking in waifs and strays.'

'What kind of waifs and strays?' Rose questioned.

'That's what I was hoping to find out. He didn't explain other than to say that the military had found the odd soldier who'd fallen behind on an exercise there.'

'Some of those exercises push recruits to the limit. Or so I've heard,' Martha qualified. 'I've also heard that some officers can be sadistic.'

'Not so different to the brutal way Hill House was run then,' Anna commented. She then asked the question she sensed Peter had been building up to. 'Did any of the runaways from Hill House seek shelter in the Tepee Village?'

'Not that I've heard.' Martha looked to Rose and Judy. Both shook their heads.

'Thank you for the coffee, croissants and information, Rose, Judy, Martha. Should we have any more questions …'

'Call in any time you think we can be of help, both of you.'

'Thank you, you're very kind, Rose. Take care, Judy, Martha.' Anna followed Peter to the door. Judy saw them out.

'Tepee Village?' Anna asked Peter as they walked to the car.

'Back to Hill House. The bureaucrats will be there by now and Joseph might need the support of the cavalry.'

'You see yourself as the brave cavalry officer?' She smiled in amusement.

'No, I see myself as the brave, *handsome* cavalry officer. Fancy some of those croissants? I could nip into the shop and get them?'

'And get crumbs all over the car. Not likely.'

'It's Trevor's car,' he reminded her.

'Get two for me.'

Trevor eyed the Health and Safety Officer across the desk.

'Are you saying, *Mr* Williams,' he enjoyed emphasising the *Mr* because every time he said it Williams cringed, 'that you have been the council's Chief Executive Health and Safety Officer for the past twenty-five years, and your duties included monitoring Hill House, yet you never went there even when it was open?'

'As I said. I was busy –'

'Doing what?'

'Pardon?'

'If you were busy you must have been doing something. I asked what you were doing.'

'I have a staff of fifty to supervise and an office to run. As I said, I sent subordinates to evaluate and monitor Hill House.'

'How often did you send your subordinates?'

'You expect me to remember that –'

'I expect you to remember if you sent in your subordinates once a quarter? Twice a year? I expect you to remember the brief you gave them. A building the size

202

of Hill House – there must have been a great deal to monitor. Roof, walls, window, electrical circuits, plumbing, was there any asbestos in the building? Was the orphanage ever refurbished to make it disabled-friendly? If not, why not?'

'I ensured that my staff adhered to the protocol, practices and regulations laid down by the relevant authority at all times while they were in the employ of the authority.' Williams ran his finger around the inside of his collar.

Trevor sat back in his chair and picked up his pen. 'So, to summarise, you never once visited Hill House when it was open?'

'I – I –'

'You just said you didn't.'

'It's years ago. I – I can't remember.'

'It's a simple question, Mr Williams, did you or did you not ever visit Hill House orphanage, either when it was open or during the closure or after it was closed?'

'The local authority has responsibility for so many buildings.'

'So now you're backtracking on your earlier assertion?' Trevor softened his voice. 'Does the local authority own a glut of isolated Victorian asylums?'

'We have several in the county.'

'Really? You surprise me.'

'We're a sparsely populated county. The Victorians chose to segregate and send the problem members of society to isolated areas where they would attract the least attention.'

'You regard orphans as problem members of society?'

'I didn't say I did. I said the Victorians –'

The telephone rang. Trevor picked it up, looked at Williams and said, 'Excuse me.'

Sarah Merchant was on the line. 'Could I have a word please, sir?'

'Excuse me please, Mr Williams.'

Trevor left his desk and went into the incident room. Sarah was standing at the door. She opened it and went outside. He followed her. The wind was keen, laden with icy needles of rain.

'An official complaint has been made, sir. We think it could have been logged by one of the local authority executives. A call was made to someone influential at the Home Office.'

'Who contacted you?'

'Chief Superintendent Mulcahy, sir. He's on the line now.'

'Tell him you can't find me and you'll ask me to return his call as soon as you track me down. After you've spoken to the Chief Superintendent put a call through to Dan Evans. Tell him it's urgent. As soon as you reach him fetch me.'

'Yes, sir.'

Chapter Eighteen

Trevor saw Anna and Peter stop at the checkpoint the army had erected on the approach road to Hill House. The sentry waved them through and Anna parked down among the military vehicles, well away from the incident room and the scattering of local authority cars and vans.

Reluctant to resume his questioning of Williams, Trevor used the excuse of his pending call to Dan to take a break. He waited for Anna and Peter to join him.

'We bear gifts.' Peter handed Trevor a brown paper bag.

'What is it?' Trevor asked warily.

Anna answered him. 'Two croissants, sir. The chef in the local pub bakes them. The landlady fed us some.'

'And they were so good we bought more in the local shop especially for you.' Peter gave Trevor an insincere smile.

'In that case, thank you.'

'From the look on your face, you were expecting us to hand you one of Patrick's specimens.'

'I wouldn't put it past you. Did you find out anything in the village?'

'Not much, sir,' Anna updated him on what little they'd discovered from Rose and Martha.

'You said Judy was incapacitated in some way?'

'If I had to make a guess I'd say she was possibly brain damaged at birth, sir. She's a little slow in walking and speaking. She obviously enjoys working in the pub and the landlady seems fond of her.'

'But you couldn't get much out of her?' Trevor unwrapped one of the croissants and took a bite.

'She hardly said a word to us.' Anna drew closer to the Portakabin and pulled up the collar of her coat as the freezing, damp-laden wind whistled down the hillside.

'Did she seem traumatised by her time in Hill House?'

'You couldn't tell after a few minutes of conversation, sir.'

'Judy clammed up as soon as we mentioned the place.' Peter reached into the bag he'd given Trevor and broke off a large piece of the second croissant.

'Peter and I thought it might be worth making a visit to the Tepee Village, sir,' Anna ventured.

'It might at that,' Trevor agreed.

'What's happening here?' Peter asked as a police car approached. It slowed when it reached the jagged line of badly parked local authority vehicles.

'If we're fortunate, the arrival of the local police to interview the officials from the authority. I asked Merchant to contact them and request their help.'

'Jobsworths proving stubborn?' Peter raised his eyebrows.

'Obdurate and sphinx-like.'

'Let me loose on them.'

'No, because I already have Mulcahy leaning on me.' Trevor watched a young uniformed sergeant climb out of the first car.

'You sent for local officers, sir.' The sergeant saluted.

'I did.'

'Sergeant Dewi Morris, sir. I have three constables

with me. The Inspector said you needed assistance.'

'I do indeed.'

'It wouldn't be anything to with the local authority being here in force, would it, sir?'

'I assume you recognise the vehicles. Do they always park like this?' Trevor asked.

'Whenever they think they can get away with it, sir.'

'I'm Chief Inspector Trevor Joseph. We'd appreciate it if you could interview the locals for us. I've made a start with the Health and Safety Chief Executive Officer.'

'I doubt Mr Williams was pleased. He's more accustomed to asking questions than answering them, sir.'

'So I've discovered.'

Dewi looked around. An army patrol was heading out on the mountain track. White-suited technicians were carrying samples into the laboratory and mortuary and ferrying out fresh evidence bags.

'Busy crime scene,' Dewi commented.

'Patrick has more assistants?' Peter asked Trevor.

'So it appears. They didn't check in with me.'

'We're not used to seeing this much activity around here in a decade, never mind a day,' Dewi observed.

'Detective Sergeant Peter Collins and Detective Inspector Anna Wells,' Peter introduced himself and Anna. 'I don't suppose you were around when Hill House was open, Sergeant Morris?'

'I was on the planet, sir,' Dewi replied, 'but not in the orphanage.'

'No need to "sir" me, Dewi, I'm plain clothes but the same rank as you. Pity you weren't on the local force when you were in kindergarten. If you had been, you might have been able to enlighten us as to what this place was like when it was operational.'

'I wasn't on the force when Hill House was open,

but my father was.'

Trevor glanced around. The local police were still in their car and the forensic technicians were too far away to listen in on their conversation. He lowered his voice. 'Was your father aware of what was going on here?'

'That's the question everyone asked him and his colleagues when so many of the staff were arrested for abuse. I can only tell you what he said at the time. Like most people in the county, he'd heard rumours, and he along with most of his fellow officers had suspicions, but although they looked into the gossip, they couldn't prove anything. What he didn't say was that every time his immediate superiors tried to open an investigation it was closed down from above. That is until the army officer found the badly injured boy on the hillside. Once the ambulance service was called and the boy reached hospital there was no hushing it up. The doctor who treated the boy before he died saw to that. There were too many witnesses from the army and medical service. And the police who attended the scene made a point of asking awkward questions.'

'What made your father and his colleagues suspect something was going on in Hill House?'

'The number of VIPs visiting the place, particularly late in the evening. There were orphanages all over the country in far more accessible places, so why did so many important people travel all the way here to have their photograph taken with the children? My father didn't believe the explanation the staff gave, that it was to generate press, highlight the positive effects of charity and the change it wrought in children's lives. The only press he and his fellow officers saw lauded the celebrities who made the visits. And some of those had strange reputations. You know how it is with the police, sir. When it comes to the private lives of VIPs rumours fly fast from one force to another.'

'Is your father retired?'

'Has been for five years, sir. He's moved to Malta but I can give you his telephone number if you want to talk to him.'

'Thank you, that might prove useful. Give it to Sergeant Merchant, she's manning the incident room.'

'I'll do that, sir.' Morris pulled out his phone and checked his contacts list for the number.

'Sir?' Sarah called Trevor from the step outside the incident room. 'I have Superintendent Evans on the line.'

'Excuse me please, Sergeant Morris. Inspector Wells, Sergeant Collins, if you take the local officers into the canteen for coffee I'll join you when I've finished my call.'

'Say hello to the brass for me.'

Sarah was working on her computer. 'I put the call through to the phone in the hall outside the small office, sir.'

'Thank you.' He wasted a smile on the authority staff who were still sitting silently, wearing their best peeved expressions.

Trevor closed the door to the office after ensuring that the door to the small office where he'd housed Mr Williams was also firmly closed. He picked up the receiver. 'Trevor Joseph.'

'You've a problem.' Dan hadn't asked a question.

'We're attempting to interview local authority personnel.'

'You alerted them to your search of the site?'

'Yesterday, I informed them we were going into Hill House. This morning we went in before they arrived. Merchant said you've received a complaint.'

'Not me. The Home Office,' Dan answered.

'You've seen the email of the photographs Patrick took in the main hall of the house?'

'Yes. I received the message you sent with them. Patrick doesn't think those body parts were left in the hall for more than a day or so?'

'You know Patrick, he'd rather stay up all night testing evidence than hazard an estimate. He wants to do more tests.'

'Do you know where those body parts were hidden?'

'Not as yet. Patrick won't allow the dogs into the building until he's finished his initial examination because of the risk of cross-contamination. We're trying to find out who lived in Hill House when it was last open and who visited there. I hoped the Local Authority employees could assist us, but ...'

Trevor's "but" hung in the air.

'You didn't really expect any official of the Local Authority to admit to visiting the home when a convicted child abuser was in charge of the place, did you? Bureaucrats are renowned for evading accountability.'

'I'm only a copper who's trying to find out how those body parts ended up here and how the people they belonged to died.'

'You're an optimistic copper. Good luck with that. I've a feeling you'll need it.'

'I also rang ...'

'To ask me to keep Bill Mulcahy off your back.'

'Please.'

'What can you give me?'

'What you've already had. The photographs of the body parts.'

'Have you sent them to him?'

'Yes.'

210

'In which case I'll need more.'

Trevor switched to official speak. 'On the basis of forensic evidence received I am opening a suspicious death enquiry into the demise of six children, one adult and two unknowns.

'Unknowns?' Dan repeated in his Welsh lilt.

'Patrick has found two more heads but he wasn't in the mood to discuss them. We also found a cache of photographs in one of the offices.'

'Hidden?'

'In a not very secret drawer in a chest.'

'What kind of photographs?'

'Vintage.'

'Of people? Staff? Inmates? Pornographic?'

'Not pornographic as far as I could see but I didn't have time to study them. Patrick ordered me out so a forensic team could do a sweep for DNA and fingerprints. I'm hoping there'll be some photographs of the inmates that will help us pinpoint just who those body parts belonged to.'

'Phone me the minute you have something to report.'

'I will. You'll speak to Bill Mulcahy?'

'He phoned you?'

'Yes.'

'And you haven't answered his call?'

'I've been busy.'

'Really.' There was a pause, Trevor sensed that Dan was pushing a peppermint into his mouth. 'Return Bill's call.'

'Yes, sir.' Trevor made a face as he replaced the receiver. He returned to the office. Sarah Merchant looked up at him as he entered.

'I'm going to the canteen to brief the locals. They'll be taking over the preliminary interviewing of the local authority staff. You have the list of questions I prepared early this morning.'

Sarah picked up a sheet of paper and handed it to Trevor. 'I haven't made copies yet, I thought you'd want to give it the once-over in case you want to add anything.'

'Thank you, you know me and my second thoughts so well.'

Trevor looked at the sheet. The ten questions were simple and straightforward but he wondered if they'd be enough to pick out the people they'd need to call back for a second interview. So much depended on the way the questions were asked, and the attitude of the person being interviewed. In his experience questions alone, no matter how searching, rarely elicited the truth.

Did you ever visit Hill House when it operated as a children's home?

If so for what reason?

Was the visit for official business or private?

What was the approximate date of your visit?

Were you aware of any rumours about child abuse in Hill House?

Were you acquainted with any of the staff in Hill House?

Were you in contact with them purely on a business basis?

Did you meet any of the staff of Hill House socially?

Were you involved in any fundraisers for Hill House?

Were you involved in any charity events at Hill House at which children were present?

Did you ever meet any of the staff of Hill House who were subsequently found guilty of child abuse?

Can you list the names of the staff you knew who worked at Hill House and the approximate date you met/knew them.

Can you list the names of any children you knew or met who were resident at Hill House and the approximate date you met/knew them.

Trevor picked up a pen from Sarah's desk and added a couple of lines.

For interviewers' eyes only. Demeanour of person being interviewed.
Circle one below.
Open? Friendly? Over-friendly? Anxious to please? Hostile? Nervous? Other?

He handed the list back to Sarah. She scanned it and smiled.

'You find it amusing?'

'Only the "other", sir. Sergeant Collins is right about you.'

'I've a feeling I'll regret asking this but what does he say about me?'

'That you hate to delegate because you think no one can do as good a job as you.'

'Is it any wonder given the colleagues I have to work with.'

'I'll print these questionnaires off now, sir. I take it they are not to be shown to the interviewees?'

'Absolutely not.'

'Will fifty copies be enough?'

'For the moment. When you run low could you run off another fifty?'

'No problem, sir.'

'I'm off to brief the locals who'll be conducting the interviews.'

'If you give me a moment you can take the questionnaires with you, sir. While you're waiting, shall I get Chief Superintendent Mulcahy on the telephone? If I succeed I'll put him through to the phone in the hall.'

'I suppose you'd better try. You're a worse nag than Superintendent Evans. You do know that?'

She picked up the telephone and hit a speed dial button. 'I try to be, sir.' She spoke into the receiver. 'Chief Inspector Trevor Joseph returning Chief Superintendent Mulcahy's call ...' she looked up at Trevor. 'Chief Superintendent Mulcahy is on the line, sir.'

'Thank you.' Trevor went into the hall and picked up the telephone.

'Joseph?'

'Sir?'

'We've received complaints about the way you're conducting your investigation.'

'Yes, sir.'

'You're aware?'

'Some Local Authority staff are not happy about being questioned, sir, but this is a multiple suspicious deaths enquiry. Deaths that were deliberately concealed, in all probability because the victims were murdered.'

'You have evidence?'

'I emailed you the photographs Dr O'Kelly took of the body parts we found inside the hall of the house this morning, sir.'

'I saw. Has he identified the victims?'

'Not as yet, sir. As you are aware the records of the inmates of Hill House are incomplete but we have found a cache of historic photographs.'

'Photographs of what?'

'I believe they are visual records of staff and inmates, sir.'

Mulcahy snapped. 'Believe?'

'They were hidden in an office. Dr O'Kelly insists that they are examined forensically for fingerprints and DNA before we study them.'

Trevor's observation was met by silence, but he was accustomed to that from Mulcahy. 'About the interviews, sir. I've enlisted the assistance of the local force. I'm about to brief them now on the questions that need to be asked.'

'Tact, Joseph, and speed. Senior people have been on the telephone threatening to demolish Hill House immediately.'

Tired of playing politics, Trevor refused to be rattled. 'And the corpse parts, sir? The photographs are already out in the media.'

'I don't need reminding.'

Peter opened the door without knocking. 'Joseph, you'd better get out here now.'

'I'm sorry, sir, I have to go. There's an emergency …'

'What kind of emergency?'

'I have to go, sir.'

'Call me …'

Trevor didn't wait to hear more. He replaced the receiver and headed for the door.

CHAPTER NINETEEN

Trevor looked ahead to the road-block. Four women were crouched on the ground in front of it. All were huddled into their hooded anoraks and all were looking up at Major Simmonds who was standing beside the guards on the Hill House side of the barrier. He appeared to be making a valiant effort to negotiate with them. His mouth was certainly opening and closing but all Trevor could hear was the screeches of the women who were intent on shouting him down.

'What's going on?' Trevor asked Peter.

'As far as I can make out, these women had children who were taken into care and brought to Hill House. The children subsequently disappeared. They're demanding to be allowed to see the body parts so they can identify them – or not – as the case may be.'

'The photographs of the body parts must still be somewhere on the internet. Why don't they just look for them there?'

'Given that the photographs were taken at night and the parts are pale bloated adipocere it's not easy for a pathologist, never mind a layman, to make out the features. Major Simmonds sent a private to ask for our help in dealing with the women. I tried explaining we're in the middle of an investigation, with people to interview and forensic examinations to evaluate but the women aren't in a listening mood. So I made an executive decision and concluded that the situation calls for someone with your superior communication skills.'

'Every time you try to soft-soap me, it sounds like sarcasm.'

'I'm not trying to soft-soap you. That was sarcasm.'

Trevor capitulated. 'I'll take over here if you pick up the questionnaires from Merchant. Take them to the local coppers in the canteen and brief them. The questions are straightforward and simple enough. Then you can supervise the local authority interviews in the incident room.'

'Don't tell me you're actually expecting the jobsworths to reveal something worthwhile?'

'Remember the phrase – "You do not have to say anything. But it may harm your defence if you do not mention when questioned something which you later rely on in court. Anything you do say may be given in evidence …"'

'So you're expecting bureaucrats to trip up and convict themselves. Dream on, Joseph.'

'Let's say I hope more than expect.'

'And that's the best plan a Chief Inspector can come up with?'

'Another comment like that and I'll order you into Hill House to clean the mess the forensics team will undoubtedly leave behind.'

'That's why I love working for you. You're so petty.'

The women's voices rose, high-pitched and hysterical above the sound of the wind and rain that lashed increasingly heavily.

'Good luck, Joseph. I've a feeling those ladies will

remain immune to your charms.' Peter headed for the incident room.

Trevor walked up to the barrier. The relief etched on Major Simmonds as he approached was almost theatrical.

'This police officer may be able to help you, ladies,' the major shouted in an effort to make himself heard above their noise. 'Chief Inspector Joseph is leading the investigation into Hill House.'

Trevor deliberately kept his voice low, calm, aiming it below the shrieks of the women. 'Can I help you, ladies?'

'You most certainly bloody well can!' A plump middle-aged woman with dyed red hair retorted aggressively. 'We want to go into that orphanage, and we want to go in now!'

'I told them that is impossible ...' Simmonds began.

'That's when we sat down here. This is a bloody sit-in, that's what this is,' a heavily tattooed woman with violent pink hair shouted. 'And we'll sit here ...'

'It's not the sixties and it's raining,' Trevor pointed out mildly.

'We can bloody well see that. It's our f ... bloody ... backsides that are getting wet. And it's here we'll stay until you let us into that house so we can see the bodies for ourselves.'

'We've a right to see them.' This speaker was painfully thin with dense black circles around her eyes that could be down to running mascara and eyeliner or bruises. Her long, greasy, black hair had escaped from the sides of her hood, most of her teeth were missing, her lips were blue and she was trembling so much Trevor wondered if she was ill, or a junkie in desperate need of a fix.

'We stand together!' the last woman in the group shouted as though she was on a picket line. The best-dressed of the four, her voice was as loud if not louder than the others.

'We stay until you show us the bodies!' All four shouted in unison, turning it into a chant. 'Show us the bodies! Show us the bodies! Show us the bodies! Show us the bodies!'

'We stay until we see the bodies!'

'Show us the bodies!'

'Show us the bodies!'

'Please, ladies,' Trevor pleaded, keeping his voice low, well below the volume of the women's shrieks. 'I can't show you the body parts because they are being examined at present by a Home Office pathologist.'

The incomprehensible babble rose to new heights.

'One at a time please, ladies.' Trevor saw Simmonds retreat to the end of the barrier and wished he could join him.

'We've been trying to get justice and a decent burial for our children for years. No one will talk to us. No one has even been prepared to listen, let alone tell us what happened to our own flesh and blood. They are ... were ... our children ...'

'And you are, madam?' Trevor asked.

'Angela Smith. My son Tyrone disappeared from Hill House more than twenty-four years ago. I've been to see everyone I can think of who might help me – and I'm sure they could if only they moved off their rear ends. I've talked to Social Services, the police, the local authority but no one will listen to me, let alone give me answers as to what happened to Tyrone. They took my son and put him in care – "Care", that was a joke. He would have been better off with my sister but they wouldn't listen to her any more than they would listen to me. And all they keep saying to me now is Tyrone "ran off." A boy of eight doesn't run off, not for twenty-four years he doesn't. I've heard "Go home, he'll be in touch" so often it circles in my head like a fault on a record ...' Angela finally stopped struggling to hold back the tears that were falling from her eyes. They flooded down her cheeks, mingling with the raindrops on her face. 'He's never ... never ...'

'Come on, Angela, you can't give up, not now.' One of the other women wrapped her arms around her.

The heavy rain suddenly thundered down in a torrent. Large heavy drops pounded the tarmac road. The icy water penetrated Trevor's thin jacket, soaking through his sweater to his shirt.

'Major Simmonds,' Trevor nodded to the women who remained crouched on the ground. 'Do you have a room I can borrow please? Our incident room is being used to interview local authority personnel.'

'Use my office, Chief Inspector Joseph,'

'Ladies, we need to talk, and we need to talk somewhere dry,' Trevor was forceful.

'We're not moving from this spot,' Angela shouted.

'I'm prepared to listen to you, and I'm anxious to do all I can to help you, but I'm not prepared to discuss it out here where we're all running the risk of contracting pneumonia. Major Simmonds's office is this way.'

The women looked at one another, Angela was the first to move. Major Simmonds led the way to his office. He went in, switched on the electric fire and moved half a dozen chairs in a circle around it.

'Would everyone like coffee?' he asked.

'Yes, please,' Angela answered for all the women who were stripping off their sodden coats.

'Please, black, no sugar.' Trevor hung his dripping coat on the back of one of the chairs.

Simmonds went to the door and barked an order at a private.

'So you're investigating Hill House?' Angela asked Trevor after they all finally sat, gently steaming in front of the electric fire.

'I'm in charge of the current investigation and I'm determined to find the identity of the corpses we found draped on the sign of Hill House and exactly how they died.'

'It's bloody obvious they were murdered ...' Angela began.

Trevor interrupted her. 'Police officers are trained to look at facts and evidence. However, I can promise all of you, ladies, three things. First, I will do my utmost to find out just who those body parts belonged to. Secondly, I will try to find out what happened to your children. And last, I will investigate to the best of my ability exactly what went on in Hill House.'

'Do you keep your promises, Chief Inspector?' Angela demanded.

'I try.'

Angela looked at the other women. 'It's an improvement on what we've fobbed off with so far. I don't think we can ask for more?'

The other three nodded agreement.

The private appeared with a tray of coffee and two packets of biscuits. Major Simmonds approached Trevor while the private distributed them.

'Would you like me to stay?'

'Please, I may need support.' Trevor waited until the women had finished stirring sugar and milk into their coffee before opening the conversation. 'You had children who were sent to Hill House?'

222

The women all began to talk at once.

Trevor looked at Angela. 'Ms Smith, would you please begin telling me what information you have about your son Tyrone and afterwards the rest of you can tell me your stories, in turn, one at a time.' Trevor took a Dictaphone from his pocket. 'If none of you have any objections, I'll record everything you say and ask one of my fellow officers to put the notes on the computer so we have a documented record we can refer to later if necessary.'

'Fine by me.' Angela looked to the other women who all murmured agreement.

'You said that your son Tyrone went missing while he was in Hill House, Ms Smith. When was that and how old was he.'

Angela didn't need to consult any notes. 'Tyrone was eight years and nine weeks old when he disappeared in November 1991. Marion Jenkins's son, Wyn, was twelve years old when he disappeared in 1995. Lynda Lewis's son, Ian,' she reached out and grasped the hand of the painfully thin woman with long, dark hair who was still shaking uncontrollably, 'disappeared in 1992 when he was just five years old. Don't try and tell us he was a runaway ...'

'I'm not trying to tell you anything, Ms Smith. Simply trying to build a picture of events. The fourth child?'

'I'm Maggie Perkins,' the oldest women in the group introduced herself. 'My daughter Alison disappeared in August 1985 when she was twelve.'

'And they're not the only children who've vanished from Hill House. Others have gone.' Angela asserted.

'How do you know?' Trevor questioned.

'A journalist told us. He's investigated all the disappearances from Hill House. He said some go as far back as the year it opened, which to him at best suggests a culture of brutality and indifference in the place and at worst a history of murder and paedophile activity.'

'Journalists earn their living from sensationalizing events,' Trevor pointed out.

'We all know that,' Angela snapped, 'but he also said that although his editor gave him the go ahead to write the article at first, he ordered him to start working on another story after two months. He told us in confidence that he was certain someone important in government had put pressure on his editor to drop the story.'

'Do you have the name of this journalist?'

'Yes, and his telephone number, but he's had so many death threats he's gone into hiding. I'll give you his name, but nothing else until I've talked to him and he's given me permission to pass on his details.' Angela lifted her dripping wet handbag on to her lap, unzipped it and produced a damp notebook. She tore out a page and scribbled a name before handing the slip of paper to Trevor.

Trevor pocketed it and made a mental note to ask Sarah Merchant to check the man out. 'All your children were taken into care by the local authority?'

'Yes,' Angela confirmed. 'None of us have ever said that we're perfect mothers. We had our reasons for giving up our children but for most of us it wasn't from choice. My husband beat me. I didn't have the courage to leave him and ended up in hospital with a fractured skull. I couldn't care for my kids in there. The coppers put my old man in jail, so my sister tried to take them. She had three girls of her own. Social Services said she could take my daughter but Tyrone would be too much for her and as there was no separate bedroom for him in her house, it wouldn't be "proper" for them to leave him with her. I was in a coma and in no condition to argue. My sister

224

tried but got nowhere so Tyrone was sent miles away to Hill House. The first thing I did when I left hospital was telephone Hill House. They said he'd run off. An eight-year-old – run off. I didn't believe them then and I don't believe them now. I've been looking for him ever since.'

'I'm an alcoholic,' Marion Jenkins volunteered. 'In 1994 I was arrested for attacking a policeman and sent to prison. My Wyn was put into care. I wrote to him but never got a reply. He was nearly twelve, bright and good at schoolwork so I couldn't understand why he didn't answer. When I was released a year later I caught a bus straight to Hill House. They told me the same as they told Angela. Wyn had run off. Where would a twelve-year-old with no money and no friends for miles around go?'

Lynda looked to Maggie. When the older woman didn't say anything she began her story. 'Like Marion I was sent to jail. I was caught dealing drugs. I have no excuse. I managed to get clean in prison and I was determined to pick up Ian as soon as I got out, and turn my life around for both of us. My social worker met me at the gate and told me Ian had been adopted. I knew that couldn't be right, as I hadn't signed any papers. She wouldn't even give me the address of the people who'd taken him. I begged her to give me a photograph of Ian – something – anything – to prove that he was still alive, but she insisted his case was closed. I kept looking for him and badgering people and getting nowhere just like Angie, Maggie and Marion. Then, a year later, the reporter Angie mentioned contacted me. He told me my Ian had vanished from Hill House in 1992 and there were no ongoing records of him.'

Angela reached out and grasped Lynda's hand again.

'My daughter Alison was put in care when I had a nervous breakdown after my husband was murdered. He was knifed to death in London. I was there, I tried to stop the man …' Maggie closed her eyes tightly against the memory, but Trevor could see pain etched deep into the lines on her face. 'She was twelve. When I was discharged from hospital they told me what they'd told Angie and Marion, that my Alison had run off.'

'How did you ladies meet?' Trevor asked.

'At the court when the master of Hill House was found guilty of child sexual abuse. The journalist I told you about introduced us.'

'You said there were other parents who'd lost children there?'

'There were. About twenty, maybe more. If anyone has an idea of the number of children who've gone missing it will be that reporter. I'm sure I heard him say that as many as a hundred could have gone missing since the place first opened.'

'He also said that some of the older ones were almost certainly runaways and some of the younger ones might have been adopted without the proper paperwork being filled out,' Maggie reminded her.

Trevor recognised the "clutching at straws" syndrome. The women were prepared to believe almost anything that offered a slim chance that their children might still be alive. 'What about the police and organisations that look for missing people? Have you approached them?'

'Some were more helpful than others. The Salvation Army was particularly kind. Many of them posted our children's photographs on their web sites, but we've never had a response worth mentioning.' Angela was despondent.

'No one contacted you with any sightings of the children?'

'No one. Every month we write to our MPs, the

newspapers and the news programmes on television and the radio. We managed to get a few interviews on the strength of the last court case. Then when we saw photographs of the body parts on the sign outside Hill House ... If it was your child who was missing?' Angela appealed to Trevor. 'What would you do?'

Trevor found the possibility that Marty could disappear from his life too painful to even contemplate.

'Please, we're begging you, Chief Inspector Joseph, let us look at the body parts so we can see if they belong to our children.'

'I'm sorry, ladies, but I cannot allow you anywhere near Hill House before the forensic teams have done their work lest you contaminate the crime scene.'

'You may have listened to us, but you're no different to all the others in authority,' Angela's voice rose precariously. 'You expect us to walk away, grateful because you spared us half an hour of your valuable time ...'

'Not at all. There is something I can do, but I'll need your help. Do any of you have photographs of your children?'

'Of course we do,' Angela snapped, 'but we're not willing to part with them.'

'I wouldn't ask you to, but it might help if you'd allow one of my officers to scan them into our computer.'

Angela looked to the others. She spoke only after they'd all nodded. 'We'll allow you do that.'

'Also, if I send for an officer and four DNA kits, would you agree to giving us DNA samples? It's quite simple. All that's required is taking a swab from inside your mouth. I assure you it's quite painless.'

'And if we do?' Angela challenged.

'I'll ask the forensic team to study the samples and

227

check if they match the DNA profiles they're trying to extract from the body parts. If they do, I should receive confirmation within forty-eight hours.'

'And you'll let us know the results?' Angela persisted.

Trevor looked out of the window. Darkness was already falling. He knew that if he nagged Patrick and Jenny he might get the DNA results by morning. 'There's an inn in Hen Parc that does bed and breakfast. How about I ask one of my officers to see if they have a couple of rooms free for tonight. You can stay there at the expense of the investigation and as soon as I have the results from the pathologist I will give them to you.'

'You'd do that for us?' Lynda was incredulous.

'I might need to interview you again so you'd be doing me a favour,' Trevor hoped they wouldn't guess that he wanted to keep them close in case they had to formally identify any of the human remains.

CHAPTER TWENTY

'I've booked accommodation at the inn in Hen Parc for the four ladies for one night, sir. The landlady told me there shouldn't be a problem if we require extra nights, as the pub is quiet at this time of year,' Sarah informed Trevor when he returned to the incident room.

'Thank you, Merchant.'

'I've also started checking through the few records we have from Hill House for the ladies and their missing children, sir, but nothing's come up so far that wasn't on the conversation you recorded with them and sent over with a soldier. I've managed to verify a couple of the facts they gave you.'

'If you come up with anything new …'

'I'll let you know right away, sir.' Sarah returned to her screen.

'Going by the absence of abandoned cars outside, I assume the local authority people have left?'

'They have. Sergeant Collins has taken the completed questionnaires into the small office so he can study them in peace and quiet.'

'Has he now?'

Trevor found Peter slumped in a chair behind the desk, feet propped on one corner, a carton of coffee and a packet of chocolate biscuits in front of him.

'Hard at it, I see?'

'This is my first break today, Joseph.'

'First break after coffee and croissants at the inn in Hen Parc?' Trevor reminded.

'The local force only finished interviewing the people from the council half an hour ago. Or to qualify that statement, the indigenous coppers finished questioning the jobsworths as far as they allowed themselves to be questioned half an hour ago. I'm going through the questionnaires now. That sergeant with a Welsh name …'

'Dewi Morris?' Trevor supplied.

'That's the one. Being as keen and eager as a retriever puppy, he offered to stay and help search Hill House. I took him into the hall to meet Patrick who screeched louder than a Welsh banshee. So, being superfluous to our requirements, dashing Dewi and his Welsh wonders have all left, but Morris said any time you need more manpower give him a ring and he and his cohorts will appear like magic genies.'

'Patrick …'

'Is in full growling mode. Won't allow anyone other than forensics near the house. Barry and Hever have returned.'

'Did they find anything?'

'After they've seen to the dogs they said they'll report in. But from what I gathered the short answer is no. Not one single solitary bark beyond the wall of Hill House. So it's unlikely that whoever arranged those corpse parts on the gate took any samples from the premises.'

'Hence your idleness.'

'Pardon?'

'You're taking an undeserved rest while waiting to receive Barry and Hever's report?'

Peter lifted up the papers in front of him. 'As I said, I'm going through the jobsworths' questionnaires. It's arduous work but someone has to do it.'

'Found anything?'

'I've learned a few new phrases, long words and novel excuses that weren't in my repertoire. Enough to seriously consider writing an idiot's guide to evading responsibility.'

'Jen?'

'Is working in the lab with one of the new forensic people.'

'How many extra forensic operatives have turned up?'

'Four.'

'How's Patrick taken to the invasion?'

'From what I can gather as I wasn't there at the time, he received them with all the warmth of Caesar welcoming a battalion of uncivilised Gauls into the Roman army. You know Patrick, he likes things done his way and no other.'

'I need to see Jen.'

'And then?' Peter asked.

'If you volunteer to debrief Barry and Hever ...'

'Which I have.'

'I'll press-gang Anna into accompanying me and the ladies down to the inn in Hen Parc and from there, we'll pay a visit to the Tepee Village.'

'You don't trust me to go there. Tut tut, those who never learn to delegate ...'

'Keep full control of the investigation.' Trevor glanced around the incident room. 'Where are Anna and Brookes?'

'Anna's with Jenny, making notes on the forensic evidence. Jenny said the laboratory wasn't big enough to hold me as well.'

Trevor smiled. 'Wise girl. You take up a lot of room. And Brookes?'

'Providing muscle for one of the new forensic people.'

'Glad to see some of my team working.'

Peter held up the file of questionnaires. 'You think it's easy staying awake to read these?' He noticed the bag Trevor was holding. 'DNA samples from the women to compare with the DNA samples Jenny recovered from the corpses?'

Trevor nodded. 'I'll drop them round to her now.'

'I heard you're putting up the women at the investigation's expense.'

'Only until the results of the DNA comparisons come in.'

'You're a soft touch, Joseph.'

'I feel for them. They've been fobbed off by officials for years and still don't know what happened to their children. No mother deserves that.'

'Having a child disappear and never knowing its fate is every parent's nightmare,' Peter added.

'You've been thinking about that too?'

'I've been trying not to. Every time I picture Miranda ...'

'The thought cuts through you like a knife?' Trevor finished the sentence for Peter.

'Fatherhood has changed both of us, Joseph. The existence of Miranda has made me more vulnerable than I've ever felt, and I hate the fear.'

After hearing Rose and Martha's warnings about the rough track that led to Tepee Village from Peter, Trevor 'borrowed' a rough terrain vehicle from Simmonds. He asked Chris Brookes to drive the women down to the inn in his car. He and Anna followed in the off road vehicle.

As soon as they'd seen the women settled into the care of a sympathetic Rose and Judy, and Chris had returned in Trevor's car to Hill House, Trevor checked the grid reference Simmonds had given him.

He and Anna finished the coffee they'd insisted on paying for, had a short final, and Trevor hoped reassuring, conversation with the women and left the inn.

The night was sodden and black. Once the few straggling streetlights of Hen Parc were behind them, Trevor found the darkness impenetrable. He turned his headlights to full beam but the rain slashed glare reflected straight back at him obscuring the road. When they left the main thoroughfare for a narrow lane, a grey mist fell, dense, thick, blanketing everything beyond the beam of the headlights. It twisted the fog into terrifying, ethereal shapes that loomed and swirled ghost-like towards the windscreen.

Sensing more than seeing that they were approaching the end of the lane and open hillside, Trevor slowed the vehicle to a crawl. The mist cleared for an instant, long enough for Anna to see the side of the road fall away sharply on their left.

'Wouldn't it be better to wait for daylight to travel down here, Trevor?' Anna pleaded.

'You saw the sheer drop to the valley floor?'

'Yes.'

'Scared?'

'Petrified,' she admitted.

'There's lights up ahead on the right. They seem to be more or less on the same level we're on. If it's a farm we'll stop and ask for directions.'

Trevor continued to bump slowly over the track, which was little more than a footpath with grass and weeds growing high in the centre.

Buffeted by the wind, the rain drove into the windscreen almost at right angles. Anna perched forward on the edge of her seat, as far as her seatbelt would stretch, peering into the darkness in the hope of seeing something – anything – ahead.

'It's a farmhouse,' Trevor said. 'There's a light in one of the windows and another outside the door.'

The front door opened as Trevor parked in front of the house. A stocky middle-aged man swathed in layers of threadbare woollen pullovers emerged. His head was bald and bare and he was holding a shotgun.

'Bit cliché,' Anna murmured. 'I feel as though we've stumbled into a Welsh *Deliverance*.'

'Let's hope the gun's not loaded.' Trevor reached for his identification, opened the car door and held it up. 'Police,' he shouted hoping the wind wouldn't carry his voice away. 'We're making enquiries into Hill House.'

'You're miles from Hill House.'

'We know. We've just come from Hen Parc village and we're visiting all the houses in the vicinity to see if anyone can tell us anything about the old orphanage.'

'*All* the houses?'

'Yes.'

'Let me see that identification.'

Trevor walked up and handed it over. The man nodded and waved him through the door but Trevor had the feeling he wouldn't have if the driving rain hadn't made conversation impossible. Keeping her head down, Anna ran inside and joined Trevor. They found themselves wedged in the entrance of a narrow passage with a flagstone floor and whitewashed walls. It smelled of chicken manure and feed, a well-remembered mix of farm odours that brought childhood memories flooding back to Trevor.

A woman opened a door at the end of the passage. She was young and slender with green eyes and long curly red hair. She stared at him.

'I saw you in town.'

'My colleague Peter Collins bought honey and candles from you in the old coaching inn.' Trevor held out his hand. 'Trevor Joseph, Anna Wells, we're with the police.'

'Alice.' She didn't volunteer a surname.

The man continued to study Trevor. He was much older than Alice with wind-flushed, corrugated skin. The tell-tale hallmark of a farmer who spent time outdoors in all weathers. 'You said you're looking into Hill House,' he reminded Trevor.

Alice retreated, but left the door open.

'We are.'

'It's been closed for years but I suppose those body parts they were talking about on the radio have set you lot nosing around again.'

'We tend to be called in whenever corpses appear.' Trevor smiled to take any unintended sting from his words.

'We're three miles even as the crow flies from Hill House.'

'As I said, we're checking all the houses in the area. We heard there's a Tepee Village down the track. We were heading there when we noticed your lights.'

Alice reappeared but she didn't open the door any wider or invite them inside. 'The people in the Tepee Village have always kept themselves to themselves. They're no bother to anyone and they'd prefer to be left alone.'

Anna smiled and extended her hand. 'I'm Anna Wells.'

Alice hesitated for a few seconds before shaking it.

'So, you can't tell us anything about the Tepee Village or Hill House?' Trevor pressed.

'It's all we can do to tend to our sheep, pigs and chickens. The farming life doesn't allow time for gossip or visiting neighbours,' the man snapped.

'How long have you lived here?'

'What's that to you?'

'I'm trying to build a picture of what life around Hill House is like now, and what it was when the orphanage was open.' When the man didn't answer, Trevor looked around the stone-built, whitewashed walls searching for a less controversial subject on which to open a conversation. 'A place this size probably started life as a longhouse. Animals one end, people the other. The walls look thick enough to be fifteenth century or even earlier.'

'Now you're an expert on farm buildings?'

'I've read up on the history,' Trevor conceded. 'I grew up in a fourteenth-century farmhouse in Cornwall.'

'So you know all about farming.'

'Enough to realise that I'd have an easier life as a police officer.'

The man unbent enough to laugh. 'So you left your father to it?'

'My brother. He loves the life and wanted no other.'

'I didn't think I was cut out for it,' the man revealed. 'But once I started helping out on a farm, like your brother I knew it was the life I wanted.'

'When was that?'

'When I was young.'

Trevor sensed the man's irritation. 'All I'm trying to do is find out what happened in Hill House.'

'Children vanished from there, that's what happened.' There were tears in Alice's eyes. 'It was supposed to be a loving, caring, safe place for orphans. But my mother said it was anything but, my mother said … it was … was …'

Anna recalled Martha Jones's description of Mair Davies. *Mair was an exceptionally pretty girl. Beautiful green eyes, long, curly, red hair, so full of life …* She could have been talking about Alice. 'I'm so sorry,' Anna grasped Alice's hand. 'The last thing we want to do is upset you. Did you know someone who was an inmate there?'

Alice shook her head. 'No …' she murmured unconvincingly.

'We can't tell you anything. I think it's time you went.' The man raised his voice as he walked to the front door Anna had closed behind her.

'We're desperate for information,' Trevor pleaded when the man lifted the latch. 'All we want is justice for the victims. We know children were abused in Hill House. We know they suffered. We've found more body parts so we can be certain that the remains of the children we found weren't even respected in death. Their corpses were dismembered.' Trevor sensed the man wavering and pressed home his advantage. 'We need to know what happened. How those children died … if only for the sake of their bereaved mothers.'

'Bereaved mothers? If they were so concerned for their kids why did they put them into care?'

'We've spoken to mothers who've been searching for their children for years – in some cases decades. Several were ill in hospital,' Anna explained. 'Unable to care for their children, they had no option but to allow them to be sent to Hill House. Others had problems that resulted in them being sent to prison or rehabilitation centres. They are the first to admit they're no angels, but they didn't deserve to lose their children. Others had family willing to care for their children but Social Services refused to allow the relatives to foster them and insisted on taking them into care. One of the mothers Trevor and I spoke to has been searching for her vanished child for over thirty years. If you can tell us something – anything – that will help us to shed light on the fate of those children or at least assist us to find their bodies and identify the abusers it may help us show the world that the law is on the side of the victims, not the paedophiles.'

'Look what's happened to those who try to tell the truth,' the man burst out angrily. 'They've been called liars to their faces, hounded, mocked and humiliated …'

'The body parts draped over the sign of Hill House, and the children who vanished from there, are the reason this investigation was opened,' Trevor explained. 'The victims deserve closure.'

'They deserve it but I can't see them getting it.'

'If you can tell us anything relevant to Hill House, we promise to keep everything you say confidential. We'll never attribute you as the source of our information, or mention your names unless you give us your express permission. And we won't ask you to do anything other than talk to us now,' Trevor pleaded.

'Have you spoken to the police before?' Anna asked.

Alice managed to control her emotions long enough to answer. 'We didn't, but my mother tried. No one would listen to her.'

Anna steeled herself. 'Your mother is Mair Davies?'

'How did you … who told you?' Alice demanded.

'I spoke to Martha Protheroe and Rose Jones at the inn.'

'Neither of them would have told you who my mother was.'

'They didn't, not intentionally,' Anna reassured. 'But they described her to me. They said how kind, thoughtful and beautiful she was, with long, curly, red hair and bright green eyes. I recognised you in that description. I watched you talk to Peter Collins in the yard of the coaching inn in town. He's not an easy man to get on with. And,' Anna smiled, 'not many people have striking green eyes and auburn hair.'

Alice looked to the middle-aged man. 'Dad?'

'Your mother tried telling the truth, and look where it got her, me and you. A lifetime of hiding, afraid to meet anyone, afraid to make a friend lest they tell the wrong people where we are. Why should anything be different now?' he challenged.

Trevor looked him in the eye. 'Because I wasn't in charge of the investigation then, sir. I am now.'

Alice opened the kitchen door wider. 'Come in, I'll make us some tea.'

CHAPTER TWENTY-ONE

Peter stared at Clive Barry. 'Nothing?'

'Nothing, Zilch, Nada, nothing,' Barry repeated to Peter. 'I'm as disappointed as you. Particularly after the way the dogs reacted to the wall last evening. And that's without mentioning the pointless miles Hever and I trudged.'

'So it's more than likely those body parts were kept hidden inside, not outside, Hill House?' Peter mused.

'Looks that way, given that the dogs only reacted to the site of the sign, front and side door of the house and garden wall. I suspect the side door and garden wall could be the exit point of our body part arranger. Unless the corpse sections were brought in well-wrapped from outside and scent leakage contaminated the joker's clothing, and it was transferred when he climbed over the wall. The question is would someone who carried the body parts in from outside have bothered to take them or himself to the front hall and dump some of the parts under the stairs.' Barry took one of the two coffees Hever brought in and prised open the lid.

'Thank you for those thoughts to ponder, Barry. So, we're agreed there's nothing we can do at present except sit, ruminate and wait.' Peter pulled a second chair closer to his own and lifted his feet on to it.

'Wait for what?' Chris Brookes walked into the incident room, peeled off his disposable white overalls and tossed them into a bin. He flashed Sarah one of his "special" smiles.

'The forensic teams to allow us into Hill House when they finally finish scraping, cutting and pasting like a kindergarten group. As you've just left them, any idea when that will be, Brookes?' Peter tossed the file he'd been pretending to read on to the desk.

'Funny you should mention that …'

Sarah swivelled her chair around to face Chris. 'Don't tell me Patrick wants us to start searching the house now. If we do, he'll expect us to stay up all night.'

'Not tonight we won't,' Barry countered. 'The dogs are kn … tired,' he amended in response to a warning look from Brookes, who abhorred even mild swearing in front of women.

'Is Patrick ready to allow us to begin searching the house?' Peter stretched his arms above his head and yawned.

'He was finishing up in the hall when I left,' Brookes said. 'He actually unbent enough to allow one of the new forensic people to collect samples and carry out preliminary checks in the old offices on the ground floor where the Chief Inspector and I found the photographs. But he did make a point of saying that he'd trained her. Nice lady, Gillian Henderson, I worked with her on another case. The laboratory must be stuffed to the rafters with all the samples Patrick's taken today, although he has left some of the larger items in the house. If he hadn't, there'd be no room for people in the lab.'

'Larger items? Like heads?' Peter asked.

'Like sections of banister on the staircase and door handles.' Brookes sat next to Sarah.

'So, a busy day again for all of us tomorrow,' Peter predicted.

'Looks like it,' Barry agreed.

'I suggest we relax while we can.'

Sarah smiled. 'When do you ever do anything else, Sergeant Collins?'

'That's insubordination from a junior to a senior sergeant.'

'I thought you were my friend, not my superior.'

'I'm both, but you don't make it easy for me to be your friend when you're being prickly.'

'We can't do anything until the Chief Inspector returns. He's called a meeting for this evening,' Sarah warned.

Peter glanced at his watch. 'Evening, it's after six now.'

'He was hoping to be back by seven, but you know what he's like when he's in the middle of a case.'

'Unfortunately I do.' Peter rose to his feet. 'I vote we go to the canteen and eat. That way if he does call a meeting and keeps it going until the small hours, at least we'll be able to sit through it with full stomachs.'

'Good idea.' Barry led the way to the door.

'I could eat a horse,' Sarah rose stiffly from her chair and rubbed her back. 'But someone should stay here and man the phones.'

'I'll do it.' Hever volunteered.

'Good man. That's the way to ingratiate yourself with your superiors.' Peter opened the door and stepped down from the incident room. Soldiers were everywhere. He saw Jenny and a group of forensic scientists he didn't recognise leave the lab. They stopped to talk to Patrick who crossed the road from the gates. Two local policemen were talking to the guards at the roadblock. Peter recognised one of them as Dewi Morris. He wondered what they were doing there but he wasn't curious enough to go down and find out.

He wrapped his arms around Brookes and Merchant's shoulders. 'Quick, let's grab the best that's on offer before the Dracula team descends.'

'I'll tell Jenny what you call her and Patrick,' Sarah threatened.

'She already knows. She chose it in preference to my old name for her and Patrick, the "Frankenstein Brigade".'

'It's a wonder they still speak to you.'

'Isn't it? But I keep working on a way of stopping them'

'Thank you.' Trevor took the tea Alice handed him. She'd set two kitchen chairs in front of the fire for him and Anna. The room reminded him so much of his mother's kitchen when he was a child he found himself fighting a wave of homesickness.

Like the passage, the stone walls were whitewashed. The range that filled most of the back wall was too large for the room, heating it to tropical temperature. The easy chairs either side of the fire that Alice and her father occupied were covered by patchwork throws. There was a battle-scarred Welsh dresser too roughly constructed to warrant the name 'antique', filled with mismatched pieces of china. The bottom shelf held two large wooden photograph frames. One held a picture of a middle-aged woman Trevor assumed was Mair Davies. She looked careworn and ill but still beautiful. The second lay face down, which piqued his curiosity.

A well-scrubbed pine table and half a dozen kitchen chairs dominated the centre of the room. A rag rug lay in front of the hearth. Cupboards and shelves had been built into the alcoves either side of the fire. They held an assortment of items Trevor recognised from his boyhood. Ointments for sheep, tools for scraping hooves, additives for chicken and pig feed, string, plasters, liniments, all mixed together with a selection of well-thumbed editions of *Farmers Weekly*. But the single overwhelming nostalgic factor was the smell. A mix of antiseptic, farmyard, wet dogs, rich meat stew and yeasty home-baked bread.

Trevor shook himself free from his memories when Alice looked to her father. He saw him give her a slight, almost imperceptible nod.

'My mother died three weeks ago.' There was a catch in Alice's throat. 'It was cancer, she'd been ill for some time.'

'My deepest sympathy,' Trevor knew what it was to lose a parent. Decades had passed since his father's death but he still missed him more than he cared to admit, even to himself at times. 'A colleague of mine met your mother many years ago in Hill House. He described her as a beautiful, caring young woman, but he also said she seemed to be afraid of someone in the orphanage. They arranged to meet in the inn in Hen Parc but she never turned up.'

'Dan Evans the police sergeant?'

Trevor was surprised to hear Dan's name. 'Yes, Dan was a sergeant back then.'

'Mair said she trusted him.' Alice's father held out his hand to Trevor. 'I'm Brian Smith, by the way.'

Trevor shook it. 'Dan Evans is a superintendent now. He spent months looking for Mair when she disappeared. He even checked the passports of people who'd left the country.'

'Really?'

'Dan was concerned for her. He knew something was amiss in the orphanage but he couldn't prove it.'

'Mair told me Dan Evans was in Hill House to watch over a friend's daughter. That concerned her, the fact that the police knew something was going on in Hill House yet did nothing about it.'

'Sensing and proving are two very different things, Brian. Police officers can't do anything until they receive an official complaint and even then they need proof to back the claim.'

'Mair said there were two female officers with him, helping him to look after a pretty little girl. Her grandparents wanted to take her but social services had other ideas.'

'I was that little girl, Brian. I wish I could tell you that I remember Mair, but I don't.'

Brian turned to Anna. 'You were in Hill House?'

'I was.'

'So you knew what went on there?'

'I knew it was a horrible place but Uncle Dan and the other officers never left me alone for a minute.'

'With good reason from what Mair told me. The things that went on there haunted her until her dying day. Mair adored children, which was why she became a social worker. She simply couldn't bear the thought of a child – any child – suffering. She used to say the problems in care began in the late sixties and early seventies when the decision was made to merge Borstals and correctional facilities for children who'd been convicted of crimes with orphanages. The idea was laudable, to provide a safe, loving environment for every child. In practice she felt that everything had been reduced to the lowest common denominator, especially when it came to attitudes and morality among both staff and children. The smaller children's homes that had opened post-Second World War, managed by housemothers and fathers, generally married couples who genuinely cared for their charges, were closed and emphasis was placed back on the larger homes like Hill House. A building programme was instigated to update the old institutions and they were staffed by social workers on shifts who rarely bothered to build relationships with the children because they were constantly moving on in search of career advancement.

'Mair knew from her training placements while she was at university that in the new regime "human rights" meant social workers were no longer allowed to keep youngsters in at night. Not even when they suspected that children had fallen prey to pimps. Hundreds if not thousands of kids in care were plied with drugs by dealers so they'd have to keep working the streets to feed their addiction and the criminals with money. Mair took the job in Hill House because she thought its isolation would protect the children there. She was so wrong.'

'Did Mair ever see any child being abused in Hill House?' Trevor probed.

'If she did, she didn't talk about it to me. She did say that she found some photographs. Disgusting things that she gave to someone she thought she could trust to take them to the police, but if he did, nothing ever came of it.' Brian stared down at his hands. 'You have to understand, Mair rarely talked about her time in the orphanage, but the impression I had was that she felt helpless. She said she often heard screams coming from the master's office, but whenever she complained she was told it was normal discipline being meted out to a "theatrical child". Injuries were explained away as self-abuse or fighting among the inmates. But she did try to help the children whenever she could. As a result she had to go into hiding to save her own life. The woman Mair shared a house with wasn't so lucky.'

'Alice Price?'

'You've done your homework, Chief Inspector, I'll give you that.'

'Rose and Martha told us that Alice Price died in a car accident.'

'My mother never believed it was an accident,' Alice warmed the teapot before dropping tea bags into it.

'Did Mair say why?'

'Because on the day she died, Alice Price confided something to my mother. Something she'd seen in Hill House. But you have to remember, Chief Inspector –'

Trevor interrupted Alice, 'Please call me Trevor, Alice … of course. Your mother named you after Alice Price. It's so obvious I can't understand why I didn't see it before now.'

'Yes, she named me after Alice. She was certain that Alice was murdered, but my mother was very ill at the end. It was difficult for her – and us – to differentiate between her reality, memory and hallucinations.'

'Mair hated talking about Hill House,' Brian explained. 'But I could tell that what had happened there lay heavy on her mind. At the end she finally began to tell us about her experiences in the place.'

'You didn't tell anyone what she said?' Trevor asked.

'How could we? We had no proof that they were anything except the ramblings of a dying woman.'

'Mum said that on the last day she and Alice worked in Hill House, Alice told her she'd taken her class up to the attic that morning so they could look out and draw maps of the hillside and valley below. Alice walked behind the children in case one of them slipped on the stairs. When she reached the attic, a boy had already opened the door to one of the rooms. There was a child's body on the floor.'

'Did Alice describe the body?'

'Alice told Mum it was a boy about eight years old. She closed the door quickly and led the children back downstairs.'

'Did any of the children see the body?' Trevor questioned.

'The child who opened the door. Possibly others but Alice told Mum she warned her class never to speak of it, even among themselves. Mum said the children would have done exactly that. Living in Hill House had taught them to keep secrets.'

'And Alice?' Trevor prompted.

'When Mum drove home late that night after her shift she saw police officers on the road. She stopped and they told her there'd been an accident. Mum said she knew straight away that it was Alice. One of the policemen offered to drive her home. After what had happened to Alice, Mum felt she couldn't trust anyone – not even a policeman – so she refused. When they asked about her relationship with Alice, she told them that she and Alice merely shared a house. That they weren't close at all, which was far from the truth, as you can tell from my name.'

'I met Mair for the first time that night,' Brian looked Trevor in the eye. 'You promise never to mention Mair, Alice's or my names to anyone outside of this room, or in any official report?'

'I promise and as you see,' Trevor held out his hands, 'I'm not even making notes.'

'Convinced that Alice had been murdered, Mair didn't return to the cottage that night. She left her car with the keys in the ignition on the road just past where the police were hauling Alice's car off the mountain. She was so convinced that she'd be the next to be killed after what Alice had told her, she hoped that someone would steal it and drive it miles away. She had a torch in the glove compartment and a university friend, an artist in Tepee Village. She hoped her friend would take her in for the night. She said afterwards she didn't think further than that at the time. It was someone's birthday in the village and we were having a party. I'll never forget the look on Mair's face when she joined us that night. Even in firelight she looked absolutely terrified. We all tried to calm her down. She said people were after her, her housemate had been murdered and they were going to murder her as well. But she wouldn't tell us who was after her.'

'Why didn't she contact the police?'

'She said the only policeman she trusted was from outside the area and the local police were in league with the people who were after her.'

'You believed her?' Anna asked.

'The one thing we all believed was her fear. It was obviously real. Her friend told her she could hide out in her tent for a while.'

'In the Tepee Village?' Trevor asked.

'I'd been living there for a few years. We all thought Alice would be safe with us because we looked out for one another. Before six o'clock the next morning a senior police officer and six constables turned up in Tepee Village looking for Mair. They didn't have a warrant and the more street-wise among us sent them packing. That's when we began to believe Mair was really in danger. That night we smuggled Mair out. I went with her.'

'Any reason why you accompanied her?' Trevor was curious.

'Call it what you will, I like to think it was love at first

250

sight. Mair was unlike anyone I'd ever met and I couldn't believe she'd ever be interested in someone like me. But I was prepared to care for her – and fight for her if I had to.'

'Where did you go?'

'Kent. My parents lived there. Mair and I moved in with them. Within a few weeks Mair was pregnant – a psychologist might say she needed to affirm life. I'd say it made me one hell of a lucky man. Six months later we rented our own farm there. I wanted to marry Mair but she wouldn't, because that would have meant leaving a record of her name that could be traced. She adopted my name unofficially and became Mrs Smith. But in all the years we lived together she never once stopped looking over her shoulder.'

'Why did you come back?'

'To live here. I was left the farm and the land Tepee Village is on by my uncle,' Brian revealed. 'I was wild as a kid and always in trouble with the law. The only people who accepted me without trying to change me or ask awkward questions about what I'd done were the people in Tepee Village. I moved there after a row with my uncle and I'd been sent to live with him by my parents because I couldn't get on with my father. When my uncle died and left us this place and his land, we thought that as Hill House had closed and so many of the staff been imprisoned it was safe. We also wanted to protect Tepee Village. Mair felt she wouldn't have survived if it hadn't been for the people who took her in the night that Alice Price died.'

'That explains why you're so protective of Tepee Village.'

'It's been a sanctuary to many,' Alice pointed out.

'Not misfits and criminals, as some would have it,'

Brian glanced at a newspaper on the table. It was folded over, displaying a photograph of the missing politician on the front page. He added, 'Just ordinary people who find life difficult as we all do from time to time.'

'Did any other staff from Hill House take refuge there besides Mair?' Anna asked.

'Not that I'm aware of.'

'What about the children? The records are incomplete but there's mention of runaways,' Trevor said.

'The one thing Tepee Village offers is anonymity. Everyone there is given the opportunity to work. If they don't want to, that's OK too. People come and go, if they want to talk there's always someone prepared to listen, but if they want to be left alone, they will be.'

'So there were runaways but you're not prepared to mention names,' Trevor said.

'There's a generator, radios, computers and internet access in Tepee Village. Given the publicity of the star witness court case, I'd say that any past inmate of Hill House who was willing to talk to the police has done so.'

'You're probably right.' The last thing Trevor wanted to do was damage the tenuous relationship he was trying to build with Brian and Alice by disagreeing with either. 'But we would like to visit there. Police work is strange. Often people have a small piece of information they think is inconsequential, yet when we put all our evidence together it can be the vital element that solves a case. Would you accompany us there?'

'If you promise to treat everyone there the same way you're treating us. You'd talk to them in confidence. You wouldn't make them visit a police station or go to court.'

'I wouldn't, but,' Trevor qualified, 'if any of the people living in Tepee Village were runaways from Hill House, I'd appreciate it if they'd confirm their identity so

I could cross their names from the list of those who've disappeared from the orphanage. What they do with their lives is their business but it might save a future fruitless and expensive police enquiry.'

'You promise not to reveal their whereabouts?'

'I promise,' Trevor reiterated solemnly.

'I don't know why I believe you, but I do.'

'Do you have a telephone number?' Trevor asked.

Alice took a notepad and pencil from the shelf, wrote down a number and handed it to Trevor.

'I'm hoping forensics will finish checking Hill House soon. Someone evidently hid those body parts in the house. Did Mair ever mention any hiding places?'

'She did say the cellars there are vast.'

'Were they used for anything?' Trevor asked.

'Storage. The central heating and hot water boilers were down there and both were coal-fired. There was an old laundry too but all bedlinen, towels and children's clothes were sent to the council laundry when Mair worked there.'

Trevor glanced at his watch. 'It's nine o'clock. I'm sorry to have taken up so much of your evening. You'll speak to the people in the Tepee Village and ask if we can visit?'

'I will.' Brian and Alice left their chairs when Trevor and Anna rose to their feet. Brian went to the door. On impulse Anna hugged Alice. It gave Trevor the brief window of time he'd been hoping for. He flipped over the photograph frame that was lying face down on the dresser long enough to see the picture.

'It's good to see that you remained unscarred by Hill House, Anna,' Alice said when Anna released her.

'Not entirely unscarred although I recall very little of my time there. I investigated the latest allegations of abuse at Hill House.'

'The star witness case?' Brian sought confirmation.

'Yes.'

'Those poor people who gave evidence.' Tears started into Alice's eyes again. 'They didn't deserve to be hurt the way they were.'

'No one does.' Brian slipped his arms around Alice's shoulders and led the way to the door. He opened it.

Trevor turned to him. 'One more thing. Those photographs you mentioned, are you sure Mair never told you who she gave them to?'

'Just someone she trusted. She said the less I knew about it, the safer I'd be.' Brian cleared his throat to conceal his emotion. 'Make the bastards who hurt those kids pay for what they did.'

'We'll do our best.' Trevor turned up his collar when he saw the rain lashing down.

'Goodnight, Trevor, Anna. For coppers you're all right.'

'Thank you,' Trevor shook Brian's hand. 'I'll take that as a compliment.'

'It was intended as one.'

Trevor ran quickly to the car. As soon as Anna climbed in he manoeuvred the vehicle out of the farmyard and back up the track.

'That was useful.' Anna huddled down into the passenger seat and pulled her coat close around her.

'What would have been more useful was what they didn't tell us.'

'You have thoughts on what that might be?'

'I'd like to know more about Alice Price's "accident". There should be a police report on the car and a record of the inquest. I'd also like to know just why the police went looking for Mair in Tepee Village the morning after Alice

254

Price's RTA, without a warrant. Someone must have said something to the police that prompted them to look for her. Without an accusation of theft or grounds for some other criminal charge, they were leaving themselves wide open to a charge of harassment and wrongful arrest if they'd taken Mair into custody.'

Anna extrapolated on his train of thought. 'Unless they could prove theft ... Do you think Mair took something from Hill House that could implicate the staff in child abuse and murder?'

He kept his eyes on the road. 'At the very least, information. Don't you?'

CHAPTER TWENTY-TWO

Peter stared at the diagrams Patrick had sketched out on a whiteboard in the incident room. 'Forgive me, highly educated scientist ...'

'You spoke, copper?' Patrick glared at him over the top of his spectacles.

'In simple layman's language can you please tell us poor foot soldiers who are delegated the hard graft, how many complete bodies you've found, how many incomplete and how many orphaned parts ... no pun intended. Can you also give us approximate numbers of adults and children?'

Patrick addressed Peter in the bored tones of a university lecturer faced with a kindergarten group of two-year-olds.

'One complete adult in six pieces. Body parts belonging to thirteen separate children. Sarah has the details and ...'

'I'll produce printouts of the forensic findings including DNA matches and descriptions of the victims. They'll be ready for distribution in the morning,' Sarah interrupted in an attempt to deflect a confrontation between Patrick and Peter.

'Welcome to our chief investigating officer and his deputy,' Peter greeted Trevor and Anna as they walked through the door.

'Sorry we were sidetracked,' Trevor apologised.

'I'd be happy for you to take over.' Patrick offered to vacate his seat in front of the assembled officers.

'No, presumably you're giving an update on forensics, we'll catch up later.'

'As I was about to say,' Patrick proceeded wearily. 'We have body parts from one complete adult and thirteen children. We've finished checking the hall on the ground floor for prints and DNA so you can go in with the dogs first thing tomorrow.'

'Anything recent?' Trevor.

'Latex glove smudges.'

'DNA?'

'If luck's on our side you'll have any match results sometime tomorrow,' Jenny advised.

'Can you give us clues as to where those body parts were hidden?'

'Other than somewhere in the house?' Patrick enquired. 'I suggest you ask the dogs.'

'We intend to, tomorrow.' Trevor glanced at his watch. 'It's late. We've had a long day and I've a feeling we're facing a longer one tomorrow. Is there anything else you've found that we need to know about?' Trevor asked Patrick and Jen.

'I'd say those body parts were dragged into the hall in a hurry. Some were damaged as they were pulled along the floor. There were two sets of footprints …'

'Sizes?' Peter demanded.

'Ten and a half and eight or in European, sizes 45 and 42.'

'So two adults.'

'You expected elves or fairies?' Patrick enquired caustically.

'You discount the possibility that those corpse parts could have been arranged by kids messing about,' Peter countered.

'I'll concede that shoes are no indicator of age given the size of children these days, but this far off the beaten track? I doubt kids would walk or cycle this far.'

'Kids, especially rich kids and hardened and experienced thieves in care, have access to cars and motorbikes,' Peter pointed out.

Bored with Patrick and Peter's sniping, Trevor looked around. 'Anyone else have anything to report.'

'What about you?' Peter asked. 'You and Inspector Wells must have been somewhere.'

Trevor looked to Anna and nodded. She began.

'We tracked down the family of a member of staff who used to work in Hill House as a social worker. She died three weeks ago but her husband and daughter were able to give us an insight into how the place was run.'

'Has anyone interviewed the ogre in connection with this investigation, sir?' Brookes asked.

'Inspector Wells and I did yesterday.' Trevor ran his hands through his hair. Had he really only been working on the investigation for a day? He felt as though he'd left home and Lyn and Marty months ago. 'The ogre talked to us but not about Hill House.'

'He spent most of the interview protesting his innocence,' Anna added.

'I think we could all do with some rest. Thank you for your hard work today, people. Meeting here at 8.00 after breakfast,' Trevor ordered. 'If the sun comes out and the clouds blow away it should be light enough for you to go in with the dogs at 8.30, Barry. If it's not we'll borrow floodlights from the army again. Hever, Brookes, you come in with us.'

'Don't go looking for too much new evidence. We have enough work waiting in the lab to last a month,' Patrick warned.

'Starting with what Brookes and I found, I hope,' Trevor reminded. 'We need to look at them as a matter of urgency.'

'I thought you knew better than to try and hurry forensics,' Patrick warned.

'As long as you know I'm anticipating a nice quiet Christmas at home,' Peter glared at Patrick.

'It will take however long it takes,' Patrick smirked back at Peter. 'Someone needs to watch where you coppers put your hobnailed boots when you go in tomorrow, so I'll spare you an hour in the morning. You going into the cellars first?' Patrick checked with Trevor.

'Seems to make sense and we'll work up. By the way I meant to ask when I came in. Where are the new forensic personnel staying?'

'Two have taken the spare rooms in our Portakabin,' Jenny revealed. 'There's a four-star hotel in town –'

'Which has an excellent restaurant,' Peter was envious. 'We ate there to break the journey here. Don't tell me the jammy so-and-sos have booked in there?'

'They said the inn in Hen Parc was fully booked.'

'It wasn't when they arrived,' Sarah pointed out.

'I warned them to be back on site by eight tomorrow.'

'You slave driver, Patrick,' Peter teased.

'Unlike some, I never ask anyone to do what I don't do myself.' Patrick rose from the desk he'd perched on. 'I'm for bed.'

'Sleep tight,' Peter called after Patrick and Jenny as they left.

Trevor stopped Merchant as she went to the door. 'Do me a favour, Merchant?'

'If I can, sir.'

'First thing tomorrow, look up the accident report on Alice Price.'

'The teacher who worked in Hill House?'

'Yes, she was killed when her car left the road between Hill House and Hen Parc. There should have been an inquest. Track down the record if you can.'

'Yes, sir.' Sarah took a notebook from her pocket and scribbled a memo. 'Anything else, sir?'

'Yes, check for records or press reports on the soldier who found the injured boy on the mountain outside Hill House. The boy subsequently died from his injuries in hospital. That was the incident that set the enquiry into motion on the ogre. I'm looking for the name of the soldier and his present whereabouts as well as anything you can find on the boy. Also investigate the present locations of the male staff of Hill House. Try and track down as many as you can who were on the payroll and are no longer on the radar, caretakers, gardeners, teachers and labourers as well as social workers. See if any were reported missing after working in the orphanage.'

'Mair Davies, sir?'

'As Inspector Wells said, she died three weeks ago.'

'It's her family you and Inspector Wells found, sir?'

'It is. Get a good night's sleep before you tackle that lot, Merchant.'

'You too, sir.' She followed Chris and Barry out through the door.

Hever left his chair. 'I'm going to the canteen, sirs, can I bring back anything for you?'

'No thank you, Hever.' Trevor pulled his chair up to Peter's desk.

'Want to brainstorm?' Anna joined them and sank down on the edge of the desk.

'I haven't a brain left to storm,' Peter rose from his chair. 'I'm off to phone the love of my life. I need a dose of sanity after the day I've had.'

'Today was nothing compared to what's heading your way tomorrow,' Trevor warned. He studied Anna. 'You don't have bags under your eyes so much as suitcases. Have an early night.'

'I will, thank you.'

'Peter has a case of beer and wine in his room. Help yourself if you fancy a drink.'

'I wouldn't mind a beer.'

'Take two.'

'You're sure Peter won't object to me raiding his stores?'

'I won't allow him to. His door will be unlocked.'

Trevor sat staring blindly at the incident board, maps and plans of Hill House after Anna left. His mind cleared as he relished and registered the silence. The only sound was the murmur of Peter's voice through the door as he spoke to Daisy.

Anna unlocked the door of the Portakabin. She stepped into the tiny hall and knocked on Peter's door without knowing why, considering she had just left him and Trevor in the incident room. A case of beer, the cardboard top already torn open, stood next to the door. She took two cans. They were cold and she reflected that there was no need for fridges in Wales in November.

She closed the door of Peter's room and opened the door to her room. Before she had time to switch on the light a figure moved out of the darkness and a hand clamped over her mouth.

Swung from her feet, she heard the door close softly behind her.

Realising he was in danger of falling asleep, Trevor left his chair, walked across the incident room and forced himself to focus on the ground plan of Hill House. He tried to put his thoughts in a semblance of order but whichever way he rearranged the few facts he could be certain of, the more confused he became.

Peter returned, banging the door behind him and shattering the peace. 'Daisy sends her love. She and Miranda spent the day shopping with Lyn and Marty. Apparently they're all exhausted. I only hope my credit card isn't.' He stared at Trevor. 'Fancy a bottle of wine and some crisps?'

'Sounds good.'

'Want to talk through a few ideas.'

'Do you?'

'Why not, it beats lying awake talking to myself. There's never any debate when I try it because I'm infallible. I'll get the wine while you phone your missus.'

'In case you're counting your cans of beer, I told Anna to help herself from your stores.'

Peter shook his head. 'Generous to a fault with other people's possessions.'

'That's me. Creep in quietly, I advised Anna to have an early night.'

Trevor returned after speaking to Lyn to find a bottle of red wine on the desk, six packets of crisps and a plate of cheese sandwiches.

'Where did you get the sandwiches?' Trevor asked.

'Canteen. I know you and your bad habits. Don't try telling me you've eaten since breakfast.'

'There never seems to be time.'

'There is now. So,' Peter filled a couple of plastic

glasses he'd filched from the canteen and pushed one towards Trevor. 'Where are we?'

'You mean with the investigation?'

'No, geographically,' Peter said caustically. 'What the hell did you think I meant?'

'I wasn't sure.'

'So, to start again, who do you think strung those body parts on the gate? Say someone wearing latex gloves and I'll take away the wine I've just poured for you.'

'If Justin Hart and his bodyguard returned here, it could be them.'

'We've been through this and couldn't come up with a single reason as to why they'd return,' Peter reminded him.

'To prove they weren't lying in court and the defendants deserved to be found guilty.'

'I'm with Anna on that one. If Justin had known there were bodies hidden in Hill House he would have produced them to strengthen the prosecution case against the defendants.'

'Brooke and I found some photographs in an office in Hill House today.'

'Hidden or forgotten?'

'In my opinion, pushed out of sight then forgotten. They were in a rather obvious secret drawer in the master's office.'

'You looked at them?'

'Patrick wants to examine them forensically first.'

'He's worse than you when it comes to hanging on to evidence. The rest of us are capable of doing our jobs, you know.'

Trevor thought it diplomatic to change the subject. 'Anna and I spoke to Mair Davies's daughter and partner tonight.' He took a sandwich and bit into it.

'The social worker who asked Dan to meet her when he was here caring for Anna and then failed to turn up?'

Trevor told Peter about the conversation he and Anna had with Brian and Alice and reminded him he'd met Alice.

'Pretty girl.' Peter sounded wistful.

'You're married,' Trevor said.

'That doesn't mean I can't look at what's available. And I don't need reminding how lucky I am.'

'Daisy deserves a medal for taking you on.'

'That's my wife, sensible in all things except one, for which I'm grateful. Do you really think Mair had evidence that implicated the ogre?'

'I think it's possible that either she or Alice knew something or took something from Hill House and the ogre was aware of it. If I'm right, the ogre and or whoever abused those kids with him must have considered it incriminating enough to kill, either to silence them or retrieve whatever it was.'

'That's if Alice Price's "accident" really was murder. You know something, Joseph, I'm not sure I buy that. A car accident isn't a sure way to kill anyone. At best it's hit and miss.'

'The car went off the road and down the hill. The body would be flung about.'

'But not necessarily killed.'

'I agree,' Trevor conceded. 'But would an extra blow to the head, where someone jerking forward would hit the windscreen, be noticed by your average pathologist? They're not all as conscientious as Patrick.'

'Do you think Mair Davies was involved in abusing the kids?' Peter questioned.

'No I don't, but I think she knew more than her partner and daughter said to Anna and me this evening.'

'Did you think that some of the new body parts Patrick found this morning could have been Mair Davies's before you met her family?'

'I did.' Trevor qualified.

'It would have been just too neat, wouldn't it? You of all people should know investigations never work out that way.'

'I was concerned about the lack of DNA for comparison,' Trevor admitted. 'Until we found Mair Davies's daughter we had no DNA to match any DNA Patrick succeeds in extracting. And now we don't need it.

'Let's hope Patrick comes up with some dental work that Merchant can cross check. Although given that the inmates and staff of Hill House came from all over the country, that might prove a dead end too. DNA is useless unless we have living relatives or samples on the national database. Our life would be so much simpler if everyone had their DNA taken and logged at birth.'

'Yes, Stalin – or is it Hitler?' Trevor sipped his wine.

'Those mothers you're putting up in the inn ...'

'What about them?'

'I don't know whether to hope that some of the kids we've found are theirs or not.'

'I think they already know their children are dead. If they were still alive, they would have looked for their mothers before now, if it was only to berate them for putting them in care.'

'Bloody social workers, playing God with people's lives,' Peter was vehement. 'They cause so much damage.'

'I've heard you swear at many people before but never social workers.'

'All I seemed to do when I first started on the force was round up kids in the early hours who should have been safely tucked up in their beds. When we returned them to whatever care home they were supposed to be living in, and quietly and gently suggested that kids ...'

'Gently? Quietly? I didn't know those words were in your vocabulary.'

'They were before patrolling the streets knocked them and tact and diplomacy out of me. To continue with the story you so rudely interrupted: kids should be kept in at night for their own safety. All I had from the bloody people who were supposed to be looking after them was "we don't set boundaries." "It's their right to live the way they choose." Their "right",' Peter repeated scornfully. '"Right" for twelve, thirteen and fourteen-year-olds to stay out all night boozing, taking drugs and thieving and selling themselves to pay for it? "Right" in which universe, that's what I'd like to know. The only thing in favour of Hill House as an institution is its isolation.'

'It's easy enough to reach by road,' Trevor sipped his wine. 'And to get back to what started this conversation, anyone with knowledge of the place, the abuse that went on here and the history of the house could have travelled up here, broken in, collected those body parts and draped them over the sign.'

'That narrows it down to hundreds of ex-inmates plus staff.'

'Merchant mentioned there was a high turnover of staff. Thank you.' Trevor lifted the glass that Peter had just refilled and drank. 'Wine isn't the same out of a plastic glass.'

'Want me to drive into town tomorrow to buy glasses?' Peter asked hopefully.

'Nice try to get out of working, but no.'

'Locals wouldn't know about the bodies unless they'd been told by a member of staff and I can't see many of those shouting about it. My money's on past staff. It's too much to hope that all the bastards who abused those kids are in jail. Some must have slipped through the net.'

'I agree. The only problem with that theory is motive. Why would past members of staff want to advertise the fact that there are corpses in Hill House when the bodies could implicate them in abuse – or even murder.'

'Please don't apply common sense to my brilliant theory, Joseph.'

'I'll try to refrain but make no promises.'

'The biggest problem I foresee is upstairs' motivation to keep the investigation operational. I can almost hear them breathing down our necks in their hurry to close it and exonerate influential VIPs. It's Anna's last case all over again. Look at it from their point of view. The kids are either dead or disappeared – the home closed. Some of the perpetrators have been imprisoned, so what can we hope to accomplish?'

'We can hope to bury the kids, bring the rest of the paedophiles to account and highlight the corruption that led to the cover up and made it possible for the abuse of children to continue here for decades.'

'Hope is the right word,' Peter agreed. 'I don't know why it should be but this case has pained me more than any other, even the child murders I've investigated. Perhaps because I can't see us accomplishing anything worthwhile.'

'Or perhaps because this is the first case you've investigated involving children since you've become a father?'

Peter fell serious. 'When I think of how tiny, vulnerable and helpless Miranda is, even when she's yelling her head off at three in the morning, I can't bear the thought of anyone causing a child pain – not just my

baby but any child. They're so trusting and innocent …'
Peter shivered. 'As for the thought of her ending up
dumped in an institution like that monstrosity and placed
at the mercy of uncaring social workers obsessed with
their own politically correct agenda and self-
importance …' Peter broke off. 'You would take Miranda,
wouldn't you, if anything happened to Daisy and me?
Daisy has no family to speak of except her mother in
Australia and she's getting on. As is my mother …'

'Of course we'd take her. Oddly enough Lyn and I
spoke about this last night, so it must be the influence of
this place. Lyn said then, if anything happened to us, you
and Daisy would end up fighting my brother and mother
and her brother and parents for custody of Marty. But we
should put it on a legal footing.'

'We should.' Peter smiled sheepishly. 'You'll look
after Miranda?'

'If you agree to look after Marty.'

'I'll drink to that.'

Peter was refilling the glasses when there was a bang
on the door followed by a shout.

'Fire!'

CHAPTER TWENTY-THREE

Anna stepped through the door into Justin's room and looked around. It was ninety per cent bed. A neatly made bed. A high shelf held a few folded items of military uniform, books and toiletries. There was a mirror on the wall, a light with a pull switch and blinds that filled a small, high window frame. Two doors, the one they had walked through and one opposite the bed that she presumed led to a bathroom.

'The words you're searching for are "compact and cosy". The rooms may be small but Lucky and I each have our own.' Justin kicked off his shoes, lay back on the bed and held out his arms.

She fell into them and embraced him. 'I thought you were dead ...'

'It was too risky to phone or text you. Not just for me and Lucky. I thought "they" might be monitoring your phone.'

'It wouldn't have made much difference. I was sent here the night after it happened and there's no mobile signal in this part of Wales.' She looked into his eyes. 'Do you or Lucky have any idea who "they" are? I saw ...' she faltered.

'Mac and Shane.' He tensed and the muscles clenched in his jaw. 'So did I.' He rolled on his side, gazed into her eyes and brushed her hair back from her forehead. 'I thought we agreed, when the court case was over you would resign.'

'How could I when my boss requested I help out with this? We're looking for evidence that could overturn the verdict ...'

'You think the powers above will allow you to uncover the secrets of the cesspit that was Hill House? There's no way they can afford to, Anna. Too many wealthy people with influence are involved for the guilty to be ever brought to book or punished. The elite have been getting away with abusing children for decades here. What chance do you think you have?'

'I can't forget the body parts, or what happened here to innocent children at the hands of sick paedophiles, and neither can the other officers working on this case, Justin. They're good police officers ...'

'I don't doubt it,' he said bitterly. 'But do they know what they're up against?'

'Yes, and they're collecting evidence ...'

He silenced her with a kiss, pressing the full length of his body against hers, evoking the responses he'd hoped for from her.

They'd been forced to stay away from one another almost from the moment they'd met after more than twenty years apart, only to fall in love. Anna knew her involvement with a material witness would taint all the police work she'd carried out on the Hill House case if it became common knowledge and it could even bring the entire investigation into question. But her need for Justin was worse than a hunger. It was an all-consuming passion.

'Justin ...'

'Just for tonight can we please forget what brought us

together?' he begged. 'Hill House and all the degradation, pain and misery of the place. I love you, Anna. I want to spend the rest of my life with you.'

She held him close as they tore the clothes from one another, and afterwards there was no need for words, only pressing, urgent action. She had never had a lover as warm and skilled, or one who had craved affection the way Justin did.

Or one she had loved as much.

Trevor was out of his seat first and charged to the door. He wrenched it open. A private was outside, fist raised, ready to knock again.

'Hill House is burning, sir.'

Without giving a thought to the howling wind or teeming rain, Trevor and Peter ran out of the incident room and raced across the road. The gates were open. Smoke and flames billowed out of a ground floor room at the back of the house. Trevor did a quick calculation and realised it was the master's office.

'Damn!' He shivered uncontrollably as the freezing rain trickled through his clothes.

'It looks localised ...'

The rest of Peter's sentence was lost in the wind and shouts that echoed from the front of the building. Trevor quickened his pace. Major Simmonds was on the gravelled terrace directing soldiers who were ferrying fire extinguishers that were being handed over the side wall from the army Portakabins.

Fire had burst through two windows to the left of the door at the front of the house, the room that Trevor recalled had been labelled *Library*.

Simmonds beckoned Trevor and Peter forward but he still had difficulty making himself heard above the clatter of shattering glass as the windows blew outwards from the heat of the fire.

'A guard at the gate saw someone climb over the wall at the front of the house. He went down to get a closer look but found nothing. When he turned back he saw flames in the front windows and raised the alarm. When our men arrived with fire extinguishers they discovered a room at the back was burning as well. They believe they caught the fires within minutes of them being set. The men operating the extinguishers said they smelled petrol.'

'They didn't catch whoever started them?'

'I'm ashamed to say they didn't. So much for their intelligence and the training they were given. None of the sentries saw any strange personnel in the vicinity. The men manning the barrier haven't allowed a car through the road block since you and Inspector Wells returned from the village earlier this evening, Chief Inspector. However, if whoever set the fires came into the grounds of Hill House over the wall, he or she could have returned the same way. In which case there would have been nothing for any of the sentries to see except the shadow they spotted.'

'Sir.' A sergeant saluted Simmonds. 'The fire's under control. But we'll have to wait for the place to cool before we can go inside the house.'

'Thank you, sergeant. Phone the local fire brigade and inform them that the fire I called in is no longer burning, but warn them we'll need their expertise tomorrow to determine the cause of the blaze.'

'Sir.' The sergeant moved off.

Simmonds turned to Trevor. 'I trust your men left nothing important in the house.'

Trevor clenched his fists. 'We'd more or less finished searching the ground floor but there was vital evidence in one of those rooms.'

'You left it unsecured?' Simmonds was astonished.

'We were waiting for forensic to check it for DNA residue and fingerprints.' The flames had died and Trevor approached the library window. Black smoke hung in a thick pall in front of the shattered frame and his feet crunched over charred and broken wood splinters and shards of glass.

'Not too close,' Simmonds warned. 'If you get singed it would mean a full Health and Safety enquiry – and even more paperwork than normal landing on my desk.'

Lost in his own thoughts, Trevor didn't even hear Simmonds. He stared at Peter. 'The photographs. They were our only chance of putting faces to the names of the inmates and staff of this place.'

'Blast Patrick!' Peter cursed. 'You should have ignored his demand that you leave them in situ. He's worse than you when it comes to delegating responsibility. The pair of you need to learn that others are as capable, if not more capable, than you of conducting an investigation.'

Trevor heard footsteps on gravel. He looked up to see Brookes, Merchant and Barry crunching towards him. All were shivering although they'd thrown coats on over their nightclothes. Patrick, Jenny and Dewi Morris trailed behind them. He held up his hand, not trusting himself to speak. He sensed rather than saw Peter shake his head behind him.

'Send someone to fetch me when the Fire Brigade arrive, Major Simmonds.

'Will do, but as the fire is under control I'm not expecting anyone to arrive from the Fire Service before morning.'

Trevor headed up to the main gate. Hever was leaving

the canteen. He stepped down into a puddle on the road.

Trevor ignored him and kept on moving, but he'd noticed that Hever's trousers were wet to the knees. Had he been walking in the wet grass in front of Hill House's garden wall?

Peter's voice cut through the sound of the wind and rain. 'I've another bottle of wine we can open.'

'As if that will solve anything.'

'A hangover will give you an excuse to bite everyone's head off in the morning.'

'It's morning now and I've a feeling I'll be lucky to grab more than a couple of hours before the Fire Brigade turn up.' Trevor halted in front of their Portakabin and felt in his pocket for the key.

'Floundering around for clues is where we'll be,' Peter prophesied glumly. 'Unless forensic pull one or two rabbits out of their laboratory.' He watched Trevor push the key into the lock.

'It's not locked.' Trevor withdrew the key.

'Anna probably left it open for us.'

'Why would she do that?'

'Perhaps she assumed we wouldn't be long. There are sentries across the road in front of the gate.'

'You mean there were sentries in front of the gate until the fire broke out. And despite all the shouting and banging on the door, Anna didn't go down to Hill House to see what the commotion was about.' Trevor stepped into the Portakabin and knocked Anna's door. When there was no reply at his third knock, he opened it.

The room yawned back at him. Anna's handbag lay abandoned on the bed. The duvet had been smoothed over, the pillows plumped up. It obviously hadn't been slept in.

'She could be in the canteen.'

'Go and check.'

Peter left. Trevor stepped into the room and closed the door behind him. He opened the drawers and wardrobe and rifled through Anna's clothes. Nothing had been hidden beneath them. He picked up Anna's handbag, unzipped it and removed her purse. He opened the back. There was a neat array of credit and store cards in a graded pocket. Next to it was a photograph folder with four slots. The first held a picture of an attractive middle-aged woman who bore a strong resemblance to Anna. Dressed in formal clothes, carrying a bouquet of flowers, she stood next to a middle-aged man with a buttonhole in the lapel of his suit. A wedding photograph? Had Anna's mother remarried? Behind that picture, in the same pocket, was a photograph of an elderly couple. Possibly Anna's grandparents. He smiled when he saw a snap of Dan in the third pocket. He looked at the last photograph for a few minutes. It was of a young man he recognised only too well ...

The door burst open behind him. 'Anna's not anywhere on site or in Hill House. Do you want to call the locals and instigate a formal search?' Peter asked.

'The locals are the last people I'd ask for help.'

Peter saw the photograph Trevor was looking at. 'Is that who I think it is?'

Trevor handed it to him. 'See for yourself.'

'What do we do? She left her handbag ...'

'But took her coat. I can't see it anywhere. Can you?'

'No. Do you think she went of her own free will or was taken?'

'I have no idea, although I'm inclined to think she would have kicked up a fuss the sentries would have seen or heard if she'd been kidnapped from this Portakabin before the fire broke out.'

'Yet they allowed an arsonist to walk into Hill House,' Peter observed.

Trevor looked down at Anna's bed. He could have quite cheerfully fallen on it and closed his eyes. He ran his hands through his hair. 'I'm fit for nothing.'

'That makes two of us. What do you want to do?' Peter asked.

'Get whatever sleep I can in what's left of the night before the Fire Brigade arrive.'

'And Anna? Do you think she's been kidnapped or run off?'

'We'll ask ourselves that question again in the morning.'

Trevor felt as though his head had only just touched the pillow when he was jerked from deep, dark, blissful nothingness by a knock on the door of the Portakabin. He picked up his phone. It was twenty minutes before six. He dragged himself upright and opened the door of his room.

A harsh Northern accent grated, 'Fire Chief's here, sir.'

'I'm coming.' All he'd done before falling asleep on his bed in his rain damp clothes was kick off his shoes. He stumbled into the bathroom, splashed cold water on his face and threw on a coat. He found and retrieved his shoes and opened his door. Peter emerged from his room at the same time. Neither spoke nor even acknowledged one another. Trevor knocked Anna's door and opened it. It was empty, exactly as he'd left it the night before.

Peter opened the main door. Rain blasted into the tiny hall on a gust of wind.

Trevor turned up his collar, put his head down and followed Peter out across the road. They walked behind the screens that had been erected over the damaged front door of Hill House and followed the sound of conversation. Major Simmonds and the Fire Officer were in the room at the back of the building that had been labelled MASTER'S OFFICE. They'd switched on the floodlights and were evaluating the damage.

Simmonds, looking more immaculate in his uniform than any officer had a right to at that time in the morning, effected the introductions.

The Fire Chief kicked a pile of burnt papers Trevor had discarded when he'd searched the place with the toe of his boot. They crumbled to grey dust. He sniffed the air theatrically. 'Arson, without a doubt. You can smell the petrol even without the can.'

'You found a can?' Trevor's voice sounded strange, slurring, thick from lack of sleep.

'Remains of one by the door. It was thrown on the blaze. It's so badly buckled and melted I doubt you'll get anything from it.'

Trevor studied the room then went to the door and looked into the library. Thanks to the swift action by the sentry who'd discovered the blaze, the fires had been confined to the two rooms they'd been set in. Papers and furniture had burned, the floors had been covered with ashes, the walls scorched and blackened by soot, but there was no serious structural damage to the building. He returned to the office. Peter was examining the remains of the carvings on the chest of drawers where they'd found the photographs.

'You were lucky the fire was caught so quickly, Chief Inspector,' the Fire Officer observed.

'Apart from the destruction of crucial evidence, I suppose we were,' Trevor conceded.

'I'm surprised anything was left here considering it's been closed for so many years. Given the risk of vandalism and fire, I assumed the council cleared everything before they decommissioned and abandoned the orphanage.'

'You would think so, wouldn't you,' Trevor agreed. 'Do you know anything of the history of this place?'

'Depends on what you mean by "history",' the Fire Officer replied. 'I've heard enough rumours about Hill House to fill half a dozen volumes.'

'No fact?' Trevor persisted.

'Nothing that hasn't been in the papers. I followed the court cases that resulted in the master and staff being gaoled for child abuse and that's about all I can tell you for certain. But,' he gazed at the blackened walls and ceiling. 'I'll make a point of talking to the council now. Isolated building like this, miles from anywhere, is ripe for vandalism. Be a shame to lose a fire officer fighting a blaze for something so worthless. Place needs demolishing.'

'My superintendent has told the council that many times.' Dewi Morris joined them. 'Good morning, Chief Inspector Joseph, Sergeant Collins.'

Peter scowled. 'Cheerful attitudes aren't appreciated by the investigating officers in this team at unearthly times in the morning.'

'My apologies, sir. But you can't criticise a man for trying.'

'I can and I am. Try less,' Peter retorted.

'We'll be working in here for at least another couple of days,' Trevor warned the Fire Officer, 'I'll let you know when we finish, so you can contact the council about demolishing the place.'

'Thank you, I'd appreciate it. As we've determined the cause of the fire, and the building appears to be no less secure or safe than it was before the blaze, I'll leave you to your investigation.'

'Do you want the lights left in place?' Simmonds asked Trevor.

'Please. The forensic teams will be resuming work soon.' Trevor looked at his watch.

'Breakfast in half an hour?' Peter suggested as he led the way back up to their accommodation.

'Just as soon as I've showered and shaved.'

'I wondered if you were going for the tramp look. The overworked Chief Inspector who sleeps in his clothes ...'

'One more gibe out of you ...'

'You're right about Anna.' Peter pointed to their Portakabin. 'She's back.'

Trevor looked ahead. Anna was watching them.

Peter carried a tray from the canteen into the section that had been screened off the incident room to serve as Trevor's private office.

'Coffee, bacon sandwiches, bananas, doughnuts, pork pies and crisps.'

'Doughnuts, pork pies and crisps? For breakfast?' Anna looked at him quizzically.

Peter shrugged as he set down the tray. 'They were on offer. It would have been ill-mannered not to take them.'

Trevor joined them. 'I've warned everyone there'll be a briefing in half an hour. So?' he opened the conversation with Anna, 'You decided to sleep out last night?'

'Justin came to see me.'

'Here?'

'My room.'

'And there's me thinking the military had security around here sewn up tighter than a Welshman's wallet.' Peter handed out the coffees.

'He was in your room?' Trevor continued.

'In my room,' she confirmed.

'Dressed as a copper or soldier?'

'Soldier. How did you know he was wearing a uniform? Did you see him?' She opened her coffee, tore the top from a sachet of sugar and tipped it in.

'I didn't have to. He owns half of the Flashing Blades who supply costumes as well as trained stuntmen. According to their website, "*Any level of skill, any military costume, any era, any century*".' Trevor quoted.

'You're well informed, sir.'

'The internet makes it easier to cover the donkey work,' Trevor acknowledged. 'I take it Justin Hart and his bodyguard are hiding somewhere close by.'

'They are. I warned them I couldn't keep anything from you. But after seeing Shane and Mac murdered ...' She looked at Trevor, 'They don't believe it was an accidental gas explosion.'

'Neither do I, but I'm still waiting for the results of the official report from Dan on that one,' Trevor took one of the coffees and opened it.

'Did they break into Hill House and decorate the sign with body parts?' Peter asked.

'No, neither Justin nor Lucky know anything about that. I asked them,' Anna said.

'I believe you, and them, but I had to check.'

'Do you really believe them or are you just saying that?' Anna looked at Trevor.

'I believe them on two counts,' Peter elaborated, 'first, they would have been hard pressed to get here, find those body parts and rig up the display in the time they had before those photographs were posted, and two, it's what you said. If they'd known about the pieces of corpses they would have told you about them to give you more evidence you could use as ammunition against the accused.'

'Tell me when Justin and his bodyguard are ready to divulge their whereabouts,' Trevor said to Anna.

'They're convinced someone is trying to silence them.'

'Given the fire last night they're probably right, but let them know I don't want to see them killed any more than they – or you – do.'

'Fire?'

'The photographs Brookes and I found yesterday have gone up in smoke.'

'Which is entirely Patrick's fault for not prioritising the DNA and fingerprint testing on them,' Peter sniped.

'Can you get a message to Justin and his bodyguard?'

Anna hesitated but only for a second. 'Yes, sir.'

'Yes?' Trevor demanded irritably at a sharp knock at the door.

Jenny opened it. 'We've something here you'll want to see, Trevor.'

'Like what.'

'Come and look.'

CHAPTER TWENTY-FOUR

Trevor stood transfixed in the doorway of the incident room. Patrick, Jenny and the newcomers to the forensic team had assembled for the meeting, but he wasn't looking at the officers. Spread out over three tables that had been pushed against the walls, was a stack of open files. In them were the photographs that he and Brookes had discovered in the drawer in the master's office.

Jenny braved the silence. 'One of our fellow forensic scientists ...'

A nervous young woman held up her hand. 'Gillian Henderson, sir.' She was clearly wary of Trevor's reaction.

'Gillian is young and keen, sir,' Jenny explained. 'After checking the photographs for DNA and fingerprints, she took them back to her room in our Portakabin last night to pinpoint racial characteristics that might help identify the people.'

'I could kiss you, Gillian Henderson!' Peter gushed.

'Sergeant Collins is not only disreputable but a married man, Gillian,' Jenny warned.

'Jealous that I might distribute my favours?' he challenged.

'Can these photographs be checked with any accuracy against the body parts for identification?' Trevor asked.

'X-rays of the skulls we have examined can be

compared to photographs of the heads. It will take patience and some fiddling to get the scale right,' Patrick warned, 'but we thought that as Gillian had made a start, she could continue. The technique may prove useful where we have no correlating DNA.'

'Would you be prepared to work on this, Ms Henderson?' Trevor asked.

'I'd be delighted, Chief Inspector Joseph.'

'Inform me as soon as you have any results.'

'I will, sir.'

'Thank the Lord for insubordinate forensic officers who don't ask permission to take their work home with them at night.' Peter beamed at Gillian.

'Is this going to turn into one of your "talking shop and Collins being funny" meetings where nothing is decided and all we achieve is the manufacture of a lot of hot air?' Patrick demanded. 'If so, Jen and I will escape now. We have work waiting in the lab. If you're fortunate we may even come up with some of the DNA results you marked urgent yesterday.'

'This is a briefing to inform everyone that Barry and I will be taking the dogs into Hill House in ten minutes,' Trevor replied.

'And you expect me to go in with you?'

'You said you would last night, Patrick,' Trevor reminded. 'As you well know, your company and professional expertise is always welcome.' He tried to sound diplomatic rather than challenging.

'And as I also said last night, if I'm not on hand, your clodhopping subordinates will blunder in with their size twelve boots and destroy any evidence before someone with half a brain has a chance to evaluate it.'

'Can I assume that you'll be coming with us?' Trevor looked enquiringly at Patrick.

'I'll go on ahead and check the fire damage. See you outside the house in ten minutes,' Patrick snapped.

'Thank you.' Trevor continued to address the rest of his team. 'If we need extra brawn, Major Simmonds has offered us his men. Hever, Morris, you'll come in behind Barry, Collins and me.'

'And me, sir?' Anna asked.

'Could I have a word with you in my office please, Inspector Wells.'

Anna faced Trevor across his desk.

'I can't ask Justin to come here, sir,' she protested. 'Not after Shane and Mac were murdered. If he and Lucky hadn't been packing uniforms in the back of the van when that explosion occurred, they'd be dead too. Anyone could be watching this place ...'

'And probably are.' Trevor updated her on the arson attack in the house.

'That proves my point, sir. Please ...'

'Go, visit Justin and Lucky. Tell them –'

'I can't in daylight, sir.'

'Yes, you can,' Trevor contradicted.

'It would draw attention to them.'

'Then give a note to Major Simmonds or one of the soldiers to push under the door of Justin and his bodyguard's Portakabin.'

'Sir ...' She stared at him for a moment before realising she couldn't contradict or lie to a superior officer. Not even for Justin's sake. 'How do you know?'

'I saw Justin walking around the night we arrived. I might not have noticed him if he hadn't pulled his beret halfway over his face. It's taken me until now to realise who he was. You should warn him that less is usually more when it comes to disguises. Talk to them, pick up all the information about Hill House from them that you can.'

'You just want me to go to their Portakabin, sir? That would alert anyone who's watching me or looking for them ...'

'As I said, arrange to have a note pushed under their door. Meet with them on neutral ground, in the pub in Hen Parc, or somewhere in the town. If anyone follows you or them down the mountain road, you'll see them behind you.'

'And if Justin and Lucky do agree to meet me, sir?'

'Ask them to meet me tonight in the small office here or in the incident room so they can take a look at the photographs Gillian saved. If they argue, tell them that no one will give any soldiers a second glance in the village or the town, not even a black one. Going by the accent, half of Simmonds's command appear to be black Londoners. As for the incident room, it's on the way to the canteen and they've obviously walked back and forth to there from their Portakabin easily enough.'

'And afterwards, sir? You expect them to stay here?'

'I'll contact Dan Evans and arrange police protection for Hart and his bodyguard.'

'Mac and Shane ...'

'Weren't under police protection. If I remember correctly from the files you compiled, you offered, they refused.'

'That's right, sir. But ...'

'But?' Trevor repeated when Anna's voice trailed.

'There was an arson attack last night. We're being kept on a tight rein with no outside internet contact. We've signed the Official Secrets Act and confidentiality agreements. Justin and his bodyguard Lucky are just as much a target as Shane and Mac were and ...' she faltered.

'I give you my word I'll do my utmost to protect them. If you want to be relieved from this case I'll give you my blessing and a commendation for the work you've done. No one could have accomplished more or brought in a different verdict on the last case. And no one could have assisted me as much on this one.'

'Has it occurred to you that you might not succeed in discovering the identity of the child abusers or murderers in this case, sir?'

'It's my case, Anna, so I have to try. As we both know, historic abuse cases, especially those involving suspicious deaths, are almost impossible to investigate. But in my experience there's always someone who's seen something significant. All we have to do is find them. That means tracking down everyone who worked in Hill House who is still alive. Not just the social workers but the cleaners, cooks, office workers and teachers. The drivers who took the children to outside venues where they were abused, the doctors and nurses who examined the children before they were admitted to Hill House, the family members, friends and VIPs who visited the children. It's our job to question them as well as gather any remaining physical evidence that points to the perpetrators. You're a trained police officer, you know as well as I do that Hart and his bodyguard may be in unwitting possession of vital information that can help us solve this case.'

'I don't want to be relieved from this case, sir, but neither do I want to put Justin and Lucky at risk.'

'Mulcahy?'

'What about him, sir?'

'Does he know about you and Justin Hart?'

'Sir?'

'You are in love with Hart?'

'Sir, I ...'

289

'When you disappeared last night, I looked in your purse. I saw Justin's photograph.'

'I should have been more careful.'

'You were careful enough when you were investigating the case that went to court, weren't you?'

'I don't think Superintendent Evans or Chief Superintendent Mulcahy suspected any emotional involvement between me and Justin Hart if that's what you're asking, sir.'

'As for being involved with Justin now, you're better placed than the rest of us when it comes to interviewing him and Lucky.'

'You want me to continue working on the case, sir?'

'I'm loathe to lose you and I promise to do all I can to protect your witnesses. You're firearm-trained?'

'Yes, sir.'

'Talk to Merchant, she'll issue you with a gun. Carry it with you at all times. It's as well you know that I've ordered Collins, Hever, Barry and Brookes to arm themselves.'

'You, sir?'

Trevor opened his jacket and showed her his shoulder holster. 'Get a message to Justin and his bodyguard.'

'I'll ask them to meet me in the coaching inn in town, sir.'

'As long as you persuade them to visit me either in our Portakabin or the incident room this evening to look at those photographs, I don't care where you meet them.'

'Yes, sir.'

'Watch your back, Inspector Wells.'

'The same advice to you, sir. Good luck with the search.'

'I'll see you later with Justin Hart and his bodyguard?'

'I'll try to persuade them to come here, sir.'

'Don't try, Anna. Succeed.'

'Yes, sir.' Anna opened the door and left. Before she closed the door, Trevor saw Hever reaching for the telephone in the small hall.

'Need to phone my girlfriend, sir.'

'It's not school, Hever. You don't need to ask permission to make a call.'

Trevor suited up in a disposable overall, hat and rubber gloves. He picked up paper over-boots and a hard hat and left his office for Hill House. The ground was sodden after the rain. Potholes in the broken tarmac were waterlogged and the gateposts of Hill House stood, skyscrapers in miniature lakes. Barry was waiting with the dogs, Peter and Hever outside the barrier that had been cobbled together to cover the shattered remains of the front door. Dewi Morris, who reminded Trevor more than ever of an eager retriever, hopped from one leg to another, joining in the conversation whenever there was a few seconds' silence.

'Patrick? Is it all right to send the dogs in?' Trevor shouted through the rough wooden panel.

'It's clear,' Patrick replied.

'Shouldn't we wait for Inspector Wells, sir?' Morris asked.

'She's working on something else, Morris,' Trevor's eyes narrowed as he turned to Morris. The local officer stepped back behind the others.

Peter and Hever pushed the makeshift board.

'Barry, send the dogs in,' Trevor ordered.

Barry unclipped the leashes. The dogs dived inside the building. Barry and Trevor pulled their over-boots on over their shoes before following. Patrick was standing at the foot of the stairs in front of one of the portable lights they'd borrowed from the military. The forensic team had cleared the area and the floor looked clean, although Trevor would have baulked at picking up anything from it after seeing the adipocere body parts swimming in dubious liquid the day before.

Both dogs dived under the stairs and began barking. Barry rewarded them and sent them down the left-hand corridor, ordering them into every room in turn, including the two the fires had been set in. There was no further reaction or bark from either of them. After an hour of sniffing and searching, Barry sent them back into the hall. Patrick opened the double doors that led into the opposite corridor. Trevor walked down the corridor Patrick had prevented him from entering the day before.

The first door on the right was labelled STAFF ROOM. While he stood studying it from the doorway, the dogs went in and sniffed around half a dozen abandoned easy chairs with splintering frames and mouldering foam cushions. The room opposite, labelled KITCHEN, was vast, the floor and walls clad in the same Victorian tiles as the hall. There were two enormous, rusting ranges, two massive Belfast sinks and an array of damp, splintering pine cupboards and sideboards that looked as though they were fit only for firewood.

A bank of full sized doors on a side wall opened into walk-in cupboards. Two were shelved and held rusting flour, rice and sugar bins. One held household cleaners and aids, firelighters, wire wool scourers, tins of black lead, brick dust and scouring powder.

He left the kitchen and moved on down the corridor, opening doors marked BROOM CUPBOARD, LINEN CUPBOARD, BLANKETS AND BEDDING. He left the doors wide for the dogs and moved on. An empty room, marked HOUSEKEEPER'S ROOM, was devoid of furniture but offered what would have been a pleasant view out over the grounds and down to the valley if the window had been clean.

He returned to the corridor and tried to imagine Hill House full of inmates. As the corridor he was in had been given over to kitchens, housekeeping and staff rooms, he doubted that the children had been allowed in that part of the house. He opened the few remaining doors in the corridor, walked to the end door on the left and tried to wrench it open. There was a keyhole and at first he wondered if it was locked. But it had swollen shut with damp and after half a dozen tugs it finally scraped open on the wooden floor.

He peered into the gloom and saw a flight of stone steps disappearing down into the darkness. According to the plans there was only one access to the cellar and this was it. He shouted down the corridor.

'Hever, find Major Simmonds and ask him if we can borrow some smaller portable lights. Bring them here as fast as you can.'

'Yes, sir.'

Trevor stood at the end of the corridor and watched the dogs go from room to room, sniffing and searching but never barking. Barry followed with Patrick. The dogs had finished in the kitchen when Hever and Morris returned with the lights.

Patrick joined Trevor and looked down the steps. 'I advise you to send the dogs in first and hang back if you're expecting to find the place where the bodies were stored.'

'Won't you need us to go ahead with the lights, sir?' Hever asked.

'Yes, but stay at the foot of the steps,' Trevor ordered.

293

'The only alerts so far, sir, have been under the stairs,' Barry reported.

'Let's hope we get more luck here. Morris and Hever are at the foot of the steps, Barry.'

Barry called the dogs and sent them down the steps. Trevor and Patrick waited until the dogs had reached the bottom before climbing down after them.

The lights Simmonds had loaned them emitted an eye-searing white glare. But beyond the range of the circle, the shadows were so black they appeared tangible. The stone steps were steep and freezing cold, even through layers of shoe leather.

Trevor found himself at the end of a long corridor that disappeared into darkness. It was similar to the one on the ground floor except it was longer and the ceiling considerably lower – barely a scant inch above Peter's head in the alcoves at the sides of the passageway.

Barry ordered the dogs forward and Hever and Morris followed with the lights. There were doors in the corridor but they were the exception rather than the rule. Most of the cellar was sectioned into open arches, several still blackened by dust from the coal they'd once held.

The cellar ended in an enormous hall the size of a ballroom. The centre was dominated by a huge square tank approximately four feet deep. It was surrounded by smaller self-contained sinks and wringers. It had evidently been used as a laundry, but the bath and sinks were cracked and when Trevor recalled what Mair had revealed to Brian about the cellar, he doubted it had been used in decades.

He shivered but not from cold.

Clovis bounded forward closely followed by Clothilde. Both dogs leapt into the tank and started barking.

Barry called them back and sent them around the area.

They paused at the sinks and sniffed the corners of the room as well as the joins where concrete floors met tiled walls. But neither alerted again until Barry ordered them back to the tank. Then they barked so loudly the sound reverberated from the walls. The dense shadows, interspersed with blinding lights and the sound of the dogs combined, lent the atmosphere an ominous, sinister air.

For the first time Trevor found himself wishing he was the most junior officer present. If he had been, he would have risked the ridicule of his colleagues by running back up the steps towards daylight and fresh, untainted air.

CHAPTER TWENTY-FIVE

Trevor noticed the enamel in the tank was cracked and had worn down to the underlying cast iron in places on the rim. The scars stood proud, crusted by rust.

'Could the segments of corpse we found in the hall and the ones displayed on the gate have been kept in this?' he asked.

Clive answered. 'There's nothing here to prove that any of the body parts in the hall or on the gate were in this tank, sir. There's no residue, deposits or dried up fluid in the bottom. All I can tell you is what you saw for yourself, sir. The dogs reacted to the tank, which suggests it once held a body or bodies. No one knows how dogs scent cadavers, only that they can be trained to do so. Drugs, blood, cadaver – teach a dog to pick up one of those scents and they will. The dogs have signalled here, but there's no saying how long ago the body or bodies, if there was more than one, were here.'

'Could the corpse of an animal, a dog or a pig for example, have been stored in the tank?' Trevor questioned.

'Clovis and Clothilde have been trained to detect human cadavers, sir, with human corpses. To my knowledge neither have ever reacted to animal corpse scent.'

Patrick elaborated. 'These dogs are trained in corpse detection using human bodies in various stages of decomposition from fresh down to skeletal. We know corpse scent is complex. After death occurs and decomposition begins, a human body will release 478 different chemicals –'

'478?' Peter whistled.

'Possibly more in your case, Collins, I dread to think what gases you have floating around your body – not to mention your brain … if you have one.'

'Thank you, Patrick. You know how to make a colleague feel special.'

Patrick continued as though Peter hadn't interrupted. 'We have no idea which scents are picked up by Human Remains Detection dogs – to the layman HRD or cadaver dogs – but what we do know is that the chemical they react to is first emitted approximately three hours after death. It is present in hours-old human remains down to ancient, including those reduced to skeletons. Whatever the dogs scent – some scientists argue it's cadaverine, others it's a different chemical – it's unique to the human body, which is why a well-trained HRD dog never confuses it with animal corpses. It's also present in several types of tissue including blood, bone and fat. HRD dogs have identified corpse scent in blood spatter, bone and cremated remains. They've even picked up the scent left in the soil after a body has been removed from a grave.'

'What about a living body?' Trevor asked.

'Trained HRD dogs simply don't react to live humans. But, as I said, a good reliable HRD dog is the product of intensive training with human cadavers.'

'Some countries even use HRD dogs to find bodies submerged in water, sir,' Barry volunteered. 'Their trainers say the dogs find the corpses not just by scent but by tasting the water. I can't confirm that, but I've read up on it. There are several well-documented cases where HRD dogs have reacted within one or two feet of bodies floating beneath the surface when they've been taken out in a boat. They've also alerted to bodies floating close to lake or river banks.'

'I believe I read the same paper, Barry,' Patrick corroborated. 'Using dogs to detect a submerged body isn't widespread yet, but given their success on land, it warrants further investigation.'

'Wasn't there a case in America recently where someone was convicted of murder without a body?' Hever ventured.

'You don't have to go as far as America,' Peter answered. 'A case was tried in Scotland in March 2012. David Gilroy was accused of murdering his on/off lover Suzanne Pilley. Cadaver dogs from South Yorkshire Police alerted to three areas: the basement of the offices Gilroy worked in and inside his car as well as the boot. Forensic scientists searched for DNA in Ms Pilley's workplace and Gilroy's car. They were unable to find Ms Pilley's DNA anywhere in the building or the car. But they testified that when they opened the boot of Gilroy's car, they noticed a fresh smell that could have been a "cleaning agent". The defence argued that the case against Gilroy was based on circumstantial evidence. The jury disagreed. They found Gilroy guilty by majority verdict. He appealed against his conviction but it was thrown out.'

'What a fund of knowledge you are, Collins.' Patrick commented.

'I try to keep up.' Collins flashed Patrick an insincere smile.

'To return to this tank, you don't think the bodies we found were ever in it?' Trevor looked from Barry to Patrick.

'Barry's right, all that can be said with any certainty is that a human corpse or corpses were in there at some time.' Patrick reached out and switched on a tap above the tank. Nothing came out. 'I take it like the electricity the water has been switched off.'

'Years ago, or so we were informed,' Trevor said.

'Then we have to take the dogs' bark for it.' Peter sat on the edge of the tank. 'A corpse singular or plural was in here at some time, but the scientists among us wouldn't like to hazard a guess as to when.'

'But not the adipocere corpse parts?' Trevor questioned.

'I agree with Barry,' Patrick said. 'The body parts were damp to the touch when we examined them and had obviously been kept in liquid. There's no liquid in this tank and, as you see, no water residue or dried stains that would have indicated the past presence of fluid.'

'So if they were kept in this building …'

'They were most probably stored elsewhere, sir.' Barry suggested.

'Please, continue searching, dogs and gentlemen. I'm returning to the incident room. I've no doubt the telephone is ringing off the hook after the fire last night. Collins, with me.'

'Do you need me, sir?' Dewi asked brightly.

'No, Morris,' I think Sergeant Collins and I can manage without you. Stay with Barry and Hever. The minute you find anything, Hever …'

'I'll notify you, sir.'

'I'll remain with Barry and the dogs until they've covered every floor, Trevor. The new forensic personnel should have finished checking the upper stories by now.' Patrick adjusted the light so he could take a closer look at the tank.

'Much appreciated, Patrick.' Trevor left the building with Peter. They shuddered as the freezing mountain air hit their lungs.

'That was a sharp wake up. I didn't think Hill House was warm until we came out here. Want coffee?' Peter asked.

'Please, but in the incident room.'

'I'll bring them in.'

Trevor stripped off his paper overalls by the door of the Portakabin and dumped them in the bin Sarah had set there for the purpose. She'd forsaken her desk for the tables and she and Gillian were sifting through the photographs Gillian had brought in. 'Like a coffee, sir?' she asked when he walked in.

'Peter's getting them. If he doesn't bring any for you two, we'll send him back out. You trying to put those photographs in order?'

'Trying to date them, sir, so they'll be easier to catalogue,' Gillian explained. 'Drs O'Kelly and Adams haven't as yet had the results of the carbon dating on the shirt that was wrapped round one of the torsos but we thought we'd start with the newest photographs – based on dress – and work backwards.'

'We're also separating them into three categories, children, staff and visitors, sir,' Sarah added.

'Give me the photographs of visitors please, Merchant. I'll start with them. Any calls?'

'About seventeen, sir, I've put the list on your desk. Chief Superintendent Mulcahy and Superintendent Evans both asked that you return their calls when you come in.'

'Thank you.'

Peter entered with a tray of half a dozen coffees, a box of mixed doughnuts and a paper bag of shortbread biscuits.

'Father Christmas has arrived,' Sarah smiled. 'And please strip that sterile suit off outside, and close the door, you're allowing a gale to blow in here.'

'One minute I'm Father Christmas, the next it's "get outside",' Peter grumbled, but he left and shut the door behind him.

Trevor took a coffee and the daunting pile of visitor and VIP photographs.

'Shall I put calls through, sir, or give you five minutes to drink your coffee?' Merchant asked.

The phone started ringing. 'Put them through please, Merchant, just give me a second to sit down.'

Sarah checked the number on the display. 'It's Superintendent Evans, sir.'

Trevor went into his office, closed the door and picked up the receiver. 'Trevor Joseph.'

'Found any more bodies.'

'No, sir.'

The line had an ominously hollow ring and Trevor was acutely aware of the warning Dan had given him. He had a vision of operatives crouched over telephone receivers listening in on their conversation and reporting – reporting – where? The Home Office? Some police department the authorities believed was secret yet everyone knew about like Special Branch or Counter Terrorism Command. But this case couldn't be classed as terrorism – unless … VIPs, paedophilia … Had that revolting mix resulted in blackmail that threatened state security?'

Dan's voice echoed down the line. 'Have you finished searching Hill House?'

'No, sir, Patrick is in there with Barry and the dogs now.'

'Are you expecting to find more bodies?'

'I have no idea, sir.'

'The photographs you found yesterday …'

'There was a fire, sir.'

'In the lab, your accommodation or Hill House?'

'Hill House, sir. It was set in the two ground floor offices. The military spotted it and dealt with it. The local Fire Service confirmed it as arson.' Trevor visualised Dan digesting the news as he sat behind his desk.

'The photographs?'

Trevor picked up on the echo on the line again and thought of the arsonist. He doubted whoever had set that fire was listening in, but even so he decided to be cautious. 'Destroyed, sir.'

'Do you need more manpower?'

'No thank you, sir. Major Simmonds is generously loaning us his men whenever we need extra muscle. Patrick has more assistants than he knows what to do with. His laboratory is too small to house more than him and Dr Adams so the second team are working in Hill House.'

'Have you told Chief Superintendent Mulcahy about the fire?'

'Not yet, sir. I've only just returned to the office from a search of the orphanage basement. The dogs alerted to a tank but Patrick O'Kelly and Barry said that although it was probably used to store a corpse or corpses it wasn't used to house the body parts that had been hung on the gate or the ones we found in the hall.'

'So basically you haven't made much progress.'

Trevor thought of Anna and Justin, Martha, Rose, Judy, Mair and the people he hadn't yet tracked down.

'No, sir, but we're beginning to piece together a few things.' He threw out a red herring for whoever was listening in. 'Have you tracked down Justin Hart or his bodyguard, the mysterious Lucky?'

'No. Their details have been circulated and the entire force is on the lookout for them. I'll inform you as soon as we find them. Just out of interest,' Dan continued casually – too casually – 'has Patrick managed to identify any of the victims or at least give us an approximate date or cause of death?'

'Not as yet, sir, although he is working on it. Neither he nor Jenny are hopeful.'

'Have they managed to extract any DNA from the adipocere of the bodies that were hung on the gate?'

'They're trying now, sir.'

'Any problems with the locals or the press?'

'No, sir, the army has set up road blocks, so we're pretty much working in isolation.'

'Get anything out of the ogre?'

'Beyond protestations of innocence, no, sir.'

'I suppose that was to be expected. Keep me updated.'

'I will, sir.' Trevor replaced the receiver.

Peter knocked the door and carried in his coffee and a packet of shortbread. 'Merchant said you might need help with the VIP photographs.'

'Merchant is right. Pull up a chair.' Trevor took the top file and handed Peter the one below it.

'Someone liked taking photographs.'

'Evidently.'

'You told Dan about the fire.'

'I did.'

'Did you tell him the photographs had survived?'

'No.'

'You mentioned them to him yesterday?'

'I did.'

'Who else did you tell?'

'I've been thinking about that.' Trevor sat back in his chair and flicked the top from his coffee carton. 'I told Bill Mulcahy about them when he phoned. Then there's the entire team. I mentioned them during the briefing. Brookes was with me when I found them.'

'You can cross Brookes off the list, aside from being straight as a die, he's too busy thinking about Merchant and their imminent offspring to even notice that he's in Wales. As for the team, you mentioned the find but I don't recall you saying exactly what you had found.'

'You're right,' Trevor agreed. 'Then there's the new forensic personnel, we know nothing whatsoever about them.'

'Aside from the fact that Patrick knows them and trusts them, and one of them did return the photographs this morning.'

'It's possible the rest of the team didn't see Gillian walking off with them when they finished for the day in Hill House. Then, another member of the team could have set that fire in the office last night, assuming that the photographs were still in there.'

'Come on, Trevor, did you see the size of the packet Gillian dumped on the table out there this morning. How do you think she smuggled those past the other members of the team when they left the orphanage?'

'Point taken.'

'If you want my opinion …'

'If I didn't I wouldn't have invited you in here.'

'I'd look no further than that little smarmy git, Dewi Morris. No copper – straight copper – new to the force is that keen and eager to please. Anyone with any sense stands back and watches which way the sheep graze

305

before bouncing like a jack-in-box with their hand up saying "Do you need me, sir?"'

'I love your mixed metaphors.'

'I made my point, didn't I?'

'But did Dewi know about the photographs?' Trevor mused.

'Look at it this way, someone obviously had access to the place and went creeping around playing with body parts in the middle of the night before we arrived here. And in my opinion that same someone went creeping round setting fire to the offices so those photographs would be destroyed before we had a chance to check them.'

'That's interesting.'

'What?' Peter demolished a finger of shortbread in two bites.

'You said setting fire to the offices.'

'So?'

'It's possible he, she or they didn't know which office the photographs were in so they set fire to both of them to be sure of destroying them.'

'There's a flaw in my argument.'

'What?' Trevor and Peter often brainstormed in a grasshopper way, flipping from one thread of thought to another and he wasn't in the least surprised that Peter had returned to his original idea.

'Why would someone want to draw attention to the bodies that presumably were hidden somewhere around Hill House one night and seek to destroy evidence that might point to those involved with the deaths another night? We're probably dealing with two separate "someones".'

Trevor looked at Peter. 'Or just one who's having trouble living with what happened to the victims and feels

306

a sense of guilt …'

'But neither do they want to be implicated in the abuse,' Peter finished for him.

The phone rang.

Peter opened the file Trevor had given him. Trevor answered the phone. When he heard the unmistakeable voice of Bill Mulcahy he put the phone on speaker and mouthed to Peter to stay.

'Yes, Chief Superintendent, I know the case is progressing more slowly than we'd hoped for, sir, but we've been hampered by our inability to access the house. Dr O'Kelly wanted to check the place for DNA and fingerprints before the dogs went in, to minimise the risk of cross contamination.'

'Are you in now?' Mulcahy snapped.

'Yes, sir. We went in this morning. Dr O'Kelly and Barry are searching the house with the dogs now, sir.'

'You've been there more than …'

'We're working as quickly as we can, sir.'

'It's not quick enough for me, or the local council. Especially after the fire. They want that place demolished.'

'You heard about that, sir.'

'Five minutes after it was under control.'

'There was no structural damage to the house, sir,' Trevor reassured.

'So I've heard. Do you need any extra equipment to expedite this investigation?'

'Yes, sir, a helicopter with heat-seeking cameras to pinpoint any areas worth digging in around the grounds and vicinity of Hill House. Also a sweep of the area around the house with LiDAR – light detection laser equipment would locate any disturbances in the soil.'

'Do you know what that would cost in relation to the

total policing budget, Joseph?'

'Yes, sir, but if you don't ask, you don't get.'

'I'll see what I can do, but I won't be able to keep the council at bay for long.'

'We've only been here two days, sir …'

'You're on borrowed time, Joseph.'

'Do you want me to investigate or whitewash, sir.'

'I'll give you as much time as I can.'

'Well done, you,' Peter said when Mulcahy ended the call and Trevor returned the receiver to the cradle.

'The equipment isn't here yet.' Trevor returned to the files he'd set out on his desk.

'Anything?' Peter asked when Trevor set a few photographs aside.

'Celebrities now sojourning at Her Majesty's pleasure for child abuse.' Trevor did a rapid calculation in his head. 'Justin Hart and his friends would have arrived at Hill House just over twenty-five years ago?'

'Give or take a year or two. What of it?' Peter watched Trevor flick through the files and pull out the ones for the relevant year. He opened it and scanned the topmost photographs before setting them aside. Then he reached for a magnifying glass.'

'Something?' Peter asked.

'You tell me.' Trevor handed him the picture and the glass.

CHAPTER TWENTY-SIX

Anna sat in the window seat of the coaching inn in town and watched two bikers walk through the archway that led from the car park. Their helmets hid their faces; their biker leathers and jackets their figures. Neither attracted a second glance from the people they passed. She recognised them from their walk, Justin's was unmistakable, confident without being arrogant, or was it that he had become such a part of her she didn't need to actually see his face to sense his presence when he was close.

'Any trouble getting away?' she asked Justin when he walked into the bar and joined her.

'No. Because we have no real orders, only pretend ones, we come and go as we please. Simmonds has hinted to the men that we're some kind of high brass on a monitoring mission so they give us a wide berth, and as you see, all you have to do is arrange to have a note pushed through our Portakabin door ...'

'And we report for duty.' Lucky removed his helmet and set it on the table.

'I expected to see you in military uniform.'

'Too noticeable in town.' Justin set his helmet next to Lucky's and sat beside her. 'But it's great camouflage in camp. In fact everyone pays so little attention to us I'm beginning to feel invisible.'

'That's life for most of us, mate,' Lucky commented drily.

'That wasn't a complaint. After four years of people shouting "Mac McLochrie Time Traveller" at me every time I step out in public, I like being invisible.' Justin closed his hand over Anna's.

'What rank have you given yourselves?' Anna was curious.

'I can just about squeeze into Simmonds's spare uniform shirt, so I'm the same rank as him, major. But it's also common sense. I was in the real army. Justin's training begins and ends with the Flashing Blades. He's all show and theatrical bluster. But he does look good when he poses with a gun, even in a lance corporal's uniform.' Lucky glanced at Anna's cup. 'More coffee or something stronger?'

'Coffee is fine, thank you.'

Lucky headed for the bar.

'So, Lucky and I are here.' Justin looked inquisitively at Anna.

'Thank you for coming.'

'It's always good to see you, but I wished you'd stayed in bed longer this morning. I wanted to wake beside you.' He reached for her hand. 'I suppose it's too much to hope that you sent the note because you couldn't live another hour without seeing me.'

'Trevor Joseph wants to talk to you.'

'The Chief Inspector himself.' Lucky returned. 'I've ordered, they're bringing it over. Tell me, how did Trevor Joseph know you could get in touch with us?' He gave Justin a hard look.

'He saw one of you walking around.'

'That would be Justin looking for you, Anna. I warned

you to stay in our Portakabin, Justin.'

Sensing an argument brewing, Anna moved the conversation on. 'Trevor found some photographs in Hill House,' Anna revealed.

'Of what?' Lucky asked.

'Group photographs of children with staff, visitors and VIPs, the sort of pictures institutions display on their walls and in glass cases in their foyers. He's hoping you will look at them to see if you recognise anyone.'

'And if Justin does?' Lucky challenged. 'Justin, Mac and Shane bared their souls at that trial, Anna. They revisited nightmares that would have best been left buried. Don't you think you've asked Justin to do enough?'

'Children were abused and murdered in Hill House.' Anna protested.

'Something Justin and I are all too aware of.' Lucky was terse.

'Someone has to be held to account and punished for those crimes. Trevor Joseph only wants the truth ...'

'Truth? – now that's a big word. Thank you.' Lucky took the tray of coffee from the waitress. 'We'll serve ourselves,' he snapped when she hovered.

'Yes, sir.' Sensitive to the atmosphere, the waitress retreated.

'Don't you want to help us?' Anna challenged.

'I think Justin has already helped you by doing more than any one man can reasonably be expected to do, Anna. He risked his life because you asked him to and so did Mac and Shane. They did what you wanted and they paid the price for trusting you –'

'That's unfair, Lucky,' Justin broke in. 'Anna offered us police protection. We refused.'

'Do you think it would have made the slightest difference if we had taken her up on the offer?' Lucky

311

retorted. 'All it would have meant is a few more dead bodies in the front yard of your house – the police protection officers detailed to look after us along with our own.'

'I won't let you blame Anna for what happened to Shane and Mac, Lucky. We all knew what happened to boys who talked in Hill House.'

'And the damned paedophiles are still abusing and killing kids a quarter of a century later.' Lucky glared at Anna.

'We need help to run a successful investigation, Lucky. Witnesses, evidence ...'

'That's just it, isn't it, Anna? No cold evidence a quarter of a century old can stand up in court, especially when the only witnesses to the crime are subjected to the kind of cross examination Justin, Mac and Shane were exposed to. I sat in that courtroom and wondered just who in hell was being tried. Justin, Mac and Shane or the defendants.'

'Yesterday, Trevor and I talked to four women who've been looking for their children ever since they were taken into Hill House. All four disappeared from there. One of the women hasn't seen her daughter for over thirty years. She was twelve when she vanished and another –'

'I'm sorry for them,' Lucky broke in sounding anything but sympathetic.

'So am I, Lucky. All Trevor is asking of you is a few hours of your time and your memories of Hill House along with anything else you can recall about the people who lived and worked there.'

'You told Trevor Joseph I was in Hill House?' Lucky glowered at Anna.

Anna had never felt so threatened or intimidated. 'Of course not. Not after your warnings ...'

'You know there are people looking for me?'

'Yes. And I would never do anything to put you at risk.'

'Like you didn't put Shane and Mac at risk.'

'Lucky!' It was Justin's turn to lose his temper.

'I was only in the place a short –'

'I know, Lucky, but it might have been long enough to recollect someone or something important. Please, abuse victims deserve closure.' Anna's pronouncement was more of an impassioned plea than a rational statement.

'There'll only be closure for me, and the other victims of Hill House, when the last one of us dies. And that won't help the children who are being abused now in institutions up and down the country as well as their family homes. I can't bear the thought of other kids going through what we went through ...'

Anna squeezed Justin's hand. 'I let you down. I should have done more.'

'You didn't let anyone down, Anna. The system did. Face it! The people who abused us are untouchable. Wealthy, all powerful, they buy, bribe and bully their way into getting whatever they want. An endless supply of children they can abuse. Entry into depraved secret societies so they can carry out their crimes in like company and enough influence to ensure that they and their friends get away with whatever they want to do without prosecution or even censure.'

'What happened to you occurred decades ago, Justin. The people who abused you are old, less powerful. Some of the staff have been punished ...'

'The only ones who've been imprisoned are the expendable ones,' Justin was bitter, 'those employed to run the homes and some of the older entertainers in the twilight of their careers who were falling out of favour.

Those who wield the real power know there's a glut of ambitious show business wannabes, ready and waiting to play court jester to the rich. No one who has real power has been punished. They remain outside of and impervious to the law, left alone to initiate a whole new generation of members into their sick clubs.'

'And so organised paedophilia goes on and will always go on while kids in care are regarded as worthless scum. Rubbish to be used, abused and tossed aside in favour of new orphanage fodder when they pall.' Lucky filled three coffee cups and handed Anna and Justin theirs.

'Trevor Joseph and his team are trying to make a difference ...'

Lucky interrupted Anna. 'Supposing Justin and I visit your incident room tonight and take a look at the photographs that Trevor Joseph has unearthed. I admit, even in the short time I was in Hill House I have vague memories of all of us children being called together in the yard to have our photograph taken with VIP visitors. Supposing Justin remembers the people who abused him and picks them out, what then? Another court case where the defence will roll out evidence of Justin's criminal and drug-taking past? I guarantee the trial will turn out to be nothing more than a charade designed to illustrate that the justice system in the UK works, which of course it doesn't. The verdict will be a foregone conclusion before the barristers make their opening remarks. The accused will be acquitted because of lack of evidence and Justin's career will be in tatters, that is, if it isn't already.'

'There's a DA-notice ...'

'You really think a DA-notice on Justin's evidence at that trial will protect him from the press vultures for ever, Anna?' Lucky challenged.

'We've been through that, Lucky. It was a risk I was

prepared to take on the grounds that I was more sinned against than sinner. I don't want to discuss it any more.' Justin was adamant.

'You'd rather spend the rest of your life waiting for another explosion every time you open the front door of one of your houses?' Lucky stared at Anna. 'Are you really prepared to take an even greater risk with Justin's life than the one that already exists?'

'It's different this time,' Anna said quietly. 'We have body parts …'

'Lucky and I have talked about that, Anna. Both of us, and Shane and Mac, saw children being taken away by adults and some of those children were never seen again. But not one of us witnessed the death – or murder – of a child.'

Lucky saw Anna watching him and turned to the window. 'I just can't see what you and your Chief Inspector hope to accomplish with this investigation.'

'You think we should ignore those corpses?'

'Of course not. But surely you realise that far too much time has elapsed for you to bring anyone to book for the murder of those kids.'

'Not one member of the team will accept that as an excuse to skimp on the investigation.' Anna recited the standard mantra. 'The point of any police enquiry is to punish the guilty and bring justice and closure to the victims.'

'No punishment of the guilty can possibly masquerade as justice or bring closure to the victims of Hill House,' Lucky said softly. 'The survivors that is. Have you any idea how many of the children who were abused killed themselves as a result of what was done to them? Those who chose suicide took the quick way out. It was a slower and far more painful death for those who self-destructed through drugs or alcohol.'

'I didn't know until I started working on Justin, Mac and Shane's case that no records were or are kept of the children who vanish in care,' Anna admitted. 'It's a disgrace that's been used, and is still being used, to cover a multitude of crimes, including murder.'

'Fred and Rose West certainly used it to advantage,' Justin agreed. 'The young women they killed simply fell through the cracks social services opened and never plugged or monitored.'

'Please, both of you, Trevor and I are desperate for help. Won't you at least look at the photographs.' Anna locked her fingers into Justin's.

'If we do, and if – and this is the biggest "if" – your investigation comes up with concrete evidence, what then? You take the new evidence to the Crown Prosecution Service so they can instigate another trial, where Justin can risk his life all over again by testifying?'

'All I'm asking you – both of you – to do is please visit the incident room and look at the photographs. By then we might even have some fresh forensic evidence.'

'And can you guarantee that the fresh evidence won't be destroyed before the case gets to court?' Justin questioned. 'You said yourself that your superiors are keeping a tight rein both on the investigation and any evidence you find. There could be more than one reason for that.'

'You think my superiors would destroy evidence?'

Lucky gave a deprecating smile. 'If they'd been got at and it suited them, I think they would. But then Justin and I have a poor opinion of most people in authority. All we want ...' he looked at Justin. 'Is to be allowed to get on with our lives. Which, for me, means continuing to work with the Flashing Blades and Justin on his films.'

Justin laughed. 'Not that an actor in hiding has much of a career to crow about.'

Anna made one final plea. 'I promise I won't ask any more of you than you take a look at the photographs.'

'Yes, you will, when we get there.' Lucky left his seat. 'If it'll shut you up, Anna, I'll go but I make no promises.' He picked up the coffee cups from the table and stacked them back on to the tray, then looked at Justin. 'You can make your own mind up as to what you want to do, mate.'

Trevor and Peter were still poring over the VIP photographs when Jenny knocked the door.

Trevor shouted. 'Come in.' He looked up, 'you've something for us?'

'The results of the DNA tests.'

Peter rose and offered Jenny his chair. 'Judging by the look on your face they're not good.'

'Depends on your point of view.' She handed Trevor a sheaf of papers.

'Are any of the children related to the women?'

'We've positively identified Angela Smith's son, Tyrone, and Lynda Lewis's son, Ian. I've left one of the trained pathologists, Neil Cummins, trying to assemble the bodies but whichever way he goes about it, neither will be a pretty sight.'

'Maggie Perkins's daughter?' Trevor asked.

'No female body parts were among the ones we've recovered.'

'Then she could still be alive?' Peter said.

'Have you forgotten that Patrick is searching in Hill House now with Barry and the dogs?'

'Momentarily,' Peter admitted.

'There's something else.' Jenny pointed to the papers

that detailed the results. 'The complete adult corpse.'

Trevor looked at her.

'We recovered his DNA. It was on file. His name was Ben Weston. He was a convicted paedophile.'

'He was a visitor here?'

'Would you believe – the caretaker?'

'I would,' Peter said sourly.

'I spoke to Sarah when I came in. She's pulling his record now. Unlike the other victims we have a clear cause of death. A knife wound to the heart made by a serrated blade at least five inches long. There were several smaller knife wounds made by a much shorter blade around two and half inches, suggesting that he was assaulted by more than one person.'

'Or one person wielding a steak knife in one hand and a penknife in the other,' Peter suggested.

Trevor picked up the papers Jenny handed him and stared blindly at them.

'Is there a problem, sir?' she asked.

'With these, no, excellent work, thank you. I was just thinking that someone has to drive down to Hen Parc and see those women in the inn.'

'I'll go.'

'You can come with me, Collins. I'd appreciate the company.'

'Could you wait a while, sir. Just in case we find more bodies …'

Brookes knocked the open door. His face was flushed from exertion. 'We've found more body parts, sir. A lot more.'

CHAPTER TWENTY-SEVEN

Trevor and Peter followed Brookes up the staircase from the ground to the first floor. It swept in a grand semicircle and, despite the damp and the grime, still held a hint of Victorian style along with a few half-buried gleams of mahogany beneath the filth that covered the banister and treads. They walked along the length of the galleried landing to the second staircase, which was narrower and more utilitarian. The one that led up to the attic floor was so narrow two people couldn't have passed side by side.

Trevor could hear the dogs long before he reached the top stair. A rough planked floor stretched ahead with equally primitive doors set either side of a narrow corridor.

'Patrick?' he called.

'Down here.'

Barry stuck his head through an open door. 'In here, sir. If you give me a moment, I'll get the dogs out of the way.' He gave a command and the dogs fell silent.

'Miserable place,' Peter observed.

'Miserable building,' Patrick commented from inside the room.

Barry walked past them with the dogs. 'I'll give Clovis and Clothilde one last run over the entire house, sir, but this is the only place they've reacted to apart from the hall and cellar.'

'Go with Barry and the dogs, please, Hever. If they signal again come and find me.'

'Yes, sir.'

Trevor, Brookes and Peter joined Patrick. The attic room was small and held four large water tanks. There was very little room between them, barely enough for a man to squeeze in upright. One corner was piled high with discarded toys.

'Want to rummage for antique bisque dolls, Collins?' Trevor asked.

'I'll pass if you don't mind.' Peter leaned against the door post.

Patrick dipped into one of the tanks and extracted a dripping arm. He held it up. 'I've sent for Jen and body bags.'

'Have you had a chance to look at exactly what's in these?' Trevor looked down into the depths of the tank Patrick had uncovered. The water was grey, murky, but he could see lighter flashes of colour in the depths.

'Give me a chance, Joseph. On a quick glance I can say there's one complete corpse that is intact and various body parts. I've had a quick look at the other tanks. One appears to be overflowing with corpse sections, another is more like this one, a thinnish broth of corpse bits, the fourth, although long since drained, looks as though it actually did just contain water.'

'Do you think you'll be able to reassemble all our jigsawed bodies?'

Patrick narrowed his eyes and glared at Trevor.

'Sorry, I shouldn't have asked.'

'If you're beginning to remember that pathologists haven't a crystal ball and can't manufacture evidence to suit the theories of police officers, I'd call that progress.'

'Jen was giving me the DNA results when Brookes

arrived. It's going to be tough on two of the mothers in the inn at Hen Parc. All they had left was hope.'

'There are times when I'm glad I chose my job, not yours, Joseph,' Patrick observed.

'You will look for DNA deposits and fingerprints here besides the body parts?'

'I've already sent down an order to two of the new assistants asking them to take a look.'

Jenny climbed the stairs. She pulled a mask over her face before handing Patrick a body bag. He set it on top of the cover of the tank next to him.

'Need any help?' Peter asked as Patrick allowed the limb he was holding to sink back into the tank. He submerged his arms up to his elbows in the open tank and pulled a complete child's body from the liquid.

'Nothing Brookes can't handle, thank you, Collins. He has a surer and lighter touch than you.'

Jenny stretched out her arms and helped lay the corpse on the body bag. Patrick adjusted it before Brookes closed the zip.

Brookes carried the bag out on to the landing while Jenny laid out a second bag.

'A suggestion, Joseph.' Patrick sank his hands into the tank again. 'Hold off informing the mothers about any DNA matches until we've had a chance to check all of these body parts, even if it means stretching the budget to pay for an extra night's accommodation. It would be better to tell them together than drip out the news bit by bit.'

Trevor was only too glad to delay passing on the information. 'I will. I'll leave you to it.'

Trevor and Peter paused when they reached the lower landing. They watched Clovis and Clothilde rush around

321

the doors of the rooms off a long corridor that stretched to a filthy window at the far end. Barry saw them and shook his head.

Trevor waved to him before he and Peter continued downstairs.

'What now, now that Patrick's asked us to hold off telling the women we've finally found their children?' Peter stepped down into the hall and headed for the open door.

'We return to the incident room, read the information Merchant has compiled, study the results the forensic teams have come up with and trust that Anna will bring in Justin and Lucky before the end of the day.'

'And if she doesn't?'

'We'll think again.' Trevor headed up the drive to the road.

'Coffee?' Peter asked as they reached the line of Portakabins.

'My head is spinning from an excess of caffeine, but yes please. Want me to get it?'

'Absolutely not, the great chief can't carry out menial tasks. It would skew the entire pecking order of the team. I know my place.'

Trevor returned to the incident room while Peter went to the canteen. Sarah and Gillian were still going through the photographs. Sarah turned as Trevor entered and handed him two files.

'The information you asked for about the soldier who found the boy on the hillside, sir, and the records of the mothers you've put up in the inn, along with copies of the photographs of their children. I used the dates they gave me to track down group photographs for comparison and made copies for you.'

'Thank you, Merchant.' Trevor returned to the small office. He opened both files and glanced through them long enough to confirm his suspicions before sitting back and mulling over their contents.

Peter walked in with coffee and sandwiches.

'Do you ever stop eating?' Trevor asked.

'Do you ever start?' Peter pushed a coffee and sandwich towards Trevor before picking up the photograph they'd been studying when Brookes had disturbed them with the news that more bodies had been found.

'You recognise the tallest man?' Trevor asked.

'Should I?'

'Imagine him with hair.'

'Bill Mulcahy?'

'His father, Superintendent Andy Mulcahy.'

'So he was a visitor here. That doesn't prove anything, Joseph. Rose Jones said her husband was a visitor here, so was Dan and so were half the minor celebrities on the contemporary show business circuit. It doesn't prove that any one of them was a paedophile.'

'No it doesn't.' Trevor took the photograph from Peter and looked at it again.

'I shouldn't have to remind you about hard evidence.'

'No,' Trevor mused thoughtfully, 'you shouldn't.'

'But you feel we're chasing shadows? And as soon as you reach out to grasp them there's nothing there to grab hold of.'

'Exactly.'

'Look at what we can, not what we can't do, Joseph.'

'Which is?'

'We can tell at least two of those women you've put up in the inn at Hen Parc that they can stop looking for their children. They can give them a funeral and a grave.'

323

'Yes, I suppose we can accomplish that much, not that's it's much consolation to the mothers – or us.'

'Those women will know the truth. Isn't that better than never knowing what happened to their children?'

'So some would say,' Trevor conceded, 'but life must be pretty bleak when you haven't even hope left to cling to.'

'You won't be happy until you arrest someone for murdering those children?'

'You want to let the killers walk?'

'Of course not, but to make an arrest we'll need highly respectable witnesses whose veracity is beyond doubt and more evidence than I suspect even Patrick can come up with.'

'When I spoke to Mair Davies's daughter and partner it was obvious that Mair spent her entire life in fear of being killed in an "accident" like Alice Price and Constables Sue Pritchard and Marilyn Smart.'

'Sue Pritchard and Marilyn Smart?' Peter reiterated.

'They looked after Anna Wells with Dan when she was in Hill House. Both were killed shortly afterwards.'

'How?' Peter dunked a biscuit into his coffee.

'Sue Pritchard was shot responding to a call in a children's playground in the early hours. Her killer was never found. Marilyn Smart was found dead lying in a road, supposedly after having been thrown from her horse.'

'The shot could have been fired by any one of the thousands of loonies we meet every day in this job, Joseph, and any number of people die after being thrown from a spooked horse, especially on a hard surfaced road.'

'And Justin Hart's fellow witnesses, Shane Jones and Robin MacDonald? You think that gas explosion was an accident?'

'Have you heard otherwise from Dan?'

'Not yet,' Trevor admitted.

'If you're right, and I'm not saying you are, but *if* you are,' Peter took one of the photographs and pushed it in front of Trevor. 'Look at some of the faces there – not the showbusiness clowns, but the churchmen, VIPs and politicians. Accuse them of paedophilia, Joseph, and there'll be bombs going off when we next open our front doors.'

'So we stop investigating?'

'No, we keep looking for hard evidence. Where are you going?' Peter asked as Trevor rose from his chair.

'To interview a witness whose veracity is beyond doubt.'

Trevor knocked on Major Simmonds's office door. A clerk opened it. The major was sitting behind his desk.

'Chief Inspector Joseph. Please come in, sit down.' Simmonds rose behind his desk and offered Trevor his hand. 'Hooper, fetch coffee for two.'

'No thank you,' Trevor refused. 'I was hoping to have a word. In private.'

The major addressed his clerk. 'Take a meal break, Hooper. When you've finished, go to the general office and make a start on the training records.'

'Yes, sir.'

Trevor waited until the clerk closed the door behind him before handing Simmonds a file.

The major opened it and glanced at the press cutting and documents it contained. 'Yes, there's no mistaking those, is there?'

'You found the severely injured boy on the mountain side?'

'Yes.'

'You were with him when he died?'

'Yes.'

'He talked to you?'

'Yes. It wasn't an easy story to listen to, and his injuries weren't easy to look at.'

Simmonds confirmed Trevor's suspicion that military officers were masters of the understatement. 'I can believe that.'

'Where did you find these reports?'

'We have a very thorough researcher. She found a document list for Ben Weston in the National Archives marked "This record is closed for 100 years" so we couldn't access it, but it did contain a list of files held within the document list. One of the files, also needless to say closed for one hundred years, was marked "Record of the inquest into Ben Weston's death including the testimony of Mark Simmonds and Wyn Jenkins."'

Simmonds sat behind his desk, reached down, opened a drawer and lifted out two glasses and a bottle of brandy. He filled both glasses a quarter full and handed one to Trevor. 'I signed the Official Secrets Act after that inquest.'

'I suspected as much.'

'However, I could tell you a story. Just two new friends over a drink.' He lifted his glass.

'I'd appreciate that.'

'You haven't a wire on you?'

Trevor removed his jacket and unbuttoned his shirt. 'As you see.'

'Thank you.'

'You were a lieutenant when you found the injured boy?'

'A raw and very new commissioned officer. But I

326

didn't find one boy. I found two.'

Trevor was surprised but adept at concealing his emotions. 'Go on.'

'One looked about sixteen or seventeen. I was amazed when he told me he was only twelve. He was carrying the younger boy, who looked about seven years old.'

'Did the boys tell you their names?'

'The younger one, who was obviously dying, was Aled Price. The older boy, Wyn Jenkins, had wrapped Aled's naked body in a blanket but Aled kept trying to throw it off, he said because he couldn't bear anything touching him. Aled was covered in blood and ... without going into details, his injuries were horrendous. One glance was enough for me to realise that he'd been sexually and physically assaulted. I radioed HQ and asked for an ambulance to take the boy to hospital. HQ contacted the air ambulance. While we waited, the older boy, Wyn, told me he'd killed the man who'd attacked Aled. He said he'd seen the caretaker, Ben ...'

'Ben Weston?'

'That was his name, lift Aled from his bed in the dormitory earlier that night. Wyn followed him when he carried Aled up to the attic. He told me it wasn't the first time this Ben had targeted Aled. A few days before he'd caught Aled trying to steal his penknife. When Aled told him he'd stolen it to kill the caretaker the next time he assaulted him, Wyn told him he could keep it.'

'You believed Wyn?'

'I believed him,' Simmonds echoed. 'From what Wyn told me that night, I believed that all the boys in Hill House were at risk of assault. Even Wyn, big as he was, had stolen a kitchen knife and kept it hidden in his trouser belt. He showed it to me. The steel blade was curved after being strapped around his waist but it was still sharp. Wyn

327

told me that when he reached the attic he heard Aled scream. He went to the room Ben Weston had carried Aled into. Weston was bleeding from the stab wounds Aled had managed to inflict with his penknife, but the blade was small and they were little more than scratches. By the time he walked in, Weston had wrested the penknife from Aled. Wyn said he saw red when he saw Weston stab Aled in the ear with it. He pulled his knife from his belt and ran straight for Weston. The blade went into Weston's chest, and he fell back and released Aled. Wyn grabbed his knife, Aled and a blanket from the room and ran.'

'Out of Hill House?'

'Wyn said he knew the kitchen door was usually left open. He carried Aled out, ran to the side wall, leaned over as far as he could and dropped Aled over it. I was out on the hill on a night exercise. By the time I reached them, Wyn had picked Aled up and was running to the road. I was hard pushed to catch up with them. And when I did, I had an even harder job convincing Wyn that I was on his and Aled's side.'

Simmonds looked at Trevor's glass. It was untouched but he still topped it up with more brandy when he refilled his own. 'The way I've told the story it probably seems very simple and straightforward. It was in fact anything but. Wyn was hysterical when I finally caught him and forced him to stop running.'

'How did you manage that?' Trevor asked.

'I took Aled from him. Wyn kept repeating over and over again that he'd killed the caretaker and he wasn't sorry. He wasn't much calmer when the helicopter arrived to take Aled to hospital.'

'You went with him?'

'So did Wyn. The police and my CO met us there. I

tried to tell Wyn to keep quiet about killing the caretaker, but he simply couldn't stop talking. However, when they heard the story from Wyn, the police officers were sympathetic.'

'Can you recall any of their names?'

Simmonds shook his head. 'No. That's if I ever heard them. The doctor who saw to Aled also examined Wyn. Not unnaturally, the boy refused to return to Hill House so the doctor agreed to keep him in hospital for observation. It took a week or so but my CO managed to get Wyn into a boarding school. After Aled died I made a point of visiting the boy and keeping in touch just to make sure that he'd be all right.'

'Wyn recovered?'

'As much as any boy of thirteen can recover from an experience like that.'

'He was never charged with the murder of Ben Weston.'

'The police assured me, and the doctor, that they wouldn't charge him and they didn't. I suspect because they only had Wyn's word that he'd murdered Ben Weston. They searched Hill House, but they didn't find a bloodstained room in the attic or any trace of Ben Weston. Shortly afterwards the man who ran Hill House was arrested and the place was closed. It wasn't justice but it was justice of a sort.'

'And Wyn?'

'He joined the army when he was sixteen. When I could see that all I was doing was reminding him of things he'd rather forget, I backed off.'

'But not entirely.' Trevor looked him in the eye.

'I sent him Christmas and birthday cards.'

'And gave him and Justin Hart sanctuary after the explosion in Justin Hart's house that killed their friends.'

Simmonds met Trevor's steady gaze but remained silent.

'Pity the police didn't find the same water tanks in the attic that you and your wife did. I saw your wedding photograph. Alice is your wife?'

'She is. Love is no respecter of age gaps. But I doubt we'd be married if her mother hadn't been so insistent on seeing her daughter wed before she died.'

Trevor looked down at Simmonds's feet. 'Your shoe size is ten and a half and hers is eight?'

Simmonds nodded.

CHAPTER TWENTY-EIGHT

Rain pattered down hard on the roof of the Portakabin. The air was still, close. Simmonds switched off the electric fire. He sat back in his chair and met Trevor's steady gaze. 'Are we still two friends enjoying a drink?'

Trevor picked up his glass and sipped his brandy. 'I've left my warrant card in my desk drawer in the incident room, so the short answer is yes.'

Simmonds rose from his chair and paced to the window. He looked out. 'Welsh mountains look dismal in the rain.'

'The orphans probably thought the same thing when they first saw that view in a cloudburst. I'm guessing that Alice's mother, Mair Davies, told you about the bodies hidden in the attic of Hill House?'

'Not until the day she died.'

'You didn't know before then?'

'No. But I did wonder if there were any bodies hidden somewhere in the house after Wyn insisted he'd killed the caretaker and the police said they couldn't find the corpse. I wasn't certain if the police or Wyn were mistaken. And I couldn't discount the possibility that Ben Weston had survived and fled. But for all that Wyn was hysterical when I found him and Aled that night, he didn't strike me as a boy who wouldn't know the difference between a dead and live man.'

'You said you spoke to the police after you found the boys?'

Simmonds turned to Trevor but remained at the window. 'I did, as did my CO.'

'They knew you came across two boys?'

'Yes.'

'There's only mention of the one who died in the press reports.'

'It was agreed early on between the doctor and the police that Wyn would be kept out of the limelight because of his fragile mental state. It was obvious he was suffering from shock. But my CO and I soon came to the same conclusion, that all the authorities, and that included the police, couldn't wait to sweep the entire incident under the carpet and close Hill House. Which of course happened within weeks of my finding the boys and much more swiftly than I imagined it would.'

'You said Mair told you about the bodies hidden in the attic the day she died. She never talked about them before?'

'Mair was haunted by the suffering of those children in Hill House. In the last few days of her life she spoke about the place more than she'd ever done before according to Brian and Alice, but she only mentioned the attic once, a few hours before the end.'

'What exactly did she say?'

'That Alice Price …' Simmonds hesitated, 'You know about Alice Price?'

'Yes. From people in Hen Parc as well as Brian and Alice.'

'Alice told Mair that she saw a dead child in one of the attic rooms when she went there with a class of children. Later she returned without the children to find the body had been removed. Alice went looking for it. She saw a

332

door open lower down the attic corridor, crept along to it and saw one of the staff dropping the body into a water tank. Terrified, she ran down the stairs and hid in the ladies' room. Mair was in there. Alice told her what she'd seen.'

'Mair had just begun her shift but she could see how shaken Alice was. She walked her to her car. Alice was understandably upset and Mair said she was talking about leaving her job and Hen Parc. Mair told her they'd decide what to do that evening after she finished her shift. Only neither of them reached the cottage they were sharing that night. That was the last time Mair saw Alice. She said for the rest of that shift she sensed she was being watched. Brian told you how Mair went to the Tepee Village ...'

'He did. What prompted you to go looking for the bodies in the water tank in Hill House when you did?' Trevor interrupted.

Simmonds returned to his desk. 'The verdict in the VIP trial. I saw the defence barrister on the news. It was disgusting. Not content with the not guilty verdict, he started lobbying to put an end to what he called "the persecution of innocent public figures by low-life criminal elements". So, I switched off the news and decided to break into Hill House.'

'To see if Mair was right?'

'I believed Mair. She was confused at the end of her life but when she was talking about what Alice had seen, I realised she was relating an actual conversation. The only thing I couldn't be sure of was if any bodies would still be there. Chances were several of the staff knew about the tanks and, afraid of being incriminated, they might well have moved the bodies after Hill House had closed. The one thing in favour of them still being there was Hill House's isolation. Its position meant that any activity there would be noticed, especially the ferrying of corpses.'

'So, you went to Hill House, found the corpse parts and draped them on the sign.'

'I knew a soldier would be passing there around midnight on night exercise. We put various things en route to test their alertness so they are trained to check their surroundings. I hoped he'd see the corpse parts, and he did. But I took photographs just in case he didn't and posted them on the internet.'

'After hacking into the Welsh Assembly's press office account?'

Simmonds shrugged. 'A man can pick up some interesting and unusual skills in military circles. And I thought an official account would attract more interest.'

'And Alice?'

'The exercise was entirely my idea. My wife only came along to try and stop me. I thought we were careful ...'

'You were when it came to DNA and fingerprints. Just not your shoes.'

'Informal chat or not, you can arrest me, Chief Inspector, but not Alice.'

'I'm not going to arrest your wife, Major Simmonds, or you.'

'Although I've admitted I carried those body parts outside of Hill House?' Simmonds questioned. 'I must have broken some law or other when I did so.'

Trevor considered for a moment. '"Any person who, without lawful justification or excuse, the proof of which lies on the person ... improperly or indecently interferes with, or offers any indignity to, any dead human body ... whether buried or not, is guilty of a misdemeanour,"' he quoted, 'but given the scale of the crimes perpetrated against defenceless children in Hill House, yours are minor. Especially when you consider that it was your actions that highlighted the crimes that had been committed and instigated this investigation in the first place.' Trevor lifted his brandy glass again. 'Two friends sharing a drink.'

'Thank you, Chief Inspector –'

'Trevor, and it's me who should be thanking you.' Trevor rose from his seat. 'Just one more thing. You obviously kept in touch with Wyn Jenkins, or rather Lucky as he prefers to be known, because he turned to you after the explosion that killed his friends and relied on you to conceal him and Justin Hart.'

Simmonds didn't attempt to deny it. 'What of it?'

'Does he know that his mother is looking for him?'

'Some people don't want to be found, Trevor. About the fire ...'

'I know who set it.'

'You do know that they won't give up trying to destroy Hill House and everyone who's aware of what really went on there?'

'I realise that the people behind the arsonist won't give up easily. I'll deal with it.'

'And guarantee Lucky's safety?'

'I'll do my damnedest.'

'They are powerless, faceless people, Chief Inspector.'

'I know.' Trevor opened the door and stepped down from the Portakabin.'

Justin and Lucky, still in their motorbike leathers, were looking through the photographs Gillian Henderson and Sarah Merchant had laid out on the tables with Anna and Peter when Trevor returned to the incident room.

'All the photographs have been scanned into the

computer, sir,' Sarah informed him as he passed her desk. 'I've dated the file and marked it "Hill House visuals 1".'

'Thank you, Merchant. I dread to think what's going to happen when you go on maternity leave.'

'Not for another few weeks yet, sir.'

'That's what bothers me. It's looming over my head like a tsunami.'

'You'll have to train up Collins, sir,' she suggested mischievously.

'He's proved untrainable,' Trevor smiled. He joined Justin, Lucky and Peter and offered Justin and Lucky his hand in turn. 'Thank you both for coming in.'

'Anna was very persuasive.' Justin wrapped his arm around her shoulders and pulled her close.

'You know I can offer you police protection.'

'A place in a witness protection programme would be a great move for an actor who relies on publicity to bring in work and feed a fan base,' Justin said wryly.

'I'm sorry.'

'It wasn't you who messed up our lives,' Justin was magnanimous.

'Anna promised anonymity,' Lucky finally joined in the conversation.

'I can guarantee that,' Trevor agreed.

'Even if there's another court case?'

'I won't ask Justin to give evidence.'

'No matter what we tell you?' Justin pressed.

'We?' Trevor turned to Lucky. 'You're finally admitting that you too were an inmate in the orphanage.'

'Considering that you've just left Simmonds's office, do I have a choice?' Lucky demanded.

'Simmonds and I shared a drink and a little off the record conversation. Nothing more.'

'Some might believe you, Chief Inspector. I don't.'

'This is an historic case. We are only interested in prosecuting the guilty, and we won't proceed until we have incontrovertible, tangible physical evidence.'

'So you really do only want information from us?'

'Yes, Lucky, we do,' Trevor confirmed.

'Right.' Lucky paused for a moment then picked up a group photograph of staff and inmates. 'According to the dates written on the back, this is the last photograph that was taken of all the inmates and staff of Hill House before it closed.' He indicated four boys sitting cross-legged in the front row, 'Justin, Stephen, Mac, Shane.' He pointed to two black boys standing four rows behind them, 'Sully, me,' he placed his thumb over a member of staff's face. 'Ben Weston.' He moved his thumb, 'the ogre ...' Once Lucky began he continued to rattle off names faster than Sarah Merchant could make a note of them.

Trevor tapped Anna's arm and whispered, 'Can I see you for a moment in the small office?'

He went ahead, she closed the door behind her when she joined him. He handed her the file Sarah had compiled of the mothers and their missing children.

'Lucky is Wyn Jenkins. I'll leave it to you to tell him that his mother is looking for him. I believe he's already aware she's been searching for him. If he allows you to mention her name, you could try telling him she's been sober for some years.'

She took the file. 'Thank you, sir. When are you going to visit the women in Hen Parc?'

'As soon as Patrick gives me the DNA results on the body parts he's just discovered. It could take another day or two.

The phone rang. Trevor checked the number. 'I have to take this.'

'Yes, sir.' Anna took the file and left.

337

Trevor picked up the receiver. 'Trevor Joseph.'

'They're shutting you down.'

'Dan ...' Trevor thought about the open line then realised it had to be imminent. 'When?'

'Mulcahy and the team are on their way, so am I.'

Trevor wrenched open the door of the office. 'Collins with me, rest of you stay here.'

Peter knew better than to shout questions as he raced after Trevor.

Trevor stepped down from the incident room, turned and saw vans, cars and lorries bearing the logo of the Local Authority at the roadblock. Some of the staff were already leaving the vehicles. He turned to Peter. 'They're shutting us down.'

Brookes walked through the gate carrying a plastic box. Trevor called out, 'How many more corpse parts are in the attic.'

'Not that many ...'

'Give me that.' Trevor took the box from him and handed it to Peter who immediately headed for the laboratory. 'With me, Brookes.' Trevor ran through the gates to the front door of Hill House. Without pausing for breath he raced up the stairs to the attic. Patrick looked up and frowned at him as he raced into the room with the water tanks.

'Joseph, in the name of all that's holy, you're not wearing a sterile suit ... or you, Collins,' he added as Peter joined Brookes in the doorway behind Trevor.

'Get all the remaining parts into one body bag and get them out of here. Now! Even if you have to throw them out of the window.' Feeling his age, Trevor placed his hands palm down on his knees and gulped in air.

'You're too old to go running upstairs, Joseph,' Patrick sniped.

'The local authority vehicles are at the road block. They're closing Hill House and the investigation.'

Patrick and Jenny stared at him as if he'd taken leave of his senses.

Voices raised in anger wafted up the stairs.

'And they're doing it now.' Trevor added.

CHAPTER TWENTY-NINE

'I gave you as much leeway as I could, Joseph,' Mulcahy insisted. 'The building is dangerous. I won't risk losing a highly trained detective or a forensic scientist.'

'There are body parts in there ...'

'It's *far* too dangerous to go inside,' Mr Williams gloated. 'The last surveyor declared the building was ready to collapse at any moment.'

'I've had people working in there ...'

'Illegally, Chief Inspector Joseph,' Mr Williams crowed. 'If you'll excuse me, I must ensure the building is properly boarded. The demolition teams will begin work on the place as soon as the heavy machinery arrives. We can't afford to have any squatters lurking inside.'

Trevor watched the man cross the road to the gate. Even Williams's walk seemed to exude an air of petty triumph.

Mulcahy read the barely restrained anger in Trevor's face. 'You should have been more diplomatic in your dealings with the local authority ...'

'Why don't you tell us the real reason why you're shutting this investigation down, Bill?' Dan challenged.

'Too many innocent people could be hurt. Both of you know how unsubstantiated allegations can ruin reputations. The real culprits have been punished and are being punished. The ogre is in jail …'

'And applying for parole – again,' Dan reminded him. 'One of these days he'll be successful and released out into an unsuspecting public. How will you feel if his next victim turns out to be a child in your family?'

'He'll be monitored.'

'Really.' Trevor was sceptical.

'We coppers can't be blamed for deficiencies in the system, Joseph.'

'We came across your father's photograph taken outside this place,' Trevor revealed.

Mulcahy narrowed his eyes. 'Are you accusing my father of something, Joseph?'

Trevor knew he was risking his job but he had to say it. 'Only if he was guilty of something, sir.'

Mulcahy pursed his lips as though he couldn't trust himself to answer.

Trevor looked around. He, Mulcahy and Dan were standing outside the incident room. Mulcahy's officers were inside. They had moved in as soon as they'd arrived and unceremoniously escorted him, Merchant, Brookes and Peter out. Neither he, nor anyone in his team, had been allowed to take a single document, file or photograph with them.

Judging by the angry shouts coming from Patrick and Jen's laboratory, the pathologist was being subjected to a similar eviction and didn't like it any better than the detectives had.

Trevor lowered his voice. 'Would we have been allowed to continue the investigation if the fire really had destroyed the photographs we found in the office?'

Mulcahy continued to stare at him.

'I see Hever's joined your team. No wonder he volunteered to camp out in the incident room. Twenty-four hour access to the only phone line in the place must have been useful to him – and you. Do you find it useful to have an arsonist at your beck and call?'

Still no response, although Trevor was aware that Dan was watching both him and Mulcahy intently.

Mulcahy broke his silence. 'Leave, Joseph, before you goad me into issuing an order we'll both regret.'

Dan reached for his peppermints. 'It strikes me that some people who visited and worked in this orphanage were guilty of concealing the most serious crime of all.'

'Child murders are indefensible,' Mulcahy said. 'I've sent officers to question the ogre, and re-arrest all the staff who have been released on parole. When my team have had time to examine the evidence you've accumulated, Joseph, we will present it to the CPS. The decision will be theirs as to whether to prosecute the ogre and his cohorts for murder – or not.'

'And the VIPs at the last trial where Justin Hart gave evidence?' Trevor asked.

'Were found not guilty of child abuse.'

'And Shane Jones and Robin MacDonald?'

'Didn't Superintendent Evans tell you?' Mulcahy glanced at Dan. 'It was a gas explosion. A broken pipe. Just one of those things that happen. A tragic accident.'

'Chief Superintendent Mulcahy ...'

'I'm coming, Hever.' Mulcahy stepped up into the incident room and turned to Dan and Trevor. 'Thank you for what you've achieved here, Joseph. Go home, take two weeks' paid leave, and that goes for everyone on your team as well as you. Use the time to think about your future.'

'Is that a threat, sir?'

Mulcahy pretended he hadn't heard. 'I'll leave it to you to pass on the good news, Joseph. I'd appreciate it if you could all be out of here in ten minutes.' He turned and strode away.

Dan clasped Trevor's shoulder. 'Time to go. 'You'll stop at the pub in Hen Parc for lunch?'

'Peter and I have just one quick call to make on the way.'

'You're sure this is the road?' Peter asked Trevor.

'I'm sure. Mark Simmonds gave me directions. It's the best and most accessible way to Tepee Village and avoids the rough track. Which is why the locals keep it secret.'

'So now they regard you as local?'

'Honorary, maybe, for the purposes of this lane.' Trevor stopped the car and stepped out. The track had ballooned into a small hard standing that held a dozen vehicles of various ages, one or two gleaming and new, three or four aged and brightly painted with flowers, birds and butterflies and a couple of rusty objects that looked as though they'd taken root, never to move again.

Peter climbed out of the passenger seat, yawned and stretched. 'I don't know why you insisted on coming here.'

'Just something Brian Smith said.' Trevor heard a noise coming from a tepee constructed of birch saplings and canvas. He walked toward it. A man tried to duck out as they approached. He wasn't quite quick enough. Trevor stepped in front of him.

'I'm looking for Michael Trenwith.'

'No one of that name here,' Michael Trenwith lied.

'Tell him if he writes to this address, the police will call off the search for him and inform his family he's fine but doesn't want to contact them. It's his right.'

The man eyed the card Trevor had handed him.

'It would be just a letter. One that could be posted

344

anywhere – even in Ealing.' Trevor smiled at the look of confusion on the man's face when he didn't understand the reference.

'I'll try to get a message to him.'

'Thank you.'

Trevor turned and walked back to the car.

Peter fell into step beside him. 'How did you know?'

'Something Brian Smith said about this place.'

'What?'

'When Alice mentioned something along the lines of "Tepee Village has been a sanctuary to many", Brian glanced at a newspaper on the table. It was folded over at a photograph of Michael Trenwith. Something set alarm bells ringing and me thinking when Brian said, "Not misfits and criminals, as some would have it. Just ordinary people who find life difficult, as we all do from time to time."'

'You and your alarm bells.'

'They're generally right.' Trevor demurred.

'I'm not disputing that, just wondering at your extra-sensory perception. As for finding life difficult, I should have financial problems like Michael Trenwith. A well off wife set to inherit more money that I can spend. A comfortable trust fund for my offspring ... Why would someone find life difficult when he has all that and more.'

'Ever thought that might be just the problem? You saw the man's diaries. It can't be easy if you feel you're leading an empty life on a pointless treadmill and your family doesn't really need you.'

Peter looked up. 'Where the hell are we walking to?'

'Simmonds told me there's a clear view of the eastern pine end of Hill House from this lane.' Trevor walked on for about half a mile.

'It's closer than I thought it would be,' Peter said when

the house came into view.

'It is,' Trevor agreed.

They both looked to Hill House. There was a face in the topmost attic window. That of a small child.

'Simmonds suggested you look at Hill House from here?' Peter checked.

'He did,' Trevor confirmed.

'It's just a trick of the light.' Peter said.

'Undoubtedly,' Trevor echoed.

'Let's go home, Joseph, but via the pub.'

'I thought you hated goodbyes.'

'Sometimes they're necessary – and I need to eat.'

'You sure you want to resign, Wells?' Trevor wasn't surprised by her announcement but he could see that Dan was.

'I need her with me.' Justin hugged Anna even closer to him. 'I have another week's filming in London, then thanks to my PR team and the DA-notice I begin work on a new feature in Los Angeles. And, after that, a pilot for an American TV series. I couldn't bear to be parted from Anna for another day, let alone the months it will take to shoot those.'

'As long as you don't expect me to hang around a set all day and watch you film. From what Lucky has said, film sets are pretty boring places.'

'You object to boring?' Justin lifted his eyebrows.

'Not if you're there,' Anna kissed him.

Trevor glanced across the bar to where Lucky was sitting with Marion Jenkins. 'Are you staying here tonight?'

'For as long as Lucky remains talking to his mother,' Justin said when Anna released him. 'But I have no idea how long that is likely to be. Lucky never appreciates anyone meddling in his private life or asking questions about his personal or business affairs.'

Dan finished his coffee and rose from his chair, 'I'm off. See you in two weeks, Trevor, Collins? Back to the Michael Trenwith case?'

'I rather think that one will solve itself, sir,' Trevor said.

'Really, Joseph?'

'You can take his word for it.' Peter made a face. 'Just don't find us any more political cases. I hate missing VIPs, especially MPs who run off with researchers just out of college. And that goes for politicians of either sex. Chances are they were on the point of being caught for fiddling expenses and wanted to hide. It's always expensive to go shopping for sexual partners in the junior department.'

'The voice of experience talking, Collins? Have you told Daisy about your murky past?' Dan enquired in amusement.

'Not my past, ask Trevor. He's the one with a wife half his age.'

Trevor stepped in and nodded towards the women sitting in the corner. 'We won't be long behind you, Dan, just a few more goodbyes.'

'Sorry I couldn't do more to keep Mulcahy off your back.'

'Nothing and no one could have kept the people pulling Mulcahy's strings off our backs. It's made me realise just how far the brass are embroiled in Hill House and cases like it. And just how many powerful people are involved in the whitewashing.'

'Let's hope the internet continues to scrape away at uncovering the truth. Times are changing, but for what it's worth, Trevor, I think a lot of people involved in the cover up of Hill House are innocent. Just leaned on to keep quiet.'

'Leaned on, how?' Peter asked.

'Dig deep enough and you'll find skeletons in any and everyone's cupboard, and not necessarily evil or perverted ones. Just ones people would like to remain buried.'

Trevor walked Dan to the door. When he returned he stopped at the table where Angela Smith and Lynda Lewis were sitting with Maggie Perkins. He offered Angela his hand but she left her chair and hugged him.

'Thank you, Trevor.'

'All I can offer is my sympathies and condolences. I did nothing for any of you.' Trevor demurred.

'You gave Lynda and me the truth and that's all we ever asked for. We can hold our funerals now and start mourning, and then we can continue to campaign against paedophiles and provide support for the victims and their families. And people like Maggie who still don't know what happened to their loved ones.'

Maggie looked up at Trevor. The pain in her eyes was almost too much for him to bear. The words remained unspoken: *there's still hope*.

'I wish you – all of you – well.'

'You too, Trevor Joseph,' Angela said brightly. So brightly her words were brittle. 'The only policeman who kept the promise he made to us and never lied.'

Trevor moved on to Lucky and Justin.

'I'm sorry about Stephen, Justin. I'll see that the search for him is kept open.'

Justin glanced at Maggie. 'Like so many others who've lost family in Hill House, I refuse to give up hope.'

'Goodbye, Anna.'

Anna rose and hugged him, then Peter, then him again.

Wrapping her arms around Trevor, she said. 'There'll always be hope when we have coppers like you fighting everyone's corner.'

'See you both at the Oscars. At least you'll be all dressed up on TV with somewhere to go.' Tired of the prolonged goodbyes, Peter waved to the room in general, kissed Rose and Judy and left the pub.

Simmonds pulled up alongside them. 'I hoped I'd catch you.'

'Don't tell me they threw you off Hill House land as well,' Peter commented.

'They couldn't throw us off the land to the side of the house, it's MOD property. Just wanted to tell you the Welsh Assembly press office has been hacked again.'

'Really.' Peter stared at the sky. 'I wonder who did that?'

'Strange really. Your people asked the advice of my people when the internet cables were put into your incident room. I thought the police would have had their own experts.'

'You'd assume so wouldn't you.' Trevor looked inquiringly at Simmonds.

'As I said, you learn some odd things in the army.'

Trevor offered Simmonds his hand. 'It was good to meet you. Thank you for alerting us as to what went on in Hill House. I'm only sorry we couldn't stay to finish the investigation.'

'I'm sorry too. Glad we met, Chief Inspector, Sergeant. Hope to see you again one day.'

'That would be good.'

'We could reminisce about the bad old days,' Peter joked.

Trevor smiled and waved through the open door to the room full of people in the pub.

Simmonds walked him and Peter to their car. 'There's talk of an inquiry.'

'Another one?' Peter mocked.

'Don't you think it will achieve anything?' Simmonds asked.

'I'd say the expenditure of several million pounds of taxpayers' money, five to ten years of lawyers' lives and a few lessons in patience for those of us who expect and want results. They'll have to learn to live with disappointment – and so will we,' Peter predicted.

'So nothing,' Simmonds forecast.

'There's always hope, Major Simmonds. Good luck to you.' Trevor climbed into the car and turned the ignition.

'And to you.'

Peter sat in the car besides Trevor. 'Let's go home.'

EPILOGUE

Trevor sat next to Lyn on the sofa. A film was playing softly on the television, too low for either of them to follow the dialogue, but both of them had given up on watching it. Trevor kissed her, long and lingeringly.

'Time for bed?' he suggested hopefully.

'You missed me enough to go to bed before ten o'clock?' she smiled.

'I'm exhausted.'

'If you're that exhausted, I'm not sure I want to go to bed with you.' She sat up. 'Is that a tap at the window?'

'It is, and if it's who I think it is, I wish he'd go home and cuddle his own wife.' Even as he protested, Trevor prised himself from the sofa and went to the door.

'You watching the news?' Peter burst into Trevor and Lyn's living room. Daisy followed with Miranda well-wrapped in a shawl.

'We were watching a film,' Trevor remonstrated mildly. He couldn't even remember what it was about but he resented the intrusion.

'Terrible film, she dies at the end. I wish it had happened at the beginning. If it had Daisy wouldn't have made me watch it.' Peter grabbed the remote and turned over to a news channel.

The photographs Gillian Henderson had rescued from

351

the office at Hill House flashed onto the screen with the faces of both adults and children pixelated. The voice of the newscaster filled the room.

'... the files were posted up by hackers who again gained access to the Welsh Assembly website ...'

Trevor stared as the photographs were replaced by snapshots of a few of the original documents Anna had assembled that were pertinent to the history of Hill House.

'The Home Office has announced that all the information posted up has been duly noted by the official investigation into allegations of abuse at Hill House. The Home Secretary has also announced that a judge will be appointed to head a new inquiry into historical child sex abuse in England and Wales. The Prime Minister has stated that the government will do all it can to expose these despicable crimes and bring the guilty to justice ...'

Trevor looked at Peter. 'The files? They're on the internet.'

'All of them, I've checked. Just like the photographs of the body parts, they've gone wild. People have been saving them to their own storage and machines. There are too many copies to track down. It's impossible for any government agency to wipe them all. God bless rogue army officers, that's what I say.'

Lyn looked to Daisy.

'Don't ask me, I'm as confused as you are,' Daisy protested.

Trevor smiled and wrapped his arm around Lyn's shoulders. 'Anyone fancy a drink? We could break out the champagne while Peter explains military justice.'

For more information about **Katherine John**

and other **Accent Press** titles

please visit

www.accentpress.co.uk

The Trevor Joseph Detective Series

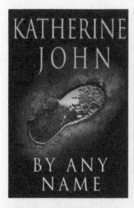

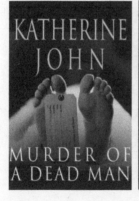

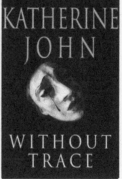

Paul Burston
THE BLACK PATH

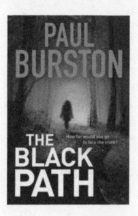

A dark tale of love and lies, obsession and betrayal, *The Black Path* will appeal to fans of 'domestic noir' and anyone who's ever wondered about the secrets people keep.

How well do you really know those closest to you?

Helen has been holding out for a hero all her life. Her father was a hero – but he was murdered when she was ten. Her husband is a hero – but he's thousands of miles away, fighting a war people say will never be won.

As bitter truths are uncovered, Helen must finally face her fears and the one place which has haunted her since childhood – the Black Path.